Button Hook Child

An Open Pond Ghost Story

Rickie Wood-Bovee

Rickie Wood-Bovee

©2011

ISBN
978-0-9818922-4-5

Library of Congress Control Number:
2010942159

Three Bars Publishing
Ponce De Leon, FL
Printed in the United States of America

Authors Note

Button Hook Child is a work of fiction. The location, DeFuniak Springs, Florida is real. The house, known here as the Cottonwood House, is actually the Burress Cawthon House and is real.

Although the Button Hook Child is fictitious, there have been strange, unexplainable occurrences in the home, as with many homes in this quaint community.

All characters in the book are fictitious and any resemblance to persons, living or dead is purely coincidental.

Rickie Wood-Bovee

For Molly

Rickie Wood-Bovee

Acknowledgements

This is my first novel and without the assistance of the following persons its completion would never have been possible.

Many thanks to Tom and Pam Hutchins for allowing me to use their home as a center piece for my story.

All my love and thanks to Molly Camosso and Brenda Wood for their positive input and advice early on. I want to thank Jeff Smalley for his help and skill with a computer.

Many thanks to Dan Owens for his advice and assistance; he is a true friend and a worthy advisor who often goes far beyond the call of duty, and for that I can never thank him enough.

Thank you to Detective John Powers of the DeFuniak Springs Police Department for his advice and to Mark Ewing of the Walton County School District who helped me out by answering my questions.

And finally, I would like to thank my husband, Jim, who encouraged me, gave me literary advice when I asked for it, and afforded me the time over the past two and a half years to complete my tale.

Rickie Wood-Bovee

1907

Nathan Cottonwood stood at the edge of the road, gazing at his new home, now just a few days from completion. Admiring the building, it was the latest addition to the town's formidable district surrounding Open Pond, the lake central to the community. *It is a grand home*, he thought. *This home tells everyone how important we are. Financially set; a pillar of the community.*

Inside, the workmen were finishing the last touches of paper and paint to the walls, preparing the home for the family to move in. Marion Cottonwood, Nathan's wife, stood nearby, giving last minute instructions. In two days time the furniture would arrive, just in time for Thanksgiving.

The fireplaces were being checked for draw to make sure that all were working efficiently. With winter temperatures beginning to set in, it was important to make sure that all was safe and prepared since each room must be heated to ward off the damp cold often felt in the Florida panhandle this time of year.

1908 would soon be here, just weeks away, and they would hold a soiree to bring in the New Year. This was so exciting; her dream home was now a reality and their place in De Funiak Springs' society was set. Nathan's timber business was a huge success, they were wealthy beyond imagination. Their only child was growing into a fine young girl, and now the perfect home was theirs. Life was perfect.

Abigail, Marion and Nathan's eight year old daughter, entered the room through the parlor doorway separating the front and back parlors. She was the light of their lives. Having arrived late in their marriage, and an only child, they doted on her. But they also made sure that Abigail stayed a gentle and humble child; lavishing her with love but not material possessions.

"Mother, where is father?"

"He is out in the front, dear, near the edge of the road."

"May I go out there with him?" Abigail asked, never assuming anything.

"Certainly, dear; I am sure he would be happy to see you"

Abigail moved past her mother and through the parlor to the front door. Peering out the window of the door, she spotted her father standing at the front path that continued past their home as it encircled the lake. As she opened the door and stepped onto the front porch her father spotted her and a huge grin spread across his face. You could say he beamed, his eyes gleaming with pleasure.

"Abigail, my little princess," he called out, "come here, dear, and behold our new home. Is it not the most grand and wonderful thing?" And as Abigail approached her father he reached out, bending over slightly, and wrapped his arms around her, giving her a huge hug. "Turn, my love, and admire our new home. It is the grandest of grand in our small, but fair city."

"Yes father, it is very beautiful."

"It is for us, Abigail. Built just for you, your mother, and I. We will have many years of joy living in our new home. We will give parties, and you will meet new friends; our life will be perfect.

Chapter 1

2007

The huge truck rumbled off the interstate highway, eighty five miles east of Pensacola, Florida, and rolled up to the stop sign. Turning left toward the city limits the driver soon reached the turn designated on his directions-sheet which took him toward the lake the town was famous for. Lake DeFuniak, one of only two perfectly round lakes in the world, lay in the center of a community well known for its Victorian charm.

The city known as DeFuniak Springs was something unique in today's world of concrete, steel and suburban sprawl with its continuous rows of look-alike houses. This quaint town still held a treasure trove of Victorian homes, many built before the turn of the twentieth century. Once derelict, they had somehow escaped the wrecker's ball. Homes rich in the traditions of quality craftsmanship, built when a man took pride in his ability to shape wood into fine creations of art. Homes laced with gingerbread trim, hand split shingles, and corner turrets designed to resemble the great castles of Europe on a miniature scale. Many of the homes recently restored to their original beauty, the town was recapturing its traditional beauty and allure. It was that allure that had drawn the Miller family to DeFuniak Springs and their new home.

Following his direction sheet the truck driver now reached Circle Drive, the mile around avenue that encircled Lake DeFuniak and provided the panoramic setting for many of the Victorian homes. Once you turned onto Circle Drive you could cruise slowly along, admiring the view of the lake on one side and the century old homes on the other.

The driver turned right and slowly drove a short distance, less than a block, before he saw the home, sitting stately between a newer replica home and the First Methodist Church; the Cottonwood House.

Most of the older homes were referred to by the names of their original owners and this house had belonged to one of the most prominent citizens of the early days; Nathan Cottonwood. Wealthy beyond imagination for his time, Nathan Cottonwood had made his money on the timber trade in northern Florida. Yellow pine; the area had been heavily forested with it and the early pioneers who took advantage of this abundant resource lived well from it. The elaborate homes were evidence of that.

Shortly after the big truck pulled up to the curb in front of the Cottonwood house, a much smaller mini van pulled up behind it. From the driver's door stepped Jeff Miller, the new owner. Speedily he moved around the front of the van, using the front fender to help him jump the curb as he bounced his way to the passenger door, quickly opening it, "Here hon, let me help you. Watch your step... that's it... be careful."

"Jeff, it's okay. I'm pregnant, not an invalid," as she chuckled lightly. "Get Chrissy out of her seat, will you please?"

As Jeff proceeded to extract their daughter, Christina, from her car seat, Karen stood there looking at her dream home. They had purchased it through an agent on the internet and the pictures did not do it justice. It was a stately home, built in 1907, and had carefully and authentically been restored by the previous owners. The covered front porch wrapped around the left side of the house and welcomed visitors with a safe refuge from the summer sun or the heavy rains that could come unexpectedly. It also provided a cool and shady respite for afternoon tea or lemonade. Just to the right of the porch, at its terminus, the front parlor window gave the outside world a fleeting glimpse into the grandeur of its interior.

Karen stood there soaking up the reality that this was hers. This gorgeous Victorian presence was now her home. She stood there looking, feeling, absorbing that fact and she had a feeling come over her as if the home were alive; speaking to her, calling her inside, trying to reveal some secret. Off in her own world with her thoughts Karen was brought back to reality suddenly when Chrissy was released by Jeff,"Here she comes. Brace yourself!"

Chrissy, full of four years of energy and exuberance, ran up and grabbed her mom by the legs, squealing all the way. The long trip combined with the adventure of a new home had her wound up like a spring and she had just sprung. She left her mothers legs and ran in through the wrought iron gate and up onto the porch. "Mommy, come here! Let's go inside, pleeease! Let's go in."

"Okay Chrissy, just give us a minute to get a few things from the car."

Jeff looked at Karen, "You go ahead with Chrissy, and I'll get the bags from the car. And hon, watch those stairs, you're not that nimble or light on your feet right now."

Karen smiled at her handsome husband. She knew all too well how top heavy she was. With only one month to go before the birth of their son, she was well aware of her lack of agility, so she carefully headed for the porch, watching her step on the cobblestone walkway. Following Chrissy up the steps she approached the front door.

Chrissy had already discovered the old fashioned door bell and turned the handle continually, ringing the bell on the inside of the door. "Mommy, this is fun. I like this house all ready."

"I know Chrissy; it's going to be a lot of fun living here." Karen inserted the key and turned the door knob, pausing briefly to look through the large window in the upper portion of the door before she pushed it open. The large heavy ornate door swung easily on its hinges and as Chrissy bolted through the doorway Karen followed with a gasp escaping her lips as she entered.

The entryway was stunning. Everything was a glorious dark honey colored wood and the upper walls, above the wainscoting, were decorated with beautiful antique style wallpaper. To the left, a series of stairs wrapped around the wall as they made their way to the second floor, a landing at each corner interrupting the ascent. At the first landing a beautiful diamond shaped cut glass window illuminated the way.

Straight ahead a doorway opened into the dining room and to the right; through a beautiful pillared archway she could see the front parlor. She was in love!

"Chrissy, where are you?" Karen could hear her daughter running through the other rooms.

"I'm back here, mommy."

"Come here Chrissy and we'll walk through the house together. Let's wait for Daddy. He'll want to go with us. We'll discover the house together."

As Chrissy came running back to her mother's legs she squealed again, "Mommy, there are more stairs back there. I want to see where they go."

"Let's wait for Daddy, and then we'll all go through the house, room by room, together."

Chrissy looked out through the front door. Her daddy was talking to the moving van driver. "Daddy… hurry! Please hurry! We're waiting for you!"

Jeff turned toward his daughters voice, "I'll be right there Chrissy!"

He said a few more words to the driver, shook the man's hand and then walked toward the house.

Coming through the front door Jeff gave out a soft, smooth whistle, "Wow! The pictures sure didn't say it all, did they?"

Karen held out her hand to Jeff, "Chrissy wants to explore the house. Let's do it together."

Clasping hands they walked forward into the dining room as Chrissy led the way. The previous owners had left a few furnishings and the dining room set was one of the most spectacular. It was original to the house, originally purchased by Nathan and Marion Cottonwood, the set was of Italian origin and was perhaps two to three hundred years old. The eight foot rectangular table had ornately carved legs at each corner below a black etched glass top. Each of the eight chairs had beautiful brocade padded seats and the ornately carved backs held an etched black glass panel down its center. Two sideboards, each in the same dark, exquisitely carved wood, had etched glass tops and a beautifully carved frame around a mirror the length of the sideboard. A huge window, to the left of the doorway, almost the width and height of the wall, sat opposite a beautifully tiled fireplace to their right. At the opposite corner of the dining room was a smaller doorway equipped with a swinging door

Karen and Jeff stood there in awe as Chrissy crawled under the table, squealing with delight, "Mommy, come here! It's neat in here. Come see!"

"Let's have Daddy check it out with you, Chrissy. I don't think mommy can bend over to see."

Chrissy giggled sweetly as Jeff got down on his hands and knees and poked his head in under the table, "Gee Chrissy, we'll have to have a tea party in here some day. We'll invite lots of people."

Chrissy giggled again, "Daddy, don't be silly. Tea parties are for ladies."

Karen turned to her left to navigate around the table, letting her left hand glide softly along the buffet as she passed, the black glass cool under her fingertips. She paused at the window, looking out onto the side yard and the church just beyond. The yard was lovely; green with well manicured lawn and the sculptured flower beds. Everything about this place was pleasing to the eyes.

As she reached the opposite door Jeff and Chrissy were emerging from under the table and she led the way through the swinging door into the kitchen. What a delight! The kitchen/breakfast room was one large room divided only by an island housing the old fashioned sink. With large windows on three walls, it had a light and airy feeling about it. To her left another door led out onto the porch just before it ended its journey around the house. Just ahead an island bar sat centered in the room, a large stained glass light overhead, and just opposite an old fashioned wood stove, conveniently converted to gas, a testament to the labors of a lost era. To the right of the stove another door led into a back room where Karen found all of the modern conveniences she could want, hidden away so as not to spoil the mood in the kitchen; dishwasher, refrigerator, washer and dryer. Just right of that door sat the divider/island housing the old fashioned sink. Open above, it conveniently sectioned the two areas yet still allowed the room to retain its open airy atmosphere.

Chrissy zipped past Karen and sped into the breakfast room which was just to the right, past the sink divider. Stopping just beyond the divider, she pointed up a stairwell, "Here Mommy, see here! Some more stairs; I want to see where they go."

"In a minute, Chrissy, let's finish the downstairs first."

Jeff paused at the stairwell, holding onto either side of the narrow opening, he looked up into the staircase as it disappeared, the wall swallowing it beyond its narrow opening, as the steps made a sharp curving ascent to the floor above, "You better watch these, hon, they look pretty steep. You might want to avoid these until after the baby's born."

Karen was looking out through the back door and windows, and not really paying attention to the stairs, "Umhuh, okay. Jeff, look at the patio. Isn't it lovely? And there's the garage, we'll have to check it out tomorrow."

Opposite the stairwell and on the same side as the backroom, another door led outside to the back patio and eventually to the detached three car garage. Hidden there was the small "apartment" that would serve as Jeff's office.

"Come on, Chrissy, lead the way. Let's see what other surprises this house has to offer." Jeff prodded his daughter past the stairway. He turned toward Karen and took her hand, gently pulling her away from her reverie to continue their exploration.

Continuing to the right and now turning back toward the front of the house they walked down a narrow hallway and into the back parlor. Chrissy was nowhere in sight. Faintly Karen heard the tapping sound of little feet running on the floor above. She looked up toward the sound and then at Jeff. With a slightly accusing tone she asked, "How did she get upstairs? I thought you were watching her?"

Jeff looked at her like she had shaken a marble loose, "What are you talking about?"

Karen called out, "Chrissy, come down here…now!"

Hearing a door open behind them they turned as Chrissy squealed with surprise, "Here I am! Look Mommy, look Daddy, a bathroom!"

Karen looked at Chrissy and then at Jeff and then up toward the ceiling, "I must be hearing things."

"You're just tired from the long drive. Maybe we shouldn't have come here until after the baby."

"Nonsense, I'm fine. It was probably old house noises. They do that."

Jeff retraced his steps into the hallway where Chrissy was standing. What had appeared as just a closet was actually a small bathroom tucked away under the stairway. "Now that's convenient." Jeff muttered.

"It will certainly cut down on the trips upstairs," Karen added.

After the acknowledgement of her discovery Chrissy sped on into the back parlor where she discovered something more to her liking; a television, set into a small cabinet next to the fireplace. Squealing with delight she clamored, "Big Bird, can I watch Big Bird?"

Karen and Jeff had followed her into the parlor admiring first the large windows on the left that looked out onto the other side yard and their neighbor's home, then the large doors just ahead and then to the right another small door that opened back into the dining room. Next to it was another fireplace, this one a free standing cast iron type, with glass doors, and just to their right, tucked into a neat little corner sat a TV cabinet which still contained the television, another item left by the previous owners. Chrissy had planted herself in front of the television, looking to them to turn it on.

"In a little while, Chrissy; let's finish with the house, okay?"

"Okay."

On the walls, around the room, were several electric light fixtures resembling hurricane lamps, but hanging overhead was a very unusual looking lamp. Jeff stood at the entrance to the room flicking the switches, the wall lights flicking on and off accordingly, but none of the switches seemed to control the overhead lamp.

"Wait a minute, Jeff. Reach up and see if the lamp will come down lower."

Jeff reached up and grabbed a small ring on the underside of the lamp and pulled gently. The light responded and soon it was down at eye level. Looking closely they inspected the lamp. Jeff said, "No wonder, there aren't any bulbs in it."

Karen chuckled lightly, "No silly. This isn't an electric light. This is an actual oil lamp, just like they used before they had electricity. I read about it in the literature on the house. Isn't that neat?"

In wonder, Jeff replied, "Yeah, pretty cool. This place is full of surprises."

"Jeff, this room has such a cozy feel to it, even without the furniture. Can't you just imagine a nice fire on a cold evening, watching a movie, cuddled up on the couch, just the three of us?"

Jeff coughed lightly, "Make that the four of us. It won't be that long, remember? Besides, this is Florida; what do you mean cold evening?"

"Jeff, I read that it can get down in the twenties sometimes, in the winter. That's cold in my book."

"Yeah, okay. I'll give you that, this is northern Florida."

Karen smiled at her husband.

Chrissy was now ahead of them again, leading the way into the front parlor. She had slid open two large oak doors, one at a time, putting all her weight into each door as it disappeared into the wall on either side. Here again, another fireplace, beautifully tiled, sat at an angle just inside to the left of the double sliding doors. As they stood in the doorway, in the opposite corner just next to the front window sat another piece that the previous owners had left and one that Karen could especially admire; a beautiful piano. "Oh Jeff, isn't it beautiful? It has to be almost two hundred years old. Look at the styling. She sat down on the stool and ran her fingers across the keys, the notes of a Chopin piece gently rising from the instrument. "It sounds wonderful; perfectly tuned," she turned to Jeff, tears glistening in her eyes, a smile spreading across her face, "Oh Jeff, I am so happy. This house is just wonderful."

"Hey, hold your judgment; we haven't seen the upstairs yet. Besides, remember, you're going to be chasing Chrissy up and down these stairs for a long time to come. You might not be smiling after a while."

"You know what? I'm going to enjoy every minute of it! Come on, let's go upstairs. Come on Chrissy; let's go check out your new bedroom."

Chrissy squealed with delight as she ran through the archway, across the foyer heading for the front stairs.

"Whoa there, kiddo, wait for us. And rule number one in the house, no running on the stairs, okay?" Jeff hollered out.

"Okay Daddy."

The three of them headed up the stairs, Chrissy leading the way. At the top a long hallway stretched off to their left toward the back of the house. Jeff looked down the long hall, "Let's see, bowling or roller skates...which will she try first?"

Karen looked at the hardwood floor that stretched at least thirty feet, "I'd guess the skates will come first." They laughed at the prospect.

Just opposite where they stood, a door opened into the master bedroom and from their position they could see a beautifully carved high backed wood bed that dominated the room; the etched design highlighted by the light from the bay windows that afforded them a beautiful view of the lake.

To their right was a type of mezzanine; a railing of delicately turned oak spindles providing protection from the stairwell and the windows affording another great view of the lake.

"I'm putting a rocker right there," Karen said excitedly. "That will be the perfect place to rock the baby or read to Chrissy; don't you think, Jeff? And another thing...we will definitely have to put baby gates at the top of these stairs."

Jeff had wandered into the bedroom across the hall. "What? Uh... yeah, what ever you say, hon. Karen, look at this bed. I know we saw it in the pictures, but look at the size of this thing. It is awesome."

The bedroom also had a tiled fireplace, which Karen seemed to notice as much as the bed. Then she turned to her left and walked slowly into a short passage through which she then entered the master bath. During restoration the previous owners had converted one of the bedrooms into a huge bathroom, complete with another fireplace. A huge old fashioned tub dominated the room, while a converted antique dresser, mounted against the far wall, served as the sink. On that same wall, just to the right, a very large, ornately cut, stained glass window threw beautiful splashes of color across the room. Looking around, Karen realized that there was no logical way the tub could have been brought in through either of the room's doors.

"Jeff, can you possibly explain something for me?"

"Sure, what is it?"

"Look at the tub and then look at the doors. How did they get that thing in here?"

Now Jeff had one on her. He motioned over to the stained glass window, "Through there."

"Through the window?"

"Yup!"

"You're joking, right? That window doesn't open. It's solid."

"Karen," Jeff said with a great deal of patience, "While they were restoring the house, before they installed the window they brought the tub up with a hoist through the window opening. You better hope we never have to change that fixture out."

"How did you know that?"

"I read the information on this place, just like you did. I remembered some things; you remembered others, like the lamp downstairs."

"I guess so."

Looking around Karen realized that Chrissy was not marveling at the bathroom wonder with them so she called out, "Chrissy, where are you?"

"Back here, mommy. I want this room. This is my room, okay?"

Karen and Jeff followed her voice out into the hall, turning right and down to the last door on their left, passing by another room on their left as they went. "I think we'll make that one the baby's; okay with you, Jeff?" Karen said in passing.

"Sure, hon. I'm leaving that stuff up to you, if you don't mind?"

"Well, it's just across the hall from us; easy access to the bathroom. It just makes sense, don't you think?"

"Absolutely; whatever you say, hon," and with a twinkle in his eye he finished with, "You're the boss."

They stepped into the room that Chrissy had claimed possession of and it was perfect. Again, a bed had been left in this room and it had a half canopy design. The delicately carved wood backboard reached almost to the ten foot ceiling. From there it extended out approximately four feet over the bed and from it, pretty white and lavender flowered fabric draped in soft folds back to the wall, creating an almost protective shell above the pillow. The bedspread matched the bed drape as well as the window curtains and the walls were covered with a soft white paper with tiny lavender flowers.

"I believe this one is called the 'lavender room'; at least that's what the website called it," Karen said. "Chrissy, I think you picked the perfect room."

Sitting on the bed Chrissy beamed at her mother. "And look here, mommy. I have my own bathroom and my own playroom." Chrissy directed her parents out into the hall where just outside her door, in what looked like another closet, and in reality, that's what it had been originally, was a bathroom with a shower.

Directly across the hall from Chrissy's bedroom was another door that opened into a compact room; perfect for her and her numerous toys. With full windows on two walls the room had a bright and spacious feel. As they entered they also noted that here was the final destination of the other staircase. A railing guarded the stairwell and Jeff and Karen both noted that here again was a possible problem. Looking at each other they simultaneously stated, "Baby gate!"

Chrissy looked at them, her arms wrapped across her chest, and with an indignant air firmly stated, "I'm not a baby!"

Jeff looked at her, "We weren't speaking of you, honey. We meant for your brother, after he's born." Jeff gave Karen a quick wink.

"Okay, that's different. A baby gate will be fine." Chrissy was very intuitive for a four year old.

"Why don't we head down stairs and I'll get the bags from the car," Jeff said to Karen, "but let's take the front stairs for now. What do you think? We can unpack the things we'll need for tonight, get cleaned up and go get something to eat. Sound like a plan?"

"Sounds good to me... what do you think, Chrissy?" Karen asked her daughter.

"Pizza!"

Karen looked at Jeff, "Pizza it is," he replied.

Chapter 2

Karen rolled over—at least that's what she called it at this stage of her pregnancy—her half opened eyes gradually adjusting to the slow creeping light that was filtering into the bedroom. She looked towards the windows, now aware that it was morning; her first morning in her new home. She laid the covers back and, with some effort, got herself up and slowly walked to the windows and watched as the sun made its way into the eastern sky. The horizon, which was actually the tops of the homes on the opposite side of Circle Drive, visible just above the lake, moved gently from deep purple to a rosy pink and then the sun made its entrance, lighting up the world for another day. The view of the lake was beautiful, the sun casting its reflection onto the smooth water as it made its way slowly, but determinedly higher.

Karen made her way through the quiet house; down the front stairs, through the dining room and into the kitchen where she began to prepare for the family's awakening. She knew it would not be long before Chrissy was up, chirping and chattering like the birds outside the kitchen window.

Rummaging through the few boxes they had brought in, boxes they knew they would need immediately, Karen found the coffee maker and conveniently packed next to it, the can of decaffeinated coffee. *'Hmmm, someone was thinking'* she thought to herself. She placed it on the counter in the back room, plugged it in and proceeded to get a pot going. As the coffee began to perk, filling the kitchen with the aroma of that fresh brew, Karen rummaged around in another box looking for the cereal Chrissy would be wanting as soon as she arrived in the kitchen. The night before they had found a Pizza Hut, and then after eating, they shopped for a few things they would need in the morning at the Winn Dixie grocery store across the highway; she would take care of the complete shopping later.

Grabbing the milk out of the refrigerator, she headed for the island counter and another box, to locate a spoon and bowl. From up above she heard the padding of little feet and then from up the back stairs she heard Chrissie's voice. Chrissy was calling for her so she called up the stairwell, "Chrissy, mommy's down in the kitchen."

A sleepy voice came back, "Okay, mommy." There was a pause and then Karen heard from the stairwell, "Mommy?"

She looked up the back staircase and saw Chrissy peering over the railing at her, "Yes, honey, what do you want? Are you ready for some breakfast?"

Rubbing her eyes Chrissy answered "Um huh…mommy?"

"Yes, Chrissy?"

"Can I come down the stairs? Here, I mean."

Karen paused for a moment, considering the dilemma of allowing her to use these steep stairs or going all the way to the front stairs and walking her down. "Okay, but listen to me. You walk to the top of the stairs and then very slowly take one step at a time. These steps are very steep and I don't want you to fall accidentally. I will stand right here until you get down, okay?

Shaking her head in agreement Chrissy made her way to the top of the stairs and slowly stepped down, first one step and then two and so on until she reached her mother's arms. "Good morning, sunshine," Karen said. Chrissy smiled into her mother's hair as Karen gave her a big hug.

"How about some cereal?"

Chrissy skittered over to the stool at the island counter, hugged it with both arms as she made her way to the top, finally arranging herself at the counter, ready for breakfast. Karen poured the bowl half full with the crispy puffs, poured some milk over it and with spoon in hand Chrissy began to eat.

Karen poured herself a cup of coffee, knowing full well she would probably end up with heartburn, and sat down on the stool across from Chrissy, "How did you sleep?"

Between mouthfuls Chrissy answered, "Fine."

"We will get your room all fixed up today and when we're done with your room we will go in and start on the baby's room. What do you think?"

Her mouth full of cereal, Chrissy nodded an exuberant yes, her eyes revealing her excitement.

A few minutes later the sound of heavy sluggish footsteps could be heard overhead, then the sound of a toilet flushing. "Sounds like someone else is finally up."

Chrissy giggled.

"Jeff, we're down here in the kitchen and the coffee's ready."

"I'm on my way."

"Come down the back stairs if you want, just take them slowly."

Then the thunk, thunk sound of steps preceded Jeff's entrance into the kitchen, scratching his head and then his slightly whiskered chin as he took the last step, "Oh, man. I slept like a log. That bed's not bad at all; how about you, babe?"

"I slept fine, or at least as well as I can at this point." and she rubbed her hand over her large belly.

Jeff was, by now, next to Karen and gave her a kiss on her cheek and then stepped over to Chrissy and gave her a big cheek rub. Giggling, Chrissy waved her daddy away.

"What's on the agenda today, boss, and by the way, are you supposed to be drinking that stuff? I thought it gives you heartburn?" Jeff smiled at Karen as he poured a cup of hot coffee.

"It probably will, but I just felt like it this morning. Chrissy and I were just sitting over breakfast discussing the day's schedule; right, Chrissy?"

"Right, mommy; we're gonna fix up the baby's room today, after we finish my room," she said to her father.

"Well, good, then I can sit back and watch."

Karen and Chrissy looked at each other and then at Jeff, both shaking their heads no. "I don't think so," they said simultaneously.

"Only kidding; only kidding. Actually, if you two don't mind I'm going to start tackling my office in the garage. The sooner I get things up and running out there, the sooner I like it."

"Jeff, I know you love what you do, but you really don't have to work you know?"

"I know. Winning that lottery was probably the greatest thing that has or ever will happen to us. It made all of this possible." Jeff motioned around the room. "But, you know I can't just sit around and vegetate. My graphic design business is something I really love doing; just can't help myself. Sorry."

"That's okay; we forgive you, don't we Chrissy?"

Looking very seriously at her father Chrissy said, "Yes, Daddy, we forgive you." Then turning to her mother she asked quietly, with a serious edge to her voice, "Mommy, what are we forgiving Daddy for?"

"Nothing honey, it's just a joke."

A bright light seemed to spread across Chrissy's face. She giggled lightly as she let out a sigh of relief, "Oh, that's good. I was worried."

Jeff and Karen laughed out loud.

Chapter 3

Chrissy's room took Karen and Chrissy most of that day to complete so they put off working on the baby's room until the next. Part way through the next morning Chrissy had become bored with the process so she had wandered off to her play area at the end of the hall.

Karen was busy putting away some of the baby's clothes when she heard Chrissy talking to someone, so Karen assumed that Jeff had finally surfaced from his office where he had been spending all his free hours for the last two days, "Jeff, come here for a minute, will you?" she called out.

After a few moments and no reply she called out again, "Jeff, are you there?"

She could still hear Chrissy talking, so she walked down the hall to the door leading into Chrissy's playroom. Chrissy was sitting on the floor having a conversation with no one. "Chrissy, who are you talking to?"

Chrissy looked up at her mother, "Abigail."

Karen looked around the room and then asked, "Abigail who?"

Chrissy's expression changed from smiling to concern as she turned back to the direction she had been facing originally, looking intently at nothing, and then asked, "Why?"

"Why what? Chrissy, what are you doing? Who are you talking to?" Karen was beginning to get annoyed and yet a tinge of concern was seeping into her voice.

Chrissy turned again to her mother, now a somewhat confused look on her face. She looked back at the emptiness she had been conversing with, paused for a moment, nodded her head lightly in agreement, and then turned again to her mother, "My friend, mommy. My secret friend and I can't tell you any more." Chrissy paused for a moment and then said, "Is that okay, mommy? I mean, is it okay if I have a secret friend?"

Karen stood there for a moment, many thoughts going through her mind, the least of which was '*All children have imaginary friends...what can it hurt?*' "Sure Chrissy, that's okay with me. You just tell Abigail— that's her name, right? — that you're not allowed to go down those stairs unless you ask first, okay?"

Chrissy visibly brightened as she answered her mother, "Okay, mommy." Then she turned back to the nothingness and smiled.

Karen smiled, turned back to return to her baby room and mumbled to herself, "I'll have to tell Jeff about this." She chuckled lightly as she returned to the baby clothes.

Several hours later Karen headed for the kitchen to make some lunch. She called up the back stairwell, "Chrissy, would you and Abigail like some lunch?"

Chrissy looked over the rail to her mother, "Abigail is gone for now mommy, but I'm hungry. Can I come down this way?"

"Take it very slowly, okay?"

Chrissy took each step one at a time, and when she reached the bottom she looked at her mother with a very serious expression and said, "Mommy, Abigail told me that these stairs are very dangerous and that I must be careful, so I'm being very careful."

"Well, Abigail is very smart. I'm glad you have her for a friend."

Chrissy literally beamed at her mother, her smile spreading across her face like the morning sunrise. "I am too, mommy."

Karen called out to Jeff, over the intercom system, that lunch was ready. When he came through the door, he grabbed

Chrissy up and twirled her around as she squealed with delight, "How's my little pumpkin today."

"Fine, daddy," and she giggled again as he set her to her feet.

"I have a new friend, Daddy."

Jeff looked up at Karen with a slight look of surprise, "Did you two go somewhere?"

"No."

"Did someone come to visit?"

"No."

Now he looked really confused. Karen said, "Chrissy, tell Daddy about your new friend."

Chrissy looked at her father, smiling at first and then her expression took on a tone of seriousness, "I met a new friend today, Daddy. Her name is Abigail."

Jeff looked at Chrissy, expecting more to come. When it didn't, he looked at Karen with a bewildered, questioning look. Karen returned his gaze with an upward nudge of her shoulders and a slight shake of her head side to side. "Okay, Chrissy, are you going to tell me anymore or are you going to keep Abigail to yourself?"

Chrissy bit her lip lightly, seemed to contemplate her daddy's question and then replied, "Right now, Daddy, Abigail is my secret friend, so I can't tell you anymore. Mommy said it was okay with her; is it okay with you?"

Jeff looked at Karen and realized that, for now, it was best to leave the subject alone. He'd find out what Karen knew later. "Sure, Chrissy, that's fine. You can tell me more when you want."

Chrissy smiled broadly, "Thank you, Daddy. I'll tell you more when Abigail says it's okay."

Jeff nodded to Chrissy, confusion written boldly on his face, and then he turned to Karen, "Shouldn't you be seeing a doctor soon? I mean, aren't you supposed to check-in with someone down here?"

"I have an appointment with Dr. Kincaid tomorrow; he's the one Dr. Davis recommended. His office is in Crestview and my appointment is for one in the afternoon. And, if I remember correctly, I told you about the appointment yesterday."

Jeff thought about it for a moment and then looked sheepishly at his very pregnant wife, "Yes, you did. My mistake, I forgot. Remind me in the morning so that I don't get into something too deep on my computer. I get out there, into my work and I am lost to the world."

Karen chuckled lightly, "And you're telling me something I don't already know? I will keep you well informed; believe me."

The next day, after sitting in the van, for what seemed like an unusually long time, entertaining Chrissy with endless games and stories, Jeff looked up with a loving smile as Karen approached the car, waddling along slowly, but surely. Looking at her wide smile he asked, "Well?"

"Everything's right on schedule. He had already looked at my records from Dr. Davis and after checking all my vitals, he said everything looks good. The baby's heart sounds good. He took an ultrasound, just to make sure, and said that our son should be arriving in two to three more weeks."

Jeff grinned from ear to ear, "That sounds so cool; our son."

Karen continued, "He also said he was afraid that the long trip here would cause me to go into labor sooner than expected, but he is now confident that everything will be on schedule."

Chrissy spoke up, "Mommy, is my little brother coming soon?"

"Yes Chrissy, in a few more weeks, so I will need your help when he arrives."

"Oh, I know that. I'm all ready to help, but I have a question?" Chrissy's expression had become more serious, "Can Abigail help with the baby? I mean, as much as she can."

Without missing a beat Karen answered, "Absolutely. Abigail is welcome to help anytime she can. You tell her for me, okay?"

Chrissy seemed to glow with pride, not only for her mother's confidence in her, but in Abigail as well. "I will, mommy, and she will be very happy. She wants to be part of the family. Oops." Chrissy slapped her hand over her mouth quickly. Her eyes grew wide as she realized she may have said too much.

Jeff and Karen looked at each other for a moment, smiled and then Karen said, "Okay Chrissy, let's get you hooked up. We'll go have some lunch and then head for home."

Chrissy called out, "Pizza!"

Chapter 4

A few days later Karen was in the kitchen getting ready to start dinner when she heard what she thought were piano sounds coming from the front room. She paused what she was doing and listened; nothing. She started to resume her preparations when she heard the sounds again. "Chrissy, are you playing at the piano?" There was no reply. *'Wait a minute',* Karen thought, *'Chrissy's out in the office with Jeff'.* Pausing for a moment Karen listened again; nothing. Karen took a deep breath and went back to her work.

Suddenly the melody came very strong, "Twinkle, Twinkle Little Star", distinct in its nature because she recognized the piece that many children learn, just as she did when she was first learning to play. And it was coming from the front parlor where the piano stood. "Chrissy, you are not supposed to play on the piano, you know that." Karen was moving toward the front parlor, turning from the breakfast nook, through the family room, drying her hands on a towel as she went, and as she approached the front parlor, where the sliding doors stood almost all the way open, she realized, there was no one there; no one at the piano or even in the room. The music had stopped, but when, she couldn't say, but there was no one in the room.

"I must be losing it. I'm going crazy," Karen said out loud as she looked around the room. Karen stood a few minutes, looking in the corners and behind the settee, to make sure Chrissy wasn't hiding somewhere. She retreated to the back parlor, still looking at the piano as she slowly sat down on the couch. "I know I heard someone playing 'Twinkle, Twinkle

Little Star' on that piano," she said out loud. She got up awkwardly and walked over to the piano again, touched the keys lightly and then tapped out the child's tune. "I knew it was on this piano. That's the exact tone that I heard," she said, speaking to no one in particular. "I don't know whether to tell Jeff about this or not? He'll think I've lost my mind."

Just then Karen heard the sounds of Chrissy and Jeff coming in the back door, calling out for her as they entered, so she carried herself into the kitchen.

"Hi, guys!" she smiled at them as she walked back into the kitchen area.

"Hi hon, is dinner ready? Chrissy and I are starved, right, Chrissy?"

"Right, Daddy," Chrissy paused long enough to draw an excited breath and then she went on, "Mommy, Daddy played a game with me on his computer and I won! I beat him!"

"Wow, the old man must be slipping. Either that or you are just getting to be too good for him. Which is it, Chrissy?" Karen smiled at Chrissy and then at Jeff.

"Daddy said I am too good for him, right Daddy."

"That's right. She's getting to be a real expert at that game. Guess we'll just have to find another one that I can beat her at." Jeff gave Chrissy a rub on her head, messing up her hair in the process, which she quickly smoothed back down with her hands, giggling and laughing all the while.

"Dinner's not quite ready. Give me a few more minutes. Say, Chrissy why don't you go wash your hands for dinner."

"Okay mommy." Chrissy quickly rounded the corner and entered the bathroom under the staircase. Karen then spoke quietly to Jeff, "Did Chrissy stay out there with you the whole time?"

"Yeah; why?"

"I mean, did she leave your sight at all, to go to the bathroom or get a drink?"

"No. What's wrong? Why are you asking?"

Karen went on to explain what had happened before Jeff and Chrissy came into the house and as she spoke Jeff's expression turned from concern to questioning. "Are you certain it was the piano and not some noise from outside? Maybe it was an ice cream wagon."

"I think I can tell the difference between someone playing 'our' piano and some horn or bird or someone talking outside. And besides, it's October. The ice cream wagon isn't running now." Karen was beginning to get perturbed. "Jeff, it doesn't make sense. How can that piano play by itself?"

"Mommy, it didn't play by itself. That was Abigail. She knows how to play the piano." Chrissy slapped her hands over her mouth again, eyes wide with surprise and guilt.

Jeff and Karen turned toward Chrissy and then looked back at each other. Turning once more toward Chrissy, Karen asked, "Tell us more about Abigail, Chrissy?"

Chrissy looked at them both, first Karen and then Jeff, and with a small voice asked, "Can we eat first?"

Karen had forgotten all about dinner and, now feeling a little guilty, answered her young daughter, "Yes Chrissy, we can eat first. Then after dinner you can tell us what you can about Abigail, okay?"

Chrissy nodded her head in agreement, looking much like a person being led to the gallows; the dread in her expression evident. Karen looked at her child and felt anger at herself for starting this whole affair over a few notes on the piano. "Come here baby, it's all right. You're not in trouble and neither is Abigail, okay?" and she hugged Chrissy tight.

When their meal was over Karen asked Chrissy to help her with the dishes; the two of them talking about any number of things except Abigail. Chrissy's mood had lifted during dinner so Karen and Jeff were not going to push the issue for now, but when the dishes were finished and put away Chrissy, letting out a big sigh, said very seriously, "Okay, I'm ready."

"Ready for what, honey?" Karen asked.

"To tell you about Abigail, but I don't know very much."

"Why don't we go in the family room with Daddy and you can tell us what you know."

Morosely, Chrissy answered, "Okay," her voice betraying her sadness. As she turned toward the hall leading from the kitchen into the family room Chrissy stopped and turned back toward the back stairwell, staring intently at the bottom steps. Quietly, she whispered, her face easing into a gentle smile, "Thank you."

Karen looked at her intently, but did not question as she then lead the way into the family room and eased herself onto the couch. Chrissy followed her in and then crawled up into the big chair and sat on Jeff's lap, "I'm ready." This time her mood was more normal and her voice reflected the lift in her spirit.

Karen started the dialogue, "Chrissy, this evening while I was getting dinner I heard someone playing the piano. You were outside in the office with Daddy, so I know it wasn't you. In the kitchen you said it was Abigail, but we thought Abigail was your pretend friend?"

"No, mommy, Abigail is real."

"How do you mean 'real', Chrissy?" Karen prodded her daughter for more.

"I met her the first day we were here, up in my room, but she asked me not to tell anyone. Then you heard me talking to her and she asked me again not to say anything; to keep her a secret, so I did. But you said it was all right, I mean, to keep her a secret." Chrissy looked at her mother with apologizing eyes.

"I know I did, honey and..." Karen paused for a moment. Looking at Jeff, her expression took on a 'what's going on' look. "Uhhh, Jeff, I think we may have to postpone this conversation."

"Karen, what's the matter?"

"I think I'm going into labor."

"Oh-oh." Quickly setting Chrissy down on her feet, Jeff motioned to Karen to stay where she was and ran to get the phone. He ran the phone back to Karen so that she could call the hospital while he got her bag out to the car. He knew there was no time to lose, because when Chrissy was born there were just a few hours between onset of labor and birth. The hospital was a thirty minute ride so time was of the essence. Returning to the house he next picked up Chrissy, bundled her into her coat and took her out to the car and got her strapped in, then he returned to the house.

By now Karen had made it to the back door, a sweat breaking out on her forehead. Jeff grabbed her coat, swept it around her shoulders and then helped her down the back steps to the car. Soon they were rocketing down the freeway, pushing the speed limit all the way until they reached the Crestview exit. Jeff swung the car onto the exit ramp, taking the wide arc as safely as he could and headed north on Hwy 85 towards the hospital. Looking over at Karen he saw the concern in her eyes as she smiled a weak and waning smile as the next wave of pain overtook her. "We're almost there, honey. Hold on...please hold on," desperation and concern lacing his words.

Jeff finished the last mile of their journey as he wheeled into the emergency entrance of the hospital. Leaving the van idling, he ran into the hospital, soon returning with a nurse pushing a wheelchair. Karen eased out of the van and into the chair as Jeff closed her door. "I'll park the car and be in with Chrissy as soon as I can, honey." Karen could only nod in reply.

Chrissy had been well prepared by Karen and Jeff about the forthcoming birth and had arranged with the hospital for a birthing suite where the whole family could be present. Chrissy was very much looking forward to witnessing the birth of her little brother and looked around the room with excited enthusiasm as she and Jeff walked through the entrance of the suite. Karen was nearing the final stages of labor as Jeff and Chrissy neared her bed. It had been only one hour and fifteen minutes since the pains had started and Jeff was concerned about the rapid progress so he asked the nurse, "Is everything okay? I mean, she's only been in labor a little over an hour. Isn't that too fast?"

"Everything's fine, Mr. Miller, she and the baby are doing just great. A very small percentage of women have very little notice leading up to labor and then have very rapid onset of contractions. It's called precipitous birth. Your wife is one of those. She's lucky, in a way. She doesn't have to spend hours upon hours in pain. Just a quick 'here I come' and then 'here I am' and it's all over. I should be so lucky," and she smiled a warm and knowing smile.

Jeff gave her a weak smile in return and then turned his attention to Chrissy, "You want to go see mommy?"

Chrissy, wide eyed, nodded her head in agreement. As they approached the bed Karen was well into another contraction and was breathing heavily as she tried to control the pain. As the contraction subsided she became aware of Chrissy's presence and turned her head toward her young daughter, "Hi, sweetie. Are you ready for this? The baby's almost here."

"Oh yes, mommy. I'm going to stand right here and help you breath and if you need to hold my hand you can."

Karen smiled at her charming child as another contraction hit, "Oooohhhh, Chrissy, help me breath...now," and Karen began puffing as the wave of pain overtook her.

Jeff looked at his wife and then to Chrissy and smiled as he watch his young daughter puffing along with his wife. The nurse entered the room followed shortly after by the doctor and as they hurried to the bedside Karen eased back on her breathing.

"Okay, Karen, everything is going great. You are almost completely dilated so I feel like we are going to welcome your little guy any moment now; ready to get this show on the road?" Doctor Kincaid patted Karen's hand lightly.

"You bet I aaaammm," and Karen started puffing again, with Chrissy puffing right along with her.

Doctor Kincaid took his position at the end of the bed where a special section had been removed permitting the doctor plenty of room to work. As Karen groaned, doctor Kincaid called to her, "Okay, Karen. He's right there; all you have to do is push. Jeff, would you like to watch your young son come into this world? Chrissy, would you like to watch your brother being born?"

Chrissy looked to Jeff and then to Karen, "Mommy, do you still need me?"

"Go baby; greet Clayton when he comes out."

Chrissy quickly moved to the end of the bed as Jeff joined her, holding her by the shoulders to keep her from crowding the doctor and nurses. "Can you see okay, baby?"

"Uh huh. I'm okay, Daddy." Chrissy's attention was focused entirely on the doctor and what he was doing. As the contractions came on harder, Karen pushed hard, her efforts rewarded by the emergence of a tiny head at the vaginal opening. Chrissy looked up at Jeff, her eyes round with wonder. Jeff smiled at her and then motioned with his head for her to look again towards the doctor. As Chrissy looked back another push could be heard in Karen's grunting sounds and with that Clayton's head and shoulders emerged. Then as the doctor cradled her new brother's head and shoulders, he reached out with his other hand to then take hold of the infant's lower torso and legs as Clayton finally exited the birth canal.

Chrissy was jiggling with excitement as she whispered over the doctor's shoulder, "Happy Birthday, Clayton." Chrissy then turned her beaming face up to Jeff and smiled the most joyful smile he had ever seen on his young, and oh so bright, daughter's face.

Jeff smiled down at her and then diverted his attention towards Karen, "You did it, momma. Baby number two has arrived, safe and sound, all fingers and toes intact,"— and at that moment Clayton disrupted things with a hearty cry— "and it seems a good set of lungs."

The nurse assisting the doctor had weighed, measured, tagged and then bundled the infant up and then walked him to Karen where she laid him gently into the crook of Karen's arm, smiling warmly as she said, "Good job, short and sweet. Here's your son, Karen."

Jeff and Chrissy walked back to the side of the bed and Karen smiled at them weakly as she said, "Well, Chrissy, what do you think? Are you ready for your brother?"

"Oh yes, mommy. He's beautiful! He is a little messy right now, but a good bath will take care of that." Everyone laughed. Then Chrissy asked, "When can we take him home?"

Jeff answered, "Chrissy, why don't we give mommy a night off and let her sleep here over night. Then you and I will come back and get her in the morning. That is, if the doctor says everything is okay to go home," and with that Jeff turned his gaze towards the doctor who was then walking up to the side of the bed.

"I would say, barring any unexpected problems, that tomorrow will be just fine, provided you are feeling up to it." Doctor Kincaid smiled at Karen and patted her on the hand, "Good job, mommy."

Karen smiled at the small group standing by her bed, took a deep breath and said, "I'll get back with you in the morning. Right now, I need some sleep," and she yawned and her eyes blinked sleepily.

Chrissy turned her head up, looking at Jeff, "I'm going to say good night to Clayton and then we better go home. I think we all need some sleep."

"I think that is a great idea, Chrissy."

Chapter 5

Thanksgiving was just around the corner and Karen and Chrissy were busy planning their first Thanksgiving in their new home. Clayton was spending most of the daytime hours sleeping, waking regularly for feeding. Jeff had resumed his computer work and the subject of Abigail had not been brought up, much to Chrissy's relief.

It happened to be a rather warm November, the daytime highs reaching the low seventies, making it nice for afternoon walks around the lake, which Karen sorely needed to get herself back into some kind of shape. So Karen and Chrissy decided to take Clayton out for his first stroll. Karen had purchased an antique baby carriage which Jeff had painstakingly restored; painting the metal and wicker, and Karen had made a new pad to go in it, making sure it was sufficiently firm, but not too hard.

After lunch Karen bundled Clayton up in a cute blue sweater set with bonnet and booties, laid him in the carriage, neatly covered with a hand crocheted blanket of light blue, and she and Chrissy set off to walk the one mile around the lake. A few blocks from home they encountered an elderly woman coming toward them, walking slowly with her little dog on a leash, pausing each time the dog stopped to sniff a bush or the ground. As the woman got closer Karen smiled at her, telling Chrissy to say hello to the lady. The older lady smiled sweetly at Chrissy in response and then spoke, "Well, hello there young lady. Aren't you a pretty one?"

"Thank you," Chrissy answered, smiling sincerely. "Can I pet your puppy?"

"Why certainly, darlin'. His name is Rosco and he loves to be petted."

Looking up at Karen, the lady spoke again, "How do you do. I'm Serena Appleton. You're the folks that moved into the Cottonwood house?" The lady held out her hand to shake Karen's.

The lady's words dripped with southern refinement and Karen just loved the sounds. It was as musical and smooth to the ear as any Chopin piece. She smiled as she responded, shaking the woman's hand as she spoke, "Yes, I'm Karen Miller and this is my daughter, Chrissy. And in the carriage here is Clayton, our newest family member."

Serena looked into the carriage to admire Clayton, "Why, he is a new one. He can't be more than a few weeks old."

"Today is his one month birthday," Chrissy spoke up, a firm hold on the side of the carriage.

"One whole month, my goodness; and how old are you young lady?"

"I'm four years and five months old, Mrs. Appleton."

"Why, you are a bright one aren't you. A real sparkplug," Serena chuckled at Chrissy's precociousness, "I tell you what, Chrissy. Why don't you call me Miss Serena?"

Karen started to object, "I don't think that Chrissy should call you by your first name Mrs. Appleton."

"Honey, down here calling a lady by her first name with the Miss in front of it is a connotation of great respect. You will find all of the young ones call their elders by their first names preceded by mister or miss. It is endearin' to us and respectful by them. So darlin', you just call me Miss Serena. Will you do that?"

Chrissy looked to Karen and when Karen smiled back at her with a nod of her head, Chrissy answered, "Yes, Miss Serena."

"Good. Now that we have that settled, may I walk along with you for a ways?"

"Certainly," Karen answered, "we'd be happy to have you join us."

As they walked along, pausing now and then to allow Rosco to sniff, Karen and Serena exchanged information concerning their background. "How long have you lived here in DeFuniak Springs, Miss Serena?"

"Honey, I was born and raised here; lived here all my life, except for my time away at college. I went to Florida State University, then came back home to marry my childhood sweetheart. There isn't a thing gone on in this little town that I can't tell you about, even before I was born. You see, I love this town and its history. I've studied just about everythin' I can about this community. I'm a member of the Historical Society, you know, and I can tell you about every house or building that has any historical significance. Why, some of these homes go back to the 1880's; that's when DeFuniak Springs really got its start. Take that house you're livin' in, for example; sad, sad case."

Karen interrupted Serena, "Sad case, what do you mean? I thought the house was built by one of the town's most prominent citizens?"

"Oh, it was; Nathan and Marion Cottonwood. Quite rich, you know, made their money from the lumber industry. Their home was built in...let me think...1907. Yes, 1907. Completed and moved in just in time to celebrate the Christmas holidays, and my goodness, they did celebrate. They shared their happiness with the community; threw some grand affairs there, they did."

"Then why do you call them a sad case? What happened?" Karen's curiosity was aroused, especially because it pertained to their home.

"Well, it wasn't what happened then, but a short time later. Seems like it was about a year; ...yes, almost one year. You see, they'd been blessed with a daughter, just the one, and a sweet little thing she was, too. She was their pride and joy. Her name was Abigail; Abigail Cottonwood."

Karen froze. She looked at Chrissy and Chrissy was looking at her, their eyes meeting, the knowledge of what she perceived showing in Karen's eyes; confusion in Chrissy's.

Seeing their expressions and the unspoken exchange, Serena spoke, "Did I say somethin' wrong?"

Karen looked at her, unable to speak, not knowing what to say. Chrissy just looked straight ahead, holding onto the carriage, her knuckles turning white as her grip tightened.

"You've seen her, haven't you?" Serena asked, excitement edging into her voice.

"Seen who?" Karen spoke warily.

"The button hook child."

"Who?" Karen responded.

"The button hook child, or at least that's what everyone around here calls her. Abigail Cottonwood, or that is, her ghost."

"No, I haven't seen her, but...," Karen's gaze went immediately to Chrissy.

Serena spoke directly to Chrissy, leaning over slightly as she did, "Have you seen Abigail, Chrissy? Have you spoken to her?"

Chrissy looked up at her mother, fear and uncertainty in her gaze. Karen gave a slight nod of her head as if to give Chrissy permission to speak. "Yes, Miss Serena, I have seen her. She is my best friend and I talk to her all the time." Chrissy turned to Karen, "Mommy, what does this mean, I don't understand." Chrissy's confusion was complete and she looked to her mother, the tears brimming over the edges of her eyes and slowly trickling down her cheeks.

"Don't cry, honey," Serena spoke softly to Chrissy, "it's nothing to be afraid of. Many people have seen Abigail, but none have actually spoken to her. My. My. My. This is excitin'. Imagine; Abigail Cottonwood has surfaced again." Serena's face took on a dreamy, far away look.

Karen interrupted Serena's reverie, "Excuse me, Serena, but I think I had better take Chrissy home. She... we are very confused at this point and I need to get her and Clayton home for a nap."

"Oh, I understand, honey; believe me, I do. Now I know you don't know the whole story, so when you're ready, you let me know and I'll come over and answer any questions you might have."

"Thank you. I will be in touch." Karen gave Serena a weak smile and then turned the buggy, Chrissy still firmly gripping the side, and walked away toward their home. Suddenly she stopped and looked back at Serena, the old woman still standing there, holding Rosco's leash, looking as if she had offended, "Oh, Serena, I don't have your phone number."

"I'm listed in the phone book, honey. You just call me anytime, you hear?" and Serena gave Karen a sad, but earnest smile.

"Thank you, Serena, I will."

Karen moved quickly along the sidewalk, neither she nor Chrissy saying a word. When they got to their house Karen stopped at the wrought iron gate waiting for Chrissy to step forward and open the gate. When Chrissy made no move toward the gate Karen spoke, "Chrissy, will you hold the gate open for me?"

Chrissy turned to look up at her mother, the expression on her face was of total disconnect with anything Karen had said, "What, mommy?"

Karen spoke again, "Hold the gate for me Chrissy, so that I can get the buggy through and then we'll go in the house."

"Okay mommy." Chrissy's answer seemed listless and uninterested so Karen knew her daughter was troubled.

"Chrissy, please don't worry. I know there is a good explanation for all of this, okay? We'll tell Daddy and see what he says, okay?"

Chrissy just nodded her head in agreement as they went up the stairs and in through the front door. Inside, Chrissy asked if she could go up to her room and Karen sent her daughter on up the stairs ahead of her. After getting Clayton down in his crib Karen moved into Chrissy's room where she found her young daughter laying on her bed, facing the window, her back toward the door. Karen moved to her daughter's bed and sat on the edge, "Chrissy, are you all right?"

Chrissy rolled over and faced her mother, "Mommy, is Abigail a ghost?"

"I don't know Chrissy."

"But I see her and I talk to her. How can she be a ghost? She isn't scary and she wears a dress and shoes. She plays with me and she goes in and watches Clayton. She helps me take care of him. She's my friend!" Each word that Chrissy spoke seemed to rise in volume as her curiosity and fear intermingled.

Karen didn't know how to answer her daughter's questions so she just reassured Chrissy with, "It's going to be all right, Chrissy. We'll talk to Daddy and maybe he can explain what's going on, okay?"

"Okay," Chrissy answered as she cuddled up next to Karen's leg and slowly closed her eyes.

Karen's only problem was, how was she going to explain to Jeff what she and Chrissy had just learned.

Rather than wait until later, Karen called Jeff on the intercom, "Jeff, could you come inside. I need to speak to you. It is very important."

Jeff's voice came from the speaker on the wall, "Does it have to be right now? I've got something I'm working on. Can it wait until I come in for dinner?"

"No, I want to discuss it while the kids are asleep." Karen's voice was edged with concern and panic.

Noticing the tone of her voice Jeff came back, "Is everything okay? Are the kids okay?"

"The kids are fine, but I really need to speak with you and I don't want to leave them here in the house alone."

"Karen we have the nursery monitor; we can hear what goes on up there."

"Jeff! In here, now; please."

There was no questioning the panic in her voice so Jeff responded with, "I'll be right in."

When he entered the back door he found Karen sitting at the breakfast table just inside. She was sitting very straight, her head looking down at her hands on the table in front of her, her fingers intertwined. As he stepped next to the table she looked up at him, worry enveloping her entire demeanor.

"Good grief, Karen, what is the matter? You look like you've seen a ghost."

Karen huffed slightly, "If you only knew."

Now totally confused, Jeff shook his head from side to side and said, "What is wrong?"

"Let me try to explain." Karen proceeded to tell Jeff about her encounter with Serena, being coy not to say too much too soon. When she came to the part about their home she explained, "Jeff, do you remember the names of the original owners?"

"Of course, it was Cottonwood; Nathan and Marion Cottonwood."

"Correct. Well, as Miss Serena Appleton was explaining the history she told me that Nathan and Marion had a daughter; an only child and evidently something tragic happened about a year after they moved into the house; this house." Karen paused for a moment because she knew that what she was about to say Jeff would not believe.

Leaning on one of the chairs, getting impatient, Jeff commented, "So? A lot of tragedy happens in life. That was a long time ago. What has it got to do with us?"

Karen took a deep breath, exhaled and then, looking Jeff right in the eyes, said, "Their daughter's name was Abigail."

There it was. She had said it. Now she waited for Jeff's reaction and she didn't have to wait long. Recognition of what Karen was suggesting was evident in Jeff's face as it drained of color. Groping for the chair in front of him Jeff slowly pulled it away from the table and sat down, all the while looking at Karen, his eyes showing comprehension and then disbelief.

After what seemed like an interminable amount of time he spoke, "Are you suggesting that this house is haunted?" Karen moved her head slowly up and down. "You mean to tell me that our daughter's play pal is a ghost?" Karen continued to bob her head. "Do you know how crazy that sounds? Karen was beginning to resemble a bobble head doll. "Have you talked to Chrissy about this?"

"We were waiting for you. She's upstairs sleeping. Jeff, she is very upset about this; she doesn't understand the implications here and she is very confused. I got her to lie down and go to sleep so that I could talk to you before we discuss it with her."

Jeff sat quietly for a few moments, his head now cradled in his hands. He looked up at Karen, "Have you seen Abigail?"

"No."

"Have you heard her voice?"

"No, but that explains the piano and the footsteps upstairs that first day. Jeff, this isn't the end of the world and it certainly explains Chrissy's 'imaginary friend'. I really don't think we have anything to worry about because Chrissy told me that Abigail watches over Clayton. It's just... how do we explain all of this to her?"

"Well, before we can explain it to her I need to know all of the facts. Does anyone know what happened to Abigail?"

"Serena told me that when we needed further explanation she would be glad to come over and fill us in with the details. We could call her now... I'm sure she has returned home from her walk. Do you want me to call her? She's really nice; you'll like her, I know I do. When we first met, despite the shock of her statements, there was something about her that I just seemed to connect with, kind of like when I first met you."

Jeff thought about it for a moment and then said, "Yeah, give her a call. Let's at least find out what we can before we sit Chrissy down for a talk."

As Serena approached the front door she looked the house up and down, scanning the windows for any sign of movement; there was none. At the door she twisted the door bell handle and heard its harsh jingle on the inside. Through the window of the door she saw Karen approach and gently open the door, "Hello, Serena, thank you for coming over on such short notice. Please come in; Jeff is waiting in the kitchen, if you don't mind sitting at the table. I thought I would make us some tea, if you would like."

"That would be lovely, darlin'. I am so glad you called. I was concerned about Chrissy. Is she all right?"

Karen was leading the way into the kitchen by way of the front and back parlors, "She's sleeping right now and that's why we wanted to get more information now, before she wakes up, so that we can explain to her what is going on."

"Well, I will surely help you as much as I possibly can."

By now they were entering the breakfast area where Jeff was still seated at the table. When Serena entered the room Jeff stood up, reaching out his hand, "Hello, Misses Appleton, nice to meet you. I'm Jeff Miller."

"Please, call me Serena, everyone does. I am so happy to meet you. You are so lucky; you have such a wonderful family. And Chrissy, she is such a little darlin'; so precious and bright for her age."

"Thank you, Serena; I feel I'm pretty fortunate all the way around."

Karen had moved to the stove where she had a pot of tea ready, "Jeff, would you like some tea? Serena and I are having some."

"That would be nice; perhaps it will settle my nerves a little after the jolt they just had." Everyone laughed lightly as Karen sat a tray on the table loaded with cups, spoons, sugar, milk, and the tea pot.

Sitting in a chair half way between Jeff and Serena, Karen reached for the pot and poured three cups of the steaming, dark amber colored liquid. As she handed the cups around, pulling one closer in to herself, no one spoke. It was as if no one wanted to be responsible for starting this conversation. Finally, after a few minutes, Karen looked at Jeff, and then Serena and spoke, "Serena, could you tell us what happened here. Why does Abigail, if it is Abigail Cottonwood, haunt this house?"

"I'll surely tell you what I can. Of course, I wasn't alive then, that was a hundred years ago, and I am old, but not quite that old," and she chuckled lightly. Jeff and Karen followed suit. Serena continued, "The Cottonwood's were preparing for their second holiday season, seems like it was just about the same time of year you folks moved in, only a hundred years before. They had lived in the house almost exactly one year. There was a tragic accident, right here in this house, but I have never been able to find out exactly what happened. The one thing I am sure of is that Abigail died, in this house, in the fall of 1908.

Afterwards, following the funeral, her parents closed themselves off to the community, not receiving any guests or inquiries, and it seems that her parents just disappeared. The house was locked and no one knew what had happened to Nathan and Marion. After some years, with no family to claim the house, it was sold for back taxes, and thus began the progression of other owners and years of vacancy.

Nathan's lumber business also faltered. With no one to lead it and ownership under question because of Nathan's disappearance, it soon failed. It was all very strange and, without explanation, left a huge question mark in the history of this community.

"Now, as to sightings; several individuals have seen an apparition, that is, what looked like a human form, but it wasn't real defined; kind of like a mist. In the 1940's a few of us kids would sneak around the house occasionally, when we were feeling very brave, and look in the windows. We'd been told stories about a ghost and the house was vacant then. One warm summer night, let's see, I was about ten, — that was during the war, you know — there was my friend Clara, myself, and…Jacob, that's right, Jacob Woodly. We were feeling especially brave so we decided to sneak over to the Cottonwood house and peek inside, hoping we would see something. We were standing out here, near the back porch.

"Now, you must understand something. Where we are sitting right now, this breakfast area, was the back porch. Where that sink is, was a wall and a doorway into the kitchen and that stairway there, behind the wall, was an open staircase, leading up to the second story porch. All of this, both floors, was open to the air. We three, Clara, Jacob and I, were standing about ten feet out, away from the porch, walking slowly towards the back door to look in when we saw her. She was standing right at the bottom of the stairs, plain as I'm sitting here. One minute there was nothing, the next she was there.

"She looked to be about our age, but her clothes were strange in some ways. I mean, her dress was longer than what we wore then and it had a drop waist, you know what I mean, the skirt was old fashioned. Her hair was dark and in braids, but the dead giveaway was her shoes; they were black, high topped and buttoned up or laced up, it was dark so I couldn't see real clear, but that's why we call her the button hook child. Those shoes were the kind you needed a buttonhook to put them on.

"Anyway, we stood there transfixed; we didn't know what to do and she just stood there and looked right at us. I don't think more than a minute went by, but it seemed forever. Finally, she put up her hand, as if to stop us, or wave, I'm not really sure, but when she faded away, we took off running, screaming the whole way, back to Clara's yard, which was a block down and back through the alley. I'm telling you right now, I have never been so scared in my life, but then I was only ten."

Karen and Jeff had not said a word, or for that matter, even moved a muscle. They were stunned by Serena's story.

Finally, Jeff cleared his throat and Karen straightened in her chair, but it was Jeff that spoke, "Serena, did she speak to you?"

"No, she never said a word, but she didn't seem to menace us either. It was as if she was warning us to be careful or stay away. I've never been sure, but one minute she was as solid looking as you and the next she was gone."

Karen seemed to shiver slightly and when she looked down, her arms were covered with goose bumps. Karen looked to the old woman, "Serena, has anyone ever heard her speak, or for that matter, utter any sound?"

"Not that I know of; just a sighting now and then. Over the years this poor old house has seen a number of owners and for some years it sat vacant. I don't know why the different owners have moved, perhaps having a ghost in the house didn't suit them, but by the time the last owners, the ones you bought from, purchased the house, it was so run down, many thought it would be torn down. But those folks, God bless them, put the time and the money into restoring this old beauty, and you see it as it is today."

"Has anyone seen Abigail recently; I mean, before us, or that is, before Chrissy? You see, Serena, neither Karen nor I have seen Abigail." Jeff asked.

"Well, I believe the previous owners had an encounter with something, but I'm not really sure what happened. I heard something about a guest in their house, saw or felt something one night, and I believe they were sleeping in the lavender room, or the lilac room; something like that."

Karen and Jeff exchanged glances and then Karen spoke, "That's Chrissy's room now; the back room, on the side towards the church. It's just across from the day room, or what was the porch, and those back stairs."

"Well, I do believe that was Abigail's room, but I'm not quite sure on that point," Serena answered.

Jeff asked, "Is that all you know, Serena? Why is she haunting the house? Is there any way to get her to leave?"

With that last question Karen turned her head sharply towards Jeff, "Why would you want her to leave, Jeff? She's Chrissy's friend. Chrissy would be heart broken if Abigail were to leave."

"I was only trying to help Abigail. Obviously she's trapped here. She needs to go… somewhere. Geez, I didn't mean that to sound like I'm trying to get rid of her. As far as I can tell, she's not hurting anything, and she's certainly not hurting Chrissy."

"We have to handle this carefully," Karen said, speaking to no one in particular, "We have to make sure that whatever we do, whatever we say to Chrissy, it has to be right so that we don't scare her."

After a few moments of silence Karen spoke again, "Serena, we need to find out why Abigail is here and why she hasn't moved on to the other side, or heaven, or what ever you want to call where we go when we die. Do you have any suggestions? Obviously, none of us have the ability to communicate with Abigail and I'm not sure I want Chrissy to be our…interpreter."

Serena sat thinking for a moment, obviously conflicted by something. The expression on her face was evidence of her thoughts and gave away her inner turmoil as she frowned slightly and then transitioned into a weak smile, that smile then melting into another frown; her eyebrows going up and down with each change. Finally, she spoke, "There is a possibility; that is, there is someone we may get some answers from." She looked at Karen and then Jeff, aiming her next words directly at him, "That is, if you have no objections."

Jeff looked back at her and then at Karen, a questioning expression on his face, "Me? Why me?"

"Because you seem to be the most skeptical person here," Serena answered.

"I wouldn't say I'm skeptical. This whole thing has caught me off guard, that's all. What or who did you have in mind, Serena?"

"Well..." and Serena paused, trying to pick her words carefully, "there is a person, an older lady, who has..." and again she paused, "special abilities."

Jeff suddenly leaned back in his chair and threw up his hands, "Geez, I knew it; a goofy crackpot. What, a ghost chaser? Or is this voodoo? Oh, no, I've got it, a psychic. She talks to the ghosts, right Serena?"

Karen turned to Jeff with a piercing gaze, "Jeff!" she spoke suddenly and with hostility in her voice. "Serena is trying to help us. The least you can do is be quiet and let her talk." Karen turned to Serena, "I'm sorry. Please, Serena, go on. Who is this person?"

"Well, I won't divulge her name right yet, for this very reason," and she motioned toward Jeff, who was now gazing at the table surface, having been duly reprimanded, "but what I will do is get in touch with her and see if she is willin' to help you. She is," Serena paused again, "rather eccentric, but few know of her 'abilities' because of the ridicule she received as a child to do with her 'talents'."

Jeff spoke then, "Look, Serena, I'm sorry if I got abrupt with you, or sounded rude, but this whole thing is somewhat overwhelming for me. I mean, here we are, in our dream home, financially set for life, the perfect family, and then wham! I get smacked in the face with this. I live in a haunted house. Haunted by a little girls' ghost who just happens to be my little girl's best friend, and now we have to bring in a psychic to find out what the heck's going on. I'm just trying to wrap my brain around all of this, and I guess my brain is just too small, 'cause it's not fitting."

Karen looked at her husband, who at that moment looked like he was about to lose it, again, "Jeff, the main thing here is Chrissy. We need to do what is best for Chrissy, and if that means doing nothing, then so be it. But I think we owe it to Chrissy and to Abigail to find out why she is still here and what she needs. Don't you agree?"

Sheepishly Jeff looked at his wife, trying to figure out why she was so calm about this whole thing, "You're right; Chrissy is what's important."

No one spoke for a few moments, each person with their own thoughts and then Jeff spoke again, "Okay Serena, get in touch with this person. Let's see what we can find out and in the mean time, you and I, Karen, will try to explain to Chrissy what we understand up to this point. Good enough?"

"Good enough, Jeff," and Karen smiled back at her handsome husband.

Chapter 6

Later that afternoon, after Serena had left, Karen and Jeff decided to wait for Chrissy to awaken and then wing it from there. Jeff went back out to his office with the provision that as soon as Chrissy was awake, Karen would call him and they would take it from there.

Karen was in the kitchen, folding laundry, when she heard sounds coming from up the stairs. Thinking that Clayton was awake, or perhaps a radio had been left on, she moved closer to the stairwell and listened. It was then she realized what she was hearing was Chrissy. Listening more intently she realized that Chrissy was talking to someone, perhaps Abigail, but she could not make out the words. Karen waited for some minutes, undecided whether to interrupt Chrissy or let her go on talking. Finally, she decided to call her daughter, "Chrissy, are you awake?"

There was a moment of silence and then Karen heard, "Yes, mommy. Can I come down the back stairs?"

"Yes honey, just be careful. You know the drill; one step at a time."

Karen heard a couple of more muffled words and then Chrissy appeared at the top of the stairs. Slowly rubbing her eyes, she looked down the stairwell at her mother, "I'm coming now, mommy."

"Okay, Chrissy. I'm here at the bottom."

After Chrissy had made it down the stairs into her mother's waiting arms, Karen picked her up and carried her to a stool at the breakfast bar in the kitchen. Setting her down Karen ran her hand down the back of Chrissy's hair, stopping at the ends, where she wound her fingers lightly in the curls. "Did you sleep okay, honey?"

"Ummhuh," Chrissy answered.

"Would you like a snack, maybe an apple, to hold you until dinner?"

"No thank you mommy. I'm not hungry."

Karen paused, not really knowing what to say next, but aware that the subject of Abigail would come up sooner or later. As Karen sat down on the stool opposite her daughter, Chrissy took care of Karen's uncertainty.

"Mommy…" Chrissy paused. Karen kept silent knowing her daughter was searching for words. Chrissy looked at her mother, "Mommy, I talked to Abigail again."

"Yes, I know. I heard you, although I couldn't hear what you said."

"I asked her something… and I don't know if I should have because her answer didn't make sense."

"What did you ask her, Chrissy?"

"I asked her why she was a ghost."

Karen sat stunned, realizing that Chrissy understood much more than even they believed. After some moments Karen asked, "What was her answer?"

"She said she wasn't a ghost. She said ghosts are dead people and she's not dead, she's just lost. Well, actually, she said her family is lost. She has looked for a long time, but, she can't find her mother or her father. That's why she is here. Mommy, I'm confused."

Karen smiled softly at her precocious young daughter, reached across the bar and took Chrissy's hand and said softly, "Chrissy, maybe Abigail doesn't know. Perhaps with someone's help we can make her understand and maybe that will help her find her family. Would you like to help Abigail?"

Chrissy's expression brightened, "Oh yes, mommy, I would. Abigail is my friend. I don't want her to be sad. But she did say one other thing."

"What was that, Chrissy?"

"She said that even though you're not her real mother and Daddy's not her real father, she would like to be part of our family. She told me that before and she said it again, just now. Would that be all right? I mean, would you and Daddy let Abigail be part of our family? And she really loves Clayton. She told me she watches over him while everyone else is asleep. Mommy, I really love Abigail."

Karen was caught off guard by the question, but she realized quickly that first and foremost, she did not want Chrissy to be hurt, in any way, by this situation. So, without asking Jeff, she answered her daughter, "You know what, Chrissy? I think that would be great! I think it would be nice to have two daughters; and a big sister to watch over you and Clayton would be... pretty awesome."

Chrissy's expression changed totally. Where once she had looked sorrowful, then hopeful, she now looked totally elated. "Mommy, can I go tell Abigail?"

Before Karen could answer Chrissy turned her head suddenly toward the staircase. With a look of recognition she smiled, nodded her head and then said, "Oh, okay." Turning back to Karen, Chrissy said, "Abigail already knows. She's been here all along, listening." Chrissy turned again toward the staircase, listening and then she turned back to Karen, "She said thank you, mommy. She's been waiting a long time for this and you've made her very happy."

Karen smiled at her daughter, shaking her head lightly in wonder, paused just a moment and then turned her head toward the staircase, "You're welcome, Abigail. I hope that some day you will allow me to hear you and maybe even see you. But until then, Chrissy can be our eyes and ears. Welcome to the family."

Chrissy beamed at her mother, her eyes twinkling with her pleasure. "Mommy, can I go back upstairs with Abigail?"

"Sure Chrissy, just be careful on the stairs. I'll call you when dinner's ready. Oh, and Chrissy, let's keep this a secret between you and Abigail and me. Okay?"

"Okay." Chrissy hopped off her stool and sped to the stairs. Looking back at her mother with a smile, she slowly started up them one at a time, "Come on, Abigail, let's go play," and she disappeared up the stairwell.

Karen sat at the breakfast bar absorbing what had just taken place. She had just accepted the ghost of a little girl, dead almost one hundred years, as a member of their family. She couldn't see her or hear her, but she knew she was there. She could feel her, and no matter how crazy it sounded to anyone else, she felt a warmth spread through her at the thought that she had made this little girl, that is, ghost happy. After all the years of waiting and searching, Abigail would once again have a family. The fact that they were of this world and Abigail another; well, that's something they would have to work out. Now, all she had to do was tell Jeff!

When Jeff came into the house for dinner that evening he realized that Chrissy had been up for some time; he could hear her playing upstairs. Turning to Karen with consternation lacing his voice, "I thought you were going to call me when Chrissy woke up? Have you spoken to her about Abigail?"

"Jeff, take it easy. When Chrissy woke up earlier she had a conversation with Abigail upstairs. I heard her talking, but left her undisturbed for a short bit, and then I called her downstairs. She seemed concerned and confused so I didn't want to bring up the subject right away, but she did." Karen then explained about her conversation with Chrissy up to the part about her accepting Abigail into the family. She felt it safer to withhold that for the moment.

"Wow," Jeff exclaimed, "Chrissy is one bright little girl. I would not have expected her to understand everything that was said, I mean about Abigail being a ghost, but you said Abigail doesn't think she's dead, only lost. I don't think we can help her until she understands that, do you?"

"What I think is we need to have Serena's friend come over. I think through her, if she can communicate with Abigail, we can better understand how Abigail died, why she is still here and what we can do to help her either transition over to the other side or be happy here." Karen already knew that for now Abigail was perfectly happy being a member of their family, and the situation was a good one for Chrissy, Clayton and her, but she also knew that the more information they had the better they could all deal with it, especially Jeff.

"Yeah, I think you're right. Why don't you call Serena and see if she can set something up with her friend and geez, I hope she's not some rattle shacking weirdo.

"Jeff, please don't be cynical about this. We need her help and I don't want to offend her. And for now, we'll leave the subject alone with Chrissy until we find out more, okay?"

"Okay. I will try to keep an open mind. Hard as it might be, I will try. And as far as Chrissy is concerned we won't bring the subject up unless Chrissy does."

Karen smiled at her husband, her little secret with Chrissy and Abigail safe, at least for now.

Karen called Serena to set up an appointment, "Hello, Serena, it's Karen Miller."

"Well, hello darlin'. I didn't expect to hear from you so soon."

"I know Serena, but Jeff and I discussed the situation, and to be honest we really just need to understand more about Abigail. Chrissy had another conversation with her this afternoon and… well…"

"I know these things are difficult to understand, dear, but there is so much in this world, and the next, that we know so little about. If people would just open their ears and eyes, and their minds, there is so much more out there to learn.

"We totally agree, Serena, and that is why I called you. Would you get in touch with your friend? We would like her to come over here and visit with us, and perhaps…" Karen paused, searching for the right words, "if she can, speak with Abigail. We want to find out some things and I really don't want to keep using Chrissy as an interpreter, if you understand what I mean. Chrissy has become very attached to Abigail and I don't want anything to be said or done that will confuse her. Although, I have to say, she has already surprised us with her perception of things."

"Yes, darlin', I know exactly what you mean. It may take me several days to set something up, if that's all right."

"Yes, that would be wonderful. Please let your friend know that we really appreciate this and please reassure her that we will not be skeptical about what she says. I would never want to offend her or you."

"I will call you back as soon as I can, and don't you worry your little self. I will take care of things on this end. You give that little sweetheart of yours a hug for me."

"Thank you, Serena. I will certainly do that, and I will look forward to hearing from you. 'Bye now."

"Goodbye darlin'."

Karen set the phone down with a sigh of relief and yet an air of anticipation as she thought, '*good, now we can get some answers. I just hope Jeff is cooperative*'.

Several days went by as life in the Miller household seemed to run at a normal pace. Clayton was growing at a rapid rate, as only newborns can. Chrissy was keeping herself busy with Abigail, which in some ways was a blessing. Karen knew exactly where she could find Chrissy; either in her room or in the playroom at the top of the stairs, although she knew from Chrissy, that Abigail spent a great deal of time in Clayton's room, especially at night.

Karen was sitting one afternoon at the breakfast table, taking an afternoon break, her mind wandering. Jeff spent most of his days hiding away in his office, at his computer, emerging now and then to get something to eat and Karen wondered why he felt the need to work so hard; it wasn't as if they needed the money.

Six months ago they were an average couple, engrossed in working, living their lives and pursuing those things that make people happy; a family, a home of their own and sufficient income to pay for it all. Then one day she stopped at a Plaid Pantry convenience store on her way home from work, bought a coke, a treat for Chrissy and at the last minute, a lotto quick pick ticket,— just one— no special numbers, just those the computer picked at random. Something she did once in a while, when the jackpot reached a high amount, never really expecting to win. But they did! More money than they had ever imagined possible. And because neither one of them had close family, they decided to move to a new location, where their financial situation would not be known. Away from the prying eyes, the requests for money and all those who wanted to 'manage' it. She and Jeff were level headed enough to take matters into their own hands. They started searching the internet for locations and homes, and when they discovered this jewel, bought the Cottonwood house. They invested enough of the winnings that the children would always have money and she and Jeff could take life easy, doing what they wanted, when they wanted, and enjoy their family. And what does Jeff do, sits at his computer all day. Karen let out a huge sigh.

Then her thoughts came back to their current situation with Abigail. She really didn't mind things the way they were. It wasn't like things went bump in the night. Other than Chrissy, they never saw or heard Abigail, although there were times when Karen could almost feel her presence. It's that feeling like someone is standing over your shoulder, but you turn and no one is there.

It seemed to Karen that Abigail's presence was most often felt near the back stairs, and she wondered if those stairs had some significance. Karen thought back to one of the first times that Chrissy had mentioned her 'secret friend', and hadn't she mentioned that Abigail said they were very dangerous. I wonder why she would say something like that, Karen mused.

Suddenly the phone rang, jolting her out of her reverie. Karen almost jumped out of her chair as she moved quickly to answer before it woke Clayton, "Hello?"

"Hello, darlin', this is Serena."

"Hello, Serena, how are you?"

"I'm just fine, darlin'. Listen, I have been in touch with Agatha. It took me a few days of talking to her, but she has agreed to come over and have a 'visit'."

"Oh, Serena, that's wonderful. I hope she does not feel pressured?"

"Well, like I said, it took me a few conversations to convince her, but I finally got her to agree. When would be a good day for you?"

"Well, I'm rather new at this Serena. Does it have to be at night time, I mean, like for a séance?"

"Oh, heavens no," Serena chuckled. "Listen honey, anytime is good for Agatha. She just needs to come in and feel comfortable and whatever can happen, will happen."

Karen paused for a moment, "Well, would morning or afternoon be better for you?"

"Anytime is good for me; I'm mostly footloose and fancy free. Honey, at my age, you look for things to occupy your hours."

"Then how about tea time, tomorrow; about four? Would that be too soon? I can brew up a pot of tea and some little goodies, and we can follow Agatha's lead."

"I will call Agatha and set it up. And remember what I said the other day; she is just a tad bit eccentric, so be prepared. Bye darlin'. See you tomorrow."

As the dial tone returned Karen set the phone down wondering what Serena meant by 'be prepared'? Karen had only known Serena for a few days yet she felt like she had known her for years. Serena had a way about her that made Karen feel comfortable, sort of warm and fuzzy, almost snuggly, like an old and familiar sweater. Part of it was her southern drawl; the words seemed to slide down like maple syrup, easy to digest, making everything she said acceptable.

But it was something else as well. Serena treated her like a close relative, almost a daughter, and Karen liked that. She had never really known her own mother, having been bounced around the foster child system from one home to the next and she had never had the closeness with a mother figure that she was now developing with Serena.

Her past was one reason that she and Jeff got along so well. Neither of them had any close relatives, Jeff having lost his parents to a car accident his senior year of high school, so when they met they immediately were drawn to each other. There was no one else to seek approval from or to distract them from each other. Now, they had Chrissy and Clayton, and for all intents and purposes, Abigail. They were a complete family. And now, as her relationship with Serena grew, she had the mother figure she had secretly desired, but never had, and she hoped that Serena wouldn't mind. Deep down, Karen knew, somehow, that Serena was also growing close to her. She looked forward to Serena's visit the next day, despite a nagging apprehension about Agatha's impending visit.

The next afternoon as Karen prepared small finger sandwiches and cookies, she was trying to anticipate what 'be prepared' really meant. She had told Jeff about the appointment so he was, at the moment, upstairs getting ready to receive their guests. Chrissy and Clayton were both down for naps, so that left them free, at least for the time being. As she was arranging the sandwiches on a plate she heard Jeff coming down the front stairs. Making his way through the parlors and then emerging into the breakfast room he was straightening his shirt, tucking it into his pants as he walked, "Is this okay, hon?"

"That's fine, Jeff. Now listen, I don't want to sound like I'm harping, but Serena had to talk like a Dutch uncle to get Agatha to come today, so please, don't say anything that could offend her."

"Geez, Karen, how will I know what I can or can't say? We don't even know this gal. And besides, I am only doing this for Chrissy. This whole thing sort of gives me the heeby jeebies. It's bad enough we live in a haunted house, but now we have to have a séance to figure the whole thing out."

"We are not having a séance. Agatha just needs to come in and she can feel or sense, or whatever she does. I don't know either, but we have talked about this and we both decided this was what was needed, so please, don't make any unnecessary comments."

Just then the front doorbell rang. Karen looked at Jeff with a weak smile and then he motioned toward the door and said, with a smile, "It's show time." Karen gave him a strong frown.

As they approached the door through the dining room they could see Serena through the glass window, which occupied the top third of the door, and she appeared alone. Karen looked questioningly at Jeff and he just shrugged his shoulders. Reaching the door Karen turned the knob and as she pulled the door open, ready to ask Serena why she was alone, Karen realized that she wasn't. Standing next to Serena, no taller than about four feet, stood Agatha. Older than Serena for sure, Agatha appeared ancient; withered like an old apple, and almost as round as she was tall. Agatha wore glasses with lenses so thick, it was a wonder she didn't start fires with them and on her head she wore a flat pill box style hat covered with large yellow and pink flowers, now faded from many years of exposure.

"Hello darlin', hello Jeff, this is Agatha Whidley. Agatha, this is Karen and Jeff Miller."

Agatha looked up at Karen and Jeff and uttered one word, "Howdy" and then shuffled through the door. As she entered the house she looked all around, moving slowly, nodding her head up and down as she mumbled to herself.

Karen said, "Serena, will you take Agatha into the breakfast room, I'm sure you remember the way. I have tea and goodies all ready for us. Jeff and I will be right along."

Serena smiled and nodded her head, "Shore, darlin'," as she took Agatha's arm in hers and headed her through the parlors and into the back.

"She looks like a dumpling with legs!" Jeff whispered. "And she waddles like a penguin."

Karen gave Jeff a jab in the ribs with her elbow. "You promised me you wouldn't say anything, remember?"

"Yeah, but Karen, the next thing you know she'll be pulling out rattles or chicken bones..."

"Jeff! Please!"

"Okay. Okay. I'll keep my mouth shut. I just hope this doesn't get too weird. I'm not sure if I can control myself if the table starts to move or her eyes roll back in her head."

Karen gave Jeff a deadly look as they moved toward the kitchen.

"I'll keep myself under control," Jeff whispered humbly.

Entering the kitchen Karen went about setting the table for tea while Jeff sat at the table opposite Agatha and Serena, smiling weakly at the two ladies. Agatha, barely visible over the edge of the table, kept looking around, taking in the surroundings. It seemed as if she were searching for something. Jeff almost offered her Chrissy's booster seat, but then thought better of it and kept his mouth shut.

Karen sat the tray down on the table and poured everyone their tea and then took her chair at the table. Everyone sat quiet for a few minutes; the tension in the air almost palpable.

"She's here," Agatha spoke, breaking the silence, her head moving slightly up and down like a cat sniffing the air, "She's here."

Jeff and Karen looked at each other, but didn't speak.

By now Agatha had homed in on the back stairs, her thick lenses like radar detectors, aimed at the opening in the wall. "Hello my dear. What is your name?"

A brief silence followed and then, "My name is Agatha, how do you do?"

Karen wanted to speak so she looked toward Serena, who gently moved her head from side to side, so Karen remained silent. She also noticed that Serena had removed a notebook and pen from her handbag and was taking notes as Agatha spoke.

"Well now, Abigail, I have a few questions for you. Would that be all right?"

Agatha paused as if listening, "Very good dear. Let's see, where should I start...? How old are you Abigail?"

Karen felt as if she was listening in on someone's private conversation, almost intruding and it bothered her, yet she needed to hear as much as she could.

"Eight; how nice. You are a very pretty girl; quite grown-up for eight."

Suddenly Karen realized that Agatha was actually seeing Abigail, not just speaking with her.

"Oh, your mother told you that. How nice; she's right you know... Abigail, where is your mother?"

Each time Agatha asked a question she would pause and then resume. It gave Jeff the creeps. He didn't understand much of what was going on and he was slightly skeptical of the whole situation.

"Lost, you say? What do you mean by lost, dear...? They went away and never returned. I see...And how long ago was that Abigail…? You don't know; just a very long time… what's that dear? You have a new mother now? Why, isn't that nice."

Karen squirmed just a little.

"Where is your new mother, Abigail?" Agatha turned and looked at Karen. "Oh, I see." Then she looked at Jeff, her eyes the size of goose eggs behind the thick lenses, "Um hmm, I see."

Jeff felt like a bug under a microscope and squirmed self-consciously in his seat.

Agatha then looked back to the stairwell, "Abigail, can you tell me what happened to you…? No dear, I mean, why you are still here?" Agatha's expression intensified as she nodded her head up and down, "Um hmmm, yes, I see. Why, that's too bad dear. Did you get hurt…? Um hmmm, yes, I understand. Abigail…?" Agatha paused and then decided not to finish her question. Instead, it seemed to Karen that she changed her tack and took her questions in a different direction, "Are you happy, Abigail...? That's wonderful dear… Yes, yes. I see what you mean. That is wonderful. Oh, and how wonderful that is. You must feel very important… Yes, you are. I'm sure they appreciate that very much… and Chrissy? Oh, I'm sure she feels the very same way…" There was a pause in Agatha's conversation and then she said, "Oh, yes dear, you go ahead. I'm sure Chrissy is anxious to see you… Oh, Abigail? Thank you for talking with me. You have been very kind to do so… Yes dear; I like you too… Goodbye dear… Abigail? May I come see you again…? Wonderful… Goodbye dear."

Agatha turned her attention back to the table and the curious observers. No one spoke, especially Agatha. She just sat there in her faded hat and thick lensed glasses, barely visible over the edge of the table.

After what seemed like an eternity of silence Karen spoke, reluctant at first, for fear of offending Agatha, "What…? I mean, you saw her, Agatha? What did she say? Oh, my, I've got so many questions and we got only half of the conversation. Please, Agatha, will you tell us what she said?"

Agatha looked up at Karen, her eyes large and round, magnified by her glasses. Silent at first, looking from Karen to Jeff and then back again. And then she spoke, "Abigail is eight years old, or that is, she was when she died. Her parents were so grieved by her passing that they disappeared from their home shortly after Abigail died, never to return. They didn't take any of their belongings, so Abigail remained here waiting for her family to come for her, but they never did."

"Yes, but how did she die?" Karen asked, perturbed.

"The stairs. She said she was running one day, when her mother called from down below, outside. They were going on a picnic and her father was waiting in the carriage. As she turned to come down the back stairs, her heel caught and she tumbled down the stairs. She believes she got hurt, because she talked about pain, but she knows nothing about dying. She just talked about her family crying a great deal and then leaving her and never coming back. So sad for such a young child, I didn't have the heart to tell her she was no longer alive."

"She mentioned a new mother..." Karen paused knowing what would come next, but not knowing how Jeff would react.

"She said that you were her new mother."

Karen turned her gaze toward Jeff at the same time he turned toward her, questions in his expression, his eyes a mixture of concern and accusation. Karen smiled weakly back at him.

"Excuse me, did I miss something?" Jeff looked at Karen and then around the table to Agatha and Serena and then back to Karen. "Why would she think you were her mother, I mean, I know she has become friends with Chrissy, but what is this business of you being her mother? I don't understand?"

Karen sat there not knowing what to say. She looked down at her hands for a few moments and then spoke, "Remember when this whole thing started and you went out to your office, waiting for Chrissy to get up from her nap?" Jeff nodded his head up and down. "When Chrissy came down and we spoke, what I didn't tell you at the time was that I also had a conversation with Abigail, through Chrissy, of course. During that conversation Chrissy told me of Abigail's desire to be part of our family, and for Chrissy's sake, I agreed." Karen paused for a moment, and then continued, "I didn't tell you at the time because I was afraid you wouldn't understand; that you would think I was crazy." Karen looked at Jeff, tears pooling at the edge of her eyes.

Jeff looked at his remorseful wife, "Jeez, Karen, give me a little credit, will you? I'm not that hard-hearted."

"I know, but you have been so... so skeptical of this whole thing, I was afraid you would laugh or even get angry about it."

"Look, what's done is done. Today we have learned more about Abigail and why she's here, thanks to Agatha. Now what we need to do is decide what, if anything, we are going to do; live with her here or somehow send her over." Turning to Serena and Agatha Jeff asked, "That is the correct terminology, right?"

Smiling gently Serena responded, "Yes, son, that's correct. May I add somethin' here?" Serena paused, looking at Jeff and Karen, and then continued, "While I'm sure it must be disturbin' to know you have a ghost livin' in your home, Abigail is by no means disruptive. On the contrary, she is quite helpful, keeping Chrissy entertained and a watchful eye on Clayton. Perhaps what you might consider is allowin' things to go on as they are for a while. It is possible that the situation might remedy itself, isn't that correct Agatha?"

Agatha looked at Karen and Jeff, "If after some time when Abigail realizes that things are not as they should be, that is, she is on the outside looking in rather than an actual part of the family, she may decide to cross over. All she needs is encouragement to go. I think she is just afraid to make that first step alone. She is a sweet thing and I'm sure that over time you will grow to accept her presence. And if she finally decides to go, it will be with your blessing." Turning to Serena, Agatha spoke softly, "Time to go."

Serena stood, along with Agatha, Karen and Jeff, and started moving toward the front door, Agatha waddling close behind her. As they approached the door Serena turned, and with a slight smile on her face, spoke to Karen and Jeff, "Take care of the girls and that sweet boy of your's. I'll be back in touch with yaw'll in a few days with a transcript of what was said, both by Agatha and Abigail, so that yaw'll have all the details."

"Thank you, Serena, and thank you, Agatha, for all your help. We do appreciate what you have done for us today," Karen spoke to the two ladies as they ambled through the door, Agatha holding onto Serena's arm for support. Just as they were about to depart Agatha turned back to look at Karen and Jeff, "One more thing. There is something here and I can't put my finger on it, but something in this house is not right. This house holds a secret, but it is not revealing it to me, at least not right now; perhaps in the future, but not now."

As they closed the door, neither Karen or Jeff spoke for a few moments, digesting what had just gone on in their home. Finally Karen spoke, "I wonder what that was all about. We get one mystery figured out just to be handed another one."

Jeff just stood there, a puzzled look on his face, moving his head slowly from side to side.

"Jeff, I'm sorry I didn't tell you about my conversation with Abigail. I didn't want to keep things from you. I just didn't know what or how to tell you."

Jeff took Karen in his arms, "Listen, honey. This has been tough for all of us and I know I haven't been the most understanding about this whole thing. Let's just go on with enjoying our life in our perfect home, with our perfect family, all five of us, and not concern ourselves with the minor details."

Karen looked up into Jeff's warm eyes, smiled and said softly, "You are one great guy. I'm so glad you're mine," and then kissed her loving husband gently on the lips.

Chapter 7

Christmas was approaching at a gallop and the Miller family wanted to really do it up right in their new home. They took several trips to the store to buy decorations and lights and spent many hours of fun putting it all together. This was also one project that drew Jeff out of his office to help, so they all worked together, enjoying each other's company.

It was a tradition in Defuniak Springs that the homes on the circle, especially the stately older ones, decorate with luxurious splendor for the holidays. The town itself had a program called "Christmas Reflections" which illuminated the lake yard park with hundreds of thousands of lights and figures depicting various aspects of the Christmas holiday. This spectacular display drew thousands of visitors to the city and the home owners decorated their houses and yards to provide those visitors with holiday splendor on both sides of Circle Drive as they drove around the lake yard.

Karen, Jeff and Chrissy divided their yard into two different themes. The side closest to the church would house a lighted manger scene, resplendent with animals, wise men, shepherds and of course Mary, Joseph and the baby Jesus. High over the manger Jeff mounted a glowing star on a tall frame which, after dark, made the star seem to be suspended in the heavens. The other side of the front yard was a winter wonderland with a miniature Victorian town, snowmen, decorated trees, a pond with moving ice skaters, and, of course, Santa and his sleigh pulled by eight reindeer flying overhead.

Chrissy was overjoyed. Even in the crisp cool air of late November, she was helping move things, set up figures, string lights, and spread tinsel on the trees; her cheeks rosy from the air and the excitement. As she was putting up a string of lights with her father, she turned to Karen nearby and said, "Mommy, I wish Abigail could come out and help us. She's been standing in the upstairs window all this time and she looks so sad."

"I know Chrissy, but from what I understand, she cannot leave the house. She must stay inside because that is where her spirit is held. But tell her that she is doing us a great favor by watching over Clayton while we are out here and she can help us decorate in the house. We'll start on that as soon as we're done here." Karen wasn't leaving anything to chance; she had the nursery monitor sitting nearby. Clayton was up in his crib, sleeping, and the monitor would alert her of his waking, but she also knew that Abigail would let Chrissy know when he awakened. Abigail seemed to be connected to Clayton in some way because Chrissy had mentioned in the past how Abigail knew when Clayton was awake even before he had made any sounds. It was nice to have that extra measure of protection, and if for no other reason, Abigail was a real asset because of her attention to Clayton.

It was nearing dark as they hung the last of the lights. Jeff stood back looking at the entire yard. "Come take a look, you two and I'll turn on the lights." Karen and Chrissy stepped out of the gate onto the sidewalk and as they turned around to see the display, the lights sprang to life, illuminating the entire yard.

Karen looked at Jeff, "How did you do that? I didn't know you had rigged a remote control."

"I didn't! As a matter of fact, I didn't turn the lights on. I don't know what happened."

"I do!" Chrissy was tugging on her dad's coat. "I do!"

"Okay. Fill me in." Jeff answered, looking down at her.

"Abigail did it. She turned the lights on, Daddy."

Jeff looked at Karen and then down at Chrissy, "How do you know, Chrissy?"

"Because she's standing at the door window, smiling and laughing. Now she's clapping her hands. Daddy, she really likes the lights. She's really happy."

Jeff looked at Karen with a questioning expression, "I didn't know she could do physical things. I mean, how could she do that?"

Karen just shook her head lightly side to side mouthing the words, "I don't know, but think about it; she did play the piano."

"Oh yeah, I forgot about that."

By now Chrissy had joined Abigail in a bouncing, clapping response to the lights, giggling and laughing all the time. Jeff looked down at his excited daughter, "Okay Chrissy. I don't want to rain on your parade, but we won't leave the lights on for now. The official light up will be Thanksgiving evening, so tell Abigail to turn off the lights for now, will you?"

Instantaneously the lights went out. Jeff looked at Karen and then at Chrissy and then at the door. "I don't get it," He said. "How can she hear me from in there? I didn't say it loud enough for her to hear."

"She can read your thoughts, Daddy. She told me she hears words without people speaking. The words just come to her."

"Oh, that's great! Now I have to watch what I think as well as say." He looked at Karen with a look of consternation.

Karen just smiled back at him, shaking her head slowly back and forth, while shrugging her shoulders as if to say, 'Oh well.' "Why don't we go in the house and I'll start supper; any suggestions?"

Chrissy hollered out, "Pizza!"

"How about hamburgers instead?" Jeff asked.

I think hamburgers would be good, don't you Chrissy?" Karen commented.

Hopping up and down Chrissy gleefully answered, "Hamburgers, hamburgers; and French fries, okay?"

"Okay, hamburgers and French fries, with a tossed salad," she came back with as they headed for the front door.

Two days later was Thanksgiving. Jeff and Karen had invited Serena over for Thanksgiving dinner and as the four of them sat down at the dining room table Karen looked to Jeff to say grace. Bowing their heads, Jeff spoke, "Dear Lord, thank you for this food you have blessed us with and thank you for the blessings that you have graced us with this past year; a new home, a new son and a new friend. For all of these blessings, we are truly thankful. Amen."

"Daddy, may we say thanks for Abigail?"

"P.S., Lord, thank you for our new daughter, Abigail. Amen"

"Thank you, Daddy," Chrissy smiled at her father.

Serena and Karen smiled at Jeff and then at Chrissy. Jeff looked back at them rather sheepishly and then lightly shrugged his shoulders as if to say, *what else could I do.*

After their meal Jeff and Chrissy moved into the back parlor to watch a football game while Karen and Serena moved into the kitchen to cleanup. As they carried the dirty dishes to the sink Serena smiled lightly at Karen as she said, "That was so sweet of Chrissy to mention Abigail and it was especially sweet of Jeff to mention her in the prayer."

"Yes, I was so pleased with both of them, especially Jeff. This has all been so difficult for him. He is not exactly a 'true believer' you might say. That is, he never really believed in the supernatural," Karen chuckled lightly, "but I guess he has been forced to change his opinions."

"I guess Abigail has been most influential."

"You could say that," and they both laughed.

The two women continued their small talk as they finished cleaning the kitchen and as they spoke, sharing small bits of information about each other, their bond grew. They were developing a friendship that they both could appreciate. Karen was the daughter that Serena had never had and Serena was the mother Karen had never been able to bond with. Each of them filled a need for the other, so without even trying they were growing to love one another.

As they were nearing the end of their cleanup Chrissy came skipping into the kitchen, all excited, "Mommy, it's almost dark, the lights will be on soon. Can I turn on the switch for our lights? Please?"

"I don't see why not unless Abigail wants to turn them on like she did the other night."

"Oh no; she already told me I could do it, if it's all right with you."

Karen looked at Serena and smiled, "Well, I guess then you will be the master of the switch."

Chrissy jumped up and down, clapping her hands with glee. Karen thought for just a moment that she heard a quiet squeal, almost as if it was coming from a long way off. Looking around, cocking her head to the side, listening, she gently shook her head and thought to herself, *I must be hearing things. It sounded like a little girl squeal, but I know that Chrissy didn't make the sound.* Pausing momentarily, Karen didn't move or say anything. *I think I will leave this one alone and not mention it.*

"Karen, are you awright, dear?" Serena asked, noticing Karen's distraction.

"Huh? What? Oh... yeah, I'm fine; just off in another world for a moment."

Serena gave Karen a knowing look, almost as if she knew what was going on with her. "Shall we go to the front to catch the lights?" she asked.

"Yes, let's get Jeff and move to the front door so we can watch the lights come on." Karen answered. "Chrissy, will you go get Daddy? Serena, I'll meet you at the front door. I'm going up the back way to check on Clayton, and I'll meet you all at the front."

"That's fine dear. We'll meet you there."

Karen went up the back stairwell, moving quickly to Clayton's room, *Maybe what I heard was Clayton making noise. It didn't really sound like him, but I don't know how to explain the squeal I heard.* Karen had reached Clayton's room and quietly peered in through the door. Clayton was sleeping peacefully in his crib. Karen walked in and stood looking at her young son. She reached down and gently smoothed his hair as she watched him breathing. *Well, I know it wasn't him; so what did I hear? Okay, I'm making way too much of this. I didn't hear anything. I just imagined I heard something. Just forget it.*

Karen moved quietly towards the door and just as she placed her hand on the door sill, she heard a whisper behind her. Freezing her movement, her hand still on the frame, she quickly turned her head back to the room, listening, but she was met with total silence. She crept back to the crib, thinking that Clayton had made the sound, but he was exactly as she had left him. She stood there, unable to accept what her brain was trying to tell her. She slowly backed away from the crib, turned toward the door and silently left the room, heading for the front staircase. As she moved down the stairs she leaned over the rail, seeing everyone else down by the front door, "Everyone ready for the grand debut?"

Chrissy squealed and jumped up and down excitedly and then she moved to the light switch for the front porch, "Now, mommy, now?"

"Let's wait until the lake yard lights go on, Chrissy."

On her tiptoes Chrissy tried to peer out the window of the big front door, "I can't see. Daddy, pick me up, please?"

Jeff reached down and picked Chrissy up and held her so that she could reach the light switch, but still see out the window. As the lights came on in sections they watched as they came nearer and when the lights went on just across from their house everyone yelled out, "Now!" as Chrissy pressed the button for the lights. Their front yard lit up and their winter wonderland and nativity scene glowed with all the wonder of Christmas. Jeff set Chrissy down as she jumped and squealed with delight. Karen was standing at the foot of the stairs and off to her right, at the first landing, she heard another squeal; this time more distinctly than the first time in the kitchen. She turned her head quickly, but saw nothing. "Did you hear that?" she asked no one in particular.

"Hear what?" Jeff asked.

"I just heard a little squeal, like Chrissy, only different." Karen was still looking towards the corner landing of the stairs.

"I didn't hear anything except Chrissy. Did you hear anything, Serena?" Jeff asked.

"No, I didn't hear anything. Are you sure it wasn't Chrissy's voice bouncing off the wall, Karen?"

"No, it was different than Chrissy. I know my own daughter's voice," Karen said, her voice sounding angrier than she really intended. "I'm sorry, that didn't come out like it should. I'm not angry; I just don't understand what I am hearing."

Serena moved to Karen's side, touched her arm lightly and said, "Don't worry, my dear. I know you didn't mean to sound angry.' She smiled softly at Karen and then said, "Perhaps the veil is lifting for you."

Karen looked at Serena questioningly, unable to understand what she was saying.

Serena went on, "Karen, imagine that there is a veil, or a curtain, that separates us from those who have passed on. Some, such as Chrissy, see right through as if the curtain is transparent. Others, like you and Jeff, and even me, cannot see through the veil. We neither see nor hear those such as Abigail. Sometimes, when we want it very much, the veil thins or lifts and we are able to see those on the other side. Perhaps, for you, the veil is thinning and you are hearing Abigail."

"Chrissy, where is Abigail? Is she here with us?" Karen asked of Chrissy.

Chrissy had run into the front parlor where she could look out a window to the front yard. She turned from the window, still excited and unaware of the conversation between the adults. "She's standing right there, mommy; by the big special window. She says the lights look even more beautiful through the special window."

Chrissy was referring to the cut glass, hexagon window that faced out towards the front yard at the first landing of the stairs; exactly where Karen had heard the squeal. Karen stood there, staring at the corner, just to her right, where Chrissy had pointed. Could it be that she had heard Abigail? Could the veil be lifting for her? *Oh my God. To think that I could actually hear Abigail; how wonderful that would be.*

Karen looked back at the others, tears welling in her eyes, "Do you think it's really possible, Serena?"

"Well, child, I don't know why not. She certainly loves you, and I have no doubt that you love her too. Am I correct?"

Karen lightly nodded her head up and down. As strange as it sounded, Karen did love Abigail. How could she not? Abigail was Chrissy's best friend, she was Clayton's guardian and she certainly didn't cause them any problems. Why wouldn't she love her? She had already agreed to be her mother, for crying out loud. Perhaps, now she could give the love and contact that the little girl truly needed; be a real mother to her.

Chapter 8

With Thanksgiving now past, Christmas was rushing toward them at a stampede pace. Karen and Chrissy, with a little help from Jeff, put up the Christmas tree in the front parlor, right at the front windows, so that everyone could see, and a beautiful tree it was. The day after Thanksgiving they had gone to a local tree farm, just a few miles east of town. In the brisk fall air, they wandered around looking at one tree after another.

Karen carried Clayton, nestled down and bundled warm, in a carrier on her chest. Serena had volunteered to stay with him at home, but this was an outing they wanted to carry on as a family tradition, so Clayton was along for the ride. Not that he was complaining; he was content to sleep close to his mother, cozy and warm.

Chrissy was drifting out ahead of Jeff and Karen, quickly looking over one tree and then another, with a discerning eye, not willing to take home anything but the perfect tree. Each time Karen or Jeff would suggest a tree, Chrissy would look it over and find something wrong and move on. They were enjoying the outing, but curious why Chrissy was being so picky, so Karen finally gave into her curiosity, "Chrissy, we have passed a number of really nice trees. Why are you being so picky about this?"

"Mommy, this will be Abigail's first real Christmas in a long time and I want everything perfect for her, including the tree. Is that okay?"

Taken aback by Chrissy's reasoning, Karen, now humbled by her young daughter, replied, "You know what,

Chrissy? I think that's a pretty good reason for the perfect tree. So you keep looking. I know we will find it."

Chrissy looked at her mother, a sweet, appreciative smile on her face, "Thank you, mommy." And she turned on her heels and took off to continue the search.

Karen looked at Jeff with wonder in her expression, shaking her head from side to side lightly.

"Wow, can you believe that kid," Jeff said. "Sometimes I think she is four going on forty. She blows me away with her astounding awareness of others. Are you sure she's only four?"

By now Karen was laughing causing Clayton to stir in his cozy domain. Karen wrapped her arms around him and whispered cooing sounds to him until he went back to sleep. "We had better find that perfect tree so that we can go home. This little guy is going to need to eat soon and we'll need to get back to the car."

"I'll track down Chrissy and get her to choose a tree."

After a few minutes of Karen following behind Jeff as he pursued Chrissy from one row to the next, they finally got her to choose a tree, Jeff cut it with a hand saw, loaded it onto a wagon provided by the tree farm and headed back to the pay station and their car. Chrissy walked ahead with Jeff, helping him pull the wagon, as the two of them carried on a conversation, Chrissy chattering like a magpie about her plans for Christmas. It had been a wonderful experience, the four of them, out together to get their tree; an outing that Karen looked forward to year after year. As she walked back to the car Karen imagined the same experience, several years in the future, when Chrissy and Clayton were both running around, knowing full well, that it would be a fun, but trying experience. Karen quietly smiled to herself relishing in her dreams of the future, *Just one of many to look forward to,* she pondered, *I'm just sorry Abigail couldn't be here with us. She so wants to be a real part of the family.* But Karen knew that Abigail was tied to the house. Her spirit, as far as Karen understood, could not leave the house,

81

unless she left to go over to the other side and right now Karen neither expected nor wanted that to happen.

Once the tree was home, Jeff and Karen set it up in a tree stand, making sure it had plenty of water at its base. They had chosen to set it in the front parlor, moving the piano off to one side to accommodate the large tree which stood almost to the ten foot ceiling. Chrissy stood back acting as supervisor, her appointed job; making sure the tree was positioned correctly. Once the tree was secured in the stand, Karen stepped back and helped Chrissy direct Jeff as to the proper positioning of the tree.

Down on his knees, Jeff's upper body was lost in the foliage of the tree, as he tilted it first one way and then another, sliding it back and forth until the perfect place was found. Backing out and then standing, Jeff turned to the two females, sweat popping out all over his face, and said with an exasperated tone, "Boy, will I be glad when Clayton is old enough to put in his two bits worth. Maybe then I won't have to be at the mercy of you two when you can't make up your minds. You girls have me outnumbered for now, but just give him a few years and we'll be even."

Chrissy was turning her head slowly from side to side, a wise smile on her face, when Jeff looked at her, "What?... Why are you shaking your head no?"

"You forgot about Abigail, Daddy. You'll still be outnumbered; three girls to two boys."

"She's got you there, Daddy." Karen smiled at Jeff a big 'gottcha' kind of smile.

Jeff just let out a big sigh and headed for the kitchen, "I need a drink of water. All this hard work has made me thirsty."

Chrissy and Karen just giggled and then began to decorate the tree. Karen told Chrissy, "You take the low branches and I'll take the high ones. How does that sound?"

"Abigail can tell us where to put the ornaments, okay, mommy?"

"Absolutely!" Karen said with a big smile. And then she thought she heard another squeal, faint, but there, and she smiled all the more.

By the time they were done decorating, some two hours later, the tree looked absolutely marvelous. Karen and Chrissy had picked out ornaments from a specialty shop and all of the decorations were period replicas of early twentieth century toys. The lights looked like candles and sat majestically perched on the branches. The ornaments resembled trains, toy soldiers, teddy bears, baby dolls, a jack-in-the-box, rocking horses, and other items depicting toys of Abigail's time. As a finishing touch, they draped beautiful gold garland around from top to bottom and the finished tree was beautiful.

Karen called Jeff, who had receded to his office, on the intercom, and asked him to come in. She and Chrissy were standing back, off to one side of the room, admiring their handy work when Jeff walked in from the back.

Letting out a slow whistle, he commented, "Wow, you girls do some good work. That is one gorgeous looking tree."

"Abigail helped us, Daddy. She told us where to put the ornaments."

"Well, I guess accolades go to all three of you then. My hat is off to you." Jeff made a sweeping motion as if taking his hat off and bowing to her.

"Daddy, you're not wearing a hat."

"It's a figure of speech, sweetie," Jeff answered, smiling at her. "By the way, Chrissy," he whispered, "where is Abigail right now?"

Chrissy whispered back, "She's standing next to you, by mommy."

Jeff turned to his side where Chrissy had indicated, made a bowing motion, and then said, "My dear Abigail, you make a wonderful supervisor. I offer you my thanks for keeping these two in line." Standing straight Jeff winked as he gave Karen a smile, tussled Chrissy's hair, and headed back out to his office.

Karen could have sworn she heard a giggle come from right next to her where Abigail stood.

After a moment Karen looked at Chrissy and asked, "How about some hot chocolate?"

Chrissy, with a big smile and a hardy shake of her head, moved toward the kitchen.

Chapter 9

As Christmas approached Karen packed Clayton and Chrissy up one day and decided to go to the Santa Rosa Mall in Fort Walton Beach, about fifty miles from Defuniak Springs. It was the closest mall and they had some serious shopping to do.

Karen had offered the opportunity to Jeff, but he had declined, shopping not being his favorite pastime, so the girls, along with Clayton, were on their own for the day. As they were getting ready, putting their coats on in the kitchen, Chrissy spoke up, "Mommy, Abigail has told me what she wants me to buy for Clayton from her, but she is sad because she doesn't have any money to spend."

Karen looked at Chrissy, "Is Abigail standing here, Chrissy?"

"Yes, mommy, she's standing right by the stairs."

Karen turned toward the stairwell, "Abigail, I will take care of the money, sweetie, don't you worry about it, okay?" Karen turned to Chrissy.

"Mommy, Abigail is smiling and says, thank you."

Karen turned back towards Abigail, "You're welcome, baby." Turning to Chrissy she said, "Okay kiddo, let's head out. We have a lot of shopping to do."

She picked up Clayton in his carrier and they headed out the door.

The drive to Fort Walton Beach took them about an hour. With no real direct route and two lane roads, Karen drove with caution as she and Chrissy discussed the day's agenda.

Once they reached the mall, Karen found a parking place a short walk from an entrance, strapped Clayton into his chest carrier and took Chrissy by the hand, "We will try to get as much done as we can here so that we don't have to go anywhere else. But in the case we can't find everything we want, there is another mall, the Destin Commons, that we can catch on the way home. Okay?"

"Okay, mommy, I'm ready to shop." And with that declaration the three of them headed for the stores.

Several hours later, they stopped at the food court for lunch and then left the Santa Rosa Mall for Destin. Heading down Highway 98, they passed through Okaloosa Island, containing many tourist shops, hotels and an aquarium. Seeing that Karen said, "Oh, Chrissy, look there; a seaquarium. Daddy and I will have to bring you and Clayton back down here this summer to see the dolphins and whales." Chrissy clapped her hands with glee.

The highway then crossed through a wide sandy beach area from which they could see the ocean on one side and the bay on the other. Then they drove over a bridge into Destin. All of this area was new to Karen; they had yet to come down to the beach since moving to DeFuniak Springs. Speaking out loud, but to no one in particular, "It is so pretty down here, and there is so much to do. And it's not really that far to drive. Who would have thought that it would be this nice, here in the Florida panhandle? This is really a well kept secret."

"What's a secret, mommy?"

"Oh nothing, honey, I'm just talking to myself," Karen laughed lightly.

After a brief stop at the Destin Commons Mall, Karen crossed over the Bay Bridge to the north side of the Choctawhatchee Bay, moved east on Highway 20 until she finally headed north on Highway 331 to Defuniak Springs. Finally reaching home, she pulled into the back driveway, being met by Jeff at the door.

"Well, do we have any money left? You girls were gone so long I figured you had spent every dime we had."

"Daddy, we didn't spend a lot of money. We just bought gifts for Clayton, Serena, Agatha, and Abigail...,"Chrissy paused, a big smile on her face, "who else did we buy for? Oh yeah, and we got some presents for you, Daddy."

"For me?"

"Yes." Chrissy lowered her voice to a whisper, "Daddy, we got a special gift for Abigail. Wait till you see it. She is really going to like it."

Jeff looked at his daughter. Her face was absolutely glowing. He could tell that she really had the right idea about Christmas. It wasn't about what she would get, but about what she could give to others. "You know, Chrissy, I think she will love it, just because it comes from you. Say, why don't we keep it out in my office. That way she won't see it before Christmas and all you have to do is not think about it. Then she will really be surprised Christmas morning. What do you think?"

Chrissy jumped up and down, clapping her hands, "Oh, Daddy, you are so smart. Then she will really be surprised. Now all I have to do is not think about it," Chrissy let out a big sigh, "Oh, boy, is that going to be hard to do."

Karen and Jeff both laughed at their young daughter. Jeff and Chrissy carried all of the packages to his office while Karen headed into the house with Clayton. Heading up the back stairs the house was very quiet, yet nearing the top stair Karen thought she heard a small voice, a whisper really, no word really discernable. "Abigail, is that you?" Karen listened for a few moments, not moving, hoping to hear an answer. But when none came she continued on to Clayton's room, placing him in his crib.

Thinking to herself, with reassurance, *it will come, it will come. Just give it time.*

Christmas Eve was a blur; Karen fixed a light dinner as Chrissy sped around the house, wired for the exciting morning to come. When dinner was ready they gathered around the kitchen table and the conversation was soon on the coming gifts.

Jeff looked over at Chrissy as she wiggled restlessly in her chair, "Chrissy, you were never clear what you wanted from Santa. Did you ever tell him what you wanted?"

"Oh yes, Daddy. When mommy and I went shopping I got to see Santa and I told him what I wanted for Christmas, and I assured him that I had been a good girl."

"Well, that's good. I hope he heard you, loud and clear." With that last comment he looked at Karen. She just smiled back and in her expression he knew she had the situation covered.

"Daddy, I told Santa about Abigail's wish for Christmas."

Having just taken a drink of water, Jeff choked, quickly covering his mouth with a napkin before he sprayed it over the table. Coughing, he looked at Karen with a panicked expression on his face and then he looked at Chrissy, "You told Santa about Abigail? What did you say, Chrissy?"

"Don't worry, Daddy, I didn't tell him that Abigail was a ghost. I told him I had a friend, but she couldn't get out of the house to see him, so I was there to tell him her Christmas wish." Chrissy paused for a moment, "I didn't lie. That's the truth. So I'm still a good girl, aren't I?"

Jeff and Karen looked at each other with astonishment and then they seemed to melt. Their eyes told each other how utterly proud they were of their little girl.

"Absolutely, the best and goodest girl I know," Jeff answered.

Chrissy giggled, "Daddy, goodest isn't a real word."

"How do you know, you're only four… or are you?"

Chrissy giggled even louder, "Of course, I'm four, Daddy. You know that." She gave a light smack on his hand.

"Sometimes I wonder."

Karen was enjoying this patter between Jeff and Chrissy. Her heart swelled when she saw the special bond that her precious daughter and her husband had. She looked forward to the time when there would be two at the table to give Jeff a run for his money. She knew that Clayton would be just as bright and glib as Chrissy.

As the two continued their bantering Karen heard a giggle, ever so light, but still there, come from behind her, from the direction of the staircase. She turned in her chair and looked toward the sound, smiled and spoke softly, "Hi Abigail. So you think those two are funny as well?" Karen listened, thought she heard a whisper, but still nothing she could discern. She thought to herself, *How I wish I could hear her. It would make things so much easier. Then she could really feel like a part of the family. Soon...I hope.*

After dinner and the kitchen was cleaned up, Karen began some preparations for the Christmas dinner. Serena and Agatha had been invited, as they had no family to spend the holiday with, so Karen wanted it to be extra special. She enjoyed cooking, and she especially liked the two elderly ladies who were coming for dinner.

And after all, this was their first Christmas in the house; the first of many to come. So she wanted everything just right. The turkey was seasoned, trussed and sitting in the refrigerator, ready to pop in the oven; the stuffing was ready for the fresh ingredients to be added the next morning. Two pies had been baked earlier in the day; pumpkin for Jeff and mincemeat for her. Plus she had made some chocolate pudding for Chrissy. Things were shaping up so that there would be more time to spend with the kids in the morning.

It was time for bed and Karen knew where she would find Chrissy. For some time she could hear Chrissy and Abigail up in the playroom. Well, she couldn't really hear Abigail, but she could hear Chrissy talking to Abigail and, from what she could hear, both girls were very excited about the coming morning. "Chrissy?" Karen called up the back staircase.

"Yes, Mommy?"

"Time for bed, honey. Get your teeth brushed and your pajamas on and I'll be up soon to tuck you in."

"Okay." Karen heard the rustle of little feet.

A little later, after checking on Clayton, Karen walked into Chrissie's room to find her in an animated conversation with Abigail, "What ever are you two talking about?" It was becoming so much easier to talk to the girls as if they both were real.

Chrissy looked up at her mother, "We were discussing what Santa was going to bring us, and…" Chrissy paused as she looked toward the end of the bed, smiled lightly and then said, "Good night…" giggled and then finished with, "see you in the morning." She turned to Karen, "Abigail is going into Clayton's room now for the night. She goes in there every night, to watch over him. She doesn't have to sleep, you know."

Karen looked at Chrissy with amazement. How could this little girl, only four years old, be so smart? "Did Abigail tell you that?"

Chrissy nodded her head as she leaned back, pulling her blankets up to her chin. Karen stood there for just a moment, bent down and kissed Chrissy on the forehead. Suddenly Chrissy reared up, connecting her forehead, hard, with Karen's chin. "Mommy," Chrissy squealed.

"Geez, Chrissy! What is the matter?" Karen was rubbing her chin.

"Mommy, we forgot to leave cookies for Santa!"

Karen looked at her daughter, "It's not a catastrophe, Chrissy! I'll go down and fix up a plate."

Chrissy was sitting up in bed now, "Be sure and put some carrots for the reindeer. And make sure you put it in the front room by the fireplace, so he won't miss it."

"I've got it covered, okay; cookies for Santa, carrots for the reindeer, by the fireplace."

Chrissy gave her mom a thumb up for 'good job', laid back on her pillow, and said, "Night, mommy. Thank you, I love you." As Karen turned out the light, still rubbing her chin, she heard Chrissy say sweetly, "Merry Christmas."

After they knew that Chrissy was sound asleep, Jeff and Karen brought in all of the gifts from the office and arranged them around the tree. After that task was taken care of, they looked at each other, smiled softly, and Karen could not help but love her man. She walked over to where he stood and wrapped her arms around his neck, gave him a soft kiss on his lips and whispered in his ear, "How about a glass of Christmas cheer?"

Giving Karen a firm hug and an extra kiss on her lips he whispered back, "Have I told you lately just how much I love you?"

"Just this morning."

"Well, I'll say it again, one more time, I love you, this much," and he held out his arms to each side, as wide as they would reach.

Karen smiled, looking deeply into Jeff's eyes, and then kissed him one more time, "I love you too, for all you do, and for all that you endure. Now, how about that drink... a little eggnog?"

"Sounds good to me." Jeff followed Karen as far as the back parlor, where she motioned him to the couch and he gladly accepted. She returned shortly carrying two cups of frothy, home made eggnog.

"Heavy on the cream and light on the rum," she said as she handed him his cup and sat next to him on the couch, bending one leg under her as she sat. "Jeff, I think I am beginning to hear Abigail. Several times, I could swear that I have heard light whispers or giggles."

Jeff didn't say anything at first, seeming to consider what Karen had just said.

"I don't think it's my imagination or wishful thinking; I think I am really breaking through."

Jeff still hadn't said anything, just looking out beyond his cup, his expression thoughtful, and finally he spoke, "Karen, I know you really want this to happen, and in some ways, so do I, but don't try too hard. I don't want you getting disappointed if it doesn't happen. Chrissy is perfectly content to act as interpreter."

"I know," Karen answered, somewhat down hearted.

"You know what," Jeff said, lifting the mood, "It's Christmas. Let's not dwell on the 'what ifs'. Let's look at the positives. We have two, or that is, three great kids, a great home, a great life looking at us, and I am positive that before daylight we will have our sleep interrupted to open Christmas presents. So, how about we finish our eggnog and head for bed."

With a smile, Karen looked at Jeff, "I am positively sure you are right. Good idea."

Very early the next morning Chrissy was standing next to Karen's side of the bed, "Mommy? Mommy, are you awake? It's Christmas. Can we go down and open our presents?'

Karen slowly opened her eyes, trying to take in the room and who was standing at her bedside. "Chrissy? What time is it? Honey, it's still dark out."

"I know, mommy, but the sun is getting ready to open up, see."

Karen was barely able to make out a glimmer of light through the window, and she wasn't totally convinced it wasn't the street light. Karen rolled so that she could see the clock; it was just making six forty five. It wouldn't start getting light for at least another twenty to thirty minutes. "Chrissy, can you give me a few more minutes? It will take me a little bit just to get your Daddy awake."

With obvious disappointment in her voice Chrissy sighed as she answered, "Okay, I'll go into the playroom with Abigail until you get Daddy up. But come get me as soon as he's awake, okay?" her voice and attitude lifting towards the end of her sentence.

Karen understood the excitement of the moment and she knew that Chrissy's enthusiasm was as much for Abigail as it was for herself. Chrissy wanted this Christmas to be exciting for Abigail because of all those she had missed.

So, although she really wanted to roll over and go back to sleep, Karen, instead, reached over and wiggled Jeff's arm, "Jeff? Jeff, are you awake? We are being summoned to the tree."

Jeff mumbled something unintelligible, but did not move.

Karen tried again, "Jeff, wake up. It's almost dawn and Chrissy is chomping at the bit to go downstairs."

Jeff rolled over, his face barely visible to Karen in the dark. His voice was almost inaudible as he croaked, "What time is it?"

"About ten to seven," Karen replied.

"Geez, Karen, it's still dark."

"I know, but it is Christmas morning. Remember what it was like; you couldn't wait to get to your presents. Come on; get your butt in gear."

"Okay, okay." Jeff rolled over as Karen threw off the covers to get out of bed.

"Come on, Santa. It's your job to hand out the gifts."

"I know, I know. I'm coming. Just give me a few minutes to get my eyes open."

Karen chuckled as she patted Jeff on his hip, "That's a good Santa; up and at 'em."

Once Jeff was up on his feet, and Karen had brushed her teeth, she collected Clayton from his crib and called for Chrissy, "Come on girls, time for the tree."

Chrissy came running down the hall and Karen met her at the top of the stairs, "Okay, slow down. No running on the stairs." She took Chrissy's hand and they walked down the stairs to the front parlor.

Once downstairs Karen laid Clayton in his buggy, pushed it into the parlor, plugged the tree lights in and then headed for the kitchen to make some coffee. Chrissy sat on the floor, a few feet from the tree. "Where's Daddy?"

"He's coming. He'll be right here. We'll just wait for him, okay. We'll let daddy hand out the presents. I'll be right back, Chrissy. You and Abigail just sit tight. And keep an eye on Clayton for me, okay?"

"Come on, Daddy," Chrissy yelled toward the stairs.

She was answered with a faint, "I'm coming, Chrissy. Just give me a minute."

Jeff came down the back stairs and into the kitchen, groaning, "Coffee, coffee."

Karen laughed as he stumbled into the kitchen, "It's coming, just a few more minutes."

"Thank goodness Christmas comes only once a year. I couldn't take many more of these early mornings."

"Your girls are waiting for you in the front parlor, Santa. I told Chrissy they have to wait for you."

"I know. Just put a cup of coffee in my hands and I will head for the tree. Ho, Ho, Ho."

Karen handed Jeff a steaming cup of black coffee and pointed him toward the front parlor and then she followed behind, her hand enveloping her own steaming cup of the invigorating liquid, laughing all the way. She just loved Jeff's enthusiasm.

Once in the front parlor, Jeff started to search through the gifts under the tree, "Let's see, who should we start with? Hmmm, here's one for Chrissy," and he handed a brightly wrapped box to his daughter.

Chrissy accepted the box, but leaned toward Jeff, "Daddy, get that one right there," and she pointed to an oddly shaped gift.

Jeff picked it up and read the tag, "Why, here's a gift for Abigail." Jeff looked toward Chrissy, still holding her wrapped package, "Chrissy, where is Abigail?"

"Right here, Daddy." And she motioned toward her right side.

Jeff laid the package down next to Chrissy, smiled softly, and stepped back toward the tree. Both Karen and Jeff watched, with interest, to see what would happen next. Chrissy looked toward Abigail, paused as if listening, and then said softly, "Okay." She set her unopened package down and then began removing the wrapping from Abigail's gift and as the content of the package was revealed Karen could swear she heard a squeal. Inside the wrapping was a beautiful antique style doll. She had a beautiful porcelain head and lavish Victorian style dress.

Chrissy began to bounce up and down and clap her hands. Turning to Karen and then to Jeff, she shrieked with excitement, "She likes it! She likes it! Oh, mommy, isn't it wonderful."

Chrissy stopped for a moment, looking concerned, "Abigail, what's the matter?"

Chrissy turned to look at her mother, "Mommy, she's crying." Chrissy turned back in the direction of Abigail, listening, and then a smile spread across her face, like the sun which was now making its way above the lake. She turned to look at her mother, "She's crying because she's happy." Then Chrissy began clapping her hands again.

Jeff and Karen watched this scene with awe and wonder and then the most miraculous thing happened. As Chrissy was clapping and squealing with delight, the doll lifted off the floor, by its self, and then disappeared. Karen and Jeff's eyes met and their mouths fell open. Neither could believe what they were seeing and they were stunned into silence. Finally, Jeff uttered an astonished, "Whoa," his eyebrows lifting in surprise.

Karen found her voice and asked her daughter, "Chrissy, where did the doll go?"

Chrissy looked at her mother with a questioning expression, "No where, mommy. It's right here. Abigail is hugging it." Chrissy beamed with pride.

Jeff and Karen looked at each other again, wonder in their eyes, and then Jeff spoke, almost in a whisper, "We have to tell Serena and Agatha about this."

After overcoming his shock Jeff continued to sift through the gifts, finding one for Karen and then one for Clayton, "Wow, look at this one. This is for Clayton; from Abigail."

Chrissy paused in her revelry and looked toward her Daddy and then toward Abigail, smiling softly with anticipation.

Jeff handed the gift to Karen and she looked toward Chrissy and Abigail, "I'll open it for him, okay Abigail?"

Chrissy listened and then nodded her head, rapidly, to Karen. Karen unwrapped the package and inside was a soft and cuddly, stuffed doggy; white with black button eyes. Karen looked up toward Abigail, "Oh, how sweet. This is so nice, Abigail. I know Clayton will treasure this, especially because it's from you." She smiled widely and then felt something around her neck. A warmth, a weight, she couldn't tell for sure and she couldn't find a word for it. She looked at Chrissy, questions in her eyes.

"Mommy, Abigail is giving you a hug." Chrissy smiled softly.

Karen lifted her arms and wrapped them together, as if enveloping something. Tears teetered at the edges of her eyes. Softly, she whispered, "I love you, Abigail. I hope you will always be a part of our family."

Chapter 10

After all the gifts were opened and the paper mess cleaned up, Karen went to the kitchen to get breakfast. "I'm going to make this a light breakfast, guys. We're having an early dinner today, and I want everyone hungry."

After all had eaten, Jeff departed to his office, with Karen's permission, for a few hours, making sure, first, that Karen didn't need his help to get ready. As he departed Karen reminded him, "Jeff, remember, we're taking the kids to church at ten thirty." Jeff waved her an acknowledgement as he entered the office.

Chrissy and Abigail headed up to the play room to share their new treasures. After putting Clayton down for a nap, Karen moved down to the playroom to check on the girls. There, laying on the day bed was Abigail's doll. "Chrissy, did you bring Abigail's doll up here?"

"No, mommy, Abigail did."

"I didn't see it move."

"I saw Abigail carry it up here."

"Okay," Karen answered, rather uncertain. *I need to talk to Agatha and Serena about this, she thought to herself.*

Karen returned to her kitchen, still trying to figure it out. As she put the turkey in the oven thoughts were racing through her mind, *first she can see the doll, and then she can't. Abigail moves the doll around, they can't see it move, yet it does.* This was definitely a question for Agatha.

Dinner was planned for one o'clock in the afternoon and she had told Serena that they were welcome to come over around noon, knowing they would definitely be home from

97

church by then. They did not attend church regularly, but Karen felt that Chrissy needed to understand the true meaning of Christmas, so they would attend the services at the Methodist Church next door. An easy in and out, and they should have no problem being back home and settled by noon.

As Karen, Jeff, Chrissy and Clayton were exiting the chapel, the Christmas day services concluded, they spotted Serena and Agatha, also leaving the church. Karen waved at the two elderly ladies waddling slowly down the aisle toward the exit, and then waited with Jeff and the kids just outside the front doors. When Serena and Agatha exited through the huge double doors, stopping briefly to shake the hand of the pastor, Karen stepped up, smiled warmly and then embraced the two ladies, "Merry Christmas, Serena, Agatha. I didn't know you two went here?"

Serena, smiling softly, replied, "We aren't really members; we just attend now and then. I suppose at our age we should be paying more attention to these types of things, but Agatha and I both feel that we have our own channel of communication with God. He knows our hearts."

Karen smiled, "Well, let's just head for the house and start our celebrating now. Besides, Jeff and I have some news and some questions…" Karen paused to look down at Chrissy, "we'll talk more at the house."

With Clayton cradled snugly in his carrier on Karen's chest, she hooked one of her arms through Serena's and the other through Agatha's as they walked slowly toward their front gate, just fifty feet down the sidewalk. "I have so much to tell you," Karen said. "This morning was so exciting; I just don't know where to start."

Serena looked down at Chrissy, walking just ahead of them, hand in hand, with her Daddy, "And how was Christmas for you, Chrissy? Did Santa bring you all that you wanted?"

Chrissy turned, trying to talk and walk at the same time, "Oh yes, Miss Serena, and he brought something special for

Abigail too, huh Mommy?" Chrissy's smile was spread as far across her face as she could possibly muster and she had a conspiratorial expression in her eyes.

Serena turned to Karen with question in her eyes, "What is she talking about?"

Karen looked at Chrissy with a loving smile and then explained, "Chrissy and I went shopping a couple of weeks ago and while out we found a perfect gift for Abigail. Actually, Chrissy had gone with me, on a mission, to find something special for Abigail. And, boy did we. In a special shop at one of the malls, we found a beautiful, Victorian style doll, porcelain head, Victorian clothes, the whole nine yards. She was perfect. And when Abigail opened her package, well actually, Chrissy opened it for her, Abigail was so happy she started to cry. It was very touching, literally and figuratively."

Serena looked at Karen, questions still in her expression, "Okay, now you've lost me."

Karen just chuckled and Chrissy giggled, sharing their little secret. By now they had reached the front wrought iron gate which Jeff held open while the family and guests walked through and then up the front steps and into the house. Through all this conversation Agatha had not said a word, just waddling along; her faded flower hat perched just above her thick glasses. But as she walked through the front door, her head went up slightly and started bobbing up and down lightly, as if she was sniffing the air like a cat, just as she had done the first time she was in their home. Once through the door, she stopped, turned slightly toward the staircase on her left, and then smiled softly as she spoke, "Hello dear, how are you today?"

It appeared as if she was speaking to the wall, but Chrissy started to smile, listening to a voice that only she and Agatha could hear. Agatha spoke again, "You did? Santa brought it for you? Why, isn't that wonderful. Where is she?" Agatha paused again, "I would love to, dear, but I'm afraid those stairs are a bit much for me to negotiate." Chrissy stood, watching the conversation, her head moving back and forth as if she were watching a tennis match. The smile on her face told the story to the rest of them; Abigail was absolutely thrilled with her gift that Santa had brought her. The fact that Chrissy had actually gotten the gift for Abigail, but was not recognized for it, did not matter one iota to her. Just the sheer joy that her gesture of giving had brought to Abigail was thanks enough for her.

As the group stood in the foyer, clustered around the foot of the stairs, Agatha once again spoke to Abigail, "All right, dear. I'll wait right here."

Agatha turned to the rest of the group, "She's gone to get her doll so that I can see it. She wanted me to come up to the play room to see the doll, but I told her I couldn't negotiate the stairs, so she's gone to get it."

Just then Agatha's attention was drawn again to the stairs. She smiled softly as she reached her arms out towards the stairs and open air. Karen and Jeff saw nothing. Chrissy smiled broadly and Serena looked expectantly toward Agatha. Suddenly the doll appeared in Agatha's hands. Karen and Jeff took a half step back, looking with awe at each other.

Agatha held the doll gently, looking lovingly at her and then at the stairs, "Why, she is just beautiful, Abigail. I know you must be so proud of her. Have you given her a name?" Agatha paused, listening, and then turned toward Chrissy, "What a lovely name, dear. I know she is very proud of that, aren't you, Chrissy?"

Chrissy just nodded her head lightly, as tears brimmed at the edges of her eyes.

"Chrissy, why don't you and Abigail take Christina up to the playroom for a while? I'm sure your mommy and daddy would like to talk for a while."

Agatha held out the doll once again toward the stairs and, as she did so, the doll disappeared again. Jeff made a move toward the front room, "I gotta sit down," he muttered, "I'm confused."

Chrissy headed for the stairs, with Karen right behind her, "I'm going to put Clayton down for a nap, and then I'll be right down." She looked at the other adults, "Don't say a word until I get back. I don't want to miss anything."

Karen returned quickly to the group seated in the front parlor. Sitting down next to Jeff on the settee, she said, "Okay, now we can talk. The girls are upstairs in the playroom." She turned her attention to Agatha, "What did we just see? I mean, I know we saw the doll, but why is it appearing and disappearing?"

Agatha looked at Karen and Jeff, "As you know, Abigail is a ghost, a soul who has not crossed over. She is here, but not here, because her soul exists in another plain, or dimension. I can see, as Chrissy does, into that other dimension. That is why I can see and talk to Abigail. When Abigail is holding the doll, it is in her dimension, therefore, you cannot see it. When she handed it to me, it was no longer in her dimension, but in ours, so it was visible to you. Do you understand?"

"Yes," Karen replied, pausing just a moment as if to digest what Agatha had just said, and then she asked, "When she received the gift this morning, she hugged me. And when she did, I felt a warmth, or a pressure… I guess you could say I felt a presence. I really don't have the words for it, but Chrissy told me that Abigail was hugging me, so I hugged her back."

Serena looked at Karen as she spoke, and a gentle smile appeared on her lips and warmth in her eyes, "It's what I told you earlier. Perhaps the veil is beginning to lift for you."

Agatha added, "It's possible that's what is happening. Your love may be bridging the gap between this dimension and hers. If that is the case, it is only a matter of time and you will be able to communicate with her."

Jeff had not spoken until now, "Are you sure this is not wishful thinking? I mean, Karen really wants this to happen. Is it possible that she is just imagining these sounds and feelings? I'm not noticing any differences."

Serena looked at Jeff, "Does it matter to you, Jeff? Do you really want to speak and see Abigail?"

Put on the spot, Jeff responded, "Well, it would be nice…I guess. I mean, I don't want to be the only one, but she is only a ghost."

Karen turned as if she had been slapped, "Jeff! She's much more than 'just a ghost'. She's a part of this house and a part of this family. We may not be able to see her, but she is as real to Chrissy as Clayton, or Agatha, or… you and I."

"Whoa, whoa, here. I'm not trying to start a fight, for cryin' out loud. I'm… look, let's just forget what I said. I'm as much on Abigail's side as you are, I just can't express myself, perhaps as well as I should, Karen… I love Chrissy and I love Clayton… and I love Abigail as well. And I especially love you. I mean that, and you know it.

Karen's anger, mollified for the moment, receded from her as she spoke, "I'm sorry, Jeff. I admit that I want this very much, but I am not imagining these things. They often take me by surprise as much as they do you. I realize this is not a normal situation, by any means, and I realize that some of this is very difficult for you to absorb or accept, so I'm sorry for jumping at you like that. I will try to control my emotions a little more, and think about what I am going to say before I say it."

Jeff put his arms around his wife, gave her a kiss on the cheek, and then said, "I'm as much at fault as you are. I know how much you want to be able to hear and see Abigail. And, I know how important Abigail is to Chrissy. I would never do anything to hurt my sweet little girl, so I will try to express myself a little better when I speak. Okay?"

"Okay. Truce?"

"Truce. Now, how about we celebrate Christmas; ladies, can I offer you some egg nog. Karen has made some absolutely wonderful egg nog; easy on the rum, heavy on the nog, or was that on the cream." Jeff smiled broadly at the two ladies.

Karen popped Jeff lightly on the back of the head as she got up from the settee, "I have some things to do in the kitchen.

Serena, would you and Agatha like to join me there? We can chat while I finish preparations for dinner."

We would love to help you, darlin', if we can. Come on, Agatha. Let's join in the fun. I haven't cooked a holiday meal in some time now; Agatha and I usually find some restaurant to eat at, don't we, Agatha?"

Agatha nodded her head in agreement as they all headed for the kitchen.

Karen started working on a salad to go with dinner while Serena washed the greens for her. Working as a team, the two seemed to move in sync with each other, as if they had been doing this type of routine, together, for years. Talking about small things, laughing together, Karen felt so at home. It felt so right to her. *This must be what it is like to have a family, that is, a mother; to do things together,* she thought to herself. Today, she felt the warmth of family, outside what she and Jeff had built together.

After they prepared the salad they moved on to setting the table in the dining room, using the new china and silverware she had bought recently. Once the table was done, she and Serena moved back into the kitchen to put the dressing together and into the oven, checking the turkey as they did.

During all of this activity Agatha had remained quietly sitting at the breakfast table, listening, almost absorbing, not only the conversation, but something else. Karen didn't question, or for that matter, bother her because Serena had warned her ahead of time that Agatha was always very quiet, speaking only when there was something important to say. She was not one for idle chatter.

As the one o'clock time crept near it seemed that dinner was going to be served right on schedule. Everything was happening according to plans, so with all the other dishes ready, Karen pulled the turkey from the oven, removed it from the pan, placing it on a large floral platter, to set before carving. While the turkey rested, she and Serena went about preparing the gravy. When that was bubbling, thick and fragrant, on the stove,

Karen called out, "Jeff, turkey time. The master chef requests the presence of the master carver, counter side, ASAP."

Jeff, who had been in the back parlor, watching a PBS program, quickly appeared at her side, "It's about time. I'm starving. Give me the knife so I can get this bird dissected and ready to eat."

Serena smiled at Jeff, "Nothing like a growing boy. Ya gotta keep 'em full and happy, right Karen?"

"Right!"

After the meal, which happened without incident, Chrissy and Abigail returned to the playroom upstairs. Jeff returned to the back parlor to watch television, dozing off shortly after he sat down, and after the dishes were done, the three ladies retired to the front parlor. Karen excused herself to check on Clayton, who was, once again, sleeping, as new babies do. When she returned to the ladies she quietly closed the doors between the two parlors so they could talk without disturbing Jeff.

Sitting down, she noticed that Serena had taken on a more somber attitude and expression, "Is something wrong, Serena?"

Serena looked at Agatha and then at Karen, "Darlin', I was speaking with Agatha while you were upstairs, and… well, I think it best to let her tell you."

Karen looked at Serena and then to Agatha, "My, God, you two look like there has been a catastrophe. For heaven's sake, Agatha, what is it?"

Agatha lifted her head slightly to gain focus on Karen, "Since I arrived today, I have felt something, but I can not define it. There is something here, in this house, I mentioned it before, but I can not figure it out. It is not another spirit, I would be able to see that, but something, a mystery, and you are the one who needs to discover the truth."

Karen was stunned into silence, as she looked from Agatha to Serena, and then back to Agatha. Seconds turned into minutes as she tried to absorb what Agatha had said. Finally, she found her voice, "I don't understand. Is this something related to Jeff and me? To Chrissy, or maybe Abigail? What kind of mystery? I don't understand?"

Agatha spoke again, "All I know and all I can tell is that it is a mystery within this house, and because your family lives here, and Abigail is a part of your family now, it involves all of you."

Frustrated and perhaps even, scared, she looked to Serena, "But what am I to do?"

"First, and foremost, don't panic, darlin'. I will help you as much as I can. We will sit down, together, and work this out." Serena reached over to take Karen's hand, squeezing it gently as she did.

Karen looked at Serena. Feeling the warmth and confidence of Serena's hand seemed to help ease her anxiety, "Thank you, Serena. I think I'm going to need all the help I can get."

"I don't want to forget to give you your gifts. With all the excitement going on around here, I almost forgot our gifts. Let me walk to the car; I will be right back."

As Serena left the house an uncomfortable silence settled over the room. Karen wanted to ask Agatha some questions, but did not know whether she should or not. Agatha sat in her chair, feet dangling just above the floor, hat perched on her head, staring ahead, not seeming to see anything, or even aware that Karen was still there.

Karen cleared her throat, "Excuse me, Agatha, but is there anything you can tell me, anything you feel, that will help me get started? I really don't know where to start."

Agatha turned her head slightly to look at Karen, "The house will show you the way. Follow your instincts and you will find the answers."

"What about Abigail? Will she be able to help?"

"This is beyond Abigail's knowledge. This is a mystery that the house holds and you must find. That is all I know and all I can tell."

Just then Serena came through the front door, her arms filled with packages, "Phew. I didn't realize what I had until I attempted to bring them all in one trip." She sat the packages down near the tree.

"Would you like me to call the girls down?'

"No darlin', let them play. You can give them their gifts later; Jeffrey too. But this one here," and she handed a small wrapped box to Karen, "I want you to open now. This one is for you."

Karen took the box and looked up into Serena's face, "Thank you, Serena." As she unwrapped the small box Serena sat down next to her, a slight smile of anticipation on her face.

Karen opened the small box and as she did so a gasp escaped her throat. Inside was a beautiful antique necklace; a pendant of intricate silver strands worked around several medium sized garnets. She looked at Serena, "Oh, my god, Serena, this is beautiful. But, I can't accept this. This is far too expensive."

"Don't be absurd! It didn't cost me a dime, darlin'. And besides, it is perfect for you. It fits you and the house. And even if I had to pay a small fortune, which I didn't, you are worth it!"

"What do you mean, 'it didn't cost you anything'?

"It didn't cost me anything because it was mine all ready. I have had that necklace since I was a young woman. It was given to me by my late husband when we became engaged."

"All the more reason for me not to accept it, Serena; don't you have someone in your family you will want to leave this to?"

"Frankly darlin', no! I don't have any children, nor do I have any close nieces or nephews. Besides, I can't think of anyone I would rather have it than you... I hope you won't mind my saying so, but in just the short time I've known you, I've come to think of you most dearly."

Karen looked at Serena, tears slowly edging to the overflow point, "Serena, you have no idea what this means to me. You have come to mean a great deal to me, much more than just a friend. And to know that you feel the same way…" Karen's voice choked, and the tears broke loose, sliding freely down her cheeks.

Serena reached over and slid her arm around Karen's shoulder, pulling her close, hugging her gently. Speaking softly into Karen's ear she whispered, "You're the daughter I never had, Karen, and Chrissy and Clayton, and even Abigail are the grandchildren I've never been blessed with. You have no idea what you have brought into my life in such a short period of time. And now, I have something to get up for, every day. Someone I know, who needs my help. You cannot know how that feels to someone who has been alone for so long. And now, we have a mystery to solve; how exciting!" Serena hugged Karen again.

Karen wiped the tears from her eyes and then her cheeks. She sniffed a couple of times and then finally reached for a tissue, loosing the battle against her emotions. "Serena, the necklace is beautiful and I gratefully accept it as a heartfelt gift from you. I will treasure it always and will gladly pass it on to Chrissy when the time is right."

"By the way, just so you know darlin', this is a true antique. My husband, Joseph, bought it right here in DeFuniak Springs from an estate sale, over fifty years ago. Just exactly who it belonged to before that, I don't know, but it has been mine ever since, and now it is yours, given with just as much love to you, as it was given to me."

Karen removed it from the box and handed it to Serena, "Would you do me the honor." Serena took the necklace and clasped it at the back of Karen's neck. Karen got up and walked over to the hall mirror, looking at the lovely piece as it lay on her chest, just below the hollow of her neck. Touching it lightly she turned her head to Serena, tears once again in her eyes, she mouthed the words, 'Thank you"; her emotions preventing her from giving the words volume.

"Well, Agatha, I think it is time to go. Karen, darlin', we have had a wonderful time. Today has been most illuminating, in many ways. You give me a call when you are ready to start on our mystery, and in the mean time, take care of those children. Love ya, darlin'." Serena placed her hand on Karen's cheek, patted it lightly, and then held her arm out to Agatha. The two ladies shuffled toward the door and as they made their way down the front steps Karen stood at the door, "Good evening, Serena, Agatha. I am so glad you came over today. And Serena, thank you again. I'll give you a call. Stop by anytime."

Karen watched the two ladies shuffle off down the sidewalk until they reached Serena's car, and as they drove away Karen waved after them until the car disappeared. Closing the front door, she leaned against it, and heaved a huge sigh, her mind reeling with all that had happened that day. *What a whirlwind of events, so much to think through,* she thought to herself.

Chapter 11

After Agatha's bomb shell, and Serena's declaration of love, Karen's mind was in a constant state of motion. Jeff slept away the afternoon and then joined her and Chrissy for some evening games, playing Chutes and Ladders, and then Scrabble Junior. Even at four, Chrissy was quite able to play a simple game of Scrabble, and Jeff and Karen encouraged her to learn every chance they could. Chrissy was also an eager and apt pupil, which made it easier for them. They both realized she had an amazing ability to understand much of what went on around her. The games also helped Karen's mind settle, at least for a brief period of time.

That evening as Karen was putting the kids to bed she placed the white puppy next to Clayton's crib, kissed him good night and headed for Chrissy's room. Chrissy and Abigail were deep in discussion. As Karen walked down the hall towards her room, Chrissy was giggling and laughing as she spoke to Abigail. Turning to the door, as Karen entered, Chrissy smiled at her mom, "Hi Mommy! Abigail and I were just talking about the gifts Santa brought. She really likes her doll, Christine. She named her after me, you know."

"Yes, I know…"

"And she is so happy that you liked the doggy she got for Clayton, and…"

"Whoa Chrissy, slow down. Boy, are you wired tonight."

Chrissy let out a huge sigh, "Sorry, Mommy. We are just so happy."

Karen leaned over to kiss Chrissy, "I know, baby, I know, but you need to go to sleep. It's lights out time."

Heaving another huge sigh, Chrissy whispered, "I know, Mommy. I am just so happy that Abigail is happy. Know what I mean?"

"Yes, Chrissy, I know what you mean."

Abruptly, Chrissy looked to the foot of her bed, "Okay, good night, Abigail. See you in the morning."

Karen turned to the end of the bed, "Watch over your little brother, okay?"

Chrissy looked to her mother, "She's smiling, Mommy, and says she will guard him with her life."

Karen looked at Chrissy and then at the foot of the bed with an amazed look, w*hat an ironic statement coming from a ghost,* she thought to herself. "Good night, Abigail."

That night, as she lay in bed, Karen's head was spinning. She thought of Chrissy and Abigail, Jeff and Clayton, the house, Abigail's house, their house. How did this all envelope a mystery?

She hadn't mentioned Agatha's revelation to Jeff. She thought, for now, she would keep it to herself. She didn't want to start another argument with Jeff. That was the last thing she wanted. So, for now, it would remain a secret between Serena and her.

The next morning, just as dawn was breaking over the lake yard, Karen went into Clayton's room, and as she bent over the crib to greet her son, she found the white, stuffed puppy dog in the crib next to his head. She picked up the toy, knowing full well she had put it out side the crib last night, when she put Clayton to bed. She laid the toy on the table next to the bed, changed his diaper and then carried him to the sitting area, at the top of the front stairs, where her rocker sat next to a window.

She sat down, cuddling him closely to her as she started feeding him breakfast. As he nursed, she rocked him gently, humming a Chopin prelude softly, watching the sky lighten slowly over the sleeping city. This was her favorite time of the day. When the house, and everything around her, including outdoors, was quiet; just before the waking process began and it was, for her, a time when she could collect her thoughts and organize herself for the coming day.

But this morning was not quite like most. She had much to think about concerning the mystery that Agatha had spoken of the day before; a mystery that, evidently, only she should or could discover, but, why her? There had been others who had lived in this house before her. Why had she been singled out? Was it because of the love and acceptance she felt for Abigail? Did that make her the 'chosen one'? The more she thought about it the more confused she became.

'Karen, you're thinking too much. Relax. Let things happen as they will. Time will uncover the mystery, Karen thought to herself, trying to relax. The tension had been building and Clayton was beginning to sense that tension, becoming fussy. "Sorry, sweetie, it's okay. Mommy will try to relax. Oh, how I love you, you sweet little boy. You are mommy's special little man." Karen nuzzled Clayton, kissed him on his cheek, and continued to hum her Chopin.

As Clayton became full and satisfied, his eyelids closed gently. His mouth gaped slightly, milk sliding softly out one corner, and his tongue moved instinctively to suckle. Karen stood easily, wiping his mouth with a soft towel and moved down the hall toward his room. She placed him back in his crib, covered him with a light blanket and kissed his cheek. As she left the room, she looked back toward the crib, paying close attention to the location of the stuffed dog.

Karen moved quietly down the hall, past Chrissy's room, peeking briefly at her still sleeping daughter, and then into the play room. There, laying on the daybed was Abigail's doll, nestled lovingly amongst the pillows. As she stood there, her mind briefly on the mystery, the doll moved slightly, and then disappeared. "Good morning, Abigail," Karen said softly to the room. She waited, listening, hoping to hear a reply, but none came. That is, none that she could hear. "I'm going down to fix breakfast. Would you wake Chrissy in a few minutes? Thanks sweetie."

Karen smiled softly at the daybed, knowing that Abigail was there somewhere, and then turned to descend the stairs.

In the kitchen Karen put a pot of coffee on, and began preparing batter for pancakes. She put a skillet on the stove, and turned up the heat. Then she laid bacon in the pan, inhaling as the smell of the sizzling bacon wafted up through the air, hopefully on its way upstairs. As the smell of the brewing coffee mixed with the bacon frying in the pan, she heard the sounds of stirring coming from overhead. The foot steps were soft, so she assumed it was Chrissy. Then she heard a small voice from the stairwell, "Mommy, I'm coming down."

"Okay, Chrissy. I'm here." Karen answered as she moved swiftly to the stairs. Looking up she saw Chrissy, taking one step at a time, coming down the stairs. "Well, good morning, sunshine," and she gave Chrissy a kiss on her cheek as she met her at the bottom. "I'm glad to see you have gotten used to the 'rules of the stairs', sweetie."

"I don't need to remember, mommy. Abigail reminds me every time I come down the stairs. 'Take them slow, one step at a time,' she tells me, every time." The last two words Chrissy said, with emphasis, bobbing her head as she said the words.

"Well, I'm glad she does. It's important that you take them slowly. They are very steep and I am almost sure that she wouldn't want you to fall and neither do I."

Chrissy just smiled, rubbing her fist in one eye as she moved toward the kitchen counter. She climbed up on a stool, working her way from one rung to the next until she was able to sit on it. "Breakfast smells good, mommy. What are we having?"

"Bacon and pancakes, unless you want cereal?"

"No, pancakes are fine, thank you."

Karen had poured some of the pancake batter in the shape of a heart and when it was cooked she placed it on a dish and in front of Chrissy. Chrissy looked down at the pancake and then at her mother with a big smile, "I love you, mommy."

"I love you, too, Chrissy." Karen reached around the counter and gave Chrissy a big hug. "Where's Abigail? Is she down here with us?"

"No, she's up with Clayton. She woke me up and then said she would be with Clayton until I was done with breakfast."

As Karen was placing the plate of bacon on the counter, they heard a loud clunking above them. Listening, they looked at each other with smiles and then, turning, they saw Jeff emerge from the stairwell. Chrissy and Karen burst into laughter at his appearance; his hair stood straight up, as if he had had a terrible fright, and he was scratching his head with one hand. His eyes were only half open and his face needed a shave, badly. His tee shirt was tucked into his baggy pajamas on one side, but hung out, loosely, on the other. He half shuffled, half staggered to the counter where he pulled up a stool and plunked his body, heavily, onto it. "God, I need a cup of coffee. I hope that's high octane you made this morning."

"Well, actually, it's decaffeinated; I still can't drink caffeine, not while I'm nursing. But looking at you, I may need to make a pot of the high test stuff just for you."

"Boy, Daddy, you look like you need to go back to bed."

"I'll be all right. Just give me a cup of java, and something to eat, and I'll be fine. I'll let you know about the high test stuff in a while."

Karen placed a cup of coffee in front of Jeff and then dished him up a stack of three pancakes. He reached for some bacon and crumbled it over the top of his pancakes and then poured the syrup, dousing his pancakes with the sweet, amber liquid. Karen looked at Chrissy, and they both moved their heads from side to side, as if men were a mystery to them both. As Jeff lifted a fork full of pancakes and bacon to his mouth,

Chrissy spoke up, exasperation in her tone, "Men, God love 'em!"

Karen busted up laughing, and Jeff choked on his food, trying hard not to spit it out, as he too, started laughing. Chrissy just smiled, hunching her shoulders slightly, and took a bite of her pancake, looking at her plate as she did.

After she was finished eating, Chrissy asked to be excused and then went upstairs to play with Abigail. After just a moment of quiet, they could hear Chrissy chattering away.

Karen looked at Jeff, "Are you sleeping okay, hon? You look like you've been pulled through a knothole, backwards."

"Yeah, I guess. I've been doing a lot of tossing and turning. Dreaming a lot, but I can't remember the dreams. I just know they aren't fun ones; pretty disturbing, actually."

"If you can't remember them then how do you know they are disturbing dreams?"

"I'm waking up, suddenly, and I feel panicked, but I can't remember the actual dream. Sure wish I could; maybe I could do something about them."

"Maybe it's just the stress of moving, and then Clayton being born, and the holidays. That's a lot going on in just a couple of months."

"Yeah, and don't forget about our friendly ghost. That sure hasn't helped. And before you jump me, I'm not complaining; just making note… It could be stress. Hopefully, with the holidays almost over, maybe things will settle down into a routine and I can get some sleep; would be nice. Speaking of holidays, what do you want to do for New Years?"

Karen thought for a moment, "I don't know; maybe just stay home with the kids, play some games. What do you think?"

"We can do anything you want or nothing at all. If you want to stay home we can do some favorite food, pizza or something like that, maybe rent a special movie, and play some games with Chrissy. That's just fine with me. Let's spend our first New Years in our new home. We'll have plenty of time to do other things and go other places for New Years."

"Okay. That sounds good to me. I'll check out some food ideas at the store. I think I'll go for things bride style."

Jeff looked at her questioningly.

Karen smiled, "You know, something old, that could be pizza, something new, that could be a new snack, something borrowed, I'll get something from Serena, and something blue, hmmm, blueberry ice cream? Whatta ya think?"

Jeff looked at her, turning his head from side to side, "Whatever you want to do, babe." He just smiled at her, the smile spreading upward, crinkling his eyes as it spread and then he leaned forward and kissed her gently. "You know how much I love you?" Without letting her answer he said, "I love you this much." And he spread his arms as wide as they would go. Smiling, once again, he leaned forward and kissed her gently one more time.

After breakfast Jeff went upstairs to clean up and then headed for his office to work. As he passed through the kitchen he stopped to ask, "I'm going out to work some...what have you got planned for today?"

Karen poked her head out of the back room, "I thought I would head over to Wal-Mart to check out the after-Christmas clearance. See if there's anything I can use. I can take the kids unless you want to watch them for me?"

"I could keep an eye on them, if you want. Can you put Clayton in his carrier and bring him out to the office, and then we can put the monitor in with Chrissy. That way I can keep track of them both."

"That'll work. I'll bring Clayton out to you when I'm ready to leave."

On her way up to get dressed Karen stopped to ask Chrissy if she wanted to go. Chrissy was sitting on the floor playing a board game, "Would it be okay if I stay here. I'm teaching Abigail how to play Chutes and Ladders."

"Sure, honey. I'm going to take Clayton out to the office with Daddy. I'll leave the monitor here so Daddy can hear you two, so if you need him, just call. Okay?" Looking opposite the board from Chrissy, Karen spoke, "I know you'll watch out for Chrissy, Abigail. Don't let her go down the stairs unless Daddy is there, okay?"

Karen got herself ready to go and gathered Clayton up, with extra diapers, and then carried him out to Jeff. She came back into the house and called up the back stairs to remind Chrissy one more time to call daddy if she needed anything. Karen left the house, poked her head into Jeff's office as she headed for the car, "I'm on my way, hon. I'll be back in a little while, and thank you for watching the kids. Love you."

She got into the van, and headed out for a morning of shopping.

Jeff's mind was on his computer project, but he was abstractly listening to the monitor. He could hear Chrissy talking about a move in her game, and then a giggle. Then he heard another child's voice; a little girl's voice. Faint, but still there. His hands froze on the keyboard. Listening intently now, he could hear Chrissy's patter, laughing, and then, there it was again; another child's voice!

Jeff sat up straight in his chair, uncertain what to do. He realized that, more than likely, he was hearing Abigail. Should he go into the house? He looked at Clayton, asleep in his carrier. If he moved the carrier he would probably wake up. He didn't want to leave him there, in the office, by himself. What to do?

Finally, he decided that he could walk into the house for a minute, just to listen at the bottom of the stairs. Quietly, he walked to the door, looking back as he stepped out toward the house. It was only thirty feet to the back door. What could it hurt?

He quietly opened the back door and stepped over to the back stairs to listen, keeping the office door within sight the entire time. Listening to Chrissy's conversation, that's all he heard; just Chrissy. Why couldn't he hear Abigail? He remained there, listening for a few more moments, and then returned to his office. Clayton was still sleeping, not even a hair out of place. As he sat down at his desk, he couldn't figure it out. He had distinctly heard another child's voice on the monitor, yet when he listened by the stairs all he heard was Chrissy's voice. Listening again, he could hear that child's voice again. *I don't get it,* he thought. *I can hear her over the monitor, but not when I'm standing near-by. Do I tell Karen or keep this to myself. She'll get upset if I can hear Abigail and she can't.* "Geez, what do I do?" he said out loud, leaning forward on his elbows, his chin resting on his palms.

Finally, he decided to keep this to himself, for now. He would mention it to Serena the next time he saw her, and ask her opinion. He really didn't want to upset Karen and he certainly didn't want a fight with her. So, for now, this would remain his secret.

Karen arrived home around noon, the car loaded with numerous bags, which contained rolls of wrapping paper, bags of bows, animated Christmas figures, and miscellaneous items of holiday interest. She also had purchased several plastic totes, red and green in color, to store the decorations until the next year.

After everything was taken into the house Jeff looked at the bags and totes, then he looked at Karen, and then back at the mound of purchases on the dining room table. "Did you leave anything for anyone else?"

Karen smacked him lightly on the arm, "Of course I did. Don't be silly."

Just then Chrissy called down from the top of the back stairs, "Mommy, is that you? Can I come down now?"

"Of course Chrissy, Daddy will meet you at the bottom." Turning to Jeff, she asked, "Where's my little man?"

"He's still asleep, if you can imagine that. He's out in my office."

Karen swept past Jeff and headed out the back door, just to return shortly carrying Clayton in his carrier. "Look at this; he's still asleep, even through being carried in here."

"I wish I could sleep like that; not a care in the world, undisturbed by everything going on around me."

"He knows he's loved and protected. I'm going to see if I can transfer him to his crib. I'll be right back."

While Karen was out of the room Chrissy and Jeff made a game of one-ups-manship going through the bags Karen had brought home. Jeff would pull something out, acting surprised and excited, oohing and aahing, and then Chrissy would pull something out of another bag, displaying the same excitement, saying hers was better, fancier, and prettier than those things her father had found.

When Karen returned, she stopped in the dining room doorway, examining the disarray in front of her. Looking at the jumble of packages she said, "Geez, you guys, could you have made any more of a mess. Talk about a bunch of..."

As she stepped into the room Karen had glanced across into the mirror on the buffet opposite her, and she froze in her tracks. In the reflection she saw, standing next to her, a young girl, perhaps seven or eight years old, with long dark hair plaited into two braids. She was wearing a light colored dress with a low waist and a ruffled skirt, and black, high topped shoes.

Karen turned quickly, looking down to her right, but there was nothing there. She turned back to the mirror, but the reflection was only hers. She looked again to her right and then back to the mirror, but saw only herself, standing alone.

Jeff was now looking at Karen, "Karen? Babe, what's the matter? You look like you've seen a ghost."

Karen's complexion had lost all its color and she stood, speechless, staring at the mirror.

"Karen?"

Karen tried to ease the words out, and they were slow to come, but she finally managed to speak, just above a whisper, "Jeff... I saw her. I saw Abigail." She turned her head toward Jeff and he saw the tears teetering at the corners of her eyes.

"Are you sure? I mean, how? Where?"

"There, right there!" Karen pointed to the mirror. "She was right there, in the mirror, standing next to me!" Karen's voice, by now, was ascending beyond her normal level, excitement edging into her voice, her finger accentuating each word.

Jeff turned to Chrissy, who was, by now, concerned about her mother, worry showing on her face. "Chrissy, where is Abigail?"

"Right there, Daddy, next to mommy."

"Then why can't I see her?" Karen asked, pleadingly. "I just saw her, in the mirror, why can't I see her now?"

Jeff was on his feet, moving towards Karen, "Karen, take it easy, take it easy." He wrapped his arms around her. "Things are evidently changing around here. Little snippets of exposure are coming through, obviously, so let's not get too overly excited. You've had one glimpse; I'm sure there will be many more, so take it easy, okay."

"I'm sorry. It just totally caught me off guard. I was stunned. I mean, I'm thrilled that I got a chance to see her; at least now I know what she looks like, but, gee, I wish it could have lasted longer."

"Mommy? Abigail is still standing next to you. Can you see her now?"

Karen looked into the mirror, but saw only her own and Jeff's reflection. Just then, she felt a warm pressure on her shoulder and she looked to Chrissy.

"She's got her hand on your shoulder, Mommy..." Chrissy paused to listen, and then continued, "Abigail says to not worry, she will be here, around you, all the time, so don't cry."

Karen placed her hand on her shoulder, as if to cover Abigail's, and then she whispered, "I know sweetie, I know."

Later, after dinner and the kids were in bed, Jeff and Karen had retreated to the back parlor for some quiet time with a movie. With the movie paused temporarily, while Karen made some popcorn, Jeff thought about the revelations of the day; first, he heard Abigail on the nursery monitor, and then Karen saw Abigail's reflection in the mirror. Jeff thought about telling Karen about his incident, and as she returned with the popcorn he decided to go for it, "Karen, I wanted to tell you about something that happened today."

"You mean besides my seeing Abigail?"

"Yeah, it happened while you were gone to the store. I think I heard Abigail." As she moved a piece of popcorn toward her mouth, Karen's hand froze mid-air. Her eyes got a little wider as her hand, slowly, returned the popcorn to the bowl, "When?"

"I was in my office, working, and I could hear Chrissy over the monitor. Out of nowhere I heard another child's voice. I knew it wasn't Chrissy's, it was different. I couldn't distinguish the words, but I could hear her, none the less."

"Why didn't you tell me before?"

"I wanted to talk to Serena about it first. I was afraid you would get upset, knowing I had heard her and you hadn't." Karen opened her mouth as if to speak, but Jeff continued, "But wait, there's more. After I heard her voice a few times over the monitor, I went into the house, to the stairs, to listen first hand, but once there I couldn't hear anything but Chrissy. When I returned to the office I heard her over the monitor again. I don't get it."

Karen thought about it for a moment, "Well, considering I got to see Abigail for a brief moment today, I guess I got the better of the two deals. And considering everything, I probably would have been upset if you had told me immediately, but now, after everything, I'm okay. No hard feelings. And actually,

I'm glad you got to hear her. It means we are both opening up to our newest family member."

"Yeah, but I still don't understand why I couldn't hear her when I was indoors, by the stairs. It was only over the monitor."

Karen considered this for a moment, "Do you suppose it has to do with radio frequency? I'm just guessing here, but maybe her voice was transported by the frequency of the radio, and you could hear her that way, but not under normal conditions.

"Maybe," Jeff paused, considering what Karen had said, "I do know this... today has been one heck of a day, for everyone. We've made some major strides, don't you agree?"

"I do indeed." Karen smiled lightly, leaned over and kissed her husband on the forehead, and popped a piece of popcorn in her mouth, "Let's finish the movie!"

Chapter 12

New Years was spent, just as they had planned, quiet, at home with the kids, and up late, just long enough to bring in the New Year. At midnight, Jeff had poured two glasses of champagne for the adults and a small glass of sparkling grape juice for Chrissy. As they held their glasses high Jeff made the toast, "To 2008; may our blessings continue as they have this past year and continue on for many, many more to come." They clinked their glasses together and drank to the toast.

Karen said, "To the future." And Chrissy repeated the phrase.

Two days later Serena called, "Hello darlin', how was your New Years?"

"Hello, Serena. It was wonderful. We stayed home, with the kids, and brought 2008 in with a toast; safe and simple. How did you celebrate, Serena?"

"About as safe as you can get, darlin'. I went to bed at nine and slept through til mornin'. Borin', but safe...been celebratin' that way since my husband died. No point in partyin' when there's no one to party with. One day's the same as the next at my age."

Karen chuckled at Serena's take on later life, "It can't be all that bad, Serena. You have other friends, don't you?"

"None I'd want to share a glass of champagne with."

Karen smiled broadly, "Oh, Serena, you are so funny, sometimes. I know you can't be serious."

"Well, yes and no. I have plenty of friends, darlin', but I've celebrated enough in my life, that it just doesn't mean much to me any more. One day leads to a week, a week to a month, and a month to another year… what's to celebrate other than I've lived to see it?"

"Well, I guess the fact that you've lived to see another year has to be something to celebrate, no matter how old a person is."

"When you put it that way, I guess you're right."

Karen expressed a big smile that she knew Serena couldn't see.

"So when are we goin' to work on this mystery, darlin'"

"Anytime you're ready, Serena. Oh, my gosh, I almost forgot to tell you… I've seen Abigail!"

"When?" Serena asked the question with great surprise and enthusiasm.

"The day after Christmas," Karen related the sighting in the mirror. "The darn thing is, it was only for that brief moment; not more than a second or two."

"It's a start, darlin', it's a start. More will come, so don't get discouraged. What are you doing today?"

"We're starting to take down the decorations. I'm starting with the tree today."

"Would you mind if I came over and helped you?"

"Why, of course not; I would love to have you over. Serena, you are always welcome in my home. And I could definitely use the help; Jeff has a project he needs to complete, and I'm not sure how much help I'll get out of Chrissy. She and Abigail have been playing board games since they got them on Christmas morning. Evidently Abigail is quite the bright little girl, so she gives Chrissy a strong learning partner."

"How soon will you be startin', darlin'?"

"Well, actually, I've just started, so anytime you want to come over is fine with me, Serena. This is going to take some time to dismantle and pack all these decorations."

"I'll be right over and we can discuss the mystery as we work. How's that sound?"

"Sounds great to me Serena, I'll see you shortly."

"Bye, darlin'"

Karen was bent over, her upper torso hidden in amongst the tree, removing ornaments from the lower branches, when the doorbell rang, "Come in, Serena, I'm in the front room."

Karen heard the door open and then close, quietly, and then she heard Serena just behind her, "Here, darlin', hand that to me and I'll place it in the box."

"I'll just keep handing them out to you as long as I can reach any more ornaments."

"You do that, darlin'. That'll keep you from having to go up and down so much. I swear, when I walked in I thought that tree was trying to swallow you up, like some big alligator. The way you were rustling around in there I thought you were fightin' for your life."

Karen laughed heartily and then replied, "I'll be lucky if I can extract myself from here. I'm so deep in you could almost say I'm in the belly of the beast. I may have to have you grab the back of my pants and pull."

"Well, you just say the word and I'll try my darndest to rescue the fair maiden from the monster."

Karen and Serena continued dismantling the tree, laughing and joking as they packed away the decorations for another year. After a couple of hours they decided to take a break for lunch. Karen prepared food for Jeff and took it out to his office. Chrissy came down from her game playing to eat a sandwich and then disappeared back up to the playroom. After everyone else was taken care of Serena and Karen sat at the kitchen table to relax, eat, and talk.

Serena asked Karen, "Have you thought anymore about what Agatha said?"

"Some. I just can't figure out why I'm the 'chosen one' to solve this mystery? I know that the first day, when we arrived, as I stood outside on the sidewalk, looking at the house, it seemed to murmur to me, as if it were alive. I know that sounds crazy and I didn't really think about it then, but it's like I have a special connection to the house."

"There are many things in this world, and the next, that we are unaware of. Things that have been hinted at, through history, but no one has been able to really define. Those who were lucky enough, if you consider it lucky, to have been blessed with the ability to see beyond normal boundaries were often considered witches or at best crazy. Today, things are getting better for those who can see beyond the veil."

"Well, I can't say I'm seeing beyond the veil, but I'm certainly seeing and feeling some strange things. I've felt Abigail hug me, I've heard her giggle, I think, and now I've actually seen her, albeit briefly. It is all very mystifying, and exhilarating at the same time. The thing that has me puzzled is this mystery. I'm totally at a loss about that. Where do we start?"

"I guess we start with the history of the house. We go through everything that has happened here that might be of a mysterious nature. And of course, we start with Abigail and her family and move through historically from there to now or vice versa."

"Serena, you know much of the history, don't you?"

"Well, yes… darlin', but much of mine is oral history. What we really need is a true history, that is, a list of each owner since the Cottonwoods, the years that each owned the house, and then try to find out if anything mysterious happened to any one of them. We can call the county clerk's office and see what information we can get from them."

"Let's do it now," Karen said excitedly and she reached for the phone book and the phone. Karen listened to the person on the other end, the phone cradled between her ear and her shoulder, as she scribbled, what looked like gibberish to Serena, on a piece of paper. When she hung-up she smiled a broad, excited grin. "This is going to be fun, at least to start with."

Serena looked at Karen, questions creasing her face, "What did they say?"

"It's all on-line! We go in and put our name, the current owner, in and it will bring up the previous owner." Karen lightly shrugged her shoulders, "Of course, I know their names, silly me." She looked sheepishly at Serena. "I'll start with their name and the address and the previous owner comes up. You just keep putting in each previous owner until you reach the original, which in this case, were Nathan and Marion Cottonwood. Once we have the list then we can look for any information we can find on each owner. Oh, I do love the electronic age."

Serena sat there watching Karen, wonder and pleasure in her eyes, amazement in her smile, "My, you sure have snatched onto this like a football and you are the star quarterback. You are off and running."

Karen smiled lightly at Serena, "I guess we should finish the tree first, huh? I'll do my homework later?"

"Whatever you say, darlin'; I'm behind you one hundred percent."

Karen couldn't wait to get started on her research, but resigned herself to the present job at hand. She and Serena worked well together, talking and laughing, about all sorts of topics. Finally, by late afternoon they had packed up all of the decorations in the plastic totes Karen had bought, ending up with four large ones and three smaller stacked up in the front hall. Standing next to them, her hands on her hips, Karen let out a huge sigh, "Boy, that was a lot of work, but also a lot of fun. I can't thank you enough for helping me, Serena."

Serena smiled at Karen warmly, "You have no idea, darlin' just how much I've enjoyed today. Spending time with you is no effort at all." Looking at the stack of totes Serena asked, "What are you going to do with these? Do you need help carrying them somewhere?"

"I think by the time I am done with all of the decorations, inside and out, there will be too much to put outside in the garage. I don't want to take up space out there I might need for something else. So I just might put them all up in the attic. We haven't opened it yet and I have no idea how much room is up there, but we won't need these for about ten months, so I think that might be the place to put them. I'll get Jeff to help me with them later."

"Well, darlin', you let me know if I can help you with anythin' else, anytime. I have more fun with you than anyone else I know."

Karen reached out and gave Serena a big hug, and as she stepped back she heard from overhead, "Mommy?"

Karen looked up and saw Chrissy's face, over the railing, looking down on her and Serena. She seemed almost spectral, as if there was no body, just her head, and it gave Karen a slight start. "Chrissy, baby, you startled me. What is it honey? Are you and Abigail done playing?"

"Yes and I heard Clayton start to fuss, so I came to tell you."

Serena patted Karen on the hand, "You have much to do, darlin'. I'll just head on home and you get back to me when you find out somethin' about the house, okay?"

Karen smiled at Serena, warmly and with affection. "I'll go online later and I'll call you tomorrow. Thank you, Serena. You are a dear friend."

Next morning, after Jeff was situated in his office, and Chrissy was busy with Abigail in the playroom, Karen went on-line and began her search. First she put in the names of the previous owners, Gene and Carolyn Hunter; they had owned the house for seven years. They purchased the home from the estate of Ida Mae Cutter in 2000. Karen repeated the process of entering the previous owners names and came up with a list of all those who had, over a period of one hundred years, owned their home.

The home was built by Nathan and Marion Cottonwood in 1907. It sat vacant from 1908 until it was purchased by Rupert and Anna Stillwater in 1918. They sold the home in

1920 to Ellis and Elizabeth McKenzie. The McKenzie's sold the home in 1930 to Connolly and Erma Anderson. They sold the home in 1947 to Gerald and Ida Mae Cutter. The house was owned by them until 2000 when it was purchased by the Hunters. They held the home until it was purchased by Karen and Jeff in 2007.

Looking at the list Karen tried to imagine the how's and why's of each purchase and sale. Somewhere, in that one hundred years, lay a mystery that she had been handed the task of solving. What had happened, other than Abigail's death? As she mused on the possibilities she heard Clayton fussing over the monitor.

Because her computer desk was located in a corner of the mezzanine she moved quickly to his room and found him awake, lying on his back, the little white stuffed dog next to his head. Clayton spotted his mother and smiled, pumping his arms and legs rapidly. "Hey, little man. How's mamma's big boy?" Karen reached down, putting her hands under Clayton's arms, and gently picked him up, her fingers supporting his head. He gurgled lightly as she moved him to her shoulder. Patting him lightly she quickly realized why he had fussed, "You need a change, don't you little one? Mamma's going to fix you right up" Karen laid Clayton on the table and quickly changed his diaper. Buttoning up his sleeper, she placed him back in his crib and turned on the mobile hanging above. "There you go, sweetie." Before she left the room she took the stuffed dog and placed it back on the table next to the crib, again.

Karen moved back to her desk and picked up the list she had made. She would call Serena and let her know what she had found.

"Serena, this is Karen."

"Why, hello darlin'."

"Serena, I have a list of all of the owners of our house and the years the house was sold. What do we do now?"

"Well, I guess we need to get together and go over the list, fill in the information that I know and research to fill in the blanks. When do you want to get together, darlin'?"

Would you like to come over for lunch tomorrow?"

"I would love to. What time?"

"Let's make it at one. That way I can have Jeff and the kids taken care of so we can sit and be left alone, at least for a short while."

"Sounds good, darlin'. I'll be there at one. Can't wait to start on this. It will be Sherlock and Watson, at work once again. With skirts on, that is."

Karen laughed, "I'll see you tomorrow, Serena. You have a good evening."

"You too, darlin'."

Chapter 13

Karen and Serena sat at the table looking over the list, "Well, we might as well start at the front and work our way backwards," Serena said, "we know that the Hunter's had an encounter, or at least a guest of theirs did, but no real surprises or mysteries there. You agree, Karen?"

Karen nodded her head in agreement.

"Okay, now the Cutters; I knew them. They bought the house in 1947; I was sixteen and met them shortly after they moved in. They were newly-weds and moved here from Montgomery, Alabama. Ida Mae was just a few years older than me, nineteen, if I remember correctly. Gerald, her husband, had been a soldier in World War II. They were such a sweet couple and very much in love. I corresponded with Ida Mae while I was away at college. Now, as far as I know, they never mentioned any encounters while they lived here, and I had told them about the ghost, so they were well aware of her. They were the ones who closed in the porches, addin' these two rooms. Gerald passed away in 1986 and I stayed close with Ida Mae until her passin' in 1992. They weren't blessed with any children and there were no heirs to move in, so the house sat vacant until the Hunters bought it in 2000. I just don't see anything mysterious about those two, do you?"

"No, I think what ever the mystery it goes much farther back."

"Okay, let's go back a little farther. Hmmm, Connolly and Erma Anderson bought the house in 1930. Now, there's a lot of Andersons in this area, and like I told you before, I've tried to learn as much history as I could, so I've picked up some

130

information on them. Connolly and Erma moved into the house along with their two children, a boy and a girl. They lived in the house for only six months before moving out, and from what I've been told, it was a fast move. They told family members there was a ghost in the house and they weren't goin' to live in a haunted house. Word got around that the house was haunted, everybody knew it anyway, and they couldn't sell the darned thing. It sat vacant until Gerald and Ida Mae bought it in 1947. My guess is, them being from Montgomery, no one ever told them about the hauntin' until they bought the house and moved in. Hmph, I guess that would have been me." Serena smiled a weak and sheepish smile.

Karen looked at Serena and chuckled lightly, "Well, that seems innocent enough. No real mysteries there. Don't you agree, Serena?"

"Oh, most definitely."

Karen continued, "Let's see, the house was bought by Ellis and Elizabeth McKenzie in 1920. They were also a childless couple…"

"How did you know that?" Serena interrupted.

"I also checked the census records for 1910 through the present and it shows that only two people lived in that house during that time, 1920 through 1930."

"Well, I'll be darned," Serena exclaimed, "You learned all that since yesterday?"

"Yup!" Karen grinned at Serena. "The electronic age is truly amazing, huh?"

"Well, I'll be darned," Serena muttered again. It took me years to find out all that I've just told you and you learned all this is a few hours."

"Actually, it was more like minutes."

"Well, roll me in sugar and call me a dumplin'."

Karen laughed out loud. As she sat there looking at Serena she laughed all the more until tears were running down her cheeks. "Oh, Serena, you are just too cute!"

Finally calming down as she wiped away the tears Karen continued, "Okay, now our last couple, Rupert and Anna Stillwater, bought the house in 1918 and sold it in 1920. They had one child, a son, and lived there only two years. My guess is they also had encounters and that is why they moved after only two years.

"What I am seeing here is a trend in the ghostly appearances. Do you see what I'm talking about Serena?"

"Let me see. The Stillwater's lived there for two years. The McKenzie's lived there ten years, probably didn't see any ghosts otherwise they wouldn't have stayed so long. The Anderson's lived there six months, and we know they saw ghosts. Gerald and Ida Mae had the house the longest and I'm sure they didn't see any ghost. The Hunter's had an encounter and that brings us up to you and your family and of course we know our little ghost is very prevalent. It is probably right in front of me, but I'm not seein' anythin'," Serena said, frustration edging into her voice.

"Those families that stayed the shortest length of time; those with children, saw Abigail. Those without children did not see her and lived in the house years longer. This tells me that she appears only when there are children living in the house."

"Yes, I see, I see," Serena agreed, "but I can't see how this is any mystery; not really. Do you?"

Karen sighed and leaned back in her chair, "No. I don't think this is what we're looking for. So, back to the drawing board; that is, the list."

"Well, the only ones left are the Cottonwoods. They finished building the house in November of 1907. Abigail died in October of 1908. Her parents, Nathan and Marion disappeared shortly after her death. That's a mystery, where they went, that is, but everyone assumed they moved away. The house sat empty until it finally sold to the Stillwater's in 1918.

"Now, I do know that the house was purchased by the Stillwater's for the amount of back taxes, so wherever Nathan and Marion moved to, they never had anything more to do with the house. They didn't even try to sell it; just disappeared…poof!"

Karen looked at Serena, "I think we need to focus on the Cottonwoods. This has to be where the mystery is. Don't you agree, Serena?"

"It appears that way, darlin'."

"So I guess I will go on to the internet again and do some research into their names; see if anything else comes up. I can search first in Florida, see if they moved to another city and if I come up with nothing, I'll move my search into Alabama and then Mississippi, and so on, fanning out across the south. Surely I will find something. There are many genealogy websites, so surely I will find something." By now Karen seemed to be talking to herself. Frustration was creeping into her voice as she spoke and she seemed to forget Serena was even there.

"Don't let this trouble you, dear. Things will come in their proper time. Just work on this when you have time. Don't make this your life's mission. You have a family to take care of. No sense making yourself ill over this."

"I know Serena, I know. I was just hoping that you and I could make some headway today."

"Well, we did narrow it down to Abigail's parents. So, really, we did make some headway, as you call it."

"Yes, you're right. We've made some progress and I guess I should be satisfied. It's just that when I get something put in front of me, that is, a challenge, I want to charge ahead, see it through, and get it done. I don't want delays. I know that sounds like impatience, but it's just the way I am. You can ask Jeff, he'll tell you."

Serena looked at Karen as if she were seeing her in a new light.

"It's not that I'm bull headed. I'm not stubborn, but I am like a bull dog in the sense that when I get my teeth into something I won't let go. I must see it to the end." Karen was getting increasingly frustrated.

"And that you will, darlin'; just in good time... just in good time." Serena reached out and patted Karen's hand lightly.

Karen placed her other hand on top of Serena's and held it gently. Looking at Serena, a sheepish expression on her face, Karen spoke, "Serena, one of the best days of my life was the day I met you. You have brought something into my life that has been missing for a long, long time." Karen paused, uncomfortable to continue, afraid of saying too much. But she looked at Serena's eyes and knew she could continue without trepidation. "I hope you don't mind my saying this, Serena, but you've become like a mother to me. I feel like you know me so well, that you can give me the guidance and the love that my own mother would have or should have."

Serena's eyes were misting lightly as Karen continued, "I never had a mother figure in my life, I moved from foster home to foster home and I never really had someone that I could feel confident in enough to share my inner feelings with. Shoot, I've never really had a best friend, except Jeff. Some how, when I met you, even that first day, as confused and concerned as I was about this thing with Chrissy and Abigail, I could tell you were going to be special to me. I hope you don't mind." By now Karen was close to tears herself.

"You know, darlin', I have felt the same way about you; I just didn't want to scare you off with the ramblin's of a dodderin' old woman."

Karen laughed, "Doddering, you are not!"

"Well, you know what I mean. You have filled a void for me as well. I was never blessed with children so I never had the chance to share my love or my knowledge with someone of the younger generations. You have definitely given me a chance to do that and I love you like a daughter and a friend. I guess you could say we have hereby formed a mutual admiration society. How about that?"

"Serena, you are so funny; I just love you to pieces." Karen reached out and hugged Serena.

"Me too, honey. Me too," Serena whispered in her ear, returning the hug.

After a few moments they drew away from each other and Serena reached out and patted Karen lightly on the cheek as she said, "Now, I want you to promise me that you will take this one day at a time; no frustration, no impatience. Okay?"

"Okay," Karen said softly.

"Things will happen in due course and you'll figure out this mystery soon enough. Now, I need to get on home. You take care, darlin' and I'll see you later." Serena picked up her coat and headed for the front door.

"Good-bye, Serena. We'll talk soon."

Later that evening, after dinner, Chrissy had gone up to the playroom with Abigail and Jeff and Karen were in the back parlor with Clayton. They were playing with him before Karen put him to bed. As Jeff dangled his stuffed doggy over him, Clayton giggled and laughed, pumping his little arms and legs as he gurgled his pleasure.

"Jeff, you're going to get him so wound up he won't want to sleep."

"Actually, I'm hoping to wear him out so he will sleep. Seriously, I can't believe how he is growing. He's like a little weed." Jeff wiggled the stuffed dog into Clayton's belly, tickling him with it and Clayton responded with another giggle.

"You know, Jeff, when I put him down at night I put that little dog on the table next to the crib. Yet, every time I go in to check on him, his doggy is lying next to his head, in the crib. I'm sure that Abigail is moving the toy."

"What can that hurt?"

"Nothing, I guess. At least for now, but when he gets old enough to start grasping and chewing on it, we'll need to be more careful. I wouldn't want him to chew off one of those button eyes."

135

"Oh, I see what you mean. Well, we'll keep an eye on things; maybe say something to Abigail about it. Whatta' you think?"

"I guess for now it's okay."

Clayton began to rub his eyes, yawning, and then became fussy. "Oh, oh, I think it's time for someone to go to bed. Here, Jeff, let me take him. I'll get him changed, fed and into bed. I'll give you a holler when he's ready and you can tuck him in."

"Okay. See you in a bit, little man."

Karen picked Clayton up and headed for the front stairs and as she left the room she heard Jeff checking the television for programs. Karen went up the stairs and into Clayton's room, calling Chrissy as she did, "Chrissy, time to get cleaned up for bed, baby."

"Okay, Mommy. Abigail and I are almost done with our game. Can we finish it first?"

"Yes, that's fine. I'll be here with Clayton for a little while, feeding him."

Karen sat down with her son in the rocking chair next to the front window above the staircase. As he nursed hungrily, she hummed Brahms Lullaby softly, rocking gently as she worked her way through the melody. Once Clayton was finished he was nearly asleep so she rose easily from the rocker and moved him into the bedroom and laid him gently into his crib. As she placed the blanket over her son she spoke into the monitor, "Jeff, come up and say goodnight to Clayton."

Chrissy walked into the room at that moment. Karen turned to her, put her finger to her lips and whispered, "Shhh"

Chrissy raised her shoulders, smiled at her mother and then tip toed to her brother's crib. Whispering softly she said, "Good night, Clayton, sleep tight." She kissed her palm and softly blew it toward her little brother. Turning, she moved toward the door and into the hall. Jeff wheeled around the corner into the doorway just as Chrissy was leaving and they almost had a head-on collision. "Whoa, there, I almost gotcha," he said.

"Daddy," Chrissy whispered, putting her finger to her lips, "Clayton's asleep."

"Sorry," Jeff whispered.

Chrissy moved on down the hall to her room as Jeff approached the crib. "Goodnight, little man. You know we love you," he whispered as he leaned into the crib and kissed his son. Clayton's lips moved in a suckling motion.

Karen literally beamed at her family. She thought to herself, *I have got to be the luckiest person on earth. I am in a circle of love.*

Chrissy called softly from her room, "Mommy, I'm ready for bed."

"Okay, Chrissy, we're coming." Karen and Jeff moved quietly out of Clayton's room and as they looked back they saw the soft, white stuffed doggy disappear from the crib side table and then almost instantly reappear in the crib next to Clayton's head. No words were necessary as they looked at each other. Jeff raised his eyebrows slightly and Karen just smiled, each knowing exactly what had just happened.

Walking into Chrissy's room they stopped at the door. Karen grasped Jeff by his wrist. Chrissy was on her knees at the side of the bed, her hands together in prayer, "Now I lay me down to sleep, I pray the Lord, my soul to keep. If I should die before I wake, I pray the Lord my soul to take. God Bless Mommy and Daddy, Clayton and especially Abigail. Amen." She stood up and then scrambled up onto the bed, smiling sheepishly up at her parents as they stood in the doorway, surprise and awe lighting up their faces. She looked as if she had been caught with her hand in a cookie jar.

"Chrissy, where did you learn that prayer?" Karen asked.

"Abigail taught it to me. It's okay, isn't it?"

"Of course, honey. That's fine. It just caught us by surprise," Jeff answered.

Karen and Jeff kissed Chrissy goodnight and then turned out the light as they left the room. Walking quietly down the hall toward the front stairs, Jeff spoke gently to Karen, "Wow! Everyday that little girl just surprises the heck out of me. Karen, sometimes I forget she is just four. She says things that seem far beyond her age."

Karen smiled softly as she responded, "Just think what she will be like in ten or even twenty years. Her experiences here and now will set the path for her life later on. I truly believe that her friendship with Abigail will provide her with a pathway to tolerance and open mindedness for her adult life."

"Whoa there, gal; let's take this a bit slower. The way you're talking we'll be retiring next month and the kids will be graduating college. Can we get them in to elementary school first before you have me old and gray?"

Karen laughed, "Sorry. I just start reflecting and my mind speeds into high gear. I'll let you get the gray hairs, one at a time, okay?"

"Works for me; let's go watch a movie." Jeff took Karen by the hand, kissed her on the cheek, and guided her down the stairs.

Chapter 14

The next morning at breakfast Jeff looked at Karen, "Say, hon', I don't mean to push because I know you're busy with the kids, but when are you going to do something with those boxes of Christmas decorations that are sitting in the front hall?"

"I planned on putting them away today; that is, if I can get you to help me for a few minutes."

"Sure, no problem, where are you planning to store them?"

"I'm going to put them in the attic, but I'll need help with a ladder and lifting them up through the attic opening."

"Just let me know when and I'll get the ladder from the garage."

"Thanks, babe, let's do it right after we eat."

"Will do, chief." Jeff took his right hand and made a military style salute to Karen and then lifted another fork full of eggs toward his mouth.

Jeff and Karen had never been up in the attic and as a matter of fact had no idea how to get into the attic. The opening or entrance into the attic, located in the upstairs hallway ceiling, had a door or hatchway covering it, but how it opened, they weren't sure. Standing underneath they noticed a short rope hanging from one edge of the hatch covering. "Do you suppose that rope pulls open the cover?" Jeff asked Karen.

"I guess we won't know until we try, but it seems logical."

Positioning the ladder under the attic entrance Jeff reached up and grabbed the short rope and gave it a slight tug, pulling the rope in several directions to try to pull down, lift up or slide in one direction or another, but nothing moved. Looking down at Karen he gave her a quizzical look. She shrugged her shoulders and then said, "Try again a little harder."

This time Jeff gave the rope a hard jerk and the edge of the hatchway moved downward and they realized it was a folding stairway. Still holding the rope, Jeff slowly moved down the ladder and when his feet hit the floor he moved the ladder out of the way as the stairs slowly unfolded to the floor.

"Wow, now that's pretty cool," he said to Karen, "let me go up and take a look before you come up. Don't want any surprise spiders or mice."

"Good idea," she replied as she shivered lightly.

Jeff slowly climbed the steps, testing the safety as he went. After he had poked his head into the entrance he called back down to Karen, "Hey, it's really pretty spacious up here. Come on up and take a look."

By this time Chrissy had heard the commotion in the hallway and was standing next to the attic stairs. Looking up she saw her father disappear into the dark entrance in the ceiling. Then she looked around at all of the green and red totes and then at her mother. With her hands on her hips she exclaimed, "What in the world are you two doing?"

Surprised by Chrissy's statement Karen tried hard not to laugh as she looked up to the attic entrance. Jeff poked his head down through the hole, "Hi Sweet Pea, we're putting the Christmas decorations away. You want to come up and check out the attic?"

"Can I go up the stairs, Mommy?"

"Okay, I'll stand here while you go up and then I'll come up behind you."

Chrissy started to ascend the open stairs as Jeff reached down to grasp her hand. Karen walked up the steps right behind Chrissy. Just at the top step Chrissy turned and looked down, past her mother, and then said, "Okay, I'll see you when I come down." Then Chrissy looked at Karen, "Abigail said she will wait in by Clayton. She's never been up in the attic and doesn't want to go up there."

Karen looked down toward Clayton's doorway, "Thank you, Abigail, for watching Clayton. You are a wonderful sister."

Chrissy got a huge smile on her face and then whispered to her mother, "Abigail is so happy and proud when you call her our sister. She smiled really big."

Karen felt a warm and fuzzy feeling spread through her. It pleased her to know she had made Abigail feel even more a part of their family.

When Karen reached the opening into the attic Chrissy and Jeff were already walking toward a big window that looked out onto Circle Drive and the lake yard. The window provided the only light for the moment. Karen looked around as she stood at the top step, letting her eyes adjust to the dim light, and then spotted a light switch on the wall just to one side of the opening. Once into the attic she walked over and flipped the switch and a small light bulb located just at the center ridge beam came on. Karen looked around to try and get an idea of the area she had to work with. On one side a solid wall traveled from the eastern side of the house, along about ten to twelve feet and then jutted back, away from the center of the attic, ending at the low point where the slant of the roof met the outside wall. On the other side the attic was open all the way to the low point of the roof with no walls or obstructions. Looking around, the one walled area was the only thing keeping the attic from being entirely open. She looked at the open space and thought, *plenty of storage area. There will be no problem keeping the Christmas decorations, or for that matter, a lot of other things I might want to store up here.*

Karen's attention was drawn back to Chrissy and Jeff as they turned from the window to admire the light Karen had found. Jeff warned Chrissy, "Stay away from the opening, Chrissy, unless one of us is with you. We don't want you to take an unexpected tumble... So what do you think, Karen? Good place to store stuff, huh, plenty of room?"

"Yeah, it's great. Let's get those totes up here."

Jeff went down the stairs to hand the boxes up to Karen, "Chrissy, you want to go down now or stay up here and help your mom?"

"I'll stay up here for a little bit and help mommy."

One by one, the totes came through the opening and as Karen set them down Chrissy would push them to a spot that Karen had designated. The outdoor decorations would go closer to the stairs, because they would be the first to come out next year; the tree decorations could go back in a little farther. Chrissy would stand behind each tote and put her arms out straight and push, using her legs for momentum. When she reached her desired location she would stop, run her forearm across her forehead, and let out a big "Whew." Then she would turn back to her mother and walk back to get the next tote.

Karen smiled as she glimpsed her daughter, hard at work, but didn't say anything. When the last tote came through the opening Karen said to Chrissy, "Well, here's the one we've been looking for."

Chrissy looked at her mother with consternation. The expression on her face was priceless and Karen couldn't help but laugh. Chrissy looked from her mother to the tote sitting in front of her and then back up at her mother. Putting her hands on her hips, she spoke, "Well, I don't know what is so special about this tote. It looks like all of the others."

Jeff suddenly poked his head through the opening, laughing as he said, "It's special because it's the last one. We're done."

Chrissy broke into one of her sunbeam smiles as she realized it was all sort of a joke. She reached out her arms and pushed the last tote into place, wiped her arm across her forehead, and let out her big "whew." Turning to her mom and dad she stated, "Now we're done."

Jeff and Karen laughed as they marveled at just how grown-up their little girl could be sometimes. Jeff looked at Chrissy with one eyebrow slightly askew and his mouth turned up on one side, "Are you sure you're only four?"

Chrissy giggled as she smiled bashfully at her Daddy.

As they departed the attic Karen switched off the light and went down the stairs taking one last look at the attic.

Chapter 15

A few days later Karen was out talking to Jeff in his office and as she headed back to the house she detoured slightly into the yard, ending up on the north side of the house. Looking up she examined the contour of the house noticing the walls and angle of the roof where it met the outside walls. Something had bothered her since they had been up in the attic, but she just couldn't put a finger on what was really bothering her. She took a deep breath and muttered to herself, *what in the heck are you looking for, Karen? Nothing seems to be out of line. You are letting your imagination run away again. Relax!*

Karen returned to the house and set about making lunch, and at the same time she threw a load of laundry into the washer. She could hear Chrissy and Abigail, well, she didn't really hear Abigail, but in her imagination she could hear them both, laughing as they played 'Candyland'. On the nursery monitor she could hear Clayton gurgling and cooing as the mobile over his bed played a tinkling tune. When she had sandwiches made she called Jeff on the intercom and then called Chrissy down to eat. While they were seated at the kitchen table she told them both, "I'm going up to check on Clayton, see if he needs his diaper changed."

Jeff interjected, "What about lunch? Aren't you going to eat?"

"I'll be right back."

Karen returned a few minutes later with Clayton in his carrier. She sat the carrier down next to the table, on a sturdy chair, so that Clayton could interact with the family while they ate. "Hey, little man, how're you doing today?" Jeff reached over and tickled Clayton in the belly and Clayton repaid the effort with a smile and a burp.

Chrissy had just taken a bite of her sandwich and proceeded to spit out some of it as she burst out with laughter. This made everyone at the table laugh even harder. Clayton joined in with an even broader smile and then he farted. That brought the house down. Lunch was over with; at least until the laughter subsided. By the end of it all, Chrissy's sandwich was demolished, Jeff was sitting with his head on the table, laughing so hard he couldn't eat, and Karen's face was wet with tears, having laughed so hard she cried.

Jeff was moaning from the effort of laughing as he sat up in his chair, "Oh my, that was just too funny." He held his sides as he looked over at his son who just smiled back at him, and then he burst into laughter again. Karen and Chrissy, by now, were laughing as much at Jeff as they were at Clayton. Jeff's face was red with the effort and he wiped his eyes as his laughter subsided. Clayton had hold of a rattle and looking around at his mom and dad and his sister, pumped his legs and arms, shaking the rattle as he did. Nothing really funny, but he smiled as he did it and this brought on a whole new round of laughter from all three. At a time like this laughter was like an avalanche; once started, it gathered momentum until it buried everyone in its path. Jeff, Karen and Chrissy were up to their necks in laughter.

After lunch Karen fed Clayton and then put him to bed for a nap. After Clayton was down Karen called Serena, "Hi, Serena, it's Karen."

""Well, good afternoon, darlin', so nice to hear from you. How are things at the Miller household? Everyone well?"

"Just fine, Serena. We had a bit of fun at lunch, today, and I thought I would call and tell you about it." Karen proceeded to tell Serena about the lunchtime fiasco.

"Oh my, how funny," Serena remarked, "I wish I could have been there."

"I don't think we have recovered from it yet." And Karen laughed some more.

By now, as infectious as laughter can be, Serena was laughing too. They both laughed and tried to talk, with little success. After a few minutes Karen gained some self control and soberly asked Serena, "Serena, have you ever been in the attic of this house?"

Serena paused for a moment, "No, I don't believe I have, darlin'. Why do you ask?"

"Well, it's just that we went up in it a few days ago to put the Christmas decorations away, and it is really spacious, but there is something odd about it."

"Odd, like how, dear?"

"I don't know, that's the problem. I can't really give you a reason. Nothing stands out as peculiar, but something is just not ringing true in my mind. Haven't you ever had something that just didn't fit; didn't feel right, and I don't mean clothes?"

Serena chuckled again, but then answered, "Karen, is this another case of thinking too much? Are you over-working things in your mind? Making more of something than is really there?"

"Maybe… I don't know… probably. Oh, Serena, I have tried to relax about this mystery thing, but some days I can do it and other days it really troubles me."

"You know what, darlin'? It's best to just push that to the back of your mind and let the fun things like today take control. The mystery will reveal itself in due time."

"I know you're right, Serena, and I promise, I'll try."

"You do that, darlin'. You know, you are so lucky to have a beautiful daughter, oops, make that two daughters; a precious son, and a husband who practically worships you. Concentrate on them and everything else be hanged!"

Karen laughed at Serena's bluntness, "Be hanged, it is, Serena… Well, I guess I had better finish up with my housework. You know what they say; a woman's work is never done."

Serena laughed, "Mine isn't, but it can be hanged. I've got me a good book and my work can wait until the book is done... You take care, darlin'. Give everyone a hug for me."

"I will, Serena. Bye now."

Karen hung up the phone and headed downstairs by way of the playroom. Chrissy was sitting on the floor with the 'Chutes and Ladders' game board in front of her. "I thought you were playing 'Candyland'?"

"We were, mommy, before lunch, but Abigail beat me so we switched to 'Chutes and Ladders'. But it isn't doing me any good, because she's beating me at this game too."

Far from being critical, Chrissy laughed as she said this. When it came to Abigail, nothing upset Chrissy. "Did you tell Abigail about Clayton at lunch?"

"Oh, I didn't have to. She was there, watching. She was laughing so hard, I'm surprised you didn't hear her, Mommy."

"Well, I might have, but we were all laughing so loud, I couldn't have heard an elephant stampeding through the house."

Chrissy started to laugh and this time Karen thought she heard the sound of another child's laughter. Karen looked to where she thought Abigail was sitting and listened again. Chrissy was laughing still, but Karen heard only her daughter's laughter. She sighed, realizing that whenever she tried to hear, nothing happened. Only when she wasn't expecting it did the little fragments come through to her. She looked once again at Chrissy, "You girls have fun. I'm going down to do some more laundry. Chrissy, I have to go to the store a little later. Do you want to come with me?"

"I'll think about it, Mommy. I'll let you know."

Karen looked at her daughter and thought *somewhere in there is a four year old. I wonder sometimes where she is.* Karen headed down the back stairs to the kitchen.

When Karen was ready to go shopping she called up to Chrissy, "I'm ready to go to the store, are you going with me?"

"Can I stay here and play? I'm finally ahead of Abigail."

"Okay, I'll call your father in. See you in a while, sweetie... bye Abigail."

Karen went to the intercom, "Jeff, can you come inside. I'm going to the store and Clayton is asleep and Chrissy and Abigail are playing upstairs."

Through the speaker Jeff's voice sounded, "Sure, babe, I'll be right there. Let me finish up what I'm doing. It'll only take a minute."

Leaving Jeff in the back parlor with the nursery monitor and the television remote, Karen headed to the store. As she walked the aisles of the Wal-Mart she kept thinking back to the attic. Something about the configuration of the attic bothered her. It didn't match the inside rooms on the second floor and it didn't work with the exterior either. Picking up a large jug of Tide detergent and placing it in her buggy she thought to herself, *something in that attic isn't right. I need to check it out again.* She made up her mind to go into the attic again... soon.

Returning home she walked in to find Jeff engrossed in a program on the sci-fi channel and she could hear the girls laughing up in the playroom. "Jeff, I'm home."

"Hi, hon. Kids are fine... Clayton's still asleep or at least I haven't heard a peep out of him."

"I'll go up and check on him." Karen headed for the front stairs and once up on the second floor she peeked into Clayton's room to see him sleeping peacefully; the stuffed doggy next to his head. Turning back into the hall, she looked up to the ceiling at the attic opening, shaking her head almost imperceptibly. Moving into the playroom she caught movement of a game piece on the 'Chutes and Ladders' board and then Chrissy clapped her hands gleefully, exclaiming, "My turn, my turn!"

Looking up, Chrissy cried happily, "Hi Mommy!"

"Are you still ahead, Chrissy?"

"I am right now... but this is a new game. Abigail won the other game. That's okay, I don't mind."

"Well, that's nice of you to be such a good sport. Abigail has a lot of making up to do on the game playing front."

Chrissy looked at her mother with a confused expression and then her expression changed to one of understanding and then a big smile spread across her face, "Boy, I guess so, about a hundred years, huh Mommy?"

Now Karen was confused, "Uh, yeah, I guess so, Chrissy." Karen thought to herself, *how could Chrissy know that?* Heading for the back stairs Karen looked back at where the girls were playing, "Have fun, kids." She continued down the stairs, her mind whirling with wonder at her daughter.

Karen proceeded to put away the groceries she had brought home, Chrissy's comment still rattling around in her head. Finally she walked into the parlor where Jeff was engrossed in his program. "Jeff, I have got to tell you something."

"What's that, babe?"

Karen relayed to Jeff what Chrissy had said upstairs and when she was finished Jeff looked at her slack jawed and incredulous, "Man, I'm tellin' ya, that kid is not four. Somewhere under that small frame and childlike façade there is a thirty year old woman hiding out. How could she figure that out?"

"I don't know. I know that we have discussed things around her, but we've been very careful not to say anything too outlandish. I know that she knows Abigail's a ghost, but to understand how long ago she died… I don't think that has ever been mentioned, at least not by us. Do you think Abigail might have told her what year she died?"

"Very possibly, but I'm tellin' ya, she's not four. She can't be. She's just too darn smart!" Jeff sat on the couch shaking his head back and forth, "She can't be four."

Chapter 16

Valentine's Day was fast approaching, and at dinner, the night before the holiday, Jeff asked Karen, "What would you like to do for Valentine's Day, my dear?"

Looking surprised Karen seemed to consider the question for a moment, "I guess we'll just stay home with the kids, maybe watch a movie."

"Are you sure?"

"Yeah, that will be fine."

Jeff looked conspiratorially at Chrissy, and she bit her lips to keep from smiling. Karen looked at them both, "What?"

"Tomorrow evening I want you to put on a nice dress because I am taking you to Bogarts, the restaurant at the Hotel DeFuniak, for their Valentine's Day special; dinner, dancing, a little wine and a lot of fun; all for my special Valentine."

Karen had a look of surprise as well as pleasure. Then she looked at Chrissy and then back at Jeff, "What about the kids? Who will watch them? We don't know anyone who can baby-sit."

Jeff held up his hand as if to halt all the questions, "All ready taken care of. Serena is coming over to watch the kids."

"That was my idea, Mommy," Chrissy blurted out, a smile bursting across her face, "You need a night out, Mommy, for all the good things you do for us."

Karen looked at her family; Jeff, her beaming daughter, and her bubbling son sitting in his carrier, watching this tableau play out. "How can I refuse?"

"You can't. Every detail is taken care of. All you have to do is be ready at seven and be determined to have a good time."

This time Karen saluted Jeff, "Aye, aye, captain."

Chrissy clapped her hands and giggled.

The next day Karen went through her closet searching for a dress suitable for a romantic evening out. Chrissy and Abigail were sitting on Jeff and Karen's bed watching as Karen pulled out one dress after another. It was tough going. Karen would pull one out, hold it up to her body and then look at the girls — well, really she could only see Chrissy, but she knew that Abigail was there because, usually where ever Chrissy was, so was Abigail — Chrissy would lean over to listen to Abigail and then would either turn her head from side to side in disapproval or shrug her shoulders with indecision. Dress after dress came out of the closet and just as swiftly returned to the rack. "Look girls, I'm running out of dresses. I'm just about down to my wedding dress, and I don't think that will work. If I don't find something soon we'll just have to go shopping."

Chrissy giggled with delight, "That would be fun, Mommy, but then Abigail can't go with us."

"That's true, Chrissy. Well, we'll just have to hope there is something here that will work." Karen continued to pull one hanger after another, looking through her closet for the perfect dress. "Wait a minute, what about this one, girls. I haven't worn this for several years, so I don't even know if it fits."

Karen pulled out a royal blue dress and held it up to her body, holding it at the waist. The neck was a shallow v with sequin work moving from below the v-neck up either side of the neckline to the shoulders. It was a slim fitting style that would show off her newly regained figure. The dress length was just above the knee with three quarter length sleeves. Karen looked at Chrissy, "Well, what do you think? Will this one do?"

Chrissy leaned over to listen to Abigail, and then a huge smile spread across her face. She held up her hand and gave Karen a thumb up, giggled and then said, "We have decided, that's the one!" and then Chrissy clapped her hands and giggled again, bouncing lightly on the bed as she did.

Smiling at her daughter's reaction to the dress, Karen suddenly cocked her head slightly, listening intently. Was that a second voice; a second round of laughter? She looked toward Chrissy and could have sworn she saw a second little girl, laughing and clapping, right next to where Chrissy sat. It was faint, but she was sure she was there. And then, just as quickly, she was gone. Karen heaved a huge sigh and then thought to herself *It's coming, it's coming, slowly but surely.*

Karen smiled again at the girls and said, "Okay, blue dress it is. I think I'll wear the necklace Serena gave me and I have some sterling silver earrings that will go well with the necklace. Now, it's just a matter of fixing me up.

At dinner, for Chrissy, that is, Karen got the final details from Jeff, "What time is dinner and what time is Serena going to be here?"

"Dinner reservation is for seven thirty and Serena will be here at seven. That way you can give her any last minute instructions about Clayton and Chrissy."

"Good. I want to be dressed and ready when she arrives. Let's see, it's five thirty. That gives me an hour and a half. I can get the dishes done and then go up…"

Jeff interrupted, "Tonight is my treat. So you go on up and relax, take a bath or shower, start making yourself look scrumptious and I will take care of the dishes; deal?"

Karen looked surprised and pleased at the same time, "You know what, buster. You're on." Karen looked at Chrissy with a big smile as if sharing the surprise with her, and then wiped her hands on the dish towel, laid it on the counter, and headed for the back stairs. Turning back, she laid her hands on Chrissy's shoulders, bent over to her ear and said, "Anytime you can get the guy to do the dishes, grab at the chance. They hate getting their hands wet doing dishes." Karen kissed Chrissy's cheek, tickled her lightly and then walked quickly to the stairs, an exuberant bounce to her steps.

Chrissy giggled and then looked at her dad, gave him a thumb up and with a sly smile said, "Another round of points for you, Daddy."

"How old did you say you were, thirty-two?"

Chrissy laughed out loud, "I'm four Daddy; you know that."

Jeff looked at her slightly sideways, "Sometimes I wonder." Turning toward the sink Jeff picked up the towel and turned on the water.

Chrissy climbed off her stool as she said, "I'll help you, Daddy. That way you can get ready to go out too." She carefully pulled her plate off the counter, reaching well above her head, and walked it over to the sink. Jeff had slung the towel over his arm like a maitre'd and with a French accent said, "Thank you, mademoiselle, I will take theees."

Chrissy held her hands out like she was holding a dress and curtsied, "Very well, monsieur," and then she giggled again. Jeff did a double take, screwed up his face as if he just wasn't sure about this mini-person standing in front of him, "How old?"

Chrissy giggled, hunched her shoulders with delighted embarrassment and held up four fingers, smiling broadly at her father.

"I don't believe it. Personally, I just don't believe it." Jeff turned back to the sink to finish his dishes, mumbling to himself.

"Daddy, I'm going up to see if I can help Mommy."

"Okay, baby, be careful on the stairs."

Jeff turned back to look at Clayton, who had been sitting quietly in his carrier through all of the bantering, "See what a crazy bunch you've gotten yourself mixed up with, little man. I can hardly wait until you're adding your two bits worth. Oohh, boy." Jeff exhaled with a huge sigh.

Karen was in her bathroom, soaking in the large tub, bubbles surrounding her almost to the point of overflowing the tub. Chrissy knocked lightly on the door, "Mommy, can I come in?"

"Of course, sweetie."

Chrissy walked to the edge of the tub. Looking at the bubbles, her eyes grew wide, "Wow, Mommy, that looks like fun." She scooped up a handful of bubbles and blew on them softly, sending them floating toward Karen.

Karen took a handful of bubbles and put them softly on Chrissy's head and nose. "There you go, my dear." Realizing something, Karen looked at Chrissy, "I guess it's been a long time since you've had a bubble bath. You're a big girl; you take showers, don't you?" Chrissy nodded her head in agreement, the bubbles bouncing lightly on her head and dripping softly from her nose. "You know what, tomorrow night you and I will take a bubble bath together. How does that sound?"

Chrissy clapped her hands and jumped up and down lightly, "Yes, yes."

Karen reached out and chucked Chrissy under the chin, "You know how much I love you?"

Chrissy looked at her mother, "Yup! This much." And she held her arms out wide.

Karen beamed at her daughter with a smile that spoke more than words could ever state, her eyes accentuating the smile like twin exclamation marks. "Okay, kiddo, I gotta get a move on here, times a wastin'."

"Can I help you, mommy. Do you need me to do anything?"

"Not right now, Chrissy. But when I get dressed, if Daddy isn't here, you can give me a hand with the zipper on my dress."

"Okay. Is it okay if Abigail and I go play for a while?"

"Of course. Go, shoo, away with you." Karen threw a few more bubbles at Chrissy as she ran for the door, stopping briefly to peek back around the edge of the door.

"Shoo, go play. I'll call you."

Karen sat in front of the vanity looking into the mirror, *hair, not too bad, make-up, acceptable; I guess it's time for the dress.* "Jeff, are you getting ready? It's six thirty; Serena will be here soon."

Jeff poked his head through the door from the bedroom, "Getting my tie on right now. I'll be ready shortly. By the way, Clayton's in his crib. I turned the mobile on for him." Jeff disappeared back into the bedroom.

Karen returned her gaze to the mirror. *Let's see, I'll put the dress on and then call Chrissy. I'll put the necklace and earrings on while she zips my dress.* Karen stepped into the dress and pulled it up and onto her arms, then sat down to place the necklace around her neck, "Chrissy, do you want to zip my dress for me."

"Coming, Mommy."

Karen was closing the clasp on the necklace when Chrissy came into the bathroom and skipped over to the vanity. Karen turned her back slightly toward Chrissy which put her reflection squarely in view of Chrissy. Chrissy had the zipper in her hand, pulling it closed when she froze mid-motion. She turned her head to her right and in the mirror Karen could see a look of consternation and then despair come over her daughter's face. "Chrissy, what's wrong?" Karen turned around to face Chrissy and could see that Chrissy was looking at, presumably, Abigail. Karen took Chrissy by her shoulders, "Chrissy, what is wrong?"

"I don't know, Mommy, but Abigail is crying. She's just standing there, looking at you, crying."

Karen looked at where she assumed Abigail was, "Abigail, what is it, dear? What is the matter?" Karen looked down at her chest as she saw the necklace move. The pendant lifted up and away from her body as if it had a mind of its own. Karen looked to Chrissy, who was by now, crying as well. "Chrissy, what is happening? Talk to me, baby."

Chrissy said softly, "Abigail?" and then seemed to listen for a moment, looking from the pendant to Karen's face and then back to the pendant and then to Abigail. Chrissy seemed to have a lump in her throat when she tried to speak. She paused for a moment and then looked at her mother, "The necklace was Abigail's mother's."

Karen gasped and reached suddenly for the pendant. Not to snatch it from Abigail's grasp, but rather as a reaction to the thought that here was a direct link for Abigail to her long lost mother. "Oh, my God, Abigail! I didn't know. Truly, I didn't know. Serena gave this to me. If I had had any idea I would not have worn it. Here, I'll let you have it." Karen reached around to release the clasp and felt a pressure on her hands, holding them in place, stopping her action, and then she felt her hands released and then drawn down to her lap. Karen looked at Chrissy, "What is happening, Chrissy?"

Chrissy looked to Abigail and through her tears she slowly smiled. Looking at Karen she softly said, "Abigail says that it is yours. You are her mother now. She wants you to wear it."

Karen reached out to where she thought Abigail's face might be, cupping what she hoped was Abigail's cheek. She whispered softly, "Abigail, darling, you weren't born of me, but you are as much my daughter as Chrissy. I love you." Karen looked to Chrissy, reached her hand to touch her cheek and whispered to her daughter, "You don't mind, do you?"

Chrissy smiled at her mother as she turned her head from side to side, tears streaming down her face, "I love you, Mommy."

Jeff poked his head through the door, "I'm read… holy cow, what's going on in here? What's everybody crying about?"

"I'll explain later," Karen said, sniffing as she looked in the mirror, "Oh my God, look at me, I've got some repairs to do."

Just then the door bell rang and Jeff said, "I'll get it."

Karen looked at Chrissy, smiled weakly, turned and looked to where she assumed Abigail was, and smiled again as she placed her hand on the pendant, "I have possibly the two most gorgeous and unique daughters in the whole world." Chrissy beamed her face-wide smile and Karen thought she saw a face, framed in dark braids and pretty white teeth, smiling back at her just to the right of Chrissy. She felt a wave of love and pride sweep over her as she stood, "Okay, girls, how do I look? Am I fit to have a fun Valentine date?"

Chrissy looked over at Abigail, nodded her head, and then looked back with a huge smile and gave her mom two thumbs up.

Chapter 17

The next day Karen called Serena, "Serena, have I got something to tell you."

"Well, good mornin' darlin'. Goodness, you're wired today."

"Serena, when you arrived last night to watch the kids, and by the way, thank you so much. I really needed that night out. Jeff and I had a wonderful time."

"I could tell when you came home, darlin'. You were one big smile."

"Well, that may have been the wine, but anyway, when you arrived, the most amazing thing had just happened and the shock was such, I just didn't want to talk about it last night."

"I could tell somethin' had happened; I could see you'd been cryin', but I just didn't want to pry. I figured you'd tell me when you were ready. So I'm guessin' you're ready?"

"Serena, remember the necklace you gave me for Christmas?"

"Of course I do, darlin'"

"Would you believe it, if I told you that that necklace had belonged to Abigail's mother?"

Serena was quiet, not a sound came from the phone for several moments, and then Serena spoke, ever so softly, "Are you sure?"

"Abigail recognized it. I was getting ready to go out and she and Chrissy came in to help me finish up and as I was connecting the clasp Abigail recognized the necklace and began to cry. It upset Chrissy and then I got upset and before long we were all crying."

"Oh my, how distressing."

"Serena, it was distressing, but it was also amazing. Do you realize what this means... this is a direct link to her mother?"

"Why yes, I guess it would be. Do you suppose that is the mystery?"

"No... no, I don't think so. I think there is something else and I believe it has to do with the attic."

"The attic, why the attic?"

"I don't know," Karen said with a heavy sigh and leaned back heavily in her chair, "there is just something that is troubling me about the attic; I just can't put my finger on it; at least, not yet."

"Well, my goodness. I don't know what to say other than things just keep getting more interesting as the days move on. So many things keep falling into place. Why, if I hadn't given that necklace to you we would have never known where it came from. How interesting... it just seems as fate has a hand in what is happening here, don't you think so?"

"It seems that way. Well, I had better get going; I've got things to catch up on around here. Serena, thank you, once again, for watching the kids last night. I do so appreciate it. You have no idea how much. I just hope the kids weren't too much for you."

"Darlin', any time. You're children are no trouble at all. Why, they practically take care of themselves. I really enjoyed havin' the opportunity to spend time with them and do somethin' for you. It was my pleasure."

"Serena, you are a peach!"

"I love you too, darlin'. You take care now, and I'll talk to you soon."

Life moved swiftly on, one day blending into the next, Chrissy and Abigail spending most of their days playing games in the playroom. As the weather got nicer Karen did insist that Chrissy spend some time outside, playing in the yard or Karen would take her and Clayton across the street into the lake yard where there was playground equipment. But Chrissy was always anxious to get back home because, as she put it, "Abigail can't come outside to play and I don't want to leave her alone for too long. It's not fair."

Clayton was growing like a weed, getting more active as the days went by, giggling, gurgling, and laughing constantly. He was now rolling himself over, grasping things with a death grip and was almost able to sit up by himself. Karen couldn't have asked for a happier baby. He had much of Chrissy's pleasant traits as an infant so she was confident that he would develop into a precocious child like his sister. Into early March he was approaching five months old and getting stronger and more active by the day.

As to the mystery of the house, it was never far from Karen's mind, but often shoved back to the deeper reaches to make room for more pleasant thoughts. One afternoon, about a week before Easter, Karen was coming out of Clayton's room after putting him down for a nap. She stopped in the hall, just under the attic hatchway, and stood there looking up at the small rope hanging down. She listened for a moment and heard Chrissy talking with Abigail, engrossed in a board game. She knew Jeff was out in his office and probably wouldn't show his face for several hours yet, so she made a decision.

She went down the front stairs and then returned with a step stool she kept in the back room. Placing it under the attic hatch, she reached up and gave the small rope a hefty yank, and the stairs began descending toward the floor. Once unfolded, she climbed up the steps, one by one, almost leery of what awaited her at the top.

Now in the attic, she reached over and turned on the light switch, although the window afforded a great deal of light. She looked around, her eyes trying to take in every little nuance; seeking something, anything, that might trigger a thought process that would help her. Seeing nothing else that prompted inquiry, she walked over to the wall that jutted across a part of the attic. She ran her hand across the wall, feeling for anything unusual, hoping for something to come to her, perhaps through osmosis. The wall seemed to be solid even though two rows of furring strips ran from floor to ceiling approximately four feet from either end of the wall, basically dividing the wall into thirds and a third strip of furring traced the line where the wall met the ceiling, running its entire length. There was no sign of a door or any form of opening. Then she ran her hands along the end wall, following the wall as far as she could toward the narrow end, seeking anything that might prove interesting. In all, the walled area equaled a space about twelve feet by six feet. It didn't look like the wall was new, that is, something that was done during the remodeling. Rather, the wood looked aged and the construction style older. Karen stood there, staring at the wall, wondering, and then an idea struck her. She reached over to the light switch, turning it off and carefully left the attic, closing the stairs up; no one the wiser for her being there.

Karen went to her computer and looked up the list of previous owners and located the phone number for the Hunters, the owners who had remodeled the house.

As she dialed the long distance number Karen tried to compose her questions in her head so that she didn't sound like an idiot. The phone rang several times and just as Karen was getting ready to hang up, now sure that her questions would sound preposterous, someone answered, "Hello?" a pleasant female voice asked.

"Hello, is this Carolyn Hunter?"

"Yes, this is she."

"Hi, Carolyn, this is Karen Miller. My husband and I bought your home in DeFuniak Springs."

"Oh, yes, how are you? How are you getting along in the house… any problems?"

"Well… no problems, per se, but I do have a couple of questions… if you don't mind?"

"Of course not; what would you like to know?"

"First of all, when you were remodeling, I know that you and your husband did some of the work yourself. Is that correct?"

"Yes, my husband is quite handy. Actually he spent his younger years working as a carpenter to pay his way through medical school."

"What I wanted to know... when you pulled out the interior walls to run the new wiring, did you or your workmen do anything in the attic?"

"No. As a matter of fact, we never really had any reason to go into the attic except to exterminate a wasp nest. There were some of the biggest wasps I have ever seen up there. My husband set off a fogger and then cleaned out the dead nest. Other than that, no work was done up there... Wait, I think they did install one light switch up there, but we never used it for storage so never had any reason to go up there. Why do you ask?"

"Well, this may sound foolish, but I recently put some Christmas decorations up there, until next year, and there was just something that didn't sit right with me. There is a walled area in the attic and I can't figure out why it's there. It's nothing really important; I just thought I would ask if you had built the wall into the attic."

"No, if it is there, it was built before we took possession of the house." Carolyn Hunter paused for a moment and then asked, "I know that you understood that there had been haunting experiences in the house. It's Florida law that anything abnormal be disclosed to prospective buyers," Carolyn paused again, "but have you..."

Before Carolyn could finish her statement Karen interrupted, "Yes, we have. As a matter of fact, my daughter..." now Karen paused, sure that Carolyn would think her nuts, "talks with her all the time. To be completely honest, they are best friends."

"Oh, how interesting. Is it a woman? Can she see her?"

Karen was starting to feel panicky; afraid she would say too much and this woman would think she was certifiable, "Yes, but it's not a woman, it is a small girl."

"Oh, how delicious, I mean, that is just fascinating. You see, we had several occurrences, but no one ever actually saw the ghost, or heard her. We thought it was the older lady who had lived there before we bought the house. After our workman was accosted—he felt a pressure on his neck, and then a friend who was staying in the front bedroom; she felt a smothering sensation while sleeping, which woke her up. And then my daughter, Jennie, was sleeping on the sun room daybed and something or someone pulled the covers down very tight across her chest— we thought that the woman's ghost was objecting to the remodeling. You know, all of the commotion. But after we were finished with the remodeling the occurrences stopped."

Karen started to lighten up a little, listening to the Hunter's experiences, realizing that maybe she didn't sound so nuts after all. "The only ghost we have experienced is a small girl, around seven or eight. Her name is Abigail Cottonwood, the daughter of the original owners of the house. She died in a fall, on the back stairs, in the fall of 1908 and has been sighted at least once, in the 1940's, until now. And to be quite frank, my daughter has become quite attached to Abigail. I have caught a brief glimpse of her, only once, but my daughter plays with her every day."

"Karen, I just thought of something. While we were remodeling we found a photo of a small girl, she looked about four or five, behind the fireplace mantel in the front parlor. How about if I email it to you? I can scan it in and send it right away and we don't have to worry about it getting lost in the mail."

Karen's heart skipped a beat, "Oh, my God, that would be wonderful. I mean, what's the chance of it being a picture of Abigail? There have been four other families living in this house, although two of them had no children, but if it were Abigail, that would give me something."

"Give me your email address and I will take care of it right away."

"I can't thank you enough. I just hope it is the right photo."

Karen gave Carolyn Hunter her email address and as they parted Carolyn added one more comment, "Please let me know what you find out. I am most curious about this. Perhaps you can find some way to finally get that little girl's spirit home to her parents. Please keep in contact."

"Thank you, Carolyn. I will surely do that."

Karen pushed the button to end the call. She sat at her computer table, motionless, unable to think clearly, her mind whirling. Then she moved quickly, scrolling her mouse through until she got to email. Then she waited. She sat in a trance, her minds eye trying to remember the brief glimpse of Abigail she had that day in the mirror. Then her computer dinged, the sign she had email. She looked at the sender, c.hunter and then the little paper clip indicating the attachment. Quickly she read the brief message, 'Here's the photo, I've got my fingers crossed. Hope it's the one you are looking for. Carolyn.'

Karen moved the cursor onto the paperclip and clicked, and then she clicked on the 'open attachment'. She realized she was holding her breath. *Breath Karen,* she told herself, and let out a large breath. As the photo eased onto the monitor, appearing from the top and opening more and more as it moved to the bottom of the screen, Karen suddenly sucked in a deep breath; there was Abigail staring back at her. The sepia tones of the photo didn't provide her with a lot of detail, but it was Abigail, younger, perhaps by a couple of years, but it was her! Karen sat back into her chair as goosebumps appeared on her arms and a shiver ran down her spine.

Karen sat there staring, motionless, and then picked up the phone and dialed, "Serena, are you available to come over here for a few minutes?"

"Of course, darlin', just give me long enough to put on something presentable; you never know who one might run into. Is everything all right? Are you okay?" The children; Jeff? You sound very excited."

"No, no, everyone's fine. I just have something very important to show you."

"Okay, darlin', I'll be right there." Serena hung up on her end.

Karen sat there for a moment longer and then called out, "Chrissy, could you come here for a moment. I'm at my computer."

"Okay, mommy."

Karen heard Chrissy move into the hallway and then she was at her side, "What did you want, mommy?"

"Look at my computer screen, baby."

Chrissy turned and looked at the photo appearing on the monitor, "Wow, that's Abigail. Neat-o, where did you get it? She looks different though."

"I think this was taken a couple of years before she..." Karen paused, reluctant to end her statement.

Chrissy continued for her in a whisper, "Died."

"Yes. It looks like she was about your age now; four, maybe five." Karen looked at Chrissy and marveled at how aware she was of her world and how adult-like she could handle what came along. "Does it bother you to know that Abigail is a... ghost?" she asked her daughter.

Chrissy seemed to think about the question for just a moment and then responded to her mother, "No. Abigail is as real to me as Clayton is. When we are playing she is right there, talking and laughing, just like you and I are right now. She isn't invisible and she doesn't scare me. I love her, mommy... just like a real sister."

Karen reached out and hugged her, oh, so grown up, daughter. "When did you become so wise? Sometimes you really surprise me."

Chrissy got an embarrassed expression on her face and then shrugged her shoulders like she often did when her parents complemented her.

"Chrissy, is Abigail here?"

"No, she stayed in the playroom."

"Do you think she would like to see this photo?"

"I don't know. I'll go ask her." Chrissy walked down the hall and returned very quickly, stopping just short of the computer desk, "See," she said pointing at the monitor.

Karen sat there watching Chrissy with a questioning expression, unable to see or hear what was happening. Karen looked hard at Chrissy, trying to get her to say something, to tell her what was happening. Finally, she just asked, "Chrissy, what is she doing?"

"She's just staring, mommy. Now she is reaching her hand out toward the screen." And at that moment Karen noticed a spot on the monitor screen that looked like a small ripple. Nothing distinctive, just an impression, as if a fingertip had been lightly pressed against the screen, right at the face of the photo. Chrissy turned her head slightly, as if listening, and then spoke, "Abigail says that her hair is different; shorter than she remembers. She said she likes her braids better." Chrissy turned to listen again and then said, "Okay, let's go." She turned to her mother, "Abigail wants to go play now."

"Okay, sweetie, you girls go ahead." Karen motioned for the girls to go on back to the playroom. *Well, that was anti-climactic*, Karen thought to herself, *I don't know what I was expecting, but it wasn't that, no response at all. Hmmm.*

About then the doorbell rang. Karen looked out the window and saw Serena's car at the curb. She hustled down the stairs and opened the door, "Hi, Serena, come on in. I've got something to show you upstairs." At the computer Karen showed Serena the image on the monitor, "What do ya think?"

"Well, I'm not sure what I'm lookin' at except... wait a minute," Serena scrutinized the photo a little bit closer, "Could that be a picture of Abigail?"

Karen raised her eyebrows a little bit and just smiled at Serena. She didn't want to bias her memory at all.

"Now, mind you, I'm goin' back over sixty years in my memory, and the ghost, that is, little girl I saw had long braids and seemed older than this child, but there are definite similarities." Serena looked at Karen with a questioning expression.

"It's her," Karen said, "I only saw her briefly, that one day, in the mirror, but I know it's her. I had Chrissy take a look and she agreed. So then I had Abigail look at the photo, and got a really strange reaction."

"Strange, like how?"

"She didn't say a word at first, just stared at the photo. Then she reached out and touched the screen and commented on her hair. Not exactly what I would have expected."

"You have to remember, darlin', this child had a traumatic death, didn't cross over, for what ever reason, perhaps because of her parents' mysterious disappearance, and then through the years has tried to come to grips with her fate. Now she has Chrissy, and you, and the rest of your family… and the life she missed out on. Perhaps all of these things that seem like revelations to you are much less important to her than you might think. It may seem to her no more important than if Chrissy saw a photo of herself. It is, after all, just a photo."

Karen seemed in deep thought, reflecting on what Serena was saying, "Perhaps you're right," she finally said.

"By the way, wherever did you get that photo?"

Karen explained her afternoon; the attic, her phone call to Carolyn Hunter, and then the email. "You know, Serena, I know you are right. I am making much more out of all of this than is necessary. What we as adults and as mortals, think is important obviously has little or no importance to Abigail. I need to lighten up and just let things happen as they will."

Serena smiled widely, chuckled a little and then said, "They had an old saying, when I was a bit younger, and I think it applies here, 'Now you're cookin' with gas.'"

Rickie Wood-Bovee

Karen started to laugh and Serena joined in. After a few minutes of rolling laughter, Karen asked, "How about some tea?"

Chapter 18

Easter was now just a few days away and Karen and Jeff had decided to have an Easter egg hunt in their yard for Chrissy. Karen planned on a nice dinner to finish the day so she invited Serena and Agatha over. The plans for the hunt were to have some of the eggs hidden in the house so that Abigail could participate and then some outside for a really challenging hunt for Chrissy.

Karen left the kids at home with Jeff one afternoon so that she could purchase all the things they needed. Plastic eggs to fill, candy to fill the eggs, larger chocolate figures as well as toys and special prizes. Jeff and Karen wanted to make one of the prizes a bicycle for Chrissy, but decided to leave that for her birthday coming up in June. Karen also bought two dozen eggs and egg dying kits to color them. The more she shopped the more excited she got. This would be the first Easter that Chrissy would really understand the egg hunt and what to do, so she wanted it special for both her daughters.

Saturday she boiled up the eggs and then put them in the refrigerator until after dinner. At the dinner table that evening she spoke to Jeff, Chrissy and Abigail. Clayton was sitting in his carrier positioned securely on a chair next to Karen. They tried to have Clayton at the table at meal times to make him feel a part of the family. "Okay guys, here is the plan for Easter. Listen up, that means you too, Clayton," Karen turned to her son and poked him lightly in the tummy, and he giggled in response. "As soon as we finish with dinner and the kitchen is cleaned up," she paused briefly and looked at Jeff.

He returned her gaze waiting for her to continue and then caught her intention, "Oh, I'll help you with the dishes, hon; we all will, won't we Chrissy."

Chrissy had just put a fork full of mashed potatoes in her mouth. She froze, for a fraction of a second, mid-motion, and looked over at her dad, the fork still touching her lips. Then she smiled, trying not to squish the mashed potatoes out of her mouth and then nodded her head up and down rapidly, and mumbled, "Ahbagaul too."

Karen looked at Chrissy, "Excuse me?"

Chrissy giggled, trying to swallow the mashed potatoes, and then said, "Abigail too."

Karen raised her eyebrows, shook her head lightly from side to side as if she was unsure who these two were who were sitting at the table and then sighed heavily. "To continue," Karen spoke again, ignoring her husband's slower than normal thinking process, "after the clean-up then we'll color the eggs before the kids go to bed. Then you and I," and here she looked at Jeff again, who was desperately trying to eat and pay attention at the same time. "will play Easter Bunny. So once we're finished here we need to move spit-spot."

Chrissy laughed, "Mary Poppins!"

The egg dying went according to plan with one minor exception. Each time Abigail would lift an egg into or out of the coloring it was a little unnerving for Karen and Jeff to see the egg floating mid-air. Because Abigail was using an implement to lift with and not actually grasping the egg, it didn't disappear. After a few times of the egg seeming to move on its own they got used to it.

Both girls had a good time; Abigail because it was something she had never experienced before, and Chrissy because she took great joy in anything that brought happiness to Abigail. The girls helped each other in making wonderful and unique designs and as Karen watched the two girls work together it was difficult to believe that Abigail was not real. And although neither Karen nor Jeff could see the child, Chrissy related and interacted with her as if she were real. She carried on a conversation, as they were dying their eggs, and it was the usual childish chit-chat when two children were playing. The only difference was that Karen and Jeff could only hear Chrissy's side of it.

When the eggs were colored and the plastic eggs filled, Karen hustled the kids off to bed. When Clayton was fed and tucked into his crib and Chrissy was tucked into her bed, then Karen and Jeff began their task of hiding things around the house. They assumed that Abigail had taken her place beside Clayton's crib so they began in the front parlor tucking eggs into the big plant by the window, under the sheet music and on the foot pedals of the piano, in amongst the fake logs in the fireplace, under a cushion of a chair, trying to make it easy enough so that it wouldn't be too hard for Chrissy or Abigail, yet challenging enough to keep them hunting.

Then they moved into the back parlor placing one at the chimney of the wood stove, another next to the television, and then Jeff decided to really make it challenging and reached up and pulled down the overhead kerosene lamp and placed one in the brass filigree, on the underside of the lamp, where the pull cord attached. When the lamp was returned to its original height the egg was visible, but the girls would have to look up. Karen looked at him, "Jeff, that's not fair. The girls won't be able to see it up there. It's too high."

"Come on, Karen, we have to challenge them a little. Who ever spots it first will get it; I'll pull the lamp down for them."

"Okay, but no clues. I want them to find this stuff on their own, if possible."

"Gotcha, no clues."

"What time do we get up to set the stuff outside; we certainly can't do it now?"

"Get up? You mean early? Why can't we put the things outside now?"

"Jeff, it is dark outside and there's no telling what might eat the goodies before morning. I can just see it now; Chrissy goes outside only to find bunnies laying on their sides, ears and legs out straight from chocolate poisoning, squirrels falling out of the trees, pink and green foil flitting down like snowflakes in their wake; and the ducks! My God, we'd have every duck around the lake in our yard, snatching up plastic eggs right and left. Oh no, buster, we're getting up at the crack of dawn to set out the eggs and hope Chrissy can beat the little varmints to the goodies."

"My, what a pleasant mental picture you paint; dead bunnies, sky diving squirrels, and rioting ducks… okay, okay, we'll get up at the crack of dawn. Better yet, why not wait until Serena and Agatha get here. They can entertain the girls while you and I hide things and then they can watch the fun. That way there won't be time for the local wildlife to raid the treasure and I can sleep in."

Karen thought about it for just a moment, "Now, why didn't I think of that; it certainly makes the most sense. I guess I've just had too much on my mind lately. We'll hold two egg hunts; the one in here, as soon as the kids are up, and then the second one, outside, after Serena and Agatha arrive." Karen turned to Jeff, patted him on the cheek and then said, "You are so smart. What would I do without you?"

Jeff just smiled for a moment, puckered up his lips, and patted his lips with one finger.

Karen leaned over and gave him a quick kiss, "Payment?"

"It'll have to do for now, but I claim the right to demand further payment at another time." Jeff smiled as he wrapped his arms around his wife and gave her a big hug.

The next morning, Chrissy was up, ready and raring to go, at seven. She woke her mother by standing next to the bed, patting Karen gently on the face, "Mommy, Mommy, wake up."

Karen stirred, groaned slightly, peeked her eyes open and looked at the clock, "Chrissy, it's only seven, honey. Could I talk you into waiting another hour?"

"Come on, Mommy. It is, after all, light outside."

Karen pulled the covers up over her head, groaned again, and peeked out at Chrissy's patient, smiling face, "You're not going to give me that hour, are you?"

Chrissy moved her head from side to side. Just then Karen heard a sharp sound, almost a scream. She jolted up, unsure of what she heard. Then she heard it again, more distinct this time, "Mother!"

Chrissy jumped back from the side of the bed, as Karen threw back the covers and sprang to the floor, running as her feet touched. As she headed toward the sound she heard the scream again, "Mother, Clayton!"

Karen careened through the bedroom door, rushing across the hall into Clayton's room, at the same time screaming, "Jeff, something's wrong." Karen lurched into Clayton's room and was next to the crib in the next stride. Looking down she saw her young son, clawing the air, his eyes wide with fear, his mouth open but no sound coming out. Karen quickly picked him up as his lips started to turn blue. She looked around quickly, trying to get a grasp on what was happening, and then she spotted the little stuffed dog, lying off to one side of the crib. One button eye was gone! Realty came crashing down. Suddenly she realized what was wrong. Her mind was spinning, but she knew she must not panic. She quickly sat down on the floor, laid Clayton on his tummy over her lap, and smacked him sharply between his shoulder blades, once, twice.

Jeff came bursting into the room, Chrissy at his heels, "What the...?"

Quickly Karen turned Clayton over and made a sharp quick push just below his sternum; again and then a third time. With that third push a small black object came flying out, hitting against the wall and falling to the floor. Chrissy picked it up and held it out to her daddy. In her palm was the black button eye.

Clayton coughed, inhaled and then began to cry. Karen lifted him to her shoulder and hugged him closely. Tears started to flow down her face as she looked up at Jeff, "It was the doggy! My God, Jeff, remember? Oh, my God, we almost lost him."

Jeff bent over to comfort Karen and then sat down next to her and Clayton. He leaned his head into the baby's back as he hugged them both.

Chrissy was standing near the wall, still holding the button, her head down, the tears seeping down onto her nightgown. She looked up toward the crib, listening and then moved her head from side to side as she muttered, "No, that's not true. Mommy, tell her it's not true."

Karen looked up at her daughter, now almost distraught, "What Chrissy?"

Through her tears and sobs Chrissy said, "Abigail says this was her fault; that she almost killed Clayton. Tell her that's not true." By now Chrissy was almost wailing.

"Chrissy, it's okay, take it easy, baby. Clayton is going to be fine… Abigail, this was not your fault. Daddy and I knew that the button was loose and could possibly come off; we just didn't think it would happen quite so soon. We didn't think Clayton would be capable of chewing it off so soon. You didn't know what could happen and that is our fault for not telling you. This was not your fault! Do you understand?"

"Yes" came a meek and soft reply. Karen froze. Still cuddling Clayton, she looked at Chrissy, then at Jeff and asked, "Jeff, did you hear that?"

"Hear what?"

Karen looked at Chrissy, but Chrissy remained speechless. "Abigail, was it you who called for help? Did you scream for me when you discovered Clayton?"

"Yes" came the same soft reply.

Then the realization of what had just occurred and what was now occurring hit Karen like a lightening bolt. The impact struck her numb. She passed Clayton to Jeff as she started to shake; a cold chill passing through her like an electric shock. She leaned back against the changing table, unable to sit up, let alone stand. She came close to fainting, but was able to resist the urge.

Jeff looked Clayton over to make sure he was okay, "Karen, are you okay? Karen? You look like you're going to pass out." Clayton was sitting on Jeff's lap, his fright now gone, unconcerned with his near death experience, flapping his arms at a space off to Jeff's side. Soon a smile spread over his face as he obviously played with Abigail.

"I'm fine. It just caught up with me; give me a minute to collect myself."

Off to one side of Jeff, Karen heard a small voice, "I am so sorry, Clayton. I would never want anything to happen to you. I will always watch over you."

Karen, realizing who she was hearing, asked, "Abigail, is that you speaking?"

"Yes, mother."

Chrissy looked at her mother, then at Abigail, and then back at her mother, each time her eyes got bigger, with realization and then with delight, "Mommy, you can hear Abigail."

Once again tears started to flow down Karen's face, "Yes... I can."

Chapter 19

Jeff looked at Karen, "Do you think we need to take him to the emergency room; maybe have him checked?"

Karen was still in shock from all that had happened and was slow to respond.

"Karen? Earth to Karen!"

Karen shook her head lightly, looking around in confusion, "What? I'm sorry, hon; I kind of zoned out there for a moment."

"Do we need to take Clayton to the hospital, have him checked out?"

"Let me call the pediatrician first."

Karen collected herself off the floor and made the call, returning shortly to the bedroom where Jeff and Clayton were still sitting on the floor, and where Chrissy, and presumably, Abigail had joined him. Clayton was reveling in the attention from all three of his admirers. Karen spoke as she entered, "The doctor said that if he isn't showing any ill effects from this to just bring him to the office tomorrow and he will check him out. Has he been okay while I was out of the room?"

"Yeah, he seems to be fine. He's been playing with the girls, giggling and laughing and... I think he needs a diaper change. Probably scared the sh..."

Karen cut Jeff off, "I get the picture. No need to go into details," and she tipped her head toward Chrissy. "Here, give him to me and I'll change him." Karen reached out to grasp her wiggling son. As she worked over Clayton, she spoke over her shoulder to Chrissy, "Why don't you go get dressed and we'll go down to hunt eggs when you're ready, and then afterward we'll get cleaned up and go to church. It is, after all, Easter."

When they were all together, downstairs in the foyer, Karen handed Chrissy and Abigail each a basket. The one handed to Abigail quickly disappeared. Karen spoke to the girls, "Now, there are real and plastic eggs hidden in the front and back parlors and the dining room. We won't give you any clues other than eggs are hidden EVERYWHERE! Up, down, and all around, so look, look, look. If you need help reaching something just ask. Okay?"

Chrissy nodded her head up and down as she smiled broadly, and Karen heard a meek, "Yes, Mother."

"All righty, then… go get 'em!" Karen held Clayton on her hip as the two girls raced around the front parlor. Karen and Jeff couldn't actually see Abigail, but Chrissy was laughing and Karen could hear Abigail giggling and squealing as she spotted the hidden prizes. Chrissy was collecting eggs, one after another, and Abigail was as well, because Karen watched as one egg, and then another, would disappear from its hiding spot. Then the girls moved into the back parlor repeating the same scenario. It was a frantic, special moment, watching Chrissy as she looked around, her gaze moving from one point to another and the moment of recognition when she spotted the next prize. Then Karen heard an excited Abigail, "Up there, up there." Chrissy's gaze moved to the lamp overhead, a big smile spreading across her face.

"Daddy, will you pull the lamp down, please," Chrissy asked her father. Jeff reached up and pulled the lamp down to Chrissy's height, but the egg quickly disappeared.

"Wait a minute! I thought you spotted that egg?" Jeff spoke to Chrissy.

"Uh-uh, Abigail spotted it first," Chrissy responded.

"That's right, Jeff. I heard her when she spotted it," Karen backed up Chrissy's statement.

"You heard her? Abigail?" Jeff asked in wonder.

"Jeff, where have you been? Upstairs, after the button, I heard Abigail speak. She's the one who alerted me. She yelled for help. And then afterward, I spoke with her. You were sitting right there; I thought you heard me talking to her?"

"No! Somehow I missed that part of the conversation. I guess I was concentrating on Clayton. But seriously, you can hear Abigail now? Everything she says?"

Karen nodded her head up and down slowly, a slight, but somewhat mystified smile on her face, "Yeah, isn't it wonderful?"

"Well, I guess I'm the last man out. Everybody else but me can, at the least, hear her, and Chrissy and Clayton can see her."

Chrissy had been standing nearby listening to their exchange, so she reached out and motioned her daddy to come down to her level by wiggling her finger. As he kneeled down in front of her, she reached out her hand and placed it on his shoulder and then said sympathetically, "Don't worry, Daddy, your time will come. You'll be able to hear and see Abigail; I'm sure of it."

Jeff patted Chrissy on her cheek, "Thank you, baby, I'm glad someone feels sorry for me. Boy, am I gonna feel left out… at least for a while."

"Okay, let's move on to the dining room," Karen said with a smile.

Later, as they were entering the church, Karen spotted Serena and Agatha, so they sat with them through the service. Karen wanted to tell the two ladies about their excitement that morning, but thought it best to wait until they were out of church. Later, as they exited the chapel, their small group walked slowly toward their home, and Karen took that opportunity to speak to the two ladies, "

Karen, walking arm in arm between Serena and Agatha, spoke as soon as they were away from the church, "Boy, have I got a lot to tell you two; this morning has been something else."

Waiting only a brief moment Karen continued, "It was bad and good, both within seconds of each other."

Serena, in that soft, southern drawl of hers, asked, "What ever are you talkin' about, darlin'? Don't keep us in suspense." Agatha, in her usual manner, said nothing.

"Well, the bad part first… Chrissy had come into the bedroom to wake us up so that she and Abigail could hunt for Easter Eggs. While she was standing by my bed, I heard a loud scream for help, 'Mother,' then a second scream, 'Mother, Clayton.' I went running into Clayton's room and found him turning blue, a button stuck in his throat."

"Oh, my God, Karen, you must have been terrified."

"At that point I was working on auto pilot. I turned Clayton over on my lap, smacked him a couple of times on his back and then turned him over and applied the Heimlich maneuver. After a few pressures on his belly, the button flew across the room." At this point Karen had started to shake again and her eyes began to tear up, the memory of the near fatal incident reliving itself in her mind. Her voice choked, a large, constricting lump having formed in her throat.

The three ladies stopped their progression along the sidewalk and Serena took Karen in her arms. The tears started to flow down Karen's face as the earlier trauma caught up with her. Serena just held her, giving her the comfort only a mother can give in a time of distress, "Go ahead, darlin', cry it out. Let the emotions go. You'll feel better afterward."

Jeff had already passed through the wrought iron gate and was going up the steps, Clayton held firmly in his arms. Chrissy had stopped midway between the steps and the gate, looking back at her mother, concern enveloping her demeanor. Jeff spoke to her, "Come on, Chrissy, let's let your mom have a little alone time with Serena and Agatha." Chrissy turned toward her dad, started to move up the steps and then paused for a moment, looking back at her mother with concern.

Jeff spoke again, "It's okay, Chrissy. Mommy will be alright. Come on; let's take Clayton in the house." Chrissy followed Jeff up the steps and into the house.

The weather was beautiful that day so Serena, Karen and Agatha made their way up onto the porch and sat down in the rocking chairs. After a few moments Karen gained control, sat quietly for a moment, and then continued the narrative, "I'm sorry. I hadn't intended on blubbering like a baby. Clayton's fine. He recovered quite quickly, really, considering he was starting to turn blue, but I called his doctor and he said just to watch him during the day for anything unusual and then bring him in tomorrow for a check-up."

Serena tried to lighten things up a bit, "Well, he certainly looked fine, you would have never known anything had happened."

"He was playing with Abigail and Chrissy within moments, as if nothing had happened. It was really remarkable."

"Well, I'm certainly glad it had a happy ending."

Karen continued with her tale, "Well, that was the bad part, I mean, not the happy ending, the whole button incident. But what came out of it is the good part."

"Okay now, darlin', you've got me confused."

Karen let out a nervous laugh, "Let me see if I can explain… I told you that Chrissy was standing by my bed when the whole thing started…"

"Yes," Serena answered slowly, confused as to where Karen was going.

"Well, it wasn't her that alerted me to the emergency, so it had to be…"

"Abigail!" Serena looked at Karen, a look of astonishment in her eyes that quickly spread across her entire face. She moved forward in her rocker, reaching out to touch Karen's hand, "My God, your heard Abigail!"

"Thank God I did or Clayton would probably be…" Karen choked once again. After a moment, she continued, "Not only that, but I have heard everything she has said since. It's as if a door has opened a crack; not enough for me to see her, but enough that I can now hear her." Karen was beaming now, a broad smile enveloping her face.

"Oh, Karen, I am so happy for you. I mean, darlin', you have wanted this for so long. I'm just sorry it had to come under these circumstances."

Serena looked at Karen for a moment and Karen could tell from her expression that Serena was playing with what she would say next, so she beat her to it, "Go ahead, you have my permission to say I told you so." Karen smiled an acknowledging smile at Serena.

"Oh my, now you can read my mind." Serena answered, a smile on her face.

"Well, maybe not your mind, but surely your expression. I know you told me that it would come, in due time. I just didn't really expect it to come like this. But this has opened a whole new world for me. It really does seem like I have two daughters now."

Agatha stirred in her chair and it drew the attention of the two other ladies. Agatha cleared her throat, leaned forward and spoke softly, "It will not last, but first you must solve the mystery of this house."

Karen looked at Agatha, her gaiety gone and a somber expression replacing her smile, "Agatha, I have tried to figure it out, but I am coming up with nothing. Can't you help me at all; any clues would help?" Karen paused and then the reality of what Agatha had said struck her, hard, "What do you mean it will not last... what won't last? Agatha, what are you talking about?" Karen was starting to sound frantic.

Serena reached out to Karen and touched her on the arm, "Whoa there child, don't get too stressed out. Sometimes Agatha expresses things that she sees, but cannot explain."

"But..."

"No buts, let's forget this for now. It is Easter Sunday, a time for celebration. Let's be thankful for those things we have… Clayton?" Serena cocked her head slightly, looking at Karen with a wise expression, and then continued, "You can hear Abigail, you have us for friends, and the list can go on. Let's not worry today, about those things that might happen tomorrow. Okay?"

Karen let out a huge sigh, puffing her cheeks as she did, looked at Serena as a child being chided, and then meekly said, "You're right. Enough for now; we will tackle this another day. Today is about food, fun and friends. Let's go inside, we've got a lot of things planned."

The rest of that day went off without a hitch. Karen's Easter meal of ham and all the special accompanying dishes was wonderful. Jeff and Karen hid many wonderful prizes for Chrissy and Abigail, outside in their yard, and although Abigail couldn't go outside the house, she was not exempt from the fun. While Jeff stood by to assist Chrissy, Karen followed Abigail's lead. As she spotted the treasures from the windows, Karen would follow her directions and retrieve the prizes for Abigail. Chrissy was more than fine with this arrangement, because it included Abigail in the outdoor fun. Serena and Agatha sat, once again, in the rockers on the porch, to follow the childhood merriment.

After all the goodies were collected and Chrissy had retreated to the house to enjoy her treasures with Abigail, Karen and Jeff joined the two ladies on the porch. Karen offered the ladies some fresh lemonade and then went into the kitchen to retrieve it. Once they were all situated on the porch Serena remarked, "That was so much fun today. Thank you both for inviting us. The Easter Egg hunt brought back such fond memories…" Serena stopped for a moment as her memory drifted back some sixty plus years, "I can remember having the same kind of fun, right here on the lake yard. Mother, and a few of the neighbors, would hold an Easter egg hunt for the local children, on Saturday before Easter. And despite the Great Depression, there were still eggs to hide. Most everyone had chickens so we had real eggs, no plastic ones, but oh, what fun we would have. It was just like today, frantically running here and there, searching high and low. I remember at one point my basket was so full that when I reached down to pick up another egg I dumped everything out. I sat there, frantically trying to pick up all my eggs, knowing I was losing valuable time. But in the end, we all had our baskets full and went home happy." Serena smiled a quaint and wistful smile, "That was so long ago and yet, things really haven't changed. The children still get as much fun and appreciation out of the simple act of hunting for prizes."

Karen spoke up, "Well, after today, I have some hunting of my own to do."

Jeff looked at Karen, "What are you hunting for?"

Karen, realizing she had opened her mouth and stuck her foot in it, tried to cover her tracks, "Nothing really, just a figure of speech… it's an inside joke with Serena and Agatha."

Jeff looked at the three ladies, "Boy, let me tell you, it sure can be chilly sitting on the outside looking in." Serena and Karen laughed; Agatha just sat there silent.

Chapter 20

The end of March heralded in the spring flowers, and the deciduous trees, that had spent the winter naked of their foliage, began to put on new, bright green attire. The Live Oaks, famous in the South for maintaining their leaves through the winter, were now shedding their old foliage and immediately replacing them with new leaves. Daffodils sprouted up throughout the lake yard almost as if a spring fairy had sprinkled the area with a dusting of yellow blossoms.

The days became warmer and the spring weather became fiercer with thunderstorms cropping up almost without warning. Karen and Chrissy's afternoon walk around the lake yard, with Clayton in his carriage, which had become a regular occurrence, was often interrupted by a chance and sudden rain.

April passed without any unusual happenings in the Miller household. Clayton was growing lickety-split and was now learning to scoot and crawl around the house which meant that baby gates went up at both stairways on the upper floor. They also secured a fine, sturdy mesh covering along the mezzanine railing spindles to prevent Clayton from getting his head caught. Karen and Jeff went around the house baby-proofing anything that looked like a potential hazard; they placed latches on all of the lower kitchen cupboards, covered all of the electrical outlets and secured any electrical cords that could easily be pulled on. They wanted Clayton to have as much run of the house as possible knowing that Chrissy and Abigail were always there to watch, even if Karen or Jeff were out of the room, even momentarily. They wanted no repeats of the near disaster of Easter morning.

As Mother's Day approached Karen began to plan a surprise for Serena. She discussed with Jeff a special day on that Sunday for them to spend together, perhaps a picnic across the street in the lake yard, or a barbecue on their own patio. Jeff felt it best to keep things small and controlled in their own back yard where Clayton and Chrissy could play in a confined area and Abigail could watch from the house. Karen contacted Serena and made the invitation.

Karen set about making her special surprise for Serena, spending every available moment working on it. Chrissy and Abigail helped with the project as did Jeff, handling the necessary work on the computer. It was truly a family affair and when it was finished, just in time for Mother's Day, it was really something to be proud of.

Sunday morning, Mother's Day, Karen started early with the preparations. She was up before anyone else, working quietly in the kitchen preparing potato salad, her own special baked beans and was applying a special blend of spices to the steaks when she heard a voice from the stairwell, "Good morning, Mother."

Knowing the voice well by now, she answered, "Good morning, Abigail. Is Chrissy or Clayton awake yet?"

"Yes, Clayton is awake, but he's playing quietly in his bed. Would you like me to wake Chrissy?"

"Yes, please, that would be nice. Tell her breakfast will be ready shortly."

Karen turned her efforts to the stove where she placed the frying pan and started the bacon cooking. Within a few minutes of her conversation with Abigail, Karen heard a soft, sleepy voice come drifting down the stairwell, "Mommy?"

"Yes, Chrissy, I'm right here. You may come down now, slowly. Hold onto the railing, please." Karen had moved from the stove to the stairwell and looked up to see Chrissy clomp clomping down the stairs, one hand on the railing, the other rubbing across her eyes. "Well, good morning sunshine," she said to her daughter.

From above Chrissy's head came Abigail's wistful voice, "My mother used to say that to me when I got up in the morning."

Karen smiled, but didn't know quite what to say. Whenever Abigail made reference to her parents, it would sting Karen' sensibilities as if an arrow were striking her heart. Not that she was jealous. On the contrary, she felt sorry that Abigail was not allowed, through fate's fickle mood, to grow up and enjoy all of the love that her mother and father had obviously felt for her.

"Do you mind if I say those same words?"

"Oh no, mother. You are Chrissy's mother and my mother, now. It is quite all right."

"Thank you," Karen replied softly. Turning her attention to Chrissy, Karen picked her up, hugged her and then placed her on a chair at the breakfast bar, "What'll you have this morning, my dear, hot or cold?"

"Can I have both?"

"Ookay. Would that be cereal and bacon?"

"Yup... please." Chrissy smiled at her mom, a sleepy, but happy expression on her face.

"Okay, one hot and cold breakfast coming up." Karen got the Cheerios, Chrissy's favorite, and placed the box, along with a bowl and spoon on the counter. After retrieving the milk she asked, "Would mademoiselle like to pour or be served?"

Chrissy giggled and Karen heard, off to one side, Abigail giggle as well. "Mad...madem.. mademswell would like to be served." Chrissy flopped her hands lightly at the wrists and lifted her head, her nose held high.

Karen curtsied lightly, poured the cereal and then the milk and then she replied, "Would the young miss like to be fed as well?"

By now Chrissy and Abigail were both laughing as Chrissy answered, "Yes, that would be lovely," her words pronounced with affectation.

Karen scooped up a spoon full of the cereal and with great pretense proceeded to feed Chrissy, but as the first spoon full made it to Chrissy's mouth she burst out laughing spraying the entire amount, cereal, milk and all, out and across the counter. Karen and Abigail joined in the hilarity of the moment, each laughing out loud, until they heard a loud clomping on the back stairs.

Jeff entered the room, Clayton in his arms, looking much like the walking dead. Looking at his two girls, laughing uproariously, he stopped dead in his tracks, as his feet hit the kitchen floor. Clayton, recognizing a good time, wiggled and gurgled in Jeff's arms, smiling and waving his arms as if to join in the frivolity. "What in Sam's hill is going on down here?" Jeff asked with consternation.

Karen and Chrissy froze mid-motion, looked at Jeff and wiggly, wormy Clayton and then burst out in another fit of laughing. Jeff stood there looking at the two females as if they were both nuts. Then he proceeded to put Clayton in his high chair and then plopped his behind in another chair at the breakfast bar. Looking at the mess created by Chrissy's outburst, his gaze went from Chrissy to Karen and then to the Cheerios and milk scattered across the counter, and then back to the two females. "Dare I ask what is so funny?"

Karen and Chrissy were both trying to suppress their laughter, rolling their lips inward and then when they looked at each other, the laughter burst forth again. Jeff just sighed, and then said, "I guess I just had to be here, right?"

Karen nodded her head in agreement, unable to answer right away. The moment was just one of those infectious things that happen, and the more they tried to suppress, the more that Karen and Chrissy laughed. Clayton by now had joined in, laughing and gurgling his approval, banging his hands on the highchair tray and pumping his legs. Watching the three enjoying the moment, it wasn't long before Jeff joined in laughing, for whatever reason, along with the rest of the family.

What Jeff couldn't hear was that Abigail was laughing along with them all.

After a few moments, the frivolity died down as Karen took a deep breath and wiped the tears from her eyes, "Oh, my God. That was just too funny."

Jeff took a deep breath and asked, "Will someone please tell me what we were just laughing about. I mean, you two were a mess."

Chrissy and Abigail were still giggling, and Clayton was watching the two girls and matching them giggle for giggle, taking pure delight in the joy of the moment.

Karen tried to explain what had precipitated the laughing outburst, but each time she got to the point of the story about the Cheerios making their exit from Chrissy's mouth she fell apart. Finally Jeff remarked, "Okay, I got the picture. You guys were play acting and it got out of hand, and then it all fell apart. Correct?"

At this point all Karen and Chrissy could do was nod their heads in agreement, a new round of laughter preventing any words.

"Well, I guess it's time for ol' Jeff to take matters in hand. Clayton, you and me are going to get some breakfast." Jeff turned to the stove where the bacon was sizzling away, on the verge of burning. He grabbed a spatula, scooped up the crisp bacon as he said, "Hah! Gotcha, saved from the fire only to be consumed by the hungry." He plopped the strips of bacon onto a plate, and when one was cool enough, handed a slice to Clayton to chew on. During the time it took to cool the bacon Jeff had cracked and added a couple of eggs to the pan and was now ready to serve them up. Once the eggs were ready Jeff sat down and ate the rest of the bacon and his eggs.

By now Karen had composed herself. Looking at Jeff with a 'what can I say,' expression, she looked toward Chrissy, "Go ahead and eat the rest of your cereal, Chrissy. I'll make you some more bacon." Looking at Jeff she shrugged her shoulders as she added, "You know, they say it's good to laugh before you go to bed; helps you sleep, but I think a good laugh in the morning starts the day out right. What do you think?"

Jeff looked at his wife, at Chrissy and then at Clayton, and then answered with a smile, "I think I agree with you."

After the breakfast fiasco Karen set about getting everything ready for the day. She already had the food for the meal prepared, the gift for Serena was wrapped so she got Clayton cleaned up after she sent Chrissy up to shower and get dressed. Abigail went in to help Karen with Clayton and the two of them talked as Karen bathed Clayton and then diapered and dressed him.

"Mother," Abigail asked. "What is Mother's Day?"

Karen thought for a moment and then replied, "Mother's Day is a holiday where all mothers are honored for their role in keeping the house and family harmonious. Did you celebrate Mother's Day before...?" Karen paused, not sure how to finish her question. "No, of course you didn't. It was a twentieth century observance started in... 1914, I think."

"I would like to honor my mother... my real mother, I mean, other than you. Is that all right with you?"

"Of course, Abigail, I understand you still have feelings for your own mother. I would not be offended at all. Abigail, may I ask you a question? It may be difficult to answer and I don't want to upset you."

"Certainly, mother."

Karen paused for a moment, looking at her wiggling son in his crib, but actually thinking of how to form the question right. She turned toward where Abigail's voice had been coming from, "Abigail, it has been a long time since your accident."

"Yes," came the answer very meekly.

"When you fell down the stairs did you see a light anywhere around you?"

"Yes," came the quiet child's voice again.

"Were you called or drawn to the light?"

"Yes," The answers were coming with less reticence now.

"Why didn't you go to the light?"

"I was afraid. I looked at my mother as she stood over me and she was crying, so I was afraid to go to the light."

Karen started to imagine the fear and anxiety that this poor child must have felt. "For all these years, I know that you have appeared to others in this house."

"Yes," the voice had gone quiet and meek once more.

"Why did you always go away? Why did you decide to make us your family?"

"All the others before were afraid of me. I don't know why," Abigail was close to tears, Karen could tell by the quaver in her voice. "But they always left me alone again... until Chrissy... and you. Chrissy wasn't afraid of me. And you... you have treated me as if I were your own daughter."

"Abigail, the others didn't understand. They may have been afraid, but their fear came from ignorance. We, Jeff and I, took the time, to learn and understand, because of Chrissy. Chrissy showed us the importance of understanding. She never once doubted you, or her love for you." Karen, herself, was close to tears. She had not intended to bring up this subject with Abigail, but the door was open now so she continued, "Abigail, have you ever wondered what happened to your mother and father?"

"Yes."

"Do you know what happened to them?"

"No," Abigail answered, the quaver stronger now.

Karen realized she was pushing the limit, but continued, reluctant to ask too boldly what she really wanted to know, "Abigail, do you understand what happened to you when you fell down the stairs?"

"I hurt my neck."

"Yes, I know you did, honey, but..." Karen didn't know how to proceed. "What I mean is... do you know why your mother was crying?"

"Because I hurt myself… I think."

"Abigail," now Karen took the conversation very carefully, "She was crying because you died that day."

"Died? But I am here. I am alive."

"No, Abigail," Karen paused. She, herself, was becoming overwhelmed with emotion. *How do you tell this innocent that she is dead; a ghost, a stranded spirit?* Karen thought to herself. *What am I doing?* "Abigail… you are a ghost."

There was no answer. Abigail was silent. Karen spoke, trying to ease the pain she knew that Abigail was feeling. "Abigail, that is why the others were afraid. But please, Abigail, don't feel badly. We love you just as if you were real. It makes no difference to Chrissy or to me or Clayton, or to Jeff. We love you as if you were our own. Do you understand?"

"Yes," Abigail's voice was as spectral as her body

"Abigail, do you understand what a ghost is?"

"A ghost is something scary that haunts old houses and chases people."

"Well, that is partially true. Let me explain, if I can." Karen proceeded very carefully here, thinking out each word before she spoke it, "When a person dies God opens the door to heaven and the bright light, that you saw, is the glory of Heaven spilling out through that open door, giving you guidance to find your way. Sometimes, for whatever reason, the person who has died doesn't follow the light. Maybe they are afraid like you were, maybe they are waiting for someone else, or… maybe they have something left to do here on earth. But for what ever reason, if they choose to stay, they become a ghost because it is their spirit that remains. Their human body has ceased. What those who are still living see is only a spectral image; a phantasm of that deceased person. So, you, as a ghost, are not meant to be scary. You are not meant to chase people, and, you are not something to be feared. Those in the past who were afraid of you were only guilty of ignorance. They did not understand your predicament. Can you understand what I have just said?"

"Yes," the quiet voice answered once again.

"Now," Karen approached her next question with more vigor, "would you like to be with your mother and father, your real parents, once again? Because I am confident they are waiting for you in Heaven."

"Oh, yes," Abigail answered with renewed energy, "But don't you want me to stay here with you?"

"Of course, dear, but what I really want is for you to be as happy as you possibly can. And if that means reuniting you with your mother and father then that's what we will work toward, okay?"

"Okay," came the reticent voice again.

"All we have to do is figure out how…"

Suddenly Chrissy's sweet voice came through the door of Clayton's room, "Mommy, Abigail, where are you guys? I'm done with my shower; can I go downstairs with Daddy?"

Karen called out, "Yes, Chrissy. Call down to your daddy and have him meet you at the stairs. Abigail and I will be right down with Clayton." Turning back to the crib Karen picked up Clayton, turned toward the door as she spoke to Abigail, "Come on sweetie, we'll figure out what to do later, okay?"

"Okay," answered the quiet, little girl voice.

Serena arrived at one o'clock, the prescribed time. The Miller family, all five of them, met Serena at the door and wished her a happy Mother's Day as she entered their home. Serena was all smiles as the family embraced her to their bosom, figuratively speaking. "My goodness, I never realized what fun it could be to be a mother. Thank you one and all."

Karen spoke, "Serena, you have been a member of this family almost since the first day we met. I know that the children, Abigail included, all consider you like a grandmother, right kids?"

Chrissy hollered out a long, drawn out, "Riight!" as she jumped up and down

Abigail added her voice to the mix, although Jeff and Serena couldn't hear her, but it made Karen smile all the more. Clayton, not talking yet, wiggled and squirmed in Karen's arms and then squealed to add his bit to the excitement, which made Serena laugh out loud.

"My goodness, I guess I'm the 'Bell of the Ball' today, how wonderful!" Serena patted Clayton on his leg.

"Serena," Karen said, "Come into the dining room. We have something we want to give you." Karen led the way out of the foyer and into the dining room. Lying on the table was a package, brightly wrapped with a huge lavender bow. Karen handed Clayton off to Jeff as she lifted the package from the table and handed it to Serena.

"Oh, my, whatever could this be? I thought we were going to celebrate you today, not me."

Karen smiled at Serena, "You are the only mother I have, Serena. I hope you don't mind?"

"Heaven's no, child. So let me see." Serena set the package on the table and began to remove the wrappings. Chrissy had hold of the edge of the table and was bouncing up and down excitedly. Abigail, off to one side, was giggling and clapping her hands, but neither Jeff nor Serena could hear, so Karen asked, "Serena, can you hear Abigail?"

"No, dear, what did she say?"

"Well, she didn't say anything, but she is giggling and clapping her hands with excitement. I wasn't sure if you could hear her."

"No, unfortunately I can't see or hear her yet."

As Serena reached the last of the wrappings and finally uncovered the gift she drew in a large gasp of air. Reaching down she opened the cover of the album that Karen, Jeff, Chrissy and Abigail had worked on furiously for the last week. On the cover it read, "To Serena, Our Mother, Grandmother, and Special Friend." Inside, as Serena turned one page after

193

another, were photos of Chrissy, Clayton, Jeff and Karen, and that special photo of Abigail. Serena pulled out a chair and sat heavily down, overcome by the love that emanated from the pages. As Serena lifted her head to look at those gathered around her, Karen could see the tears welling up in Serena's eyes.

"Wy, Ah don't know what to say. Ah am just ovahwhelmed." Serena's smooth, southern accent had grown thicker with emotion.

"There is nothing to say," Karen said, "Just accept it with our love and thanks for all that you have done for us."

"Darlin', Ah will treasure this always."

Later that evening after Serena had left and the kids were in bed, Karen and Jeff sat on the couch in the back parlor. Karen snuggled into Jeff's shoulder, letting his arm which enveloped her shoulders, wrap more firmly about her. She laid her head against his chest and let out a huge dreamy sigh.

"Are you happy, hon?" Jeff asked her.

"If I were any happier I would pop like corn." Karen answered.

Jeff smiled softly to himself. "You know, today was supposed to be all about you; you're the mom in this house."

"I know, but Jeff, I couldn't have had a nicer day. Having the opportunity to show Serena just how much I truly appreciate her meant more to me than any special gift. Your help and the kids pitching in... I mean... it just meant so much to me to do it all, as a family, together. The love and appreciation it made me feel for you guys, and the awesome family we have. Oh, my God, I am so happy. Today was everything I could have hoped for." Karen sat up, looked at Jeff and then gave him a kiss.

Jeff lifted his eyebrows, "Wow! If that is all I have to do to get this kind of reaction, I'll go out and print up some more photos."

"It's more than just the photos, and you know it." Karen knocked Jeff lightly on his shoulder.

"I know, silly." Jeff reached out, wrapped his arms around Karen and pulled her to him. He quickly gave her a tickle on her ribs, knowing she was exceptionally ticklish there and she squealed and wiggled away from him. Then a sort of wrestling match ensued with a lot of laughing and squealing.

After a few moments of this child's play they heard a light cough at the doorway into the breakfast nook. They froze mid-motion and looked toward the doorway. Chrissy stood barefooted, nightgown to her ankles, leaning one arm against the door sill, with a look of attitude, the other hand on her hip, "Excuse me," she said, "some of us are trying to sleep." She turned on her heels and headed back into the breakfast nook and turned, out of sight, toward the back stairway.

Jeff and Karen looked at each other, having been duly chided, and busted up laughing. Jeff spoke first, "How old is that girl?" Karen just laughed all the more.

Chapter 21

With Mother's Day now past, June was quickly approaching and with it came Chrissy's fifth birthday. Karen and Jeff were all a twitter with plans for a surprise birthday party. Serena was helping with the plans as was Abigail. The trick for them all was to keep it a secret from Chrissy.

Karen had taken special effort to include Abigail in the planning of the party and swore her to secrecy. Abigail was thrilled to be included as an important member of the family. Karen had discussed with her the plans for the cake, chocolate or vanilla, chocolate was the winner. The ice cream, chocolate, vanilla or strawberry, strawberry was the winner there. And most of all, what they would get Chrissy for her birthday.

Abigail had expressed the wish that she, personally, could pick out a gift for Chrissy. So Karen made a deal with Abigail that she, Karen, would go to a few stores, scout out some choices, bring back a list of those items, and then Abigail could pick out what she wanted to give Chrissy. That way the gift would truly be from Abigail to Chrissy.

Jeff and Karen had long ago decided they were going to get Chrissy her first bicycle for her birthday. One day Jeff had nonchalantly walked with Chrissy through the toy department at the local Wal-Mart, discussing various items they spotted on the shelves. As they approached the aisle where the bicycles were located Chrissy's eyes really lit up when she spotted a Barbie bicycle. It was pink and white, with pink handle bar grips and pink tassels hanging from the grips. The fenders were shiny chrome and it had a white wicker basket on the front. The bicycle was sitting on display at floor level so Chrissy climbed on board, the training wheels holding the bike upright. Her feet barely made it to the pedals, but that didn't stop her from imagining. She turned the handle bars from side to side, squealing as if she were taking a hard turn.

"Whoa, tiger, I hope you're not going to be screaming down the sidewalks one of these days. You'll be sending the old ladies running for the curb."

Chrissy giggled as she climbed down from the bicycle. She smiled at her daddy as she said, "No, silly, I won't chase the old ladies. I will be very polite when I get my new bicycle." Chrissy looked at Jeff, wrinkling her face up in a contorted wink and winked at him, twice. "Hint, hint," she said.

"I heard you." Jeff rubbed Chrissy's head, messing up her hair in the process. Chrissy reached up and smoothed her hair back into place as she said, "Daddy, don't do that. You're messing my hair."

"Oh, excuse me. I didn't know you were expecting to run into mister right today."

"I'm not, silly. I just like my hair to look nice."

Jeff looked down at his daughter, "You women; you are all alike. Comb the hair, put on the make-up, and squirt on the perfume. Yikes!"

Chrissy just giggled and softly said in a demure manner, "Daddy."

So the day before her surprise party Jeff had gone to the store and purchased the Barbie bicycle, still in the box. When he arrived home, Karen looked at him as if he was nuts, "It's still in the box. Can you put it together?"

Jeff looked back at her, a wounded expression on his face, "Of course I can put it together. All men are at least a little mechanically minded; at least enough to put a bicycle together." Jeff hauled the box out of the van and muscled it into his office, away from Chrissy's view.

"Well... I hope you can get it together before tomorrow."

Jeff looked back at her with an expression of 'Are you kidding.' "Come on, Karen, it'll only take me an hour or so," was his reply to her doubting statement.

Several hours later, as dinnertime approached, Karen walked out to see what progress Jeff had made. She opened the door to find him sitting on the floor amidst a number of nuts, bolts, pedals, fenders, handle bars and pink streamers, a large set of instructions in his hands. Karen cleared her throat, "Excuse me, mister mechanic, how soon do you think you'll be finished? Dinner is just about ready."

Jeff looked up at her like the proverbial kid with his hand in the cookie jar. He sighed heavily, letting out a final puff of air, laid the instruction sheet down, looked around at the mass of parts yet to be assembled, contemplated his situation and then replied, "Call when it's ready. If I'm not done I'll finish up after dinner."

Karen closed the door behind her, a fervent prayer on her lips, *Please, oh please, have it done before tomorrow.*

After dinner Karen sent the girls upstairs to play before bedtime, she lifted Clayton from his high chair, looked at Jeff and said, "Come on, I know that thing isn't done yet, so I'll help you before I put the kids to bed." Karen headed for the back door, Clayton bouncing happily on her hip, as Jeff headed out the door behind her.

As they went out the door Jeff called back, "Chrissy, Mommy and I will be out in my office. If you need us for anything just call us on the intercom."

When Jeff turned to follow Karen he found her waiting for him on the patio, the nursery monitor in her hand. She held it up, "I'm way ahead of you. The other half is in the playroom. We'll know right away if she heads down the stairs."

As they entered the office Karen closed the door and locked it. Smiling at Jeff, she said, "Just in case."

Within an hour, with Karen reading the instructions and locating the parts, and Jeff doing the actual assembling, they stepped back to look at their handy work. Karen reached out her hand to shake Jeff's, and with a smile said, "We work pretty well as a team, don'cha think?"

Jeff smiled back as he shook her hand, "Indeed we do, my dear." He leaned over and kissed her cheek.

Picking up Clayton, they headed for the door, and as they left they switched out the lights. Karen said softly, "I can't wait to see her face tomorrow." They both walked happily back into the house, smiles of satisfaction lighting up their faces.

The next morning, Karen was up bright and early. She immediately checked on Clayton, who was sleeping happily in his crib, and then headed downstairs to the kitchen. As she put the coffee on she was silently running through her list, *Get things ready for lunch, get the bow on the bicycle, check with Serena about the cake, send Jeff to get the balloons at Wal-Mart...*

"Mother?"

Karen turned toward the voice, "Good morning, Abigail."

"Good morning."

"Have you gotten your gift for Chrissy wrapped?"

"Well, no. that was what I wanted. Could you help me with it?"

"Certainly, Abigail, where is it?"

"I'll go get it. It is upstairs. Would you like me to wake anyone while I'm upstairs?"

"No, why don't we just let them sleep until after we get the gift wrapped."

"Very well, I'll be right back."

Although Karen couldn't see Abigail, she could almost feel when the spectral child left the room. It was just a feeling, nothing more; like there was a void where the child had been.

Only moments passed, and Abigail was back, "Here, Mother. I just couldn't seem to get the paper to work right."

Karen smiled lightly to herself as the tiny box appeared on the counter. "Okay, let's see. I've got some wrapping paper here somewhere." Karen turned into the back room and returned shortly with a roll of paper, some tape and a pretty bow. Showing the paper to Abigail where her voice had last come from, she said, "Will this do?"

Abigail replied, "I'm over here, Mother."

Karen turned to her other side, "I'm sorry, dear, I hadn't realized you had moved. What do you think of this paper? Will it be okay?"

Abigail replied, "Yes, it is very pretty. It suits Chrissy very much." Her voice projected the feeling that she was smiling and that pleased Karen.

As Karen started to wrap the box she spoke softly to Abigail, "You know, Abigail, I think you chose very wisely. I really think that Chrissy is going to like this more than even her bicycle."

"Really?" Karen could tell that Abigail was proud of her choice, "Do you really think she will like it?"

"Oh, absolutely. She will think it is the best thing, ever. You mark my words."

Unseen to Karen, Abigail was smiling so widely that it seemed her face would crack. She was very proud of her choice.

Just then Karen and Abigail heard a noise at the stairs. A sleepy voice called down from the top, "Mommy? I'm ready to come down."

Karen walked over to the stairwell, "Okay, honey, come on down, one step at a time."

Chrissy let out a heavy sigh, "I know Mommy, you always say that." When she reached the bottom and stepped into Karen's arms Chrissy stated in no uncertain terms, "Mommy, I am five years old now. Don't you think I'm old enough to come down these stairs by myself?"

Just off to Karen and Chrissy's side came Abigail's voice, "Chrissy, I was eight years old, and I thought I was old enough, and look what happened to me."

Karen stood upright, surprised by Abigail's comment, but she felt it best not to say anything. Chrissy looked at

Abigail, contemplated what Abigail had just said and then replied, "Welll," stretching out the word for several counts, "I guess that's true. Okay, mommy, you can keep watching me AND reminding me about one step at a time. I don't mind... I guess."

Karen nuzzled Chrissy for a moment and then whispered to her, "Good morning, birthday girl."

Abigail added with a squeal, "Wheee. It's Chrissy's birthday. Happy Birthday, Chrissy."

Karen moved the celebration over to the counter in the kitchen, setting Chrissy down on a stool. "So, what would the birthday girl like for breakfast?"

"Hmmm... pancakes with maple syrup, bacon, crispy please, and grape juice."

"Well, let me check with the cook and see what Karen's Diner can come up with."

Chrissy giggled and Karen could hear Abigail giggling, too. Karen looked at Chrissy and where she assumed that Abigail stood, and thought to herself, *Oh, my God, how I love these times with my sweet girls. Just me and them, here in the kitchen, talking and laughing, without a care in the world.*

Just then Karen's thoughts were disrupted by that, all too familiar, clomping on the stairs. All three of the girls turned to the stairs as Jeff, carrying Clayton, appeared from the stairwell, "Well, good morning my beauties, and a Happy Birthday to my youngest beauty." Jeff walked over and kissed Chrissy on the head as he moved past her to place Clayton in his high chair.

As Jeff kissed her head Chrissy hunched her shoulders and lowered her head, assuming her usual stance when she was embarrassed.

After placing Clayton in his chair, Jeff took his place at the counter on his usual stool. He grabbed a knife in one hand and a fork in the other, placed his hands firmly on the counter and in a stern and gruff voice, said, "Okay, Ma, what's fer breakfast. Ah'm hongry."

Chrissy looked at her daddy and then over at her mother and started to laugh, because just as Jeff finished his statement Karen threw the dish towel and it landed on Jeff's head, one portion draping down and covering his face. Jeff grabbed the bottom of the towel that was covering his face, stuffed it into the neck of his shirt and reached up to the top of his head, smoothed the towel down off of his head and face and onto the front of his shirt, like a bib, uncovering his face as he did so, and assumed his original stance with the knife and fork. All of this in minimal movement, as if it was rehearsed and well practiced.

Chrissy was laughing so hard she almost fell off her stool and Karen could hear Abigail laughing almost as hard. She looked at Jeff and then commented, "You know dear, you never fail to amaze me with your dexterity and talents." And then she started to laugh.

Jeff just looked at her, cocked his head slightly, raised his eyebrows as if to say, 'I am so glad I please you.' And then he started to laugh.

Karen thought to herself, *Ahh, this is going to be a great day*. And she smiled at her wonderful crew.

After breakfast Karen sent the girls up stairs with orders to play games until lunch time. She had already discussed with Abigail the plan for her to keep Chrissy busy while everything was set up for the party.

Serena was due at noon, bringing with her the cake and ice cream. Karen had arranged for pick-up of the balloons at eleven thirty so that Jeff would have time to get back and arrange them.

Karen set about making up the tuna salad for sandwiches, Chrissy's favorite. She got down from the cupboard the bag of barbecue potato chips, also Chrissy's favorite. She made up some broccoli salad, another of Chrissy's favorites. This was to be a special meal for her special girl. Karen's only wish was that she could do the same for her other special girl, Abigail, but that would have to remain a wish unfulfilled.

Clayton was playing happily in his play pen while Karen fixed the food. Every so often she would check on him, check his diaper, talk with him a bit and then tickle and play with him. Clayton somehow sensed that today was something special and was content with the few moments his mother had to spend with him. He luxuriated in her attention, but was totally content to play with his toys, by himself. When she looked at the time, she spoke to Clayton, "Oh, my goodness, Clayton. It's time to send Daddy to the store. I had better go call him, right?"

Clayton was sitting up, smiling at his mother and at the mention of daddy, he waved his arms up and down as if to send her on her way. Karen moved over to the intercom and pushed the call button, "Jeff, it's eleven. You're supposed to pick up the you-know-whats at eleven thirty. You better get going."

"Okay, hon, I'll be right in."

Karen turned to Clayton, "Do you want to go with Daddy?"

Clayton bounced up and down, as much as he could while sitting up and not fall over, waved his arms some more, and then gurgled and giggled. A big smile and a lot of slobber spreading across his face.

"Well, we'll just check with him when he comes in, okay?" Karen reached down and tickled Clayton lightly on his tummy.

Jeff came through the door. Karen turned to him, held her finger to her pursed lips and pointed to the ceiling, "The girls are right upstairs, playing."

Jeff stopped in his tracks. Then he proceeded across the room, on tip toe, to where Karen stood, next to the playpen. Clayton looked up at his daddy, squealed lightly, and began bouncing once more on his little diapered bottom, waving his arms, trying to get his daddy to pick him up. Jeff leaned into the playpen and picked Clayton up, the child obviously happy with his daddy's choice.

"I think he wants to go with you," Karen said. "Do you mind taking him with you?"

"Heck, no! I'd take my little man to the moon, if that's where he wanted to go." Jeff tickled Clayton in his belly. The child scrunched up and giggled.

Jeff grabbed his wallet and the diaper bag and headed to the car. "We shall return," he proclaimed as he and Clayton headed out the door to the car.

"There's supposed to be one hundred latex and ten mylar balloons, all filled with helium, so go prepared to fill the car," Karen called after Jeff. Realizing she was being louder than she wanted to be, she almost whispered the last part of her statement. She closed the door and moved back into the kitchen. Then she decided to check on the girls so she moved to the back stairs and quietly moved up each step looking through the spindles as she approached the floor level. When she could see well enough, there was Chrissy, sitting cross legged on the floor, the game board in front of her. Just as Karen was about to ask, a game piece moved two spaces up the ladder printed on the board; they were playing 'Chutes and Ladders.'

"Hi, girls, how are things going?" Karen asked.

Chrissy looked over at her mother, "Ohhh, they're going fine, but I sure hope someone gives me a new game for my birthday."

"For heaven's sake, why?"

"Because I can't beat Abigail anymore; she has won every game we've played this morning and this is the third."

Karen heard a small giggle come from the opposite side of the board from Chrissy.

"It's not funny, Abigail. It is polite to let your guests win, now and then." Chrissy said to Abigail.

"Well now, wait a minute, Chrissy. Isn't Abigail your guest?" Karen asked her daughter.

"Well, not really, mommy. I'm Abigail's guest."

Karen thought about this for a moment and then said, "Chrissy, how do you figure that you are Abigail's guest?"

Chrissy looked at Karen as if she were a dummy, "Mommy! This was Abigail's house first! So, I'm her guest because I came second."

"Okay, I got ya. You're correct, technically." Karen stepped back from the side of the stairwell where she was standing, impressed by her daughter's logic. "Uhm, I'm going back downstairs, girls. I'll call you, Chrissy, when lunch is ready, okay?"

"...Okay, mommy," Chrissy was already back to her game, intensely studying the game board, her right elbow resting on her knee and her right hand cupping her chin.

Karen went back down the stairs, stepping out into the kitchen as Serena knocked lightly on the back door. Karen waved her in. Serena quietly asked, "I know I'm early, I hope you don't mind?"

"Heck no," Karen said, smiling at Serena, "Is there anything I can carry in from the car?"

"I left the cake and the ice cream, until I knew the coast was clear. Let's both go get them."

Karen and Serena went back out the door and retrieved the party treats from the car. "Let's put these things in the refrigerator in Jeff's office. Then Chrissy won't accidentally discover them," Karen spoke to Serena conspiratorially.

After they stowed the cake and ice cream in the office fridge Serena went back to her car and retrieved a wrapped present. "For Chrissy," she smiled. "Hope she likes it, it's another game, a new and more advanced game."

Karen smiled a knowing smile, "I think she will probably love it. As a matter of fact, I could almost bet on it."

The two women moved into the house and then Serena mentioned, "Where's Jeff? I noticed the van is gone."

Talking quietly, Karen pointed to the ceiling, "He's on a balloon run. He took Clayton with him and the two of them should be back shortly."

Just about then Karen heard the soft whisper of the van pulling into the carport outside and then said, smiling at Serena,

"Speak of the devil, and who should appear?" They both laughed and then moved toward the door to help Jeff unload.

Karen moved quickly to get Clayton out of his car seat and then carried him into the house and placed him in the playpen. Then she returned outside to help with the mass of balloons. The back of the van was full; the middle seat, where Clayton had been, was almost full, and the front seat was also full, except where Jeff had been sitting. Looking at the mass of balloons, Karen started to laugh. "I wish I could have seen you coming out of the store; I'll bet that was a sight."

Serena was laughing as well as they pulled the bundles of balloons from the car. The balloons were tied into groups of twenty-five; each group having been placed into a large clear plastic garbage bag, one string extending out of the bottom of each bag and the bottom of the bag tied securely to avoid losing any balloons. There were five bags in all. Jeff looked at the two women, and while chuckling, himself, he explained, "The sales associate helped me tie each bag to my buggy. I had Clayton in the child seat, and these bags tied all around the edge of the buggy basket. Thank goodness those buggies weigh what they do or we'd have lost Clayton into the stratosphere. Up, up and away he would have gone. Not only that, but I'm sure you couldn't see me pushing the buggy across the parking lot, because a number of people going into the store, as I was leaving, stopped to peak around to the end of the basket to check on who or what was moving the basket. I'm sure it was quite a sight."

Karen and Serena laughed all the more as they imagined the buggy rolling across the parking lot, propelled by balloons. They each carried the bundles into the house and then into the dining room where the party action was going to take place. Karen stayed inside while Serena and Jeff returned to get more balloons. Karen untied the bags of balloons, one by one and released them from their confinement, watching them drift up to the ten foot ceiling as they bounced and scattered out. As each bundle was released the ceiling filled up and by the time Karen released the last bag of latex balloons, the ceiling looked like it was covered with confetti; spots of yellow, green, blue, red, pink, orange, and white hovering above their heads, the strings hanging down to brush their heads as they walked under them. Then the last bundle, the ten mylar balloons, with 'Happy Birthday', 'Birthday Girl' and various other pertinent sentiments, was released, the much bigger balloons squeezing in amongst the smaller latex balloons. When all were released, the ceiling was full. Not a speck of the ceiling could be seen. The cooling system came on and the resulting breeze from the vent caused the balloons to bounce and jiggle, almost as if they were dancing to an unheard tune.

Karen, Jeff, and Serena laid out the table with Barbie party plates, napkins, pink plastic eating utensils and party noise makers, and then started bringing in the food. Karen brought out the plate full of tuna sandwiches, the chips and the salad, while Serena and Jeff went after the cake and ice cream. Karen had retrieved Clayton's high chair from the kitchen and had Clayton secured at one end of the table. When everything was in place, Serena and Jeff waited by the table while Karen went to the stairwell, "Chrissy, Abigail," she called, "Lunch is ready." Karen moved back to the dining room and they waited until they heard Chrissy coming down the stairs and then Karen called out, "Chrissy, we're in the dining room."

Chrissy pushed through the swinging door and when she saw the dining room and the table, she stopped dead in her tracks. Standing very still, her arm still holding the door open, she surveyed the room and its occupants. Her eyes grew wide and then she started to cry. Karen could hear Abigail laughing and squealing with delight, while Chrissy just stood there and cried.

Karen looked at her daughter and then at Jeff and Serena, incredulous at her daughter's reaction. Then Karen stepped forward and bent down to Chrissy's level, "Honey, what's wrong? Why are you crying?"

Chrissy stood immobile, wiping her eyes with the back of her hand, "I thought you forgot."

Jeff stepped forward, sweeping Chrissy off her feet and into his arms, "Forgot? Are you kidding? This is all we've been thinking of for the past couple of weeks. Forget your birthday? Not on your life." Jeff gave Chrissy a big kiss on her cheek and then replaced her in a standing position near the door. "Come on, everybody, it's party time!" Jeff grabbed a party noisemaker from the table and started to blow on it, grabbing another and twirling it to make even more noise. Serena and Karen joined in and then Chrissy did the same. Soon they were all laughing and making noise; Clayton, all the while banging on the tray of his high chair with a rattle and laughing along with the merriment and noise. The balloons on the ceiling bounced along with the merriment.

Everyone pitched into the food and took a place at the table, Chrissy relishing in the attention. After the food was finished Karen retrieved all the gifts from the back room; all except the bicycle. Chrissy opened the gift from Serena first, a new game, Chinese Checkers! She looked at Serena and then got up from her chair and walked over to where Serena was seated. She curled her finger, back and forth, indicating to Serena she should bend down. When Serena bent over, Chrissy wrapped her arms around Serena's neck, hugged her firmly and then kissed her on the cheek, thanking her for the game. Chrissy released her grip on Serena and then turned to where Abigail was standing and said, "Now, maybe I can beat you at this one."

Karen heard Abigail giggle and then say, "Maybe."

Chrissy smiled at Abigail's response.

Then Chrissy returned to her chair where two gifts were waiting; one gift from Clayton and one from Abigail. Chrissy chose to open Clayton's first, finding a book inside the wrappings. She walked over and hugged her little brother and thanked him for the book. Clayton had no idea why his sister was hugging his neck, but he loved it just the same, giggling and slobbering joyously.

When Chrissy returned to her chair the last of the wrapped gifts was awaiting her attention. She looked at the small box, neatly wrapped with a pretty bow and then she looked off to one side and asked, "This one is from you?"

Karen heard the soft reply, "Yes, I picked it out myself. Mother helped me."

Chrissy looked at her mother with a question in her eyes.

Karen replied with, "I'll explain how later, but yes, she picked this out, all by herself."

Chrissy quickly, but very carefully removed the wrappings, easing the taped ends gently apart. When the wrappings were off, lying in front of her was a small, jewelry type box. Chrissy looked to her mother and then to the empty area to her left, her hands lying softly in her lap, almost as if she was apprehensive to open the box. Karen nodded her head and smiled softly, as if to encourage Chrissy to go ahead and open the box.

Chrissy reached her hands up and grasping the box on two sides, she gently pried the box back on its hinge, exposing a small silver pendant, lying on a black satin base. The pendant was half of a heart; a jagged shaped edge down one side, as if the heart had been broken in two. On the pendant was the letter A, prettily engraved. Chrissy didn't move nor did she say anything. When she looked up, she had tears watering her eyes. She looked over at Abigail and whispered, "It is beautiful, Abigail. I absolutely love it!"

Karen, knowing what was coming next, had tears in her eyes as well. Watching Chrissy's expression, she realized what Abigail was doing, and then she heard Abigail say, "I have one, too, see." Chrissy reached out and hugged the empty air, or at least that's what Jeff, Serena, and Karen saw.

Jeff and Serena looked at Karen and then Jeff said, "What's happening? What's going on?"

Karen smiled softly at what she knew was going on with her daughter and then turned to Jeff and Serena, "Abigail has the other half of the heart and it has a C engraved on it. She has shown it to Chrissy and now Chrissy is hugging her… I think."

Karen heard Abigail say, "I will never take it off and I will wear it forever."

"Me, too!" Chrissy responded. "I will wear it forever and ever. It is the best gift, ever."

Karen couldn't see Abigail, but she could pretty well guess that she had a huge smile on her face. Karen looked to where she thought Abigail stood and said, softly, "See. What did I tell you?"

"Thank you, Mother, for helping me," Abigail whispered.

Just then Jeff stood up, "Okay, Birthday Girl, now the final reveal. I'll be right back." Jeff left the table only to return a few minutes later, a large handkerchief in one hand. Okay, kiddo, turn around while I put this blindfold on you and then I will take you with me." After he had tied the handkerchief around her eyes, he picked her up and said, "Okay, partiers follow me." Everyone, including Abigail, followed Jeff out to the back door. Jeff continued out onto the patio, Karen, holding Clayton, and Serena, followed him out the door. Karen heard Abigail say, "I will wait here, Mother," as they all went out the door.

Jeff set Chrissy down and then pulled the blindfold off, exposing the new bicycle. Chrissy squealed and Karen heard another squeal come from the back door. Chrissy immediately ran to the bicycle and climbed on. Jeff had put the seat on its lowest position and Chrissy was well able to reach the pedals. She immediately began moving the bicycle, turning in an ever widening circle, the adults moving out of her way.

"Daddy, can I take it out on the sidewalk?" Chrissy pleaded with her daddy.

"Why don't we keep it in the driveway out here in the back until we know you have full and complete control? Remember the old ladies."

Chrissy giggled and then said, "I remember… okay, driveway it is." Chrissy let out a huge sigh and headed out to the driveway. She stopped for a moment, looked at her mother and father, and then at Serena. Smiling happily, she said, "This has been the best birthday, ever." She turned back to the house and smiled again, reached up and rubbed the heart necklace hanging around her neck, and then pedaled off down the driveway.

Chapter 22

June played out as only a Southern June can in Northwest Florida; the days were hot and humid, the evenings warm and humid and the rain showers came hot and heavy. Karen and Jeff, coming from another part of the country, had not anticipated the warm weather that now embraced them. Any outdoor activity had to be planned so that it could just as easily take place in-doors in case it rained. The forecasters could give their ideas of what the weather would be, but Mother Nature definitely had her own ideas.

The spring flowers had long ago shriveled in the intense heat, to be replaced by green; green leaves, green grass, and sometimes a green sky. The first two greens were welcome, but that green sky meant trouble; stormy weather was ahead.

The month of June dissolved in the heat and before they knew it the Miller Family was preparing to celebrate the Fourth of July

Now, in Defuniak Springs, the residents take the celebration of our country's independence quite seriously, as most small towns do. This year the Fourth of July fell on a Friday which meant that many families would be escaping the doldrums of everyday life by taking a three day week-end. Many of those families came to the Emerald Coast of Florida for those week-ends and many of those made DeFuniak Springs one of their daily destinations, because this small city had the perfect setting for a special day trip; the perfectly round Lake Defuniak, its mile-around park that encircled that lake, providing an absolutely perfect place to picnic. The fourth of July festivities at the lake yard began in late afternoon with a parade. Then a program was planned at the amphitheater, with a flyover of jets from Eglin Air Force Base, and then, the big finale of the day; a huge fireworks display over the lake just after dark.

Jeff and Karen had been discussing the fourth with the children for several weeks. The discussion actually started right after Chrissy's birthday. What they would do that week-end really depended on the weather, but after some insistence on the part of Chrissy and Abigail, it was decided that they would all stay home to enjoy the festivities. A picnic was planned on their patio so that it could be taken in-doors in case of rain, and then they would sit on the front porch to watch the parade and then later the fireworks.

As the day grew closer Chrissy and Abigail became more and more excited. Abigail had been there, in the house, to see the parade and fireworks, since they had started the tradition many years before. And as the big day approached she would describe the past parades and the fireworks displays to Chrissy, getting her all the more excited.

The week before the fourth Karen called Serena and invited her and Agatha to their house for the picnic and to stay and watch the parade and fireworks. Serena immediately accepted even though her house sat on Circle Drive and she had a good view from her own front porch. As Serena put it, "Darlin', I'd much rather watch somethin' like this with friends and family, than all by my lonesome."

The morning of the fourth you'd have thought it was Christmas morning. Chrissy was up before dawn, trying to drag her mom and dad out of bed, "Mommy, wake up, it's the Fourth of July, America's birthday!"

"Chrissy," Karen groaned, "Honey, it's not even day light. Nothing starts until much later today." Karen let out another groan, rolled over and was back asleep immediately.

Chrissy decided trying to get her folks out of bed was useless so she went into Clayton's room to get Abigail. "Abigail, I can't sleep. Do you want to play some games?"

Abigail was watching over Clayton's crib and looked up at Chrissy when she entered the room. "All right, Chrissy. Clayton is still asleep, so we can go to the playroom. If he wakes I'll still hear him."

Some hours later the Miller household was still sound asleep; all except Chrissy and Abigail, that is. Finally, as the sun raised its shining corona up from the East and spread its golden rays across the still water of the lake, Karen stirred. She laid there for a few moments, getting her eyes used to the light, blinking back the sleep that had recently engulfed her. As the cobwebs in her brain cleared, she thought about the dream she had earlier; Chrissy was standing by the bed, all excited about the Fourth of July festivities. *Wait a minute,* she thought, *was that a dream?*

Karen got up and moved to Clayton's room; everything there was as usual. Clayton was still asleep. Karen asked quietly, "Abigail, are you here?' She was met with silence. Karen then moved into Chrissy's room. Looking at the bed, which was empty, she realized that maybe it hadn't been a dream.

As she turned toward the closed playroom door, she called out softly, "Chrissy?"

Her question was answered, "Yes, Mommy?"

Karen let out a sigh of relief. Not sure where Chrissy might have gone in her excitement, Karen was relieved to see she had gone no further than the playroom. "Good morning, baby. I wasn't sure where you would be. I'm sorry I didn't get up with you earlier."

"That's okay, Mommy. Abigail and I have been playing games and Abigail has been telling me more about the parade and the fireworks." Chrissy's excitement was mounting as she spoke and by the time she reached the end of her sentence she was clapping and bouncing where she sat.

Karen looked at her daughter, myriad memories of months gone by flowing through her mind, *I look at her here and she is so much a little five year old girl, and then, at other times, she talks like she is a grown-up, wise with age. What a dichotomy. She is my little old soul.*

"Okay, Chrissy, that will all come later. How about we go down stairs and get some coffee going and get you some breakfast. Sound like a plan?"

"Sounds like a good plan, Mommy. I'm famished."

"Famished, Chrissy, where did you get that word?" Karen looked at her daughter, trying to figure out if she was actually a little girl. *Famished? What child uses that word?*

Chrissy hunched her shoulders and looked down, her hands folded in her lap. Embarrassed by her Mother's comments, she said quietly, "I don't know, is it a bad word?"

Karen chuckled, smiled lightly at her precocious daughter, leaned down and lifted Chrissy's chin with her fingers, "Not at all, Honey. It's just one of those big words that adults usually use, that's all."

Chrissy let out a big, "Whew! Boy, I thought I was gonna get in trouble for that one!"

Karen just laughed as she headed for the top of the stairs, "Come on, oh famished one. Let's get something to eat."

As the girls sat in the kitchen, the familiar clomping on the stairs heralded the arrival of the men of the house. Jeff came in to the kitchen, looking every bit like warmed over death. Clayton, being carried by his daddy, was smiling, bouncing and waving his arms, slobbering and giggling. Jeff put him into his high chair and dropped his own body onto a stool.

Jeff hung his head and cradled it in his hands, his elbows supporting it all on the counter. He groaned lightly as he rubbed his face with his hands, his one day growth of beard sounding like sand paper. "I don't know why I'm so tired, my gosh, I slept well enough last night, a few of those nightmarish dreams, but that's all. Did I hear Chrissy by the bed early this morning, I mean last night, I mean… I don't know what I mean."

"No…no, I don't think so," Karen replied, "you must have been dreaming, dear." Karen looked over at Chrissy and gave her a conspiratorial smile. Chrissy just hunched her shoulders and looked at her plate of pancakes. Karen heard Abigail giggle off to one side. Clayton just looked from one person to the next, and then over to where Abigail giggled, and then he laughed as he pounded his hands on the high chair tray.

Jeff looked around the counter at all of the early morning gigglers ending up looking at Clayton and then muttered, "It's a conspiracy, and you're all in on it. You're all plotting against me, I know. I can tell. And you!" and he pointed at Clayton, "You're the worst. You're supposed to side with me. You know, guys against the girls. Come on, buddy!"

Clayton just looked at his daddy, not comprehending one bit what he was saying, but when Jeff was finished, Clayton's eyes got a big sparkle to them, his mouth curled into a big wide grin, showing off his four, new, pretty white teeth, and then he burst forth with a loud gurgled giggle as he pounded his hands on the tray. Through all of this, everyone sitting there focused on him and began to laugh, and it became one of those rolling laughter's; gaining volume and intensity as it moved around the room. Then the laughter was trumped by the sound of passing gas. Everyone turned to look at Clayton. His hands froze in midair as all eyes in the room were on him. His expression had taken on an uncertain look, just for a moment, and then he resumed the beating and laughing. Everyone else absolutely exploded with laughter; Clayton had farted!

After the roar of laughter subsided everyone got down to the business of eating, Jeff consuming a stack of four, plate sized pancakes as well as four slices of bacon. Karen and Chrissy looked at him as he finished off the last bite; a smile of complete satisfaction spread across his face.

Chrissy looked at her daddy and her eyes grew wide and took on an expression of disbelief, "Daddy, my goodness! If you keep eating like that you're going to get fat like a hippopatamumus."

Karen broke out laughing as did Jeff. Clayton looked at his parents and joined in the laughter.

Chrissy looked indignantly at them all and then asked, "And what was so funny about that?"

"It's pronounced hippopotamus, honey," Karen corrected.

"That's what I said, hippopotamumus."

"No, no," Karen was trying very hard to stifle her laughter, "hip-po-pot-a-mus" she corrected again, emphasizing each syllable.

"Whatever," Chrissy answered, "May I be excused now?"

Jeff had remained mute throughout this exchange, but now answered, "Yes, you may be excused. Would you like help getting down?"

"No thank you, I'm a big girl now, Daddy. I'm five, remember?" Chrissy wiggled down from her stool and when her feet touched the floor she called out, "Come on, Abigail, let's go play upstairs." She took off for the back stair case.

Later that afternoon, while Clayton was down for his nap and Jeff was out in his office, working, Karen was walking down the hallway, upstairs, when she eyed the cord hanging down from the attic access door. She stopped just underneath it, transfixed by the idea of the wall up in the attic that seemed to have no reason. She stared at the attic door and thought to herself, *One of these days I'm going up there and check out that wall. It just makes no sense to me at all.* Just then she heard Chrissy squeal from the playroom, bringing Karen out of her reverie.

Karen moved toward the playroom door and as she opened it she heard Chrissy squeal again, "Chrissy, keep it down please, Clayton's sleeping."

"Sorry Mommy. "

Chrissy was obviously delighted about something. She was absolutely beaming, even though she had just been

217

chastised. "My goodness, Chrissy, what prompted the outburst?"

Chrissy hunched her shoulders as she usually did when embarrassed, and then looked up at her mother, a big smile on her face, "I finally beat Abigail!"

Karen could hear Abigail laughing and then said, "Well, my, my, my. Looks like you've finally met your match, huh Abigail?"

"Yes, Mother. Chrissy is getting better all the time. When I was first learning she would win all the time, but once I got the idea of the games, then I was able to out-play her. Now, with this new game, Chinese Checkers, she has once again gained the advantage. But I will get better and then I will win once more."

Karen looked over at Chrissy and she had a triumphant look on her face. Karen spoke out, "Better watch out, Chrissy, pride cometh before the fall."

Chrissy looked at Karen with a confused expression and said, "Huh?"

Abigail just giggled, "What she means, Chrissy, is, don't get too cocky or I'll beat the pants off you the next time."

Karen tried to alleviate Chrissy's confusion, "It's an old saying that basically means that when a person gets too arrogant about oneself, they get overconfident and then fail. Do you understand?"

Chrissy remained confused looking for a few moments, and then as if a light bulb had come on in her brain, a smile slowly spread across her face and she looked at her mother as an embarrassed expression replaced the smile. "I understand, Mommy. I need to be humble when I win, right? That way I can beat her again."

"Something like that, Chrissy, but don't expect to just keep on winning because Abigail learns quickly and one of these times she will win, right Abigail?"

"Right," Abigail returned quietly.

The one thing that Karen could always count on with Abigail was her kindness. She was never arrogant or mean when it came to Chrissy. Karen could depend on Abigail to be considerate of Chrissy and Clayton. One thing Karen knew for certain, Abigail was a nice, sweet little girl, uh, ghost.

Karen looked at her watch and realized it was three o'clock, "Okay, girls, let's get the game picked up. Serena and Agatha will be here in thirty minutes and I would like to have everything set up and ready. Chrissy, you can help me with the stuff on the patio and Abigail; you can help with the things in the kitchen. Okay, hup to, kiddos." Karen clapped her hands together as the girls giggled.

Chrissy and Abigail began setting the marbles and the game board back into its box. It always mesmerized Karen to watch the two girls work together. Items would disappear from the play area and then appear suddenly in another place. Karen knew that these items were being picked up by Abigail, so she understood, but it never failed to fascinate her. Sometimes, it even unnerved her, just a bit.

Once the game was put away Karen said, "Okay, chop chop, let's go," as she clapped her hands again.

Heading for the back stairs Karen heard Abigail warn, "Chrissy, go slow. Never underestimate these stairs. They are dangerous."

"I know, I know, you don't have to remind me," Chrissy was growing petulant at Abigail's continual reminding about the stairs.

"Yes, I do. And I don't have to tell you why."

Karen had already started down the stairs, stopped, and then turned to look at Chrissy during this exchange. When Abigail mentioned her last statement Karen watched Chrissy's expression go from petulance to sadness.

Then Chrissy responded, "I'm sorry, Abigail. I know why you always remind me, and I love you for it, really, I do."

"Alright, then, take them slow, okay, 'because I love you too, and I don't want anything to happen to you."

Karen stayed silent during this entire exchange between the two girls and her feelings were mixed. She felt great pride in her daughter and great sadness for Abigail.

Once into the kitchen Karen started to disperse orders. She grabbed the red, white, and blue dishes she had purchased, just for this occasion. Chrissy picked up the container with the colored plastic ware and followed her mother out the door. Together they spread the white cloth on the patio table. As her mom set out the plates, Chrissy followed behind setting a white fork, a red knife and a blue spoon at each place. Once the glasses were in place, Karen placed an arrangement with red and white flowers and blue sparkly stars in the center of the table. The table had the most patriotic look that Chrissy had ever seen, "Wow, Mommy! That looks terrific. You're a real Martha Stewart."

Karen looked over at Chrissy, "Well, thank you... I think.

Just then Jeff came out of his office and looking at the patio and the decorative table expressed, "Wow, that looks terrific. You're a real Martha Stewart, hon."

"Thanks, dear. Seems I've heard that somewhere before." Karen looked down at Chrissy and smiled lovingly.

Looking around, Jeff asked, "Is there anything I can do? Something you need from inside?"

"Not right now, Jeff, not until Serena and Agatha get here, then we'll need the sweet tea."

Jeff moved past his girls and headed for the back door, "Where's Clayton?" he asked over his shoulder.

"Up in his bed. I haven't heard anything over the nursery monitor, but you might go check on him anyway."

"I'll do that. See ya in a bit," Jeff said back to Karen.

Karen and Chrissy moved back into the kitchen to find the chips, napkins, salt and pepper shakers, the butter dish and an empty pitcher for the tea waiting on the counter. "Wow," Karen called out to Abigail, "You've been busy. Good job, Abigail!"

No reply came back, but Karen heard a light giggle from one side of the room. She looked at Chrissy who was looking in the direction of the giggle and smiling. Chrissy held a thumb up as she looked to where the giggle had come from and then she giggled as well.

Just then Karen heard the door bell jangle from the front. Karen moved through the dining room and as she came through the front dining room door looked out through the front door window to see Serena standing outside. As she opened the door she greeted Serena and Agatha, who was standing next to Serena, too short to be seen through the window.

"Welcome, ladies, happy to see you. Please, come in." Karen stepped aside to allow the two ladies in. She then led the way through the dining room and into the kitchen.

All the way through Karen noticed that Agatha had raised her head slightly, in her sniffing manner, and continued it all the way through to the kitchen. When she stepped into the kitchen she immediately turned her head, looking in the direction of where Abigail had been. Smiling, her eyes wide and enormous looking through her thick glasses, she said, "Hello, Abigail. How are you today?"

"I am fine, thank you," came the demure reply.

Karen heard the reply and smiled lightly, but Serena, as yet unable to hear Abigail, just looked at Agatha and then at Karen, aware that she was the odd one out.

"Shall we go into the parlor and sit or would you rather we go outside in the heat?" Karen asked the ladies.

"The parlor will be fine, thank you, Karen," Serena replied. "I am afraid the humidity is buildin' to a rainstorm later. Hope the parade gets through before it hits."

"Oh, I do too. Would you ladies like some sweet tea?"

"That sounds wonderful, darlin', just easy on the sweet. Gotta watch my waistline, ya know. Actually, things seem to settle more to my bottom than my waist nowadays."

Karen chuckled lightly, "Serena, you look wonderful. I just hope that I'm in as good a shape when I'm your age." Karen reached into the refrigerator and retrieved a large plastic pitcher of tea, poured it over into the glass pitcher that Abigail had set out, placed that pitcher on a tray with several tall glasses and then headed toward the back parlor with the tray. The two ladies followed.

As they entered the back parlor from one side door, Jeff entered through another door with Clayton in his arms. "Good afternoon, ladies." Clayton wiggled in Jeff's arms, gurgled a little bit, laughed and then smiled broadly at the two elderly women. "Clayton says welcome, as well." Jeff continued across the room to place Clayton in his playpen, now positioned in a corner of the room. He sat down next to Karen.

They sat and talked until shortly after four o'clock, when Jeff mentioned, "Should we move to the front porch and get settled before the parade starts?"

After getting seated in the rockers on the front porch Karen went back inside to make sure that Chrissy and Abigail were aware of the time, "Chrissy, Abigail, it's almost time for the parade."

"Okay," Chrissy's voice came from just above Karen on the upper floor.

"Chrissy, where are you?"

"We're up here by the front window, Mommy."

"We'll be out on the porch, Chrissy, if you need us."

"Okay, Mommy. Abigail and I will watch from up here. Is that okay?"

"Certainly, Chrissy."

Karen returned to the porch, bringing Clayton's playpen so that he could move around, at least a little bit.

The crowds began gathering along the sidewalk, congregating near the amphitheater, the Chautauqua building and the library. The Miller's home sat between the library and the Chautauqua building so the crowds were sparse in front of their house.

Circle Drive was the perfect location for a parade. The units formed at the middle school, just one block south of the lake. The parade would enter onto Circle Drive, move around clockwise, the little more than one mile around, and then exit out at the middle school.

As Karen, Jeff and the others sat on the porch, the late afternoon heat was oppressive, even in the shade of the porch. They could see the large cumulus clouds gathering and building, pushing together and gaining density. The white billowy clouds soon became darker and grayer, compacting together until the sky was a solid steel gray. A storm was definitely brewing, but just how long before the skies opened up was another matter.

"Oh, I do hope the parade has a chance to get through before it rains," Serena said with a worried expression, "These folks have gone to a lot of trouble just to get rained out."

Just then they heard coming from their right the sound of a band playing. The crowds along the side walk stepped out into the street, straining their necks to see the coming parade. As the sound of marching music grew louder, the rumble of thunder could be heard in the distance.

The parade watchers on the porch looked to each other, hopeful yet doubting expressions on their faces. The music became louder and then, just down the street came a brief siren. The parade was approaching.

A police cruiser came into view, and then a sheriff's cruiser. As the cruisers came closer, a military color guard could be seen in the distance. As it approached the group on the porch stood as the American Flag and the Florida State Flag were carried past. Spectators along the street removed their hats and placed their hands upon their chests, allegiance to our flag was evident. The Air Force personnel carrying the flags marched with pride; in their flags, in their country, in their uniform.

Once the color guard was past the marching music became quite loud as the military band came past; the Air Force band from Eglin Air force Base. The music was patriotic as well as grand. Karen looked over at the two ladies, still standing, and could see the moisture in their eyes, their hands still over their hearts. Their feelings of patriotism were apparent.

Karen then looked down at Clayton, still in his playpen and watched as her son beat his hands and bounced in time with the music. She looked to Jeff and could see that he was watching Clayton as well, a huge smile across his face.

Overhead Karen could hear the sound of small feet, pounding to the rhythm of the marching music.

Once the band had passed then came the cars of dignitaries; the city mayor, the council members, the county commissioners, and a few others. Then came a bicycle built for two, ridden by a local radio personality and his wife, who were dressed in gay nineties costumes. Next, a unit of Confederate Civil War re-enactors followed by a wagon carrying a contingent of ladies dressed in anti-bellum attire. As the parade continued, still the rain held off, but it was only a matter of time, for the thunder had gained intensity.

The parade contained a tribute to our Revolutionary soldiers, a man dressed as Uncle Sam, a float carrying someone dressed as Lady Liberty, an Elvis Presley impersonator, a Brownie troupe dressed in white shirts, a red vest and blue shorts; each waving a small American Flag. There were antique cars, a local Boy Scout Troupe and a float from Eglin Air Force Base showing our military personnel past and present. Many individuals were interspersed among the floats, all dressed to express their love of country.

As the parade wound down, last but not least, the fire trucks and ambulances representing our local first responders. Sounding their sirens, they alerted the bystanders that the end of the parade had arrived. Just as the last fire truck passed and the crowds had dispersed, the first rain drop fell. The drops slowly gained in frequency and as the small group on the porch moved inside, the sprinkle had developed into a full blown downpour. The wind had increased, coming in off the lake, and was now blowing the rain in under the porch roof. Jeff had plucked Clayton out of his playpen before the rain increased and he and Clayton were now safely inside.

Karen rushed to the other end of the house, running out the back door to retrieve what she could from the table. She gathered everything up in the table cloth and carried it quickly inside. When she stepped into the kitchen she was met by Jeff, holding Clayton, Serena and Agatha. Chrissy quickly popped her head out of the stairwell. They all stood there, staring at Karen.

Karen stood in front of them, dripping wet, clutching in her arms, the table cloth full of plates, silverware, and poking out of the top of the wad of table cloth, one sparkly blue star. She smiled weakly as the water, from her drenched hair, trickled down her face, eventually dripping off her chin, only to be caught in the bundle taken from the patio table. A pool of water soon collected on the floor under Karen's feet.

Chrissy started with, "Gee, Mommy, what happened to you?"

Jeff started to laugh, and then Serena added, "Darlin', you look like a drowned rat, or at best, the one the cat drug in."

Karen brushed the next trickle of water from her chin and then everyone started to laugh, Karen included. Even Agatha joined in the fun with a faint smile.

Karen pulled the sparkly blue star from the bundle, waved it around a bit, and then said, "Happy Fourth of July everyone."

Chapter 23

Serena moved to Karen and said, "Here, darlin', let me take this stuff. Let's see what we can salvage and we'll set up the table in here."

Karen released her grip on the bundle and allowed Serena to take the table cloth full of dishes.

"You go on up and get some dry clothes on, darlin'. Chrissy and I will get this all set up, won't we, Chrissy?"

"Yes, Miss Serena." Chrissy smiled at Serena and then at Karen, "We'll be just fine, Mommy. Go get dry, okay?"

Karen just nodded her head in agreement and headed for the back stairs. As she moved past Jeff, still holding Clayton, he just shook his head from side to side and laughed. Karen could almost read his thoughts as if he were thinking; *I can't believe you did that.*

Chrissy and Serena moved to the round breakfast table and set the bundle down. They carefully opened the jumbled mass of plates and eating utensils. One by one, Chrissy and Serena removed the pieces until all that remained was the table cloth.

Serena contemplated their dilemma and then said to Chrissy, "I think this one is a bit too wet, don't you?"

Chrissy nodded her head in agreement.

"Do you know where Mommy keeps the other table cloths?"

Chrissy moved into the back room and returned with another white table cloth. By the time Karen returned, considerably drier, the table was all set; including the arrangement with the sparkly blue stars, and the rain had stopped. In this part of Florida, the rainstorms stopped with the same suddenness as they began.

"Wow, you guys work fast. That looks wonderful... I don't know about the rest of you, but I'm hungry, how about something to eat?"

Chrissy jumped up and down and clapped her hands in agreement.

"Well, we're all set up in here, so there's no sense in moving everything outdoors, but we can still cook on the grill. Jeff, will you go fire up the barbecue and I'll get the burgers and dogs."

"Will do, oh mighty captain of this ship." Jeff saluted Karen and then headed out the back door to prepare the grill for cooking.

They had a great meal of hamburgers, hot dogs, potato salad, baked beans and then Karen presented a cake she had prepared that was decorated like the flag, including all fifty candy stars. When she set it on the table, everyone ooohed and aaahed appropriately.

Jeff commented, "Wow, babe, you really outdid yourself, today. This is great! That cake really looks terrific!"

"I helped, Daddy. Actually, Abigail and I both helped. We put the stars on it, didn't we, Mommy?" Karen smiled in acknowledgement.

"You and Abigail did a most spectacular job, I must say," Jeff replied. "Congratulations to the chef and the assistant chefs."

"Here, here," Serena added.

Karen and Chrissy both smiled. Chrissy looked to one side of the room and her smile broadened, and at that point Karen knew that Abigail was smiling as well.

Karen looked at the wall clock and then exclaimed, "We had better get going. We will miss the flyover. We can come back and have the cake later while we wait for it to get dark. Jeff, you grab Clayton and Chrissy, get your hat and sunglasses;

it's still hot enough out there, you need to protect yourself. Serena, your going up to the amphitheater with us, aren't you?"

"I'll walk with you darlin', but I think Agatha would probably prefer to wait here, if that is alright?"

"Of course, she can keep Abigail company. Abigail, we will be gone only a short time and then we will be back so that you and Chrissy can watch the fireworks together."

"All right, Mother. I will stay with Miss Agatha."

The Miller's, along with Serena, moved out to the sidewalk and walked the few blocks to the amphitheater, arriving just in time to hear the announcer alert the crowd, "Here they come folks, watch overhead at twelve o'clock." Jeff gently applied his hands to Clayton's ears. Everyone, gathered at the amphitheater, craned their necks, looking in all directions, and then the loud whine of the engines alerted the on-lookers to the approaching jets. Whoosh! Four large jets shot overhead in an arrowhead formation. They sped across the opening just above the trees.

Everyone was looking up. Chrissy was straining her neck, holding her sunglasses, with one finger, at the bridge of her nose, and the sound was so loud she dropped her hand from her glasses and clapped both her hands over her ears. The planes seemed to be just above the tree tops as they sped across the lake and disappeared in the distance. Chrissy looked up at her parents in wonder, "Wow!" was all she said. Clayton clapped his hands and kicked his legs.

The announcer returned to the P.A. system, "Get ready folks, here they come again."

Chrissy, this time, ready for the loud noise, did not cover her ears, but rather ducked down as if she feared the planes would scoop her up, all the while watching them as they shot by.

"Oh, my goodness, that was wonderful!" Chrissy exclaimed, a bright smile of wonderment enveloping her face. Clayton just squealed with glee, kicking his legs and clapping his hands.

"Gee, Chrissy, did you think they were going to get you? The way you ducked I thought you might think they were gonna drop a hook and swoop you up and take them with you," Jeff chuckled a little as he teased his daughter.

"No, Daddy," Chrissy answered back, "I knew they couldn't get me." Chrissy hunched her shoulders and swung lightly at her daddy's leg, smacking him lovingly on his thigh. Chrissy loved these moments when her daddy teased her. She was always embarrassed by them, but she knew they were done with love, and that, most of all, was why she enjoyed them, because she loved her daddy just as much as he loved her.

"Okay, everyone, how about we head back to the house and connect with that cake. I didn't slave over that hot oven just to look at a pretty cake."

Their small group turned and headed back to the house; Jeff carrying a wiggling, gurgling Clayton and Karen keeping a watchful eye on Chrissy. Noticing Karen's eye on Chrissy, Serena reached her hand out to the little girl and whispered, "I don't suppose you'd be willin' to help an old lady down the street. It would sure make me feel a lot more secure with you holding my hand."

Chrissy beamed a big, proud smile up at Serena as she took the elderly woman's hand and said, "I would be proud to help you Miss Serena. I just hope I'm big enough to help steady you," and then she smiled at Karen, her expression telling Karen just how good it made her feel to be needed.

"First one back to the house gets to clean the cake plate," Jeff said back to the rest of the group. He and Clayton were already well ahead of the ladies and he knew full well that he and Clayton would be the first to arrive back at the house.

As the afternoon melted into the twilight of evening the Miller's and their guests settled in to await the fireworks. With the two girls up stairs on the mezzanine at the front windows, the rest of the friendly group moved out onto the front porch to sip iced tea, and discuss the day's events. Karen and Jeff had decided to let Clayton stay up to enjoy the fireworks. Karen also knew that once asleep, the first loud bang from the fireworks would have him awake anyway, so they might as well just let him stay up.

Chrissy and Abigail had brought the Chinese Checker board up to the front window area to help pass the time. Every so often Chrissy would peek out the window to check on the progress of the darkness. Each time she would come back to report the progress to Abigail, "It's almost dark, but I can still see the water, so I don't think it is quite dark enough yet."

A short while later, as the ignition time approached, Karen went inside to check on the girls. From upstairs she heard Chrissy say, "Darn, darn, darn!" Then she heard a quiet giggle, and then Chrissy again, "That's not fair, Abigail!" and then, "Yes, it is. I did it right!" "Yeah, but I'm your guest."

Finally, Karen broke in, "Chrissy, what's going on up there?"

"Oh, nothing, Abigail just beat me at Chinese Checkers… again."

Karen heard a petite chuckle from overhead and then she chuckled herself, "Boy, it didn't take Abigail long to figure that game out, did it?"

With a huge sigh Chrissy let out an exasperated, "Noooo."

Karen smiled a secret smile to herself in the fading light and then said, "It's almost nine o'clock, girls. They will be starting the fireworks in just a few minutes. You might want to position yourself at the windows." Karen heard the shuffle of two little feet as Chrissy ran to the front window.

Karen returned to the front porch; a smile still creasing her face.

"What's got you smiling like the Cheshire Cat," Jeff asked her as she sat down.

"Nothing, but sisterly rivalry; isn't it wonderful." Just then a loud whistle sounded from the opposite side of the lake and all their attention was focused on the black sky overhead.

Boom! The sky exploded with bright sparks of gold and green and the ooohs and aaahs of the spectators carried around the lake. On the first boom Clayton, sitting in his playpen, jumped, an expression of uncertainty on his face as he looked around, and then his eyes grew wide as the gold and green sparks reflected in his eyes. Karen just smiled at her brave little boy.

Overhead and inside, Karen heard the squeals of delight coming from Chrissy and Abigail. Another whistle sounded the launching of another fireworks bomb followed by an explosion of red sparks that then branched off into a number of new explosions of blue sparks that each, in turn, exploded into a mass of white, glittering sparks. Everyone on the porch let out their own ooohs and aaahs. Clayton joined in with each and every explosion, voicing his approval with gurgles and squeals. Not put off or even frightened, he seemed enthralled by the noise and the lights. Upstairs, Karen heard more of the ooohs and aaahs and then more squeals.

This went on for over thirty minutes; one burst of light and sound after another, each seeming to be better, brighter, and louder than the one before. Finally, there was a massive explosion, numerous whistles and then bang after bang as many blasts were sent up into the dark and humid night; the smell of burnt powder drifting heavy on the air.

"Well, I think that ends the evenin's festivities." Serena said as she moved to the edge of her chair, "Karen, you have once again given Agatha and myself a holiday to remember. I can't remember when I have had more fun on a Fourth of July. This has been most enjoyable." By now, standing, Serena reached over and gave Karen a big hug as she whispered in Karen's ear, "Thank you, darlin', for includin' me in your family. I do so love you all."

When she finally pulled away, Karen's eyes were moist with emotion. She smiled softly at Serena and then said, "Agatha, Serena, I am so glad you could both come and be with us today. I hope that we can make this an annual event. You two ladies are always welcome in our home. Karen reached out and squeezed Serena's hand.

Jeff had picked Clayton up from his playpen and was heading for the door, "I think it is time to get this guy into bed. Karen, I'll get him ready to put down. You stay with the ladies. Good night Serena, Agatha. Thank you both for coming." Jeff disappeared into the house.

As he passed through the door Karen heard him call out to Chrissy, "Okay, girls, time to hit the hay. Chrissy, go brush your teeth and get your pajamas on while I get Clayton ready for bed."

Karen smiled as the two ladies headed down the front steps, pleased with the way the day had turned out, "Serena, call me soon, will you?"

"That I will, darlin'. You take care now. Goodnight." Serena and Agatha slowly disappeared into the night.

Chapter 24

July soon melted into August; the weather in the small city now humid and oppressive. One particularly bright afternoon Karen looked out the front door window at the sidewalk, the park and the lake across the street. Everything seemed to be shriveling in the heat. Karen noticed the cooling system kick on as a nearby vent began blowing cool air in her direction, *thank goodness for air conditioning. I wonder how anyone survived down here before air conditioning.*

Karen turned toward the front stairs and moved up them, taking each one slowly, her mind many decades in the past. When she reached the top step she turned and moved toward Clayton's room. She peeked into the door only to see her young son, sleeping soundly, his mouth making small suckling motions. Karen then turned back into the hallway to check on Chrissy and Abigail. As she did so she noticed, once again, the cord hanging down that opened the attic access door.

Karen looked at the cord and then contemplated the wall in the attic. For weeks now, that wall had not been far from her conscious thoughts. The thought plagued her that the wall did not make sense. Why was it there with no access from the inside or outside? No windows and the wall did not conform to the outside walls. It just did not make sense.

Karen had made a decision. She moved toward the playroom door to check on the girls, seeing that they were playing quietly and intent on the game before them she decided to check on Jeff. Down the front stairs, she moved quietly so as not to disturb Clayton, and then out through the kitchen and into the garage office. Poking her head through the door she smiled at Jeff and asked, "Hi hon, just checking to see if you needed anything?"

"No, I'm good for now. What are you up to?"

"Nothing special; just the same ol' things. Housework stuff. Clayton is asleep and the girls are playing a game. Ummh... are you going to be busy for a while?"

"Yeah, I'm pretty tied up here for now. I've got this on-line catalogue I have to finish for a client, so I'll be busy for some time. Just call me when dinner is ready, okay?"

"Sure, babe, I'll see that you're not disturbed. I'll call when dinner is on." Karen closed the door, now assured that she could proceed, undisturbed. She moved to her storage room located next to Jeff's office. Retrieving a ladder and a hammer she walked around to the front door of the house and carried the tools up to the second floor.

Placing the ladder under the attic door, she gave a quick jerk on the cord and then pulled steadily as the stairway unfolded down to the floor. Once again she walked over to the closed playroom door, listening to assure herself that no one would discover her.

Karen moved quietly up the stairs and once she was into the attic she reached over and turned on the lights. The heat in the attic was so overwhelming it almost sucked the breath from her lungs. The stifling heat made it difficult to breath. Quietly she moved over to the wall, lightly moving her hand over the surface. Something inside her was telling her that whatever secret this house held; whatever mystery lay undiscovered; the answers were behind that wall. Despite the heat she was determined to follow the course she had set for herself.

She took the hammer and slid the claw portion of the hammer under one of the slats that ran up and across the wall. Gently applying pressure she pried up the slat. As it popped free of the nail holding it in place, she moved on to the next nail location. The slat popped up with very little resistance. Karen slowly moved along the slat until she reached the end. Grasping the slat she removed it and laid it onto the attic floor. Turning back to the wall she discovered what she had suspected. The slat covered a seam in the wall; a small, straight break in the wood covering the wall. She moved on to the next slat. When all three were removed she discovered a distinct pattern of seams. What appeared as a solid wall, in reality, was a wall, with an opening that had been disguised.

A door maybe? Karen pushed lightly on the seamed area and met with total resistance. She surmised that she would have to determine at which side the hinges were.

She hurried down to retrieve a flashlight and checked once more on Clayton and the girls. Once back in the attic she slowly shined the light into the crack, moving slowly to find the hinges. As she followed the crack she finally found a hinge in the seam to the left. Following the crack down she spotted another hinge; the obstructions so minute, so indistinct that she almost missed them.

Now that she knew where the hinges were, she moved to the right side of the door and pushed, slowly intensifying the pressure. Eventually she leaned her back against the wall, using her legs for leverage. Slowly; ever so slowly, the door gave way under the pressure.

Karen slowly slid her back down the wall until she was sitting on the floor. Breathing hard from the effort, she turned to look at the now partially opened door, *I knew it! I knew it!* She thought to herself. *I knew there was something here!*

Karen turned onto her knees and applied pressure with her hands to the door. With a scraping, slightly metallic sound the door slowly gave way. Once the door had swung open enough for Karen to crawl through she moved forward through the opening on her hands and knees. The room was dark. There were no windows, so Karen reached back for her flashlight. Slowly she moved forward, one hand then one knee, then the other hand and the next knee, all the while Karen is thinking to herself, *Karen, you've got to be nuts! There could be rats or spiders or who knows what in here. What are you looking for, anyway?* She didn't know, but by now curiosity had taken hold of her.

As she moved into the room she turned her head to the area behind the door. Legs; metal legs of something were right against the backside of the door. Some one had placed it against the door to block it.

Once inside only the flashlight provided light; that and the little that seeped in through the opening in the door. Still on her hands and knees, using her flashlight, Karen scanned the small room; the narrow beam providing very little information. Nothing really distinct, just a small room, very confining in space, probably not more than six feet by ten to twelve feet. Karen shined the light up and realized there was room enough to stand so, getting off her knees seemed like a good idea; besides, her knees were beginning to hurt.

Karen scanned the room. A lot of dust; not much in the way of spider webs, *whew, that's good.*

Suddenly, the flashlight beam picked up something as she turned it toward the wall at the door. Something… some kind of furniture; the door had been blocked by an old metal bed. She moved closer to the bed. Something was on the bed. In the frail light of the flashlight beam, something white, no not white; something yellow. She couldn't tell, so she moved closer, bending down to see clearly in the gloom.

She reared back, a scream stifled by her hand. Karen started to gag but then she stopped to calm herself as much as possible. She had backed up and was now against the back wall beginning to hyperventilate, *calm down, calm down, take it easy until you know what you're dealing with.* She stepped toward the bed, looking closer once again. She leaned down to see two empty orbs looking back at her and she reared back again, *Oh, my God, what?*

Slowly, ever so slowly, she moved to the bed and, with her thumb and forefinger, she lifted what appeared to be an old blanket away from whatever it was staring back at her. The flashlight beam exposed a skull. No, wait, there was a second.

Two, together, what in heaven's name was this? Karen looked at the two yellow skulls; empty eyes, their old, yellowing teeth, closed in peaceful death, the two skulls next to each other, one slightly smaller than the other. Karen stepped back again, unsure what to do; unsure what to think.

Karen's legs could no longer support her and she slipped slowly to the floor, one hand holding the flashlight on the macabre scene before her, the other covering her mouth, trying to hold back the bile that was slowly creeping up her throat.

Minutes ticked by. Karen couldn't move. She just kept the beam of light on the two skulls, unable to decide what to do. Finally, she decided she had to do something. She moved forward, once again, lifting herself onto her knees. As she kneeled next to the old iron bed, almost in reverence of what lay before her she lifted the old, decaying blanket, just a little bit more; touching as little as she possibly could. The blanket crumbled under her touch, but she was able to move it just enough to reveal a hint of the skeletal forms that lay under it. Two hands, one from each form, were clasped together, as if the deceased had lain peacefully together, accepting their fate.

Then the light beam picked up what looked like a scrap of paper; held in one of the two hands. Karen eased forward enough to grasp the paper and then settled back on her legs to examine it. Using the beam from the flashlight, she scanned the folded sheet of paper. It seemed to be a letter, written in a feminine and very articulate hand.

As Karen read the letter she let out a huge sigh, "Oh, my God," she uttered out loud.

The words of the letter echoed through her mind, the immensity of feeling that the words conferred,

'To Those Who Discover Our Passing,

So profound is our grief that we wish only to be with our darling Abigail. And it is our belief that we will reunite with her once more at the Heavenly Gates, to spend eternity together.

Nathan and Marion Cottonwood

By the time Karen had finished reading the note tears were streaming down her face. She could only imagine the grief that this poor couple felt. To have been that distressed that they evidently closed themselves up in this room, only to lie together until they died, *Oh, God. Oh, my God, what grief they must have felt.* Karen just sat there, unable to move, consumed by that grief.

After some minutes, sitting absolutely still, the letter still held in her hand, Karen heard a small voice come from out in the attic, "Mommy... Mommy... where are you?"

"I'll be right there, Chrissy. Just stay where you are... I'll be right there."

Karen moved swiftly, not wanting Chrissy to witness the grisly discovery she had found. She moved out into the attic, pulling the door closed behind her, leaving just enough room for her fingers. She turned out the light and then moved to the stairs. She found Chrissy waiting for her at the bottom.

Chrissy, noticing the look of distress in her mother's expression and the tear stains on her cheeks, asked, "Mommy, are you okay? What's wrong?"

Karen moved quickly down the steps, each step bringing her closer to her daughter, whose face was asking many silent questions. At the last step she kneeled down to look Chrissy directly in her face, "Mommy's okay, Honey. It was just so hot up there in the attic that it made my face red and my eyes run. I'm okay, nothing to worry about." Karen could see the immediate look of relief on her child's face. The tense lines around her eyes relaxed and a light smile inched across her mouth.

"Why did you go up there, Mommy? I heard noises, something scraping or being moved."

"I was just looking for something. I didn't find it so I guess I put it somewhere else. Why don't you go on back and play with Abigail." Karen wanted to get out of the house. No, she needed to get out of the house.

"Abigail's in with Clayton. She heard him fuss, so she went in to be with him."

Karen turned back to Clayton's room. Entering, she said, "Thank you, Abigail, for checking on Clayton. You can go back to play with Chrissy. I'm going to take Clayton down to be with his daddy."

"All right, Mother," Abigail answered, her voice soft and demure as always.

Karen gathered Clayton up, changed his diaper, and then carried him down to the kitchen where she placed him in his carrier. Making sure that Chrissy and Abigail were back in the playroom, she called up the back stairs, Chrissy, if you need anything, just call Daddy on the intercom, okay? Also, I've left the monitor on the table by the door so he will be able to hear you."

"Okay, Mommy."

Karen moved out the back door to Jeff's office. Popping in through the door, she said abruptly, "Jeff, I have to go out for a few minutes. I won't be gone long. Watch Clayton for me, please. Chrissy and Abigail are upstairs; here's the nursery monitor. I told her if she needs anything just to holler for you. Bye!"

Jeff looked back at his wife, his mouth gaping open, his fingers poised above the keyboard, not sure what to think. She had caught him by surprise to the extent that he couldn't utter a word.

She set Clayton down next to Jeff's desk, smiled at her husband and then closed the door as she departed. Before he even had a chance to ask anything, she was gone.

All of this had been accomplished in a matter of less than ten minutes. She needed fresh air to breath and no interference in order to think. She moved quickly out to the front yard, out the gate and then crossed the street.

Down the block, passed the Chautauqua building was a children's playground. Beyond that, just a matter of yards, was a wooden pier that extended out into the lake at least one hundred feet or more. At the end of the pier was a gazebo with benches. Karen was moving quickly, not really knowing where she would end up; she just knew she had to get away from the house.

No one was on the pier or in the gazebo, *thank God*, Karen sighed as she sat down. At first she leaned forward, her elbows on her knees, her head cradled in her hands. She took one deep breath after another. Finally, she sat up straight, looking calmly out to the water that lay in front of her.

Her thoughts were running rampant, *those poor people, their grief must have been monumental... What do I do now? Do I call the police; they'll think I'm nuts or some sort of a murderer. What do I do?* Karen groaned and dropped her head into her hands once again.

Sitting up, her thoughts took over once more, *how ironic is that! Those people take their own lives just to be with their daughter for eternity and she's still here... I've told her I will help her cross over to be with her mother and father... but how? How do I do that?* Karen groaned out load again and dropped her head into her hands.

She just sat there; minute after minute, unsure what to do. Slowly Karen became aware that someone was standing next to her; she saw the feet as she looked at the ground. Looking up she saw Serena staring at her, a distant, but loving expression on her face.

"Serena, oh my God, am I glad to see you! I haven't heard from you in weeks; have you been alright?"

"Yes dear, I'm fine. I've been here all along; all you had to do was call. Now, what is botherin' you, darlin'?"

"Oh, Serena, I have made the most ghastly discovery. I have figured out the mystery of the house."

"And what was it, dear?"

"Serena, I am so upset. I found the bodies, no, really, the skeletons of Abigail's mother and father, today, in the attic. They were so grief stricken they closed themselves up in a small room and just laid down and died. Oh, God, what am I to do? I feel so badly for Abigail. She wants to be with her parents. Her parents died to be with her, and…" Karen began to shake and then the tears started to flow again as she dropped her head into her hands once more.

Serena sat on the bench next to Karen and put her arm around Karen's shoulders. "Karen, darlin', if anyone can help that child, it's you. You just hang in there and follow your heart."

By now Karen had calmed down and the tears had ceased. She sat up, heaved a big sigh and said to Serena, "I know you're right, Serena. I just need to think things out. I need to talk to Jeff."

"I think that is a good idea, darlin'. I need to get going now, dear. You pull yourself together and then go take care of your family. Bye for now. And Karen, if you ever need to talk, remember, I'll never be far away."

Karen sat there a while longer, first watching Serena disappear down the pier, slowly working her way back to land and then the gravity of the day's events took hold of her and she dropped her head into her hands. Karen sat there, lost in thought, until finally she realized that it had been more than mere minutes. The sun was receding from overhead and slowly making its way toward the western horizon.

Her thought process was moving at tortoise speed and it took her a moment to realize, *oh crap, Jeff doesn't know where I am. He must be worried out of his mind. I have got to go home. Besides, maybe he can help me figure all this out.*

Karen tried to stand, but found that her legs were reluctant to move, *come on, legs, I don't want to go back there anymore than you do, but we have people waiting for us. NOW, GET UP!*

Karen used her arms to push off the bench and once her body was committed, the rest of her moved along with the decision. She moved back toward the house at a much slower pace than she had left it, but she knew she had to go home. When she reached the gate she just stood there, staring at the house with its dark secret that she had discovered. *How do I go back in there? How can I keep Abigail from discovering what I know? How do I hide my depression from Chrissy? And, Karen, there's no denying it, you are definitely depressed at this point. Why, at this time in my life, when everything seems to be so right, can so much be wrong?... Okay, feet, get moving.*

Karen pushed the gate open and moved up the steps and then walked around the porch to the side kitchen door. Opening this, she stepped into the kitchen. Not seeing anyone she called out, "Yoohoo, anybody home."

Karen heard a squeal of delight from two fronts, Chrissy and Abigail; Chrissy came running into the kitchen from the back parlor, followed closely by Jeff, carrying Clayton. Karen knew that Abigail must be nearby.

"Mommy! Where have you been, for heaven's sake?" Chrissy demanded, hands on her hips, "We have been worried sick!"

Jeff's expression told it all, accusation, worry, concern; they were all there. His eyes almost watery, "Karen, thank God! Where have you been? I didn't know where you had gone. The van was still here and I couldn't imagine... no, let me rephrase that, I was imagining all kinds of things. Practically every possible scenario ran through my head; kidnapping, rape, murder; the kids and I were sitting here feeling very abandoned, we..."

"Whoa, hang on... I'm sorry, there's no excuse, but then again, when I explain it all to you, Jeff, I think you'll understand, but I don't want to do that now. Let me make some dinner, we'll get the kids down for the night and then we can talk. I am very depressed and confused and I need some good advice. "You're still my number one beau, okay?" Karen reached out and touched Jeff gently on his cheek, reached over and kissed Clayton on his little fuzzy head and then bent over and kissed Chrissy on her cheek, "And you're still my number one girl, and Abigail, you're my number two girl, Okay?"

Chrissy smiled and Abigail replied softly, "Yes, Mother."

Karen quickly pulled together a meal of hot dogs, which delighted Chrissy no end. To that she added a can of pork and beans and a tossed salad. When she placed it all on the table, she looked at her gathered clan and stated, "Well, it's not steak tar tar, but I think it will do for tonight."

Chrissy looked at her mother with a curious expression, "What is tar tar, Mommy?"

Karen studied her daughter for a moment and then said, "Steak tar tar is raw beef steak, with very little fat, all ground up, piled up on a dish and then served raw, with a raw egg in the middle."

As Karen described the dish Chrissy's nose began to wrinkle up and as her nose wrinkled more and more, her lip soon joined the ride up her face until it couldn't move any farther up. Finally, Chrissy let out a long, drawn out, "Eeewwww. Mommy, that sounds disgusting."

Karen did everything she could to not laugh, but Jeff just couldn't help himself and started to laugh out loud. Finally he was able to control his laughter and said, "I'm with you, Chrissy. It does sound disgusting, but there are places in the world where people eat that stuff with great relish." As soon as he had said his statement, Jeff knew he had opened another can of worms.

"You mean like pickle relish? Eeewwww."

Karen really didn't feel much like laughing, but this fiasco of words was becoming too much and the smile on her own face was beginning to take on an edge of laughter. Then she heard Abigail laughing off to one side and the reality of the day came crashing down on her. She stepped back from the table and turned her back to the others and then the tears started to flow.

"Karen, what's the matter? Are you crying?" Jeff asked.

Stifling her emotion enough to speak, Karen said, "I'm okay, really. I just need some fresh air. I'm going to step outside on the patio, but I won't go anywhere, I promise. You guys just go ahead and eat, I'm not hungry."

Karen stepped out the back door, taking deep breaths of the heavy, summer air. Jeff stepped out the door after her and grasped her by the shoulders, "Karen, what the heck is going on? You haven't been right for hours. Can't you explain to me what's happened?"

"Jeff," Karen said between sobs, "I found something today, but I cannot go into it now. I want to wait until the kids are in bed. After dinner, once I've got everyone down, and Abigail is in with Clayton, we can come down here and I'll explain everything. I don't want either one of those girls within ear shot, at all!"

Seeing just how emotional Karen was Jeff realized it was something serious so he just backed off and said, "Okay, whatever you say. We'll get the kids upstairs and out of hearing and then I want to hear everything. Okay?"

"Okay," Karen replied, and then lost herself in another sob.

Later that evening, after everyone was fed, bathed, and tucked into bed, Karen went outside to the patio, where she awaited Jeff. Seated in one of the lounge chairs Karen decided it was best to begin all the way back to Agatha's message at Christmas and then bring him up to the grim discovery of today.

Karen was lost in her thoughts when Jeff came out the door, a wine glass in each hand, "Here, I thought you needed this to calm down." Jeff handed one of the glasses to Karen. Jeff lifted the other glass in his hand as he said, "And I think I'll need this to get through whatever it is you have to tell me." Sitting down in another lounger Jeff prompted his wife, "Okay, lay it on me. Tell me all the ugly details."

Karen looked at him, "You have no idea..." and then she told Jeff everything; about the mystery, the wall in the attic, and finally her discovery that afternoon. When she was finished she leaned back into the lounger and just looked dazed, letting out a huge sigh. "Jeff, what do we do now? I mean, I guess we have to call the police."

Jeff had listened without comment, a serious and intense expression on his face; Karen could tell he was deep in thought. Finally, he looked at Karen and said, "I guess that would be the smart thing to do. We'll call them in the morning. I have no idea what they will have to do, so we'll just go with the flow and work it out as need be. Agreed?"

"Agreed."

"And as far as Abigail? We'll just work that one out as we go as well. Agreed?"

"Agreed. But I don't think we should mention Abigail to the police. They'll think we're nuts." Karen thought to herself *I'm not so sure I'm not crazy.*

"I don't want you anymore distressed than you already are and as to Chrissy; the less trauma to her, the better, so Abigail will remain our secret." Jeff looked at his wife, "Do you think you can sleep?"

"I don't know, but I certainly need to try. I've just about cried out my last tear."

"Come on, let's go to bed and start over in the morning." Jeff stood up in front of Karen's chair, held out his hands to her. Once on her feet, they walked hand in hand, into the house to face the new day together.

Chapter 25

"Hello, police department? My name is Jeffrey Miller and I live at 66 Circle Drive. Yesterday... my wife, umm... found a, uhh... couple of, umm... skeletons in our attic." Jeff was having a hard time getting the statement out. He didn't want the operator to get the wrong impression, "I didn't call nine one one because I didn't think it was a real emergency, plus, we think we know who the dead people are."

"Sir, I have your address and I'll send an officer over as soon as possible."

"Uhhh, thank you, I guess."

Jeff hung up the phone and turned to Karen, "Well, now the fun begins. We'll just have to wait and see how it goes from here."

Karen just let out a huge sigh and smiled weakly at her husband.

Not five minutes later there was a knock at their front door. Jeff went to the door and could see an officer standing on the outside. As he opened the door, the officer said, "Hello," and the officer looked at the note pad in his hand, "Mister Miller, I'm Officer Williams of the Defuniak Springs Police Department. You called that you had found a skeleton in your attic. Is that correct, sir?"

"Well, partly. Actually there are two skeletons."

"Can you show me to the attic, sir?"

"Sure, follow me." Jeff moved up the front staircase, Officer Williams following right behind him and Karen just behind him. A parade of solemnity moved up the stairs. Once at the top, Jeff turned to his left and moved down the hall to the attic entrance, "Up there. I'll need to get a ladder to open the stairs."

"I'll wait right here, if you don't mind, sir?"

"No, no problem."

Karen spoke up, "Jeff, I'm going to check on Chrissy and…" Karen almost slipped and mentioned Abigail, "make sure she stays in the playroom and then I'll check on Clayton and I'll meet you back here. I'll need to go up there with you."

Officer Williams looked at Karen, "That won't be necessary, ma'am. Just the one who found them should go up to show me."

"That would be me, Officer. I found the…" Karen just couldn't bring herself to speak openly of what she had found.

Once Jeff returned with the ladder, Karen watched as he brought the folding stairs down. Karen went up first, followed by the officer, and then Jeff. Karen reached over and turned on the attic light.

"It's over here, Officer. I hope you have a flashlight because there is no light in this room." Karen moved over to the wall and indicated the door by the small opening she had left. "You'll have to duck down, the doorway isn't very high. I went in on my hands and knees."

Karen looked over at Jeff and he returned her gaze with a quizzical expression. Karen said to Jeff, "Don't ask?"

The officer pulled a flashlight from his service belt and bent down as he slowly pushed the door open. Then he got down on his hands and knees. Moving the flashlight from side to side, he scanned the room as he entered, moving very slowly, almost with a cautious air.

"Um, Officer?" Karen spoke almost in a whisper, "the bed that they are laying on is just behind the door, and I think once you're inside you'll be able to stand up; I did."

"Thank you, ma'am."

Karen looked at Jeff, "I'm staying out here; I don't need to see that, them… that again. Once was enough."

"That's okay, hon, I'll stay here with you. Frankly, I don't care if I see them or not."

Just then the officer crawled out of the opening in the wall. Once again standing, he reached for the radio on his shoulder and pressed a button, "Station, this is Officer Williams. I'll need a detective at..." he turned to Karen and Jeff, "What's the address here?"

"Sixty six Circle Drive."

"Sixty six Circle Drive," The officer repeated into the radio. After releasing the radio button he then spoke to Karen and Jeff, "I'll be out in my cruiser writing up an initial report and I have to establish a crime scene report and then when the detective arrives we'll need to get back up here. If I could ask you folks to go down to the main floor and wait there I would appreciate it. We need to make sure access to this area is limited. Oh, and I'll need to know the names of everyone who has been in that room?"

"That would be me, Officer. My name is Karen Miller. I'm the only one who has been in there."

"Thank you, Mrs. Miller. Now, if you folks would move downstairs, I'll head down to my cruiser."

"Sure, no problem officer," Jeff answered. "C'mon Karen, let's go down to the kitchen." Jeff moved Karen toward the stairs and then the two men followed behind her.

At the bottom of the stairs, Karen turned to the officer, "Excuse me, but my daughter is playing just down the hall in her playroom. Do we need to move her down into the kitchen with us?"

"No, ma'am, just make sure she stays in there and doesn't find her way up into the attic."

"Oh, I can assure you, she will not go up there. I will make sure of that. I don't want her to see what is in that little room; she's only five."

"I understand ma'am. I'll be downstairs in my cruiser. We'll see you in a few minutes, and I apologize for all the inconvenience."

Karen and Jeff moved to the kitchen, by way of the playroom, to inform Chrissy about staying in there.

"No worry, Mommy. Abigail is beating the tar out of me and I'm trying really hard to beat her. It looks like it's going to be a tough afternoon. Know what I mean?"

Karen just chuckled, "Yeah, sweetie, I know exactly what you mean."

Jeff looked at Karen as they moved toward the back stairs and then he whispered to her as soon as they were down into the stairwell, "Are you sure she's only five; sounds more to me like she's thirty-five?"

Karen just chuckled a little more and then smiled as she looked at her husband, "Yes, I'm sure she's only five."

It was only a few minutes, when Karen and Jeff, sitting in the kitchen, heard the door bell jangle. Karen hadn't even had time to boil water for a cup of tea.

"I'll get it, hon," Jeff said as he rocketed up out of his chair and moved quickly toward the front of the house. Karen was through with the whole mess for now. Emotionally drained, she just sat at the kitchen table waiting for her water to boil. She needed her cup of tea a lot more than she needed to follow the officers up and down the stairs. *If they need to ask me any questions they'll just have to come back here and ask them.* Karen was determined to distance herself from all of this as much as she could. Her nerves needed the break. She had solved the mystery of the house, she was sure. She had had enough. Now it was time for her to relax.

The whistle of the tea kettle pulled her away from her thoughts. Karen moved from the table and poured some of the boiling liquid into a cup and moved back to the table, cup in hand. She settled herself, looking forward to that first hot sip of tea; Typhoo, her favorite. A rich, dark British tea she had discovered several years back.

Karen was holding the cup next to her mouth, waiting for the tea to cool enough, inhaling the aroma from the amber liquid, when Jeff walked through the kitchen door from the dining room. His expression told her she would not like what he was going to say.

Karen set the cup down, looked at Jeff and then asked, "What is it? You look distressed. What did they find?"

"It's not what they found; it's what they have asked of us."

"What, for heavens sake?"

"Well…" Jeff let out a big sigh as he lowered himself into a chair, "they are calling in the FDLE, the Florida Department of Law Enforcement. They are setting up a crime scene and sealing off the house."

Karen just looked at Jeff until she realized what Jeff had just said, "Sealing off the house? Does that mean what I think that means?"

"Yup!" Jeff waited a moment before he continued. "The FDLE has the forensic team. They will come in, collect evidence, and then send it off for analysis. But, we have to stay out of the house, the entire house, to prevent contamination of the crime scene."

"What crime scene? There is no crime. Jeff, for crying out loud, the letter says it all. There is no crime, these people curled up and died. They were heart sick; is that a crime." Karen's voice was gaining volume as she spoke until finally she was practically yelling.

Jeff put his index finger to his lips, let out a shushing sound, and pointed to the ceiling trying to get Karen to lower her voice.

Karen lowered her voice immediately, "How long is this going to take?" she asked impatiently.

"Officer Williams and Detective Howard said that the forensic team would be here by this afternoon. They will remove the bodies, I mean skeletons, and the whole thing should be over with by late tomorrow; only about twenty four hours in all, so here's what we're going to do. We'll take the kids and any pertinent beds, playpens, etc. and take them out to my office. We'll go out for dinner tonight. Pizza, I'm sure, if

Chrissy has anything to say about it, and then we'll just tough it out until they leave tomorrow. Thank god my office is equipped like a small apartment, bathroom, shower, and all. It won't be so bad. We'll live through it and I'll bet Chrissy will think it's some kind of adventure."

"Jeff! What about Abigail? I don't want them spooking her, no pun intended, and I don't want her going up into the attic, at least not for now. And, heaven forbid, one of them might see her."

"For crying out loud, Karen, WE can't even see her!" As soon as the words were spoken he was sorry. "I'm sorry, hon, that was uncalled for." Taking a deep breath he continued, "When we go in to collect the kids you can give Abigail special instructions, okay?"

"Okay," Karen answered like a small child. This was becoming too much for her; one crisis after another. *When will all this end?* She thought to herself. Karen let out a very tired sigh as she cradled her head in hands, her elbows supporting it all on the table. She was tired. All she really wanted was to be a good wife and mother. She had a great husband, two, no, really three, beautiful kids, heck, she even had a surrogate mom now. If it weren't for all the drama, life would be perfect. *Well, maybe, when this part of the picture is through, things will quiet a bit and we can get down to a normal life.* Even her thoughts were tired.

"Can we get the things we need now?" Karen asked.

"Yeah, as a matter of fact Officer Williams suggested we go ahead and get the things we need, collect the kids and vacate the house. He will stay on duty upstairs until the FDLE team arrives."

"Okay. I'll go up and get some things for Chrissy and collect her if you'll go get Clayton's playpen, carrier, and anything else we'll need. We'll get the kids after everything is set up for them in the office."

"That's fine. I'll handle the boy's side of things if you'll handle the girl's" Jeff smiled at his wife, trying to lighten her spirit a little. She returned his smile with her own, only hers was a little more forlorn.

Karen moved up the back staircase, passing the two girls at their game. She moved into Chrissy's bedroom to retrieve her pajamas and some extra clothes. Then she went into her own room, passing Officer Williams along the way, smiling weakly as she passed. She felt like an intruder, in her own home yet. *Boy, would she be glad when this was all over with!* Karen thought as she passed the officer. She went into the master bath and retrieved some underclothes for her and Jeff and then some clothes for the next day.

Heading down the front stairs, she passed Jeff in the midst of his chores, "I've got clothes for us," she said in passing. "I'm heading down to the office and then I'll come back in for Chrissy. When you're done will you get Clayton, and don't forget extra diapers and, let me think…"

"Karen, I've got my end covered; already got the diapers and all of his necessary equipment, including his high chair. I even got extra formula. I'm on my way to get him now. I'll meet you in the office."

"Okay," Karen answered.

Heading back up the back stairs Karen went through her mind of what she was going to say to Abigail. Once she was in the playroom, she said, "Chrissy, honey, we're going to spend the rest of today out in Daddy's office, even sleeping there tonight. I need you to gather up anything you want to take out there with you."

Chrissy looked at her mother with a shocked expression, "Why are we going out there?" She demanded.

Karen looked at her daughter, "There are going to be a lot of people in the house tonight, and… we need to be out of their way, so they've asked us to leave the house."

Chrissy looked at her mother, at first like she was crazy, and then a look of defiance came over her face, "Well, that is just crazy! I'm not leaving!"

"Excuse me?" Karen replied.

"I'm not leaving! I can't leave, even for one day!"

"Chrissy?"

"Mommy, I am not leaving Abigail here, all by herself, with a house full of strangers. I don't want her to be alone. And she certainly can't come out there with us."

"It will be all right, Chrissy. I'll be fine," Karen heard Abigail answer.

"No! I'm not going!" Chrissy crossed her arms on her chest and then took on a rebellious stance.

Karen looked at her diminutive daughter, "Well, I'm sorry young lady, but you don't have a choice! I want you to go down the stairs and out to the office, right now! I'm going to speak with Abigail for a moment. Now go. If there is something you want, I'll get it for you."

By now, Chrissy's defiance had melted into tears, "But Mommy, I don't want to leave Abigail alone. I don't want her to be alone." The tears were flowing freely and Chrissy was dissolving into a tantrum, stamping her foot with each word.

Karen had never seen Chrissy like this. It was totally out of character for her and, right now, she was not in a mood to handle it, "Chrissy, go down stairs, now, or I will get Daddy to come get you, physically. NOW!" Karen pointed to the stairs.

Chrissy stood there defiantly, for just a moment. Then she turned and stomped to the top of the stairs. She turned to look back at her mother, her expression a pleading one.

Karen returned her gaze with, "Remember, take the stairs slow; one at a time."

Chrissy let out a huge sigh, dropped her arms to her sides, dropped her gaze to the stairs, and as she took the first step down another huge tear rolled down her cheek.

Now, Karen turned her attention to Abigail, "Listen, Abigail, while these people are in the house, there will be a lot of activity. These people will be coming and going, in and out of the house. What I need from you is to stay in one room, whichever one you pick, and just stay there. Can you do that?"

"Yes, Mother."

"Good. Now, which room will you be in, just so I know?"

"I'll stay here in the playroom. That way I can watch out the window at the office door. Would that be all right?"

"That will be fine, dear. I will make sure that the people use the front stairs and you won't be disturbed. Now, it is very important that you stay in this room, just in case any of those people can... see or hear you. Do you understand what I mean?"

"Yes, Mother. I am a ghost and they would wonder about me... I wouldn't want to scare anyone."

"Yes, I think you do understand," Karen smiled softly at just how smart and intuitive her little spectral daughter was. "If I could I would hug you, you are so smart."

Karen heard Abigail whisper, "I love you, Mother."

"I love you, too, Abigail." A small tear made its way down Karen's cheek. "Okay. I need to get downstairs and out to the office. Chrissy will be back to play tomorrow, probably in the afternoon. Remember, just stay here in the playroom. I'll close the door so that the people will know to stay out, okay?"

"Okay, Mother. I'll be good, I promise, and I won't go out into the rest of the house."

"Bye bye, sweetie, I know you'll be fine."

Karen closed the playroom door and then moved back to the stairwell. When she got out to the office Chrissy was sitting on the floor, with her daddy, playing with Clayton, all of her defiance had dissolved. She was smiling and laughing as Clayton threw another soft and squishy block at her.

Jeff looked up at her as she entered and then said, "I told Chrissy we were going out for dinner. Remember what I said about pizza?"

Karen just chuckled, "Yeah, I remember."

The rest of the day went like a breeze, especially after she explained to Chrissy that Abigail was going to stay in the playroom, that she had shut the door, and that Karen had told Officer Williams to instruct the others to use the front stairs.

And, that Chrissy could look out and see Abigail in the playroom windows because she would be watching.

With that last statement Chrissy ran to the door and opened it, waving up at the window. When she turned, she looked at her mother, a huge smile on her face.

"Is she there?" Karen asked.

Chrissy nodded her head rapidly, her smile widening, "Uh huh."

"See, everything will be fine."

Chrissy closed the door and walked over to her mother, wrapping her arms around her mother's neck, "Love you, Mommy," she whispered to her mother.

"Love you too, sweetie."

With that hug, Karen knew that everything would be just fine.

The next day Detective Howard came to the office door to let Jeff and Karen know that they could go back into the house. The officers from the forensic team had finished with their evidence collection and the crime scene was now open. Jeff and Karen stepped outside to speak with the detective, closing the door behind them.

"What will happen with the …" Karen looked to see if Chrissy was listening, "bones?"

"The remains will be taken to the lab in Tallahassee, where they will be identified. After that they will be turned over to whoever claims them. The identification could take as long as six months, especially because of the lack of any identifying tissue."

"But what about the letter?"

"Well, that will obviously hold some sway. If no other evidence shows contamination of the scene at an earlier time, the letter will definitely help."

"Thank you, Detective," Karen said.

"I apologize for the inconvenience, but it was necessary for us to do our jobs. You folks have a nice day." The detective tipped his head and then left.

Karen looked at Jeff, let out a sigh and then said, "Boy, am I glad that is all over. Let's get the kids and all the stuff moved back." Karen opened the door to the office, "Chrissy, you can go back into the house now. Be careful on the stairs, please."

Chrissy let out a whoop and took off running for the house.

"Slow, please," Karen called out after her, "those stairs are just as bad going up as coming down." Karen knew exactly where Chrissy was going.

Jeff and Karen smiled at each other and went about gathering up the toys, playpen and all of the other equipment. Clayton was in his playpen, laughing and bouncing, happy as usual.

Chapter 26

Several days later, after the furor of Karen's find had calmed down, and the reporters had departed, the Miller household could finally relax. Jeff and Karen had spent two days trying to dodge the real reason for all of the intruders in their life to Chrissy. But when the questions came they fibbed to her that her daddy had discovered some bad people doing some bad things on the internet. Luckily, she was easily distracted by Abigail.

Abigail. Oh my God, what about Abigail? Karen thought. *I promised her I would help her get home to be with her mother and father.* Karen's nerves were beginning to unravel. Her peace and privacy had been so fragmented by all that had come about in the last few days; she just didn't know how much more she could handle. The gravity of it all was just too much.

Sitting at the kitchen table one morning with a cup of tea, brooding about the dilemma of Abigail, she was staring out the window, lost in thought, when she felt a presence. Turning, she saw Serena standing near the wall, next to the staircase opening.

"Serena, oh boy, am I glad to see you. I see you so seldom anymore and there has been so much going on..."

"I know darlin'. That's why I'm here. I knew you were beginnin' to stress over Abigail again, so I came to see what I could do to help."

Karen smiled a weak, but loving smile, "Serena, just knowing you're near gives me the strength I need."

"So, what's troublin' you darlin'?"

"It's Abigail. I promised her weeks... no, months ago, that I would help her cross over so that she could be with her mother and father... and I don't know how." Karen was beginning to crumble. Tears were forming in her eyes and her hands, holding the cup, were beginning to tremble. The amber liquid in the cup developed ripples that soon resembled title waves.

Serena had taken a chair next to Karen's and now reached out and touched her hand to steady Karen's. "You know what, darlin'? Just like I've told you before, let things happen in their own time. This, like all other problems, will work itself out. Abigail will be reunited with her parents when the time is right. And for now, you need to relax and take care of yourself and your family."

"I know Serena, but every time I hear that sweet little voice, it breaks my heart. She sounds so lost; so frail. I know she has been here for almost a hundred years, and she's managed just fine on her own..., but I've made promises to her..." Karen was beginning to choke up, the words not making their way to vocalization, and the tears were beginning to flow, "promises I don't want to break... and I don't know that I can keep."

Serena looked lovingly at Karen, "You know what, darlin'? I don't think Abigail will hold it against you if she has to be content with you and Jeff as her mother and father, and I know that she is completely satisfied with Chrissy and Clayton as her siblin's. So, why don't you just relax, go with the flow, as they say, and just let one day move into the next. I am confident that, before too long, all of her problems will be solved."

Karen listened to Serena carefully, mulled over what she had said, and then answered, "You're right, Serena. I am making another mountain out of a little mole hill again." Looking at Serena directly, Karen continued, "I will do my very best to just let things happen as they will, on one condition."

"And what is that, darlin'?"

"That I can count on you to be here when I really need you; I know you will be, and it's silly of me to think otherwise, but right now, I just need the reassurance that you will cover my back, so to speak."

"Darlin', you have my word. I will be here, for you, no matter what happens. You can count on me; I will not let you down. But keep in mind, darlin', you still have Jeff."

"I know, Serena. I know that Jeff is there for me, but sometimes I still doubt his commitment to Abigail and this whole ghost thing, crossing over, you know?"

"I know, dear, but you must remember, no matter what happens, that Jeff has your, and the children's, best interests at heart. He loves you very much, and he thinks the sun rises and sets on those two children."

"That's the problem, Serena, the two children. I wish I could count on him to be as committed to Abigail's welfare as he is to Chrissy and Clayton."

Serena patted Karen's hand again as she said, "Don't you worry about a thing, darlin'. In the end, when all of this is over and done, you will see just how strong Jeff's commitment to you and all three of the children really is. You just wait and see." Serena patted Karen's hand once more. "Well, I've got to be goin' now, darlin'. I've just about used up my time. Now, remember what I said, I will be here when you need me, and that promise comes straight from the heart."

"Thank you, Serena." Karen watched as Serena moved toward the back door to leave, "Good bye, Serena, I'll talk to you soon."

"Good bye, darlin'. You take care of that family of yours, don't get too stressed out with what life throws your way and I'll be back soon. Take care, darlin'." Serena disappeared out the back door and was gone.

Not thirty seconds later Jeff came in, through the door, from his office.

"Did you see Serena?" Karen asked him.

"No, I didn't see her."

"Well, you must have just missed her, like two ships passing in the night, only it's daytime. She was just here. I was feeling a little down, but she helped a lot; she really cheered me up."

Jeff looked at Karen for a moment, deciding whether to say something or not, and then decided on the latter. Instead, keeping his mouth shut, until later.

Later that evening, after the kids were all tucked neatly in to bed, Jeff suggested they just relax in the back parlor with a glass of wine and talk. Karen thought it was a great idea. Jeff sent her off to put some soft music on the stereo, she preferred Chopin, while he went after the wine.

Returning to the back parlor with two glasses of wine, white for her, red for him, Jeff found Karen snuggled up on the big couch, her eyes closed, listening to the music. Chopin's Waltz in C Sharp Minor was playing. Karen played this piece so Jeff was particularly familiar with it, and Karen was lost in the music; her head moving as if she were sitting at the piano, playing. Jeff made it to the couch and she was still unaware of his presence. Holding her glass of wine out to her he cleared his throat, interrupting her musical mood.

She reached for the glass, "Wow, I didn't even hear you come in; thanks, babe."

Karen accepted the glass.

Jeff sat down next to Karen, drew his feet up under him as he placed his arm around her shoulders, pulling her close to him. "You were really lost in the music, hon. You feeling okay?"

"Yes; it's just been so long since I could play, with all the drama going on in this house. I really miss it. It's very relaxing, you know."

"I've watched you play. If you call that relaxing…"

"Well, I do. I may be intense when I play, but most musicians play… because they like it… and because it relaxes them."

"If you say so," Jeff countered, speaking with skepticism.

They sat there quietly listening as the Chopin CD played on, going through a repertoire of pieces, some sullen and moody, others light and sprightly. Chopin was definitely a composer for all.

Not wanting to break the peaceful mood, but needing some answers, he finally spoke, "Karen? This afternoon, when you mentioned Serena, you said that you were feeling down. Is everything okay with you? I mean, you're not becoming depressed are you. I mean... if you need help... we could see a doctor..."

"Jeff, I'm not depressed, for heaven's sake. I said I was feeling a little down, that's all."

"Can you... or will you... tell me what you're feeling down about?"

Oh, boy, now the moment of truth, Karen thought, *if I spill it all he'll get mad and think I'm nuts, worrying about a ghost, but if I can't tell Jeff, then what good is our relationship? Okay, so tell him.*

"Jeff, a few months ago..." Karen took a breath, "I made a promise to Abigail," Karen felt Jeff let out a huge sigh, but he didn't say a word, "a promise I don't know if I can keep, and it's tearing me apart." Karen rushed the last of her statement, almost running the words together. "That's what I'm feeling down about."

Slowly thinking over what Karen said, Jeff took the next moments very slowly and gently, "Okay, let me see if I can help, but first I need to know what you promised her."

Now, it was Karen's turn to sigh, "Well... I promised her that I would find a way to help her cross over to reunite with her mother and father. That was before I found their skeletons in the attic and before I read the letter. Since then, knowing all the facts that I do, the weight of the promise has just been pressing more and more on me."

Jeff kept silent, allowing Karen to vent all of her frustrations.

Karen continued, "I just don't know how!" Karen's frustration was beginning to show as her words became more adamant, "Serena said to just let things happen in their own time; that it all would resolve itself."

"Sounds like pretty good advice to me."

"I know, I know! But… it is just so frustrating. I want to help the poor child… and I can't!"

"Okay, okay, calm down; I don't want you upset anymore and I certainly don't want you having a nervous breakdown." Jeff thought for a moment, "Have you talked to Abigail about this, that is, about your promise. Maybe it's not that important to her. Good grief, she has Chrissy and Clayton, she has you… and she has me. That's more family than she had to start with."

Karen sat up with a start, "Really?"

Jeff was lost, "Really what?"

"What you said."

Now Jeff was really lost, "What did I say?"

Karen let out a sigh of exasperation, "That she has you."

"Well, of course. I am her surrogate father, am I not?"

Karen couldn't speak; she just smiled at Jeff, all the love she felt for him welling up in her throat. Her eyes began to sparkle from the flooding tears. All of her doubts had been swept away; all her fears gone, with just a few words. "Have I told you lately how much I love you?"

"No, but I'm willing to listen." Jeff smiled softly at her.

"I love you this much," and Karen spread her arms as wide as they would go.

"Hey, that's my line," Jeff smiled at her.

Karen just smiled back. Then Jeff reached out, taking her in his arms, hugging her tightly.

Chapter 27

The next few days were uneventful. Karen was trying to figure a way to bring up the subject of her promise with Abigail. In the afternoon, Karen went upstairs to check on Clayton, to see if he had awakened from his nap. She stepped in through the door of his room only to find him, toes in the air, playing quietly in his crib. "You are such a good boy," she said softly to him. Since he was born, Karen was so proud, and thankful, that he was such a happy baby. He never really fussed. It seemed she had been blessed with two really happy children.

"I've been watching over him, Mother. We have been playing. He is such a good baby." Abigail said, her voice tender and loving.

"Oh, hi Abigail. I thought you were in playing with Chrissy."

"She got sleepy so she went in to take a nap, so I came in to watch over Clayton. He is such a sweet baby. I like just sitting here watching him sleep."

"I know, Abigail. Thank you for being such a good big sister to him."

Abigail was silent for a moment, "I love my family, Mother, all of you."

"I know sweetie, we love you too. Abigail, do you remember what I promised you a few months back?"

There was silence in return to Karen's question.

"You know, about reuniting with your real mother and father?"

"Oh, yes, mother, I remember. You said you would try to help me get over to them."

"Yes, that's correct. But I have a problem."

Karen's comment was met with silence.

"Abigail, I don't know how?" Karen was starting to get upset and her voice was developing an emotional quaver. "Short of someone dying, and heaven forbid that happening, to escort you over, I don't know how we can get the light to reappear for you."

"That is all right mother. Please don't cry. I don't want anyone to die because of me."

"Abigail, I made you a promise and I don't want to fail on that promise, but I just don't…"

Karen felt a slight pressure on her lips as if someone had pressed their finger to them, and then she heard a whispered, "Shhh."

Karen was silent, potential sobs silenced for the moment.

"Mother, please don't worry. I have not thought about the promise since then. Please, I am happy here. I have Chrissy and Clayton, and I have you and father. That is more family than I had before."

Karen smiled and said in just above a whisper, "That's what Jeff said."

"I'm happy if you are happy."

"Abigail, I do have one concern."

"What is that, Mother?"

"As Chrissy grows, she will grow older than you and her interests will change."

"I'll still have Clayton."

"Yes, but even he will eventually grow up. I'm worried about you, sweetheart. I don't want you forgotten."

"Will you forget me, Mother?"

"Of course not, Abigail."

"Then I will be happy, just to be here with you and father."

Karen was silent for a moment, and then she said, "You are such a sweet, lovely little girl... and I'm proud to be your mother."

Karen couldn't see Abigail, but she could almost bet she was smiling.

Chapter 28

Several days later, after breakfast was through and everyone had dispersed throughout the house; the girls in the playroom, Jeff in his office, and Clayton in his playpen, Karen happened to look at the calendar hanging on the wall. She homed in on the day's date and then had a startling moment. It was August twelfth. She turned and rushed up the stairs.

When she reached the top she turned to see Chrissy sitting on the floor, in her usual spot, playing a board game with Abigail.

"Chrissy, I just realized something very important."

Chrissy turned to look at her mother, smiling at first and then her expression took on a look of concern, "What's that, Mommy?"

"School starts in two days and you get to start kindergarten this year." Karen smiled at Chrissy, her own excitement showing in her smile. "I thought maybe we would go buy you some new clothes to start school with."

Chrissy looked back at the board game, "That's okay. I'm not going to school."

"What do you mean, you're not going?"

"I'm not going. I don't want to go to school."

"Chrissy, you don't have a choice; you have to go to school."

"No I don't."

"Yes, you do!"

"Mommy, I already know my numbers and my letters, remember, I play Scrabble Junior, and, I can write my own name."

266

"Chrissy, you have to go to school!"

"Well, I'm not going!"

"For heaven's sake, why not? I thought you would be excited about starting school."

Chrissy turned to her mother, placing her hands on her hips, "Mommy! I don't want to leave Abigail."

Karen was starting to get exasperated, "Chrissy, Abigail will be just fine for a few hours, besides, she won't be alone, I'll be here and so will Clayton and Daddy."

Abigail, having remained silent until now, spoke up, "Chrissy, you must go to school. You are very smart and it will help you get even smarter. I went to school until…"

Chrissy turned back to look across the board at where Abigail sat and then turned quickly back to look at her mother with an a-hah expression on her face "I know, you can teach me here."

"You mean home school? Here? Me?"

"Yeah mommy, and then Abigail can go to school with me, right here."

Karen stood there not saying a word, just looking at her daughter, "I'll have to talk to your father about it… and I'll have to call the school system about it. So don't get your heart set on it. You may still have to go to school anyway."

"Okay." Chrissy's attitude had perked up considerably.

Karen started to turn away and then she turned back to Chrissy, "Where did you learn about home schooling, anyway?"

Chrissy shrugged her shoulders in an 'I don't know attitude.'

Later, when Jeff and Karen were alone, Karen told Jeff of her conversation with Chrissy. Once she was finished she was not happy with Jeff's reaction. He just laughed.

"What are you laughing at? What is funny about this?"

"It's not that I think it is funny; I'm just amazed at her reaction. The idea that our little girl would think of home schooling; I'm just amazed that she would do that," Jeff laughed again.

"Well, I don't think this is a laughing matter, Jeff. She has to get over this idea that she can't or won't leave the house because of Abigail. Our lives have to remain normal despite Abigail's presence." Karen was silent for a few moments, thinking of the alternatives facing her. *Either she could go along with the home schooling, giving Abigail the benefit of more learning. And on that side of the argument, Abigail could act as a good learning partner, but on the bad side, Chrissy would lose out on the social side of going to school; learning to get along with other children her own age. Or, she could have an enduring fight with Chrissy over going to school. Jeez, she would never have thought that Chrissy would not want to go to school. What was she to do?*

Karen let out a huge sigh. She was tired of all the drama. She just wanted things to go along quietly and without turmoil. She wanted her perfect life back!

"Okay, here's what we are going to do. And I say we because you are going to help with this. I will call the school board tomorrow and find out what I have to do to home school Chrissy. We will try this for one school period, what ever that is; six weeks, nine weeks, twelve weeks, whatever. If we are not happy with her learning by that time, then, like it or not, she will start public school; no arguments, agreed?"

"Hey, I'm with you, all the way, and I will help with her lessons whenever you want, no questions asked. Okay, Hon?"

"Okay," Karen responded in an unenthusiastic sigh.

"Karen, why don't we give it until Christmas? That way we will give her at least four months. We know she's smart and with Abigail helping…"

"Okay, Christmas it is," Karen agreed, letting out another heavy sigh.

Chapter 29

August slipped into September and the home schooling was going pretty well. Because, at the age of five, there was no real need for them to follow school district protocol, Karen and Jeff fixed up an area of the mezzanine as a school room, complete with a dry erase board and little antique school desks they had found at an antique store. Chrissy was responding well to the home schooling, taking her learning very seriously. Abigail helped, keeping Chrissy paying attention each time she wanted to go play. Although Abigail was several years older than Chrissy when she died, Karen found her to be very much more advanced than modern children her age. So, in many ways, Karen's teaching helped little in advancing Abigail's knowledge. But that was okay with Abigail, she just liked helping Chrissy. So one day, in class, Karen proclaimed Abigail her official teaching assistant.

Karen kept the two girls in class from ten in the morning until noon and then from two until three in the afternoon, Monday through Friday. These were Clayton's nap times so it afforded Karen the time to put to the girls usually undisturbed. Karen tried to maintain as much normalcy as possible so that in the event Chrissy did end up in public school it would not be difficult for her to fit in.

Karen was actually enjoying the time with both girls and so she let Jeff substitute only once in a while, and that was okay with Jeff. He much preferred to be in his office at his computer. In the evening, after the kids were in bed, Jeff and Karen would sit in the back parlor and discuss the day's events, most of which was the girl's schooling.

One evening, in late September, as they sat on the couch, the kids safely tucked in bed, Karen spoke softly to Jeff, "Can you believe it has been almost a year since we moved in?"

"Yeah, I know. It seems like just yesterday. And... in less than a month our little man will be one year old. Boy, I feel old."

Karen chuckled and then she smiled, "Well old man, I'm about ready for bed, how about you?"

"Sure... if I can get these old bones to move. I think next time I want the lawn mown and the weeds pulled I'll just hire it out. I am just beat." Jeff groaned as he moved to stand.

"Wow, you're all of thirty-two. How are those old bones gonna be when your sixty-two?"

"If today is any indication, immovable."

Karen chuckled a little louder. Standing in front of Jeff, she reached out her hand to pull him to his feet. "Come on old man, let's go climb Mount Everest to the next floor and get ready for bed."

The next morning Karen was up bright and early, first to prepare breakfast and then to get ready for school. Although Chrissy was not necessarily a morning person, she had been getting up earlier. Each morning when she came down for breakfast, she was bright and alert, ready to meet the next day of school with enthusiasm. Today was no exception. Karen was in the kitchen, at the stove, when she heard, from the stairwell, "Mommy?"

"Yes, Chrissy, come on down."

Karen listened for the sound of her tiny feet on the stairs, counting each one as she came down. Karen knew exactly how many steps there were so she knew when to move to the doorway, "Good morning sunshine. How are you this morning?" Karen reached out her arms as Chrissy stepped down from the last step, giving her a big hug.

"Good morning, Mommy," Chrissy answered, a big, bright smile on her face.

"Wow," Karen exclaimed when she looked at Chrissy. She was already dressed for the day in the clothes Karen had bought for her for school. Chrissy's smile broadened with pride.

"How about some breakfast to get those brain cells ready for incoming knowledge?" Karen asked.

Chrissy nodded her head as she climbed up on the breakfast stool.

Karen moved back to the stove, "Chrissy, do you know what is coming in just a couple of weeks?"

"Ummmh, Halloween? I want to be a Barbie Princess."

"Okay, we'll see what we can do, but that is over a month away, so we can discuss what costume you'll wear later. What I was asking about comes sooner than Halloween. It's Clayton's birthday,"

Chrissy squealed and then clapped her hands, "Oh boy, another birthday party, yay."

Karen heard another squeal from off to one side, "Good morning, Abigail," she said.

"Good morning, Mother"

"What are we going to get Clayton for his birthday?" Chrissy asked.

Karen responded with, "I don't know, Daddy and I haven't discussed it yet, but I thought you and Abigail might want to get him something by yourselves."

"Mommy, Abigail can't go to the store."

"I know, Chrissy, but I thought you and I could go shopping together, you could pick out some items to tell Abigail about and then the two of you could make a decision together. That's what we did for you for your birthday and it worked out well. What do you think?"

Chrissy looked over to where Abigail's voice had come from and then Karen heard, "Chrissy, it really is a good idea. That is how I picked out your necklace. Once we have decided what gift we want you can go back to the store to purchase it."

While Abigail spoke Chrissy's head bobbled up and down in agreement and then she said, "Yeah, that's what we'll do."

Abigail responded with, "After breakfast, before school, we'll go up stairs and discuss some ideas, so when you go to the store you'll have some idea of what to look for. How does that sound?"

"As Tony, the Tiger, would say, Grrreat!" Chrissy nodded her head in one firm movement as she said grrreat to emphasize the word.

Karen heard Abigail laugh and she laughed as well. Just as Chrissy said her emphatic statement, they, all three, heard a noise at the stairwell and turned to see Jeff clomp down the last step into the kitchen, Clayton in his arms, bright eyed and bushy tailed as usual.

"Daddy!" Chrissy yelled.

Jeff looked at his three girls, assuming Abigail was there, "Good morning, ladies," he groaned, "The men have arrived." He walked over to the highchair and placed Clayton down and fastened the tray. Then he moved over and sat down at his stool, groaned slightly, put his elbows on the counter and then dropped his head into his hands.

"Are you okay, Hon?" Karen asked with concern. Jeff seemed to be dragging a little bit more than usual.

"Yeah, I'm okay, I just didn't sleep well; had another one of those nightmares. I woke up suddenly, terrified, and then I couldn't go back to sleep; afraid to, I guess. Can't remember a dang thing about it either, that's what's so frustrating. If I could remember the nightmare, maybe I could figure out what it means, if anything."

"Wow, I'm so sorry, Hon, why didn't you wake me?"

"What good would that have done?"

"Well… at least I could have kept you company," Karen commiserated with Jeff.

"That's okay, Babe. One of us has to be awake today. Sooo, what's happening today, beside school?"

After listening to her daddy with a sympathetic, saddened expression, Chrissy spoke up excitedly, "Clayton's birthday is coming soon and Abigail and I are going to pick out a gift for Clayton just like she and Mommy did for my birthday, and then I'll go back to the store and buy it." All of that was said in one breath.

Jeff looked at his daughter and a big smile spread across his face, "Wow, all that and more," and then he broke out in laughter, "Girl, you are going to have to learn to come up for air once in a while."

Chrissy looked at her daddy, dropped her head slightly and hunched her shoulders in embarrassment. Feeling badly that he had embarrassed Chrissy, Jeff bent down to look at her and could see a smile on her face. Then he reached over and chucked her lightly under the chin as he said, "That's okay, Chrissy, I know you are excited about Clayton's birthday. Can you believe he will be one year old? You better hurry up or he's gonna catch up with you. Oh, wait a minute. He can't catch up with you... you're actually thirty-five, not five. What was I thinking?"

Chrissy reached out and lightly swatted her daddy's arm, smiling the whole time, "Daddy, I'm not thirty-five, I'm only five, see," Chrissy held up her right hand, fingers spread, and then she counted out, "One, two, three, four, five," as she pointed out each digit.

"Oh, my goodness, the kid can count." Jeff smiled broadly at Karen, knowing he and his daughter were playing their favorite game.

Chrissy swatted Jeff's arm again, "Daddy, I've been going to school, remember?"

Karen looked lovingly at the two of them, a smile on her face, as they bantered with each other. She especially loved these times when father and daughter could lovingly tease each other, no hurt feelings, just plenty of love. This was what she so longed for; just normal days, no drama, other than the normal drama that comes with kids. With this, her life truly felt perfect.

After breakfast, Chrissy and Abigail departed to the playroom to discuss Clayton's birthday gift.

Karen and Jeff remained in the kitchen, drinking coffee and discussing various things, "Jeff, I want to have a party for Clayton. Do you mind?"

"Heck no, Babe, I figured we would. How much do you want to do, he won't really know what's going on anyway?"

"Well, this is his first. I want to give him a big one, well, that is, about the same as Chrissy's. You know, cake, ice cream, party favors, decorations. I'll invite Serena..."

"Have you spoken with Serena lately?"

'No, not for some weeks, not since I discovered the... bones. I've called her home several times, but all I got was her answering machine. I've left messages, but she hasn't returned my calls. To be honest, Jeff, I'm a little worried."

"Do you think she went out of town?"

"I don't know."

"Why don't you call Agatha?"

"I don't have her number. Serena always took care of contacting her and I've looked in the phone book, but her number isn't listed."

"Do you have any other way to get hold of Serena, any other phone numbers?"

"No, and that's what bothers me. Serena didn't have a cell phone. I've driven by her place, but there was no sign of anyone home. I don't know if she had friends that she would have gone out of town to visit. I don't think she had any relatives, at least not anyone directly related to her. She might have had a few distant cousins by marriage, but she told me once she didn't have anyone close. When she gave me the necklace at Christmas, she said she wanted me to have it because she didn't have anyone else she wanted to give it to.

"Jeff... I just don't know what to think. When I last saw her I was so upset, I really didn't pay much attention. She was there, on the pier, when I needed her, and she said she would be around. No, wait a minute, I saw her one more time, right here in the kitchen, a few days after the… find. I was really upset about something, and she was there again to comfort me. Jeff, she told me that she would have my back; that she would be there when I needed her, but it's been almost a month. I just don't know what to think."

"You know what, Hon? You need to just relax and don't get yourself worked up about this. Serena is just out of town, gallivanting around somewhere, and when she needs to be here, she will be. She's just that kind of gal. So don't go off, thinking the worst. I hate to see you get all worked up. If something has happened I'm sure someone will let you know. So, with that said, let's talk about the party." Jeff smiled once more at his wife.

One week later on a Saturday, with no school, Karen went up to the playroom after breakfast. Chrissy and Abigail were hard at work trying to beat each other at Chinese Checkers. "Chrissy, would you like to go to Wal-Mart and look for some gift ideas for Clayton? I need to go order his cake and balloons."

Chrissy looked over to Abigail and then turned her glance back to her mother, "Yes, today would be good. Abigail and I have some ideas and I want to check them out."

"Okay, I'm going to change my clothes, take Clayton down to the office and then I'll come back to get you. Get your clothes changed and I'll be back in a few minutes." Karen changed the direction of her gaze to the opposite side of the game board, "I'm sorry to interrupt your game, Abigail. I hope you don't mind if I steal your fierce opponent for a couple of hours."

"Oh no, Mother, that is quite all right. Chrissy and I have been looking forward to this for a week. I will wait here until you get back." Karen could hear the excitement in Abigail's voice and she knew that this was as much fun for her as it was for Chrissy.

Once they parked and entered the store Karen could tell that Chrissy was all business. At the entrance Karen took a buggy and looked down at her daughter, "Okay, what will it be, riding or walking?"

Chrissy stood there for just a moment quietly contemplating her choices, her Barbie purse hanging from her bent arm, "Ummm, walking!"

"Walking, it is. Now where do you need to go?"

Chrissy opened her purse and pulled out a folded paper. She snapped back the latch on her purse and then proceeded to unfold the paper and then study it very intently, "Let's see, I need to go to the toy department, the baby department and the department where they sell movies." Chrissy looked up at her mother with a big smile.

Karen was looking at her diminutive daughter, total surprise and wonder in her expression, "Chrissy, did you just read that... I mean, do you have all that written down there?"

"Well, kind of."

"May I see your notes?"

Chrissy nodded her head in agreement

Karen took the note in her hand, not knowing what to expect. She knew that Chrissy was precocious and could be very advanced for her age. She also knew that at times, and in certain circumstances, Chrissy was every bit the five year old. So when she looked at the paper in her hand, a huge smile broke out on her face. Chrissy's notes were in symbols, not letters. There was a drawing of a toy block; below it a baby bottle, and below that a drawing of Mickey Mouse. Karen's smile broadened as she realized just how smart her daughter was.

"Okay, I'll tell you what. I have to go to the bakery to order the cake, and the floral area to order the balloons. Let's do those two things first and then we'll wander the other areas you need. Then, when you have explored all the possibilities, we'll get the groceries we need. Okay?" With that said, Karen handed the note back to Chrissy.

Chrissy nodded her head in agreement as she snapped her purse open and then replaced the note inside.

Pushing the cart forward, Karen looked down at her little girl and with a smile said, "Let's go shop!"

Several hours later they returned home with a number of bags. When Karen popped her head inside the office door she smiled at Jeff and said, "We're home. I'm going inside to unload the groceries. You want me to take Clayton?"

"No, he's fine. We've been discussing the issues of the day, the latest football scores. You know, man stuff."

Karen looked over at Clayton sitting upright in his playpen, a broad smile showing all six of his pearly white teeth.

"All righty then, I'll see you guys later, at lunch." She closed the door and headed into the house. Chrissy had gone on ahead and was already up stairs discussing her finds with Abigail. "Chrissy, lunch will be ready in a short while," Karen called up the back stairs.

"Okay, Mommy."

Chapter 30

September was gone and the cool October weather had arrived. The leaves were changing and the big Pin Oak trees were beginning to shed their leaves in anticipation of the coming winter. Clayton's birthday was now just one week away.

At breakfast, after each one of the Miller's had sated their appetites, Chrissy reached over and tugged on her daddy's sleeve, "Daddy, Clayton's birthday is just around the corner."

"Yes, I know, sweetie."

"Well," Chrissy let out a huffing sound, "I have got to go to the store and get Clayton's present. Abigail and I have decided on what we want to get."

"Oookay," Jeff let out a long extended sigh, "and you're telling me, why?"

Chrissy let out another sigh, "Daddy, you told me that you would take me to the store and pay for our present for Clayton."

Jeff smiled a teasing, mischievous smile, "I did?" he said.

Chrissy put her hands on her hips. Let out a bigger huffing sound and said, "Yes, you did, last week. Well, now I'm ready. I need to go now so that I have time to wrap it properly."

Jeff looked over at Karen, that same mischievous expression in his eyes. He was trying hard not to laugh, counting off on his fingers, he said, "Well, let's see. I have this to do today, and that to do today, and then some more of this…"

"Daddy, please. I beg you, please, take me today." Chrissy had put her hands together in a begging manner.

Karen had gotten up from the table and turned her back on the two of them. It was becoming too difficult for her to keep a straight face. Once under control, she turned around and said, "Chrissy, I'll take you if Daddy is too busy."

Chrissy crossed her arms over her chest, let out another huffing sound, "But he promised!"

Karen looked over at Jeff and, looking at his expression, she could tell he had taken the teasing as far as he was going to. Jeff spoke up, "You know what, Chrissy? I did promise you, sooo, later today we will hop in the van, leave Mommy and Clayton and Abigail behind, and we will go get your surprise gift for Clayton. Okay?"

Chrissy's face broke into a huge smile and she quickly nodded her head up and down in agreement. Chrissy looked over at her mother, "Mommy, may I go up stairs with Abigail until Daddy is ready to go?"

"Yes, Chrissy, You and Abigail go ahead up stairs. I'll call you when Daddy is ready."

After the two girls had disappeared up the back stairs Karen turned to Jeff, "You almost took that bit of teasing too far, don't you think?"

"Yeah, I think she was getting a bit feisty with me."

"Sometimes you two just don't know when to quit."

"Yeah, but she loves every minute of it and so do I."

"Jeff, she didn't look like she was loving every minute of this last little go around. She was getting down right frustrated and I don't blame her."

"Okay, okay, I'll make it up to her. She knows I'm teasing, at least most of the time. I just took it a little too far. I'm sorry."

Later that day, just after lunch, Jeff had gone out to his office to finish up a project with the promise he would be done by one o'clock. Chrissy and Abigail were up stairs in the playroom and Karen and Clayton were in the breakfast nook. Clayton was very close to taking his first independent steps and

Karen was working with him. His playpen was near the opening to the back stairs and Karen was sitting at the table.

Clayton was standing next to the playpen, holding a tenuous grip on the netting. Karen was reaching out to him, prompting him to step toward her. He was contemplating that first step away from his security when Jeff stepped through the back door.

Jeff stopped dead in his tracks when he realized what was going on. Clayton looked up at his daddy just as his foot moved forward for that first monumental step and his hand released his grip. A big grin on Clayton's face exposed those bright white teeth of his just as he plopped down on his diapered behind, his momentum forward suddenly stopped.

"Oh, darn," Karen exclaimed, "I thought he was finally going to make it."

"I'm sorry, Babe, I didn't know what was going on in here, otherwise I wouldn't have barged in."

"That's okay, I know he'll get up and try again."

Clayton looked at his mommy and daddy, sheer joy enveloping his face. He turned around to face the playpen and worked his way back up to a standing position.

Jeff watched his son proudly, "Man, I can't wait until he is walking," he said.

Karen turned her head, looking up at her husband, "What? I'm the one who will be chasing him around this house. We will have to keep baby gates at the top and bottom of these stair cases just to corral him."

Jeff chuckled lightly, "I know, but it just means he'll be closer to being the pal I can do things with. I can't wait until he's old enough for the two of us to do things together."

"You mean, like sit at the computer, mow the grass, watch television? All of those really important things in life."

"Yeah! We'll watch football, basketball, baseball, all of those really important things." Jeff was smiling; that mischievous expression once again in his eyes.

Karen turned her attention once again to Clayton who was now standing up waiting for his chance to try again, but he wasn't about to try until his Mommy's arms were out waiting for him.

"Well, I've got to get going. I'm sure Chrissy will be biting at the bit, ready to go," Jeff said.

Just then, from up the staircase, came Chrissy's voice, "Daddy, are you ready to go? I'm all set."

Jeff turned and smiled at Karen, "Yeah, Chrissy, I'm ready. Come on down and we'll head out the door. Easy on the stairs, though, okay?"

Jeff heard the slow, repetitive sound of Chrissy's steps coming down the stairs. When she emerged out from the doorway, purse hanging from her arm, she looked every bit the five year old, yet she carried herself like a much older person. Erect, poised… and ready to shop.

"Okay, kiddo, get your coat on, it's a little bit chilly out there. We will shed this mantle of domesticity and hit the store aisles. Whatta ya say?"

Chrissy smiled at her daddy, not really understanding what he just said, but knowing his intent. She turned to go get her coat, hanging in the front entry hall, and soon returned with coat, hat and purse, looking every bit the young lady.

"Okay, I'm ready!" she declared to her audience in the kitchen.

Jeff turned to Karen, "We won't be long, Hon. We'll get whatever Chrissy is after, and I'll pick up what we discussed." Jeff leaned over and kissed Karen softly. "Ummm, I'll have to come back just for some more of that."

Chrissy smiled at her Mother and Father. She could see the love they felt for each other.

Karen spoke, "Maybe by the time you get home he'll have taken his first steps."

"In a way, I hope not," Jeff said with a wistful smile, "I sure would like to see those first steps."

"Well, I can almost guarantee, there will be plenty more where those came from, that you'll be able to see at another time. Something tells me he's gonna be a terror on two feet, if you know my meaning."

Jeff's face broke into a big smile, "I can't wait! See you later. Come on, Chrissy, let's go."

Jeff and Chrissy disappeared out the back door as Karen returned her attention to Clayton, "Come on, baby, let's get started. Come on, Clayton," Karen encouraged her son to take those first steps.

Clayton gave his mommy that big toothy grin and stepped out where many men have gone before. His first step forward was almost stopped because he failed to let go of the playpen, trepidation written on his face. Suddenly he let go, the smile returned, and he launched himself forward, one quick step after another, his body almost moving faster than his feet. Crossing that vast openness, of the two feet he had to travel, he fell into his mother's arms, smiling all the way. Once in Karen's arms he laughed loudly as Karen hooted and hollered her joy. Karen then hugged her little man and said, "Oh boy, wait until your Daddy gets home; he will be so happy."

Clayton giggled all the more. Then he twisted around, his attention drawn to the hallway opening that led into the back parlor. Karen followed his gaze and saw Serena standing in the hall, "Serena!" she exclaimed, "I am so happy you're here."

Serena smiled a soft and wan smile and then said, "Hello, darlin'. I just came by to see how you're doin'."

"Oh, Serena, I have missed you so much, where have you been?"

"Well, darlin', something came up and I just had to take care of it."

"Well, anyway, you're here now. First of all, Clayton's birthday is next week and I wanted to invite you…"

"Darlin', I need to talk to you. It's very important so please listen." Serena's expression, once soft and friendly was now very serious.

Karen hesitated for just a moment and then answered slowly, "Okay."

Serena looked at Karen, "There are dark clouds comin' darlin' and I wanted you to know I will be here for you, don't you fear."

Karen was confused, "Dark clouds? Serena, what are you talking about?"

"Darlin', I can't say any more. Just know that when you need me, I will be here for you... I have to go now, bye darlin'." With that last statement Serena turned and walked toward the back parlor and was quickly gone.

Karen sat there holding firmly onto Clayton, totally confused as to what had just happened. She looked down at her little boy and said, "Whoa, what was that all about?"

Clayton just looked back at his Mommy and smiled his loving, toothy grin, slobber trailing down the side of his mouth, totally unaware of what had just transpired. Suddenly Clayton turned his head away from Karen and looked toward the stairway opening.

Once again Karen turned her gaze toward where Clayton was looking and what she saw caused her to suck in a great breath. Standing in the doorway was a pretty young girl, dark pigtails draping over her shoulders, and wearing, among other things, black high button shoes. "Abigail," Karen exclaimed, "Sweetie, I can see you!"

"Yes, Mother, I know."

"But why? I mean, I'm grateful, but why now?"

"I just wanted you to know how much I love you; Daddy and Chrissy, too, but especially you."

Karen was speechless at first and then quietly she responded, a weak smile on her face, "I love you too."

"Mother? I also wanted to say thank you for loving me."

Karen smiled wider, "It's very easy to love you, Abigail, you're a sweet girl, but why now? I'm confused; first Serena and now you. I'm grateful, but so very confused.

Abigail walked over to Karen, who was still holding Clayton. As Abigail approached, Clayton's smile widened as he reached out for her. As she neared Karen, Abigail reached out and placed her hand softly against Karen's cheek and as Karen felt the warmth of her touch Abigail whispered, "Remember the promise." And then Abigail faded away.

Chapter 31

Jeff fastened Chrissy into her child safety seat, gave her a quick tickle in the ribs, and smiled as she giggled in return.

"Let's head for home, okay, kiddo?"

Nodding yes, Chrissy smiled, "Daddy, I want to show mommy what we bought for Clayton's birthday."

"Your wish is my command, mi' lady."

Chrissy's face broke into a huge smile as Jeff slid the van door closed and headed for the driver's door, opened it and slid inside. Hooking his seat belt, he looked back over the seat at Chrissy, gave her a thumb up and said, "Hold onto your seat, your chariot is about to leave."

Chrissy giggled again.

Jeff put the car in gear and eased it forward through the parking lot and then out onto Bob Sikes Rd, turning right toward Hwy 331, where a light controlled the flow of traffic. Just as he was slowing down for the red light it turned green, so Jeff accelerated into the intersection. Suddenly he saw a movement from the left and as he turned his head toward the driver's window Jeff saw the grill of a huge truck just outside his door. The last thing he heard was the screech of brakes, the crunch of metal compressing, and the sound of glass shattering.

Then Jeff saw and heard no more.

Karen looked at her watch again, wondering what was keeping her two loved ones, knowing all too well, they were probably buying out the Wal-Mart store. Karen had tried to get Jeff on his cell phone, but he must have turned it off because her call would not go through. She looked out the back window again to see if they had driven into the carport. Not seeing them, she walked to the front parlor, drawing back the drapery to look out the window. Perhaps they had parked out front.

Just as she was letting the drapery go she noticed a car slowly pull up to the curb. A cold chill slithered down Karen's spine and she stiffened as she noticed two people— no, they were police— get out of the car and walk through the front gate.

The door bell jangled. Every nerve in Karen's body was alert, yet her feet were immobile, as if nailed to the floor. The bell jangled again. From the kitchen, the phone rang and Karen stood paralyzed, unable to move in either direction. The door bell jangled a third time, followed by a firm knock on the door. Karen's mind started to float, her brain seeming to lose contact with her skull. All sense of time and place was drifting away.

A voice called from the other side of the door, "Mrs. Miller, are you in there? Mrs. Miller, this is Officer Griggs, Defuniak Springs Police Department. We need to speak with you."

The voice brought Karen back from her benumbed place as she finally eased her way to the door, her hand moving slowly to the door knob as she approached. Faintly, through the window of the door, she could see the silhouettes of the two officers standing at the other side. Karen slowly, automatically, turned the knob, her inner self sensing impending doom, screaming to her, "*Don't open the door!*"

"Life goes on." "They're in a better place." "You still have Clayton." "Jeff would want you to keep going." "Jeff and Chrissy are together." The words went on and on. The days oozed by, one after another, each in its own gray haze. People came and went, offering their condolences. Their sympathies! How could that bring them back! How could that change the reality? Jeff, her rock, was gone! Chrissy, her shining little angel, was gone! What was life without them but empty. Yes, she had Clayton, and she would do all she could to take care of him, even through her numbness, but for now, My God, it was so hard. How could she ever feel alive again?

Thank God for Serena. She was there almost immediately helping to care for Clayton. If Karen ever needed a mother it was now and Serena was happy to fill the need. She gave her comfort, a shoulder to cry on, when the tears would come. But most of all, she was there, filling the void.

The funeral, or was it funerals, was a blur. Karen sat stiffly in the front pew, Clayton on her lap, unable to look at anyone in the chapel, which was full. Serena had stayed at the house to get things ready for visitors. Although they had lived in DeFuniak Springs such a short time, the community offered her overwhelming support and yet gave her as much privacy as she needed.

She needed the privacy; to grieve, to mourn, to fall apart, to get herself back together. She needed to know Jeff and Chrissy were all right. How would she know they were all right? How could anyone know they were all right?

The next day, after the funerals, at home alone, despair overtaking her, she cried out, "My God, what am I going to do... no, what are we going to do?" She mustn't forget Clayton; her beautiful, little Clayton. She walked into Clayton's room and found his bed empty. She started searching the house, becoming more frantic as she went from room to room, fearing somehow, that he too was gone, and when she found him, safe with Serena, playing in the kitchen, the relief was overwhelming. Karen moved out of the kitchen and into the front parlor where she fell into a chair and dissolved into tears.

Through her grief Karen suddenly realized that she had not seen Abigail since the accident. "Abigail? Are you here?" Karen waited. "Abigail? Honey, are you here?" Karen waited longer. "Abigail, if you are here in the house will you come to me, please? I really need you."

Karen waited what seemed like a very long time yet nothing happened. Even Abigail seemed to be gone. They were all gone. Karen also realized that the laughter in the house had died as well.

Later that evening, Serena had left and Karen had put Clayton down to sleep so she drifted into her bedroom and laid heavily on the bed, a new wave of despair sweeping over her. Even though she had her sweet, darling little boy, she felt utterly alone. All those she loved, except Clayton, were gone. The love and laughter in the house were gone.

Karen drifted in and out of sleep, the night seeming to drag on endlessly. The nights were the worst; the darkness allowed her mind to run rampant with worry. In their bed, the bed she and Jeff had shared, she felt the most despair. *Oh, my God. Why did this happen? Jeff, why did you leave me? God, why did you take my little angel, my Chrissy?* Her thoughts ran a gauntlet of anguish.

Karen turned toward the windows, noticing the first signs of light sneaking through the glass as the sun slowly worked its way into the morning sky, relieving her of the darkness. Slowly Karen became aware of a glow, ever so soft, coming from the wall behind her. She didn't recall leaving a light on in the adjoining bathroom. She rolled over, believing she would have to get up to turn out a forgotten light, only to discover where the light was emanating from.

Near the fireplace, just right of the door to the bathroom, a light— no, it seemed more like an orb— seemed to grow with intensity, slowly gaining a glow that soon became almost too much for her eyes. Then Karen realized that within the orb a form was taking shape. It seemed to be almost pyramid-like. As the glow became more intense, the form became more distinct; it was not a pyramid, it was a person. No, wait. There were three figures; one large and two smaller. Then Karen realized that it was an adult and two children.

Karen was now sitting up in bed, the glow so intense that she held her hands up in front of her eyes to shield them

288

from the aura, yet still allowing her to see. The light was now behind the figures, making them grow more distinct with each second that passed. Suddenly, Karen's mind grasped the element of recognition; it was Jeff and on one side holding his hand stood Chrissy, and on the other, stood Abigail.

"Oh God, Jeff!" she screamed. "Chrissy!" The tears were streaming down Karen's face as she moved off the bed, reaching out for them, her hands moving through thin air, feeling only coolness where there should be warmth.

Karen stepped back, unable to quite comprehend what she was seeing. *I'm losing my mind. Oh, my God. I'm going crazy!* She thought.

Then Karen felt, rather than heard, Jeff chuckle. She couldn't tell if the sound came through her mind or ears, but she didn't care. She knew that sound too well. That was Jeff.

"Jeff, where have you been? I don't understand what's happening. There was an accident; a funeral. I don't understand."

Again, the words came through her mind, "It's all right Karen. I had to come back to let you know we are all right. I couldn't stand the agony you were going through. Please, don't suffer this way."

"But Jeff…"

"Karen, please listen to me, I don't have much time. Abigail has her family now and can finally be at peace. We are all together here and we are well. Things are good here on the other side. Chrissy and Abigail are really together and, I have it on good authority, that you and Clayton will be fine. You'll get over this in time, but I wanted you to know, that for as long as you need me, I will be here for you. All you need to do is ask for me and I will be here. Do you understand?"

"Jeff, I love you. I don't want you over there; I want you here, with me. I want Chrissy here with me. Please Jeff…"

"Karen, this is the way it was meant to be. Have you ever heard the expression, 'it is written'?"

Karen nodded, a heavy sob escaping her.

"This was written, long before we came upon this earth, and nothing could change it. Everything in my life; every step I have taken, every path I have followed, has led me to this moment. This was my time to go. This was Chrissy's time to go. Karen, you will go on; you will grow old. Clayton will grow up to be a great young man —just like his old dad— and I'll be with you all the way, all you have to do is call for me. Please honey, have peace with that."

Karen stared at Jeff's figure for a few moments, unable to speak, not knowing what to say; her grief choking out any words. Then a feeling of peace came over her as a gentle wave caresses the sand. The feeling seemed to remove all sorrow and doubt from her mind. Calmness replaced her agony; and fortitude, her despair. "Okay, Jeff, I understand… But Jeff, I will always love you."

"And I you."

"Chrissy, mommy will always love you."

"She knows."

As the glow began to dwindle, their shapes becoming less distinct, Karen realized that her time with them was almost gone.

"Goodbye, Jeff. Goodbye, Chrissy. Goodbye, Abigail."

"Karen, remember I love you this much." And as the light faded she saw Jeff spread his arms wide.

Epilogue

A few days after the funeral, Karen heard the door bell jangle. Moving from the kitchen she could not see anyone at the door. As she opened the front door she saw Agatha standing there, too short to be seen through the window.

"Agatha, what a pleasant surprise," Karen exclaimed, holding the door wide for Agatha to enter.

"I hope you don't mind, Karen, I just thought I would stop by and see how you were doing?" Agatha raised her head in that all too familiar fashion, as if she were sniffing out something in the air.

Karen looked at Agatha with astonishment.

"I'm doing fine, thank you, Agatha. I'm managing quite well, with Serena's help, of course."

Agatha looked at Karen with a peculiar expression. "What do you mean?" Agatha asked.

Now Karen had the peculiar expression, "What I mean is exactly that, Serena has been here to help me almost every day since…" Karen couldn't finish the sentence.

Agatha looked around the front foyer, smiled lightly and then said, "Yes, I see. She's here."

Karen looked at Agatha again, confusion showing in her expression, "What are you talking about, Agatha?"

Agatha smiled lightly once more, her big eyes, behind her thick glasses, crinkling at the corners, "Honey… Serena passed away July fifth…" Agatha paused and looked around the room once more, "but she's still here."

Rickie Wood-Bovee

Button Hook Child takes place in an existing Victorian home in DeFuniak Springs, Florida. It is the first in a series named, **The Open Pond Ghost Stories,** currently being written using real homes in that quaint, Victorian, historic community. The second in the series is in the writing stage so watch for

Don't Move The Coat!

Coming soon